Business To Kill For

Rosie & Joe
This book proves it's smart
to stay in Emmett —
Love to all
Mike

Business To Kill For

Mike Brogan

Lighthouse Publishing

This novel is a work of fiction. Names, characters, places and incidents either are the product of the author's imagination, or are used fictitiously. Any resemblance to actual persons, living or dead, events, corporations or locales is entirely coincidental.

Published by Lighthouse Publishing
Birmingham, Michigan

Book cover design by Marge Kelly
Cover photography by Steven Kovich
Production by Katherine Cosgro

Library of Congress Cataloging-in-Publication Data applied for.

ISBN 0-615-11570-5 (Hardcover)
Printed in the United States of America
January 2001
First Edition

For Marcie, Brendan and Chloé

ACKNOWLEDGMENTS

There are a great many to whom I owe a great deal. For his suggestions and words of encouragement early on, I thank Elmore Leonard. For her masterful guidance in building characters, stories and writers, I thank Leslie Kellas Payne. For suggesting Leslie, I thank Natasha Kern. For his wise counsel on advertising and the automobile industry, I thank Thomas B. Adams, former chairman of the board of Campbell-Ewald Company. For support and occasional nudging, I owe my writing buddies, Gary Devine and Bill Garvey. For enlightenment on things medical, I thank Dr. John Brooks and Dr. Bill Sheppard.

I also extend my heartfelt thanks to Marge Kelly for her exquisite sense of design and graphics, Steven Kovich for his inspired work with a Hasselblad, Kathy Cosgro for guiding us through publishing, Kathleen Lawrence for de-weeding the manuscript, some very creative agencies for advertisements described herein, and my friends in the agency business and at General Motors, Chrysler and Ford for inspiring me, whether they knew it or not. And finally, I'd like to thank my wife and family who bring labyrinthine dimensions to the word patience.

One

LUKE TANNER sat in a hushed alcove of Detroit's cavernous Renaissance Center, staring at shimmering silver coins in a nearby fountain, unable to look away, even though he should have been writing a television commercial with a cool forty million dollars riding on it.

Sipping lukewarm coffee, he forced his attention up to the multi-floored atrium. It reminded him of a concrete canyon. Balconies hunched over balconies, people leaning over them, peering down, watching people. He liked watching people watch people.

Tanner had slipped away from his office upstairs, where he was creative director of Connor Dow Advertising. He often tried to escape in the afternoon to work in his creative cranny, a quiet refuge that, he noticed, was quickly becoming less quiet.

Men, unseen and mumbling, scraped chairs up to a table on the other side of the alcove abutment that blocked his view of them.

He considered leaving, but decided to stay and finish the commercial for a prospective client with an amazing new glue. He wanted to create a commercial as exciting as the product, but so far his ideas packed all the excitement of a wet sock. And he did not have much time. His producer wanted a concept for the commercial in thirty minutes.

The men were whispering now. Terrific, he thought, knowing he was hooked. He leaned closer to hear.

"Let's get this over with," said a deep, impatient voice. "Is everything arranged?"

"Yes, everythin'," said a man with a thick Spanish accent. "What about these Siamese Twins guys? They still hunt in same place?"

"Yes," the first man said. An American accent.

"*Excelente.*"

"Their accident is arranged?"

"*Sí.* Yes."

"It must look like an accident."

"It will."

"Tell me about it," the American said.

"*Cuatro Narices.*"

"What?"

"'Four Noses' we call them. Six-foot black *serpientes.* Snakes. Killers. Jungle full of them. The Twins will walk into a nest. We help a little."

"And if the snakes don't kill them?"

"*Amigo,*" the man said, chuckling, "when this many *cuatro narices* bite you, you die."

"This Sunday," the American said.

"*Sí.*"

Luke Tanner grinned. This had to be Berger and the bozos from the office, faking accents. They almost had him. He started to shout, "What time Sunday?" then something told him not to.

Spanish voice cleared his throat. "You never tol' us how come you wan' these two men, these Twins, killed so bad."

"Business decision," the American said.

"What kind of business?"

"When they die, their advertising business will switch from their present agency to another one."

"This business—it's worth a lot?"

"Yes."

"Many millions?"

"*Many* millions."

"Maybe we should get bigger fee, eh?"

Another man grunted, "*Sí.*"

"Look—Goddammit!" the American said. "It's four hundred thousand! For you two and your colleague. That's it!"

"Easy, *amigo*, just kidding," Spanish accent said. "But when do we get our fee?"

"Half was deposited in the Banque Bruxelles Lambert account in Brussels this morning. The rest, as agreed, will be deposited when you handle the Twins."

Tanner broke out in a cold sweat. *Jesus—this is real.* These men were finalizing plans for a hit, talking about a fee sent to the Banque Bruxelles Lambert and *cuatro narices*, things his agency pals wouldn't know about.

Luke saw Herb, the ancient waiter, working tables nearby, start to walk toward him, coming to warm up his coffee. Luke tried to wave him off, but as usual the old man's eyes were drilled to the floor. Herb's foghorn voice would boom over the alcove wall and let the men know Luke had overheard them.

Luke looked down, pretending to concentrate on the script, praying Herb would go away. But Herb's feet clomped closer and stopped.

"Care for something?"

Luke looked up, then realized Herb was on the *other* side of the abutment.

"No," the American said. "My friends and I are leaving."

Luke exhaled like a slow leak. He heard chairs scraping, the men walking away. If they turned right, they'd see him, know he knew. He pretended to write, white-knuckling his pen. The footsteps faded left, the way they'd come, along the balcony. Luke had to see them.

He stood, peered around the abutment and saw two short, dark-skinned men wearing blue-black windbreakers and walking with a tall, blond, bearded man in a grey suit. They vanished into an elevator heading up.

Luke sat back down and stared at the floor. *Incredible.* He'd just overheard men plan the murder of two businessmen connected to an advertising account, two men called the Siamese Twins. He couldn't recall anyone in the business referred to as Siamese Twins. Which meant he had to phone his pal, Hank Redstone, a lieutenant with the Detroit Police. Hank's people would somehow have to identify the two men in an industry which employed hundreds of thousands—and warn them before Sunday.

Today was Wednesday.

And the police had nothing to go on. No personal names. No company names. No clues. Unless, Luke wondered, the men left something on their table. A cup with fingerprints. A matchbook. A crumpled note...

* * *

Two levels above him, the three men stepped off the elevator and walked along the balcony, circling behind the alcove tables below.

Mason Bennett was pleased. Despite the Mexican's absurd request for a larger fee, things were progressing exactly as planned. And they would. Bennett wasn't about to fail on this assignment. He had a reputation to maintain. He *delivered*. The

Siamese Twins would suffer a most unfortunate snakebite accident and die in the jungle, which would make him a wealthy man. And he had a secret plan to make this assignment—his most lucrative ever—even more lucrative.

He glanced at his watch. Time to update Klug.

Suddenly, something caught his eye on the lower level.

Quickly, he jerked the two Mexicans, Carlos and Paco, over to the balcony and pointed down at a tall, chestnut-haired man getting up from a table next to theirs. *He's been sitting there,* Bennett realized. The man walked around the wall, carefully inspected their table and the surrounding area, then hurried toward the elevators.

Mason Bennett squeezed a waste-bin lid, turning the plastic white.

"Think he hear us?" asked Carlos, the taller Mexican.

"Fuck yes, he heard us," Bennett whispered. "He checked our table for clues, then rushed to the elevators."

Bennett watched the man waiting for the elevator. The guy looked anxious, worried. He *had* heard. Bennett turned to the Mexicans. "Wait in your car. I'll phone you there."

"Why you wan' us to wait?" Carlos asked.

"You may have another assignment."

"What?"

"*Him.*"

The two men nodded and left.

Bennett turned and studied the man. Casual, but expensive clothes. Beige leather folder. Seemed to know the Ren Cen. The man stepped into a 400 Tower elevator going up. He probably worked here.

Bennett saw the old waiter clear a coffee cup from the man's table. Perhaps the old guy knew him. He took the escalator down to the tables, walked over to the waiter and pointed. "My friend was just sitting here. When I came down to see him, he'd left. His name escapes me."

The waiter smiled. "That'd be Luke. Luke Tanner. Nice fella."

"Yeah, Luke. Works upstairs."

"Yep. Connor Dow."

Mason Bennett thanked the waiter, then entered an empty elevator and headed up. He pulled off his blond beard and hairpiece and stuffed them into his pockets. He combed his oily, brown hair straight back, and crammed a silk handkerchief into his breast pocket. He jammed the floor button repeatedly, as though it would accelerate the elevator's ascent.

So, he thought, someone named Luke Tanner, who works at Connor Dow, has overheard us. But what did Tanner know? He knew about the Siamese Twins. He knew they would have a hunting accident and be killed by snakes. But he didn't know *who* the Twins were, *who* wanted them dead, *where* the accident would happen. He also didn't know *which* piece of business would be switched, that it was worth over *one billion dollars,* or *which* agencies were involved.

And he wouldn't live long enough to find out.

The elevator door whooshed open and Bennett walked briskly into the distinctive, mirrored lobby of Kennard Rickert Marketing Communications.

Moments later, he stepped into Forrest C. Klug's sprawling office, with its panoramic view of the meandering Detroit River. Bennett crossed the purple Isfahan carpet, sat in a burgundy leather chair and stared over the mahogany desk at Klug, who was carving off the tip of a Porlaranaga cigar as he spoke on the phone. Klug's diminutive size made the desk and office seem enormous.

Slowly, Klug's face turned. His left eye, the glass one, pointing slightly in and down, seemed to stare at Bennett's neck. The good eye, a shade greyer and very intense, scrutinized Bennett, as usual, for any hint of unwanted news.

Klug lit the cigar, smacked his thick lips like a carp, and billowed smoke upward where it was sucked straight into a small ceiling ventilator.

"Give me prime time," Klug shouted into the phone, "or I switch forty million over to ABC."

Klug at his arm-twisting finest, Bennett thought as he watched the silver-haired chairman of Kennard Rickert, a four-billion-dollar global advertising and media conglomerate. A self-absorbed man, Klug had charmed, cajoled, bullied, bludgeoned, and sometimes blackmailed CEOs in order to get their multimillion-dollar advertising budgets.

Bennett had known Klug since Vietnam. Once, when he told Klug his soldiers were disembowelling Viet Cong prisoners and playing tug-of-war with the intestines, Klug had looked at him and asked, "What's your point?"

"By end of day—or no deal!" Klug said, slamming the phone down and straightening the sleeve of his grey, three-thousand-dollar suit. His good eye found Bennett.

"You met them?" Klug asked, smoke curling up his cheek.

Bennett nodded. "Everything's on schedule."

Klug examined his stubby manicured fingers.

Bennett knew he had to level. "But we have a minor problem."

Klug's good eye froze and turned toward him like a laser.

"A guy overheard us," Bennett said, "but—"

"Overheard y-you?"

Bennett hadn't heard Klug stutter in years.

"You s-s-stupid—"

"But he didn't learn anything important."

"*I* decide what's important!" Klug said. A vein puffed up like a fat worm on his temple. "*What* did he hear?"

Bennett explained while Klug hurled clouds of thick smoke toward the ceiling.

"But I know who he is," Bennett said.

"Who?"

"Luke Tanner."

Klug blinked at the name, stood and paced behind his desk.

"He works—" Bennett said.

"I know where the fuck he works. Tanner's in my profession. He's smart. He might put this all together. You're positive you didn't mention Kennard Rickert?"

"Positive."

"Or the name of the account?"

"Positive."

"And that he didn't follow you here?"

"Positive."

Klug drew hard on his cigar, stretched his five-foot-four-inch frame, walked over to the window and stared down at the river for several seconds. Smoke curled from his lips. He turned and huffed a shaft of smoke toward Bennett.

"Tanner only learned what you've told me?"

"That's all.

"Then he won't learn any more."

"Why?"

"Dead men have flat learning curves."

Bennett nodded. "How you want it handled?"

Klug picked a speck of tobacco from his tongue. "He's in advertising, isn't he?"

Bennett nodded.

"So be creative."

Two

LUKE TANNER hurried down a shadowy hallway and leaned over a balcony, scanning the maze of walkways and clusters of people for the three men. They had vanished.

It was easy to vanish among the Ren Cen's sixteen thousand people. It was also easy for someone you didn't see to follow you through the web of hidden alcoves, overhanging balconies and winding hallways that twisted and meandered through the four joined, thirty-three-story office towers.

Luke watched people trail after each other like ants through tunnels, from one tower to the next. The towers, massive and cylindrical, stood alongside the river like sentries. They formed General Motors new World Headquarters complex, a modern Fortress Detroit surrounding the seventy-three-story Marriott Hotel.

Tanner decided to go upstairs to his office at Connor Dow Advertising.

As he entered, he was greeted by the smiling face of Marie, his trusted secretary. Her calm, light-brown eyes told him no disaster had occurred in his absence. Marie Chamberlain was a friendly, forty-seven-year-old married mother of two. She brushed back her short blonde hair, revealing tiny smoker's lines beside her eyes.

"Your calls," she said, handing him a few message slips.

"Any urgent?"

"Nothing that can't wait," Marie said, nudging horn-rims back up her nose. "But Jenna called. She wondered what time you're going to pick her up to go rafting Friday.

"I'll call her."

Marie nodded her obvious approval. She reminded him weekly how terrific Jenna was. The reminders were redundant. He knew.

Luke entered his office, settled in behind his large glass-topped desk and saw that work had stacked up, some requiring his immediate attention. He'd come in early tomorrow and crank it out. Right now he had to call Hank Redstone. A street-smart cop, Hank would believe him and know how to proceed.

Luke grabbed the phone, dialed and got Redstone's voice mail. He left a message for him to call as soon as possible.

Staring at Jenna's phone slip, he pictured her large, cobalt-blue eyes that seemed to see into him where no one saw, her smile that could microwave people, her thick brown hair that would look good in a hurricane. Jenna Johannson, Doctor of Medicine. Her flaws, if she had any, were buried beneath more levels of nice and compassion than he'd ever known.

But sometimes her compassion for a patient's health hurt her own. Like Michele, her teenage cancer patient.

Detroit Memorial's switchboard put him through, and amazingly Jenna picked up.

"What's happening?" he asked.

"We just fixed a cute little guy with a navy bean stuffed up his nose."

"Anything serious going on?"

"That *is* serious. Beans can grow up there."

He paused. "Come on..."

"Really. It's warm and moist. Perfect climate."

"So what'd you do?"

"Scott's herbicide. Squirted it right in up there."

Luke smiled.

"Actually, he sneezed it out."

"And maybe nailed Doctor Stickles?"

"No such luck," she said, laughing.

Luke flipped through his other phone slips, seeing a couple of client calls he should return soon. "How's Michele?"

Jenna sighed as though the air had been crushed out of her and he wished he hadn't asked.

"Still weak. She doesn't appear to be responding to the new treatment." Her words were heavy with frustration. "So how goes the big, bad ad game?"

He hesitated, wondering if he should burden her with what he'd just overheard. "The big, bad ad game took a bizarre twist this afternoon."

"Really?"

"Yep," he said, hoping to shift the subject. "Hey—before I forget, what time can you leave to go rafting Friday morning?"

"Around nine. But what's this bizarre twist stuff?"

"It's difficult to explain on the phone."

"So e-mail me."

"How about I swing by around seven, we'll catch a movie and I'll reveal all the sordid details." He heard a hospital loudspeaker paging her.

"I like sordid. Gotta run. See you at seven."

They hung up.

Luke looked at a small photo of Jenna on his desk. As usual, he felt better just from talking to her. He'd never really known anyone who *always* made him feel better. But then, he'd never known anyone like Jenna. Friday's rafting trip would be fun. They both needed time away from offices and phones, the concrete and traffic, their patients and clients.

His mind snapped back to the Siamese Twins. *Two men about to die.* He wondered if anyone at the agency had heard of them. Perhaps Elizabeth Blakeley. Elizabeth, a trusted friend, managed the agency's Reference Center and over the years had met hundreds of people in the business. He dialed her number but was told she was in a meeting.

Maybe Baines Thomas, agency chairman, his friend and mentor, might know the Twins. Luke trusted Thomas, who'd hired him six years ago and told him to raise the agency's level of creativity. Since then, Thomas had helped Luke sell several original, provocative advertising campaigns to somewhat conservative clients. The campaigns had been huge successes.

Thomas, with over forty years in advertising, knew every CEO since God. His encyclopedic knowledge of corporate heavy breathers might well include two men referred to as the Siamese Twins. Luke dialed Thomas's office.

"Baines is in Sweden attending an international conference for the week," Thomas's secretary said.

Luke had forgotten about that. He thanked her and hung up. He called Hank Redstone again, got his voice mail and left another message.

He looked down at the unfinished MegaGlue television-commercial script. He should finish it. MegaGlue was a copywriter's dream—a unique product with real consumer benefits, like twelve times more bonding strength than anything on the market, *and* the stuff didn't stick to your fingers. It was incredible. His commercial was not.

The *right* commercial concept, Luke knew, could help them win the lucrative new account. Connor Dow was competing against four other excellent agencies. Winning the account might also help his chances to be named agency worldwide creative director, a position up for grabs in three years.

Luke wanted a commercial with a hook—something that kept viewers from zapping to another channel. He stared out the window at Jefferson Avenue's grey stone buildings. He marveled at several of the new ones, evidence of Detroit's renewal. Traffic surged past gaudy billboards, one for AIDS prevention, another that showed the sleek profile of a red Chevy Corvette.

Luke clapped his hands and stood.

What if, he thought, the commercial opens with a close-up of a robot arm applying a thick, one-foot-wide strip of MegaGlue to a flat white surface? Slowly, the camera pulls back, revealing the side of a red Corvette just inches from the white surface. The robot then applies glue to the car's side. The car's side gently eases against the white surface, glue to glue. The glue hardens within seconds.

The camera pulls back slowly, and we see the car is stuck to an outdoor billboard forty feet above a busy expressway, suspended only by the glue. An announcer, off camera, says something like, "MegaGlue. If you get the idea it sticks, you get the idea." Fade to black.

The commercial should work. Product tests proved it had the adhesive strength. As he scripted the commercial on his computer, the phone rang.

"Luke, it's Elizabeth, returning your call."

"Got a minute?"

"Sure."

He hurried to the hall exit, then took the stairwell down three floors. The agency occupied six. Over seven hundred sixty people were nestled into fifty-two-thousand square feet of comfortable office space.

He thought of Elizabeth Blakeley, a consummate professional who'd nurtured the Reference Center from a small room with an encyclopedia to a two-thousand-square-foot complex with six librarians on line to over five hundred specialized computer databases updated daily. If someone wanted to know about pickles in

Abu Dhabi, the Reference Center could tell them what percentage were eaten by pregnant Shiite Muslims.

On the phone, Elizabeth waved him into a chair beside her desk. The petite, fifty-three-year-old mother of two, as usual, looked stunning. Streaks of grey hair accented large blue eyes that reflected her warm personality and keen intelligence. Gold teardrop earrings matched her necklace. Her double-breasted, white-plaid jacket and straight skirt revealed a figure that women thirty years younger would kill for.

She smiled as she spoke. Her desk, as usual, was immaculate. The chrome in-box held one memo, even though she probably processed as much paperwork as anyone. Beside the in-box sat a dark-green, malachite-based silver pen and pencil set, an elegant tribute to her twenty-five years at the agency. A laptop case leaned against her black leather tote bag.

She hung up and smiled at him. "What's up?"

Luke explained what he'd overheard.

Elizabeth stared back amazed, then amused. She shook her head from side to side. "Luke, this *has* to be a prank."

"I wish it were."

Again, she stared. "You're positive?"

He nodded.

Her eyes hardened as she toyed with the gold pendant on her necklace. "And these two men will be killed Sunday?"

"Yes."

"Incredible. We'll start trying to identify the Siamese Twins immediately. My sense is it won't be easy. We'll search the Internet, of course."

"That should give you some quick answers."

"A partial answer. An Internet search engine like Alta Vista, for example, only indexes around eighteen percent of the Web. Which gives us a one-in-six chance of finding *all* Siamese Twins references."

"What if we combine Alta Vista with Yahoo and other search engines?"

"Combining search engines will improve our chances to about

forty-eight percent or half of all Siamese Twins references."

"A fifty-fifty chance."

She nodded. "But these could help. She spun toward her computer and tapped in a code. Her blue screen filled with a long list. "Our special advertising and marketing databases. We can search them for any printed reference to Siamese Twins. Last month we purchased special access to the *Advertising Age* and *Adweek* archives, from 1965 to the present. We also have *Campaign* from the United Kingdom and *Strategies* from France loaded in. We're on-line to the *Wall Street Journal*, the *New York Times* and the *Financial Times of London*. We'll also check other major business media. If the Siamese Twins are mentioned, we'll know."

"How many special databases do you have?"

"Over five hundred."

His hope sank like lead. "When can you know?"

She paused. "If we're lucky, a couple of days. If not, a worldwide check of all major business media will take a couple more days."

"We have four, counting today."

She nodded and typed something on her keyboard.

Luke stared out the window. A lone gull coasted on the wind currents between the Ren Cen towers, then dove toward the river. On the Canadian shore, an inky sky crept like soft asphalt over Windsor. Rain was coming. He looked back at Elizabeth. "Would the *size* of the account help?"

She ran her finger along her keyboard. "Perhaps. If we knew the size, we could just check accounts that size for any Siamese Twins reference."

"They hinted the account was large."

"Five-million-dollars large?"

"Larger, I think."

"Twenty, thirty million?"

"Possibly. Maybe much larger."

"Did they say whether the account was domestic, or worldwide?"

"No."

"Any hint of the product category—soap, airline, beer, shampoo?"

"No."

Her brow tightened in a frown. "It's so little to go on. Based on what we know, the account could be one of several hundred. Identifying it before Sunday may be impossible."

He knew she was right.

Elizabeth tapped on her keyboard. "Still, we have to try. First, we'll check the Internet and advertising databases for any reference to the Siamese Twins. Next we'll compile a list of five-million-dollar accounts and larger, and search those accounts for any Siamese Twins reference. In the meantime, I suggest you phone your police friend."

"I called. Hank's out."

Luke stood and moved to the door. "I'll try again. And, thanks, Elizabeth."

He returned to his office and sank into his chair. He hadn't expected to identify the Twins immediately, but it was becoming clear that uncovering their identities might prove very difficult, perhaps impossible, if Siamese Twins was a code name. He saw a phone message from Redstone and dialed his friend.

"Redstone," said a gravelly voice.

"Tanner."

"Hey, Luke, you wimpin' out on next week's 10-K run? Or do you need a handsome black cop for a TV commercial?"

"I need a handsome black cop to stop the murder of two men Sunday."

Redstone paused. "I missed the punch line."

"No, you didn't."

"Talk."

Luke told him what he'd overheard.

Redstone was silent for several seconds. "The only Siamese Twins I heard of is that Thai sister act, the nude gymnasts over at that Windsor club."

Luke smiled.

"Could you identify the three men?"

Luke tried to visualize them. He'd only glanced at them before they disappeared into the elevator.

"The two Latins, maybe. Early thirties. Broad, oval faces. Perhaps Mexican or Caribbean native. Short, maybe five-six. One had a scar on his right cheek."

"The tall guy?"

"Six-two. Hundred ninety pounds. Blond hair. Full beard. Expensive, Italian-cut grey suit. He looked about forty-five."

"You see his face?"

"The right side."

"Can you look at some mug shots now?"

"I'm on the way."

Luke put the phone down and stared at the MegaGlue television commercial script. He should refine it, but his mind wasn't on glue. It was on preventing murders. On the way out, he handed the script to a television producer, who said she really liked it and would storyboard the concept.

Two minutes later, Luke got behind the wheel of a red Ford Mustang he'd borrowed earlier from the company's car pool. He liked to check out cars competitive to the agency client's World Motors cars. He steered the Mustang out of the Ren Cen parking garage and turned east onto Jefferson Avenue.

As he drove into the black shadows of the Ren Cen towers, he saw pedestrians leaning like tilted statues into a brisk May wind. Some Asian businessmen clustered around a flapping map, then trundled off toward nearby Cobo Convention Center.

The hint of rain streamed through the vents. Black clouds had crept over the city. He turned onto the I-75 entrance, passed a cement truck dripping sandy water and eased into swift-flowing traffic.

He would look through Redstone's mug shots. Perhaps he'd get lucky and identify one of the men. Failing that, he wasn't sure what more he could do.

In the rearview mirror, a large, silver Mercedes passed a rusty pickup and pulled in two cars behind him. Traffic was moderate since most auto plants had changed shifts two hours ago. He passed an expressway interchange and eased into the inside lane to take the exit in about a mile.

The Mercedes was suddenly alongside him.

It inched even, then *stayed* even, although there were no cars ahead.

Luke slowed a bit. The Mercedes slowed a bit. Why didn't it pass?

Something was wrong.

He glanced over and his body turned to stone.

He was looking into the vacant eyes of the scar-faced Latin. The man smiled, then slowly raised a handgun.

Luke ducked—as two shots shattered his window. Glass sliced his temple, warm blood skidded down his cheek.

They know!

Head down, he tried to visualize the vehicles ahead, but focused inexplicably on a green Doublemint wrapper on the carpet. Horns honked.

He *had* to look up. Or crash.

Glancing up, he saw a garbage truck from nowhere—ten feet ahead. He swerved around it and sped up.

The Mercedes was behind him. Slouching, he kept his head low, eyes just above the instrument panel. He passed a van, darted to the outside lane and floored the accelerator. The speedometer leapt to ninety.

The Mercedes was on him.

Where the hell are the police?

Luke accelerated to ninety-eight miles per hour.

He saw an Allied Moving van and a chemical tanker crawling in the two lanes ahead. A slow VW clogged the inside lane. He was blocked.

He slowed, glanced in the mirror. The Mercedes was gaining.

Ahead, the van and tanker grew enormous. He braked.

Bullets slammed into the trunk.

Then he saw it. A slim chance. He hit the brakes, cut across three lanes, shot up the exit ramp. Maybe...

He checked the mirror.

Nothing.

Then tires screeched.

Looking back, he saw the Mercedes racing up the ramp.

Three

MASON BENNETT didn't believe in luck. He believed in backup plans. Even though the Mexicans that were following Luke Tanner from the Ren Cen should nail him easily, Tanner might get lucky. If he did, Bennett needed to find a way to control him. Forrest Klug had given Bennett the way—Tanner's girlfriend, a woman named Jenna. Klug had met her at some advertising event.

Bennett phoned Connor Dow's main switchboard and was put through to Tanner's secretary.

"Luke Tanner's office. This is Marie."

"Is Luke there?" Bennett asked, knowing he wasn't.

"I'm afraid he's left for the afternoon."

Bennett paused. "Oh...this is Arnold Williams, a friend of Luke's Uncle Raymond in Grand Rapids," Bennett said softly, pumping a little sadness into his voice. "I'm afraid Raymond passed away this morning."

"Oh my..."

"It was sort of a blessing. He had cancer. Raymond's sister is having the funeral Friday. We wanted to tell Luke or Jenna. Do you know where I might reach him?"

"He's driving over to see a friend, Lieutenant Redstone."

Bennett's muscles hardened. Tanner *had* overheard them. Now he was telling a cop—a *friend*, who'd believe him. Not good. "I see. Would you have this lieutenant's number?"

"Of course," she said and quickly gave him Redstone's number. "You said the funeral's this Friday?"

"Yes." Bennett heard concern in her voice. "Does Luke have an important meeting?"

"Oh no. It's just that he and Jenna we're planning a rafting trip." She sounded a little disappointed.

"That's unfortunate," Bennett said, filing away the rafting information. "If I can't reach Luke, perhaps I could let Jenna know. Would you know her number?"

"I have it right here, Mr. Williams. Just a moment."

Bennett heard pages flipping, then she gave him Jenna's work and home phone numbers. He smiled. Like taking candy from a baby.

* * *

Three miles away in Detroit Memorial Hospital, a respected medical complex in the city center, Doctor Jenna Johannson looked into the glazed, sunken eyes of fourteen-year-old Michele Krammers. Jenna brushed matted strands of ash-blonde hair back off the skeletal girl's forehead, then smoothed glycerine onto her cracked lips.

Jenna saw no indication the new treatment was controlling her disease.

Holding Michele's pale, scrawny fingers, Jenna recalled how fast the girl's condition had deteriorated. Three months ago, she'd been walking around the ward, playing Nerf basketball, joking with the staff. Then her cancer, a rare leukemia, had roared back angrily, as chronic myelocytic leukemia, CML, almost always did, and began squeezing life from her.

Jenna's eyes moistened. *Detach*, she reminded herself. She tried often, but despite all the advice she'd received from peers and in med school, she'd become close to Michele. It was hard not to after she'd found out no adult had ever been close to the young girl. They spent hours talking, sharing moments from their very dissimilar lives.

Michele attempted a smile and whispered, "Thanks for hanging with me."

"Hey, kid, I'm always here for you." *Even though no one else ever was.* Born addicted to heroin, Michele had been deserted by her mother and father at six months, bounced from foster home to foster home and was sexually abused in some. She'd finally escaped to the streets where she'd lived until eleven months ago when she stumbled into Detroit Memorial's Emergency Room.

Jenna remembered the night. Michele had been chalk-white, anorexic-thin, sweating from a high fever. Her white-blood count was over 600,000/Ul, her spleen enlarged, her Ph chromosome and tests all confirmed what Jenna had feared. Michele had CML. Medical evidence said it would kill her.

But Jenna refused to accept it. She would find a treatment that would send the deadly cancer into remission. New treatments and drugs were found every month. Miracles *did* happen. Michele would be one.

Glancing down, she saw that Michele had dozed off. Jenna studied her chart and saw that the young girl's white blood cell count was still climbing. *Damn! The alpha-interferon and ARA-C combination simply isn't working.* Bone marrow transplantation was not a good option, because Michele had no known, tissue-matched close relatives to act as donors. And her cancer was simply too far advanced.

Jenna walked to the window and tried to think. Perhaps Oncology could suggest some new interferon combination.

Turning back, she caught her reflection in the window and shook her head. She looked like a cattle butcher. *T-bones today, sir?* Her white coat, which hung on her slender frame like a Sears tent, was blood-spattered, thanks to a three-year-old who'd grabbed a hedge trimmer that trimmed his finger a bit. The same kid who'd smudged her lipstick into a demented grin. No wonder her last two infant-patients shrieked.

She wiped off the lipstick with a tissue, fastened her hair back and left to go consult with a friend in Oncology.

Entering the hall her stomach clenched. Doctor Norman Stickles, Chief of Administration, was hurrying toward her. No time to escape. Stormin' Norman. Short, pudgy, close-cropped blond hair, bifocals clinging to a button nose, clipboard clutched to his chest like protective armor. Stickles was an adequate doctor with the bedside charm of a pit bull. As usual, he appeared on the verge of a hissy fit. His eyes looked like eggs escaping his skull. He reminded her of a demented toad.

"There you are," he said, as though she was a fugitive. "You're behind on your paperwork, Doctor. Again. Administration is less than pleased. We want it caught up immediately."

She nodded. She was behind. Again.

"Is there a particular reason?" he asked, clearly unwilling to accept any explanation.

"Sick kids."

"Pardon?"

"We've been very busy."

He peered over his glasses, pursing thin, moist lips that looked like strips of veal. "We're *all* busy."

"So are the diseases killing these kids."

"Yes, yes. But it doesn't take much time to fill out forms."

"Only about half my time. Which is obscene." She felt herself getting worked up again over the mountain of administrative and insurance forms she had to fill out.

"All doctors must fill them out," Stickles said as though that made it right.

"That's my point."

"What point?"

"America's most frightening medical emergency."

Stickles, bored, stared back. "What?"

"Paper. Paperwork. Forms. It's choking American medicine."

"Paper, Doctor, is what runs business. And hospitals are businesses."

"They used to be where doctors treated patients."

Stickles' cheek began to twitch until his manicured finger brought it under control. "I would strongly suggest you complete your paperwork immediately. If you don't, it will not bode well for your upcoming performance evaluation."

Late paperwork, she knew, would get her into serious trouble, perhaps get her suspended, a black mark her career and bank account could ill afford. "I'll have the paperwork in your office tomorrow."

"It will help."

She nodded, as though the toad had imparted profound advice, which she admitted begrudgingly, he had.

Stickles pirouetted in triumph and waddled off looking for his next paper felon. She reminded herself to add a Stickles de-stress mile to her treadmill jog tomorrow.

Turning toward the nurses' station, she saw Nurse Anna Benoit approaching, waving frantically for her. Anna looked very concerned. Had the preemie developed lung problems?

Anna grabbed Jenna's arm and gasped for breath. "A man just called from the lobby. He works with Luke..." Benoit paused, avoiding Jenna's eyes. "There's been an accident nearby. I'm afraid...Luke's been...injured."

Jenna felt her knees buckle. The corridor began to tilt. She leaned against the wall, closed her eyes. *I just spoke to Luke at the office. There's a mistake. It can't be him.*

"The man's coming up now. He'll take you to Luke. The accident just happened."

The elevator door hissed open. A tall, blond man in a grey suit hurried out and turned toward Jenna. He looked down at Jenna's name tag.

"Doctor Johannson," he said, a concerned look on his face.

"Yes."

"I'm John Rasmussen. I work with Luke. Research and Strategic Planning department. I'm afraid Luke's been in an accident just off I-75. He asked me to bring you to him."

Again, she had to steady herself on a nearby gurney railing. "Yes, please. Where are they taking him?"

"Henry Ford Hospital. It's closer."

She grabbed her purse and hurried with the man into an open elevator.

As they drove along East Warren, Jenna tried to control the emotions surging through her. Her heart pounded against her chest. Panic hit her in waves, each worse than the previous. "How bad is it?"

"Not good," he whispered.

"What happened?"

"Someone in another car shot him."

She swallowed the hot lump in her throat. "Was he conscious?"

"No."

She closed her eyes. This was not happening.

Please let Luke live. I'll make him better. Please may he not be in pain.

Four

L UKE SPED down side streets and alleys, changing directions,
heading east toward Grosse Pointe, checking the mirror,
making sure he'd lost the Mercedes. How did the Latinos know
he'd overheard them? He might never know. He *did* know they
wanted him dead.

All the more reason to brief Redstone—fast.

Twenty minutes later, holding a blood-spotted tissue to his
cheek, he parked next to Detroit Police Department 13th
Precinct on Woodward and Hancock.

He stepped from his car, shook tiny chunks of glass from his jacket and walked into the crowded, noisy reception area. He passed a young sergeant escorting a bosomy blonde wearing a gold-sequined mini skirt and smelling like a car-wash air freshener. A teenage boy, slumped in a chair, held a blood-soaked towel to his head. Beside him, a young women with pin-prick, heroin eyes stared into the next decade. Phones rang without being picked up. In the corner, a large woman gnawed on barbequed ribs that dripped on her yellow dress. *NYPD Blue*, Detroit style.

Luke walked down the narrow hall to Redstone's office and found him standing at the window, looking out and talking on the phone.

Unnoticed, Luke walked in and sat in a brown vinyl chair with patched armrests. He caught the scent of gunpowder and saw a Beretta 9mm handgun, tagged for evidence, on the cluttered desk. Beside the gun, a transparent evidence bag revealed a bloody white blouse and bra. Two empty Big Mac cartons and a french fry container were next to the phone.

Hank, who weighed two-twenty, had porked up a bit in the last few months, and occasionally jogged with Luke to help control his weight. Behind the desk, stacks of case folders leaned against each other on a file cabinet.

Redstone was describing a scam in which men posing as gas company employees robbed older women. His eyebrows tightened above angry brown eyes as he explained how the men had beaten an old woman senseless, then robbed her. His light-brown jaws hardened into knots. He twisted the phone line around his fingers until his forearm veins looked like ropes.

After sixteen years in the job, Redstone was still passionate about helping victims and nailing their perpetrators.

He hung up, turned around. His eyes widened when he focused on Luke's bloody Kleenex.

"Close shave?"

"With a .44 Magnum."

Redstone walked around and examined Luke's cheek. "Talk."

"The two Latins just tried to paint me to I-75."

Redstone stared at him. "We've had expressway snipers. You

sure it's the same guys?"

"Do the Japanese make cars?"

Redstone sat down and fingered a thin grey scar on his jaw, a remnant of his ghetto youth. "So they know you overheard them."

"They know."

"Which means they saw you there, or someone you talked to told them."

"I talked to one person. Elizabeth Blakeley. I trust her."

Redstone nodded.

"Elizabeth's also looking for any media reference of the Siamese Twins."

"That could help," Redstone said, scratching his short, wiry black hair. "Meanwhile it's show time." He crushed the Big Mac containers in his powerful hands, stuffed them in a basket, and flipped open a large binder of mug shots on his desk. "Have a look."

Luke began searching the faces, profile by profile, scar by scar. An hour and a half later, he arched his shoulders, rubbed his eyes and closed the last binder.

"They're not in the books."

Redstone did not appear surprised. "Detroit's not exactly teeming with Latino hit men. We grow our own talent. I'll get some out-of-town mug shots."

The phone rang. Redstone picked it up, listened briefly, then covered the mouthpiece. "Who knows you're here?"

"My secretary."

"He's got a deep voice." Redstone handed him the receiver.

"Mr. Tanner?"

Luke recognized the voice immediately. The American he'd overheard in the Renaissance Center. "Yes..."

"We've just given Doctor Johannson a ride from Detroit Memorial Hospital. She's quite beautiful. But if the police investigate what you overheard, or if they search for her, she won't be. She'll be dead. Do you understand?"

Luke opened his mouth, but couldn't form words.

"Mr. Tanner?"

"I understand." He felt like something was crushing his chest against his backbone.

"If you've already told the police, just tell them you misunderstood, now that you've thought about it. Got it?"

"Yes. But how do I know she's ..."

Luke heard the phone changing hands.

"Luke, is that you?" Jenna's voice trembled.

"Jenna—"

The phone receiver was slammed down so hard he flinched. He hung up, unable to speak, his mind racing, wondering how they'd found out about Jenna, wondering if he'd see her again. He felt Redstone's eyes on him.

"They have Jenna," Redstone whispered.

Luke looked down at the floor.

"And if we pursue them," Redstone continued, "they'll do something to her, right?"

"They'll *kill* her," Luke whispered.

Redstone stood, walked over to the soot-covered window, and looked out for several seconds. "Did he say they'd release her if we did not pursue?"

"No."

Redstone turned and stared at Luke for several seconds. "You know what my professional advice is?"

Luke nodded. "Undercover."

"It's the right thing."

"Maybe, maybe not."

Luke felt like a razor blade was stuck in his throat. Would he jeopardize Jenna's life more by not searching for her, or by permitting an undercover search? The kidnapper would carry out his threat. Still, the appropriate procedure in a kidnapping was to inconspicuously—and quickly—search for the kidnapped person. Reason suggested he follow professional wisdom.

"How undercover is *undercover?*"

"Deep. A couple of informants who know what's going down. We grease some palms, call in some chits. Maybe we find out."

41

Luke hesitated, anguishing over what he should do. Going undercover or doing nothing seemed equally lethal. There was no good choice. Could he live with himself if his decision resulted in her death?

"Well?" Redstone asked.

After several moments, he nodded agreement, yet felt sickened by the possibility he'd just risked Jenna's life.

"In the meantime," Redstone said, "lay low. Don't go home tonight."

"Why?"

"They may still want you dead."

Five

LUKE FELT like someone was grinding football cleats into his stomach as he drove the bullet-riddled Mustang north on I-75 toward his cottage and his .38 Smith & Wesson.

Is undercover the best way to find her? The more he thought about it, the less certain he was. The kidnappers might release her, they might not. Nothing was certain—except that Jenna was terrified.

He thought about his .38. It had been years since he'd fired the

---

43

gun, but if people were going to take target practice at him, he'd return the favor.

How could a day like all others become like no other? A couple of meetings, a television commercial screening, the alcove for a few creative moments...moments that created pain for Jenna and might have helped end her life. A life to which he'd become profoundly linked last Saturday night when they'd first made love. The memory warmed him as he recalled her fragrance, the softness of her skin.

A truck horn blasted in his ears.

Luke glanced in the mirror and saw enormous headlights bearing down on him. A large Amoco Oil tanker pulled out and roared past. He realized he was only doing the speed limit, lethally slow on I-75. He sped up.

As he drove past the Pontiac Silverdome, the air turned cooler. Inky darkness painted the night sky. Another pair of headlights crept up behind him. Could it be the silver Mercedes? He sped up a little and relaxed when the car exited moments later. He passed an Allied moving van, and two haulers loaded with white Cadillac Cateras.

Soon he'd be at the cottage. He'd purchased it six months ago as a weekend getaway, a place where he and his father could hang out and do some fishing. Only his dad, Jenna and Redstone knew about the cottage, which faced Whistle Lake, a secluded, sixty-three-acre lake, forty miles north of Detroit.

He and Jenna had been looking forward to stopping by the cottage Friday, then going rafting in some nearby rapids that had been recently created when county officials diverted water from the Flint River.

His tires crunched onto the gravel road that bordered the lake. Moments later he turned into the drive and eased into his one-car garage, avoiding the water skis jutting out from the wall.

He stepped from the car, closed the creaky garage door and walked toward the front porch. Spongy grass sucked at his shoes. A chilly lake wind carried the scent of fresh, clean pine and the hint of rain. Overhead, stars flickered like a chandelier, but seemed dimmer than when Jenna had marveled at those same stars a few nights ago.

Something moved. In the black shadows of the porch, a few feet ahead. He squinted, but couldn't see anything.

More noise, feet moving.

He jumped back as two enormous raccoons bolted from the porch shadows and scampered into the woods. He breathed out through his teeth. *Little edgy, Tanner?*

Stepping inside the cottage, he turned on the lights and glanced around. Everything seemed normal. He opened a window to let in fresh air, then walked over to a large, oak table and flipped through the stack of junk mail that a kind, elderly neighbor woman brought in for him every few days.

He walked into the kitchen, realized he wasn't hungry. Still, he should eat. His doctor's warning echoed in his mind: *"Remember, Luke, you can help prevent a relapse of your illness by eating regular, balanced meals."*

"Sorry, doc, this was not a regular, balanced day," he whispered.

He opened the ancient Frigidaire and grabbed a can of icy Killian Red. Lots of healthy oats and barley in beer. He walked to the den, dropped into his favorite chair, sipped some and stared out at the lake, waiting for the serene water to soothe him, like always. Not tonight. His eyes followed a ribbon of moonlight across the lake to the small, wooded island where he and Jenna had canoed.

Is she injured? In pain? Have they abused her? Beer ran down his knuckles, and he realized he'd crushed the can.

He thought back to when they'd met three months ago. They were coaching kids at a Special Olympics track meet and he'd tripped over his own shoelace. She'd tried to help him up, but had fallen, butt-first, into a water cooler. They'd been together ever since, growing closer, closer than he'd ever felt to anyone.

But he'd sensed himself beginning to hold back, to move very cautiously. A familiar feeling. He glanced down at the reason on his forearm, a small white scar, a relic of when a nurse accidentally ripped the injection syringe sideways. He'd been sixteen, and dying.

He remembered the headaches, the debilitating weakness. At first doctors thought he had a persistent flu, maybe mono. Then they saw the tiny red spots on his arm, little pockets of blood under the skin. Bone marrow and blood tests confirmed he had leukemia, something called acute nonlymphoblastic leukemias, ANLL. His doctor's eyes confirmed it could kill him.

He underwent chemotherapy and radiation, transfusions of platelets and red cells, antibiotics. His eyelids, hands and feet swelled. His hair fell out, leaving three-inch-wide bald spots. His skin yellowed and burned around his IV catheters. His mouth sores bled when he vomited. Night after night, his father, still recovering from the death of Luke's mother, sat by his bed and wondered why his family was being destroyed.

The leukemia finally went into complete remission, but his doctor had warned him. *"Live cautiously. Stay rested. Your disease could relapse any time. Manage your stress."*

Tough to manage stress dodging bullets, Luke thought.

The phone rang.

"It's Hank. Just checking in. Any visitors?"

"Two guys wearing black eye masks."

"What?"

"Raccoons."

"Asshole. Any *human* visitors?"

"No."

"And no one knows about the cottage?"

"You, dad and Jenna." Suddenly he envisioned the kidnappers torturing her for the cottage location.

"I put a guy down the road from the cottage," Redstone said. "Keeping an eye on things."

"No one followed me."

Redstone paused. "They may arrive later."

"Or they may leave me alone now that they have Jenna."

"Maybe."

"Your undercover people learn anything?"

"It's too soon."

Or too late. Luke felt despair wash over him.

"Hank..."

"Yeah?"

"Level with me."

Redstone paused. "About what?"

"Jenna's chances are not good."

Redstone cleared his throat and paused. "They could be better."

A tree branch slapped a nearby window and Luke tensed. Thunder cracked in the distance, causing Canada geese to honk their departure from the lake.

"But," Redstone said, "I've got more mug shots coming from Texas, Miami and L.A. *Muchos Mexicanos* and *Latinos*. You can look at them tomorrow."

"No way. They said they'd kill her if they see me helping the police."

"They won't see you. Tomorrow morning your secretary will receive a beautiful floral arrangement. The flower base will be mug-shot binders. If you identify one of the photos, we might get closer to Jenna."

Luke knew he was right. "Okay."

They hung up and Luke looked outside. Lightning painted the lake white, thunder exploded and sheets of rain hammered his windows like pebbles. Branches screeched against the gutters as they had last Saturday night, when Jenna and he'd made love just a few feet away from where he sat now.

They'd driven out to the cottage in the afternoon to meet his father and go fishing. When they arrived, they found his dad's note saying he'd "gone to play poker and trade lies with some old farts."

"Parental desertion," Luke had complained.

"Their cruelty knows no bounds," she said.

"Would a cruise on my personal yacht ease the pain?"

"A smidgeon."

As they paddled his canoe around the lake, a violent storm

erupted, and they were suddenly reeling through four-foot swells and whitecaps. The canoe capsized, dumping them into neck-deep water, fifty feet from land. Jenna swam ashore as Luke pulled the canoe in. Drenched, they'd run inside the cabin, stared at each other, watched rain drip from their noses, and burst out laughing.

"Look! We're land-locked," Jenna said, pointing outside to a river of rainwater, four feet deep, cascading over the only road to the cabin. "You obviously caused this storm to keep me captive."

"Yep." He grinned up at the soot-black sky. "Seeded them clouds myself."

They changed into clean sweat suits, and walked into the tiny kitchen where Jenna swung open the doors of the old Frigidaire. He could still see her eyes, gleaming like blue ice in the refrigerator light. He could still hear her laughing at what she saw.

"What?" he'd asked.

"The cheddar fungus from hell. A decent bottle of red Bordeaux and four Hershey bars."

"All major food groups."

They ate, became slightly zippy on the wine and chocolate, laughed a lot, moved to the sofa in front of the glowing fireplace, and listened to the storm blend with George Winston's *Summer* CD.

When lightning exploded over the lake, she moved closer. He placed his arm around her shoulder, felt his pulse accelerate, savored her closeness, her perfume, her body's delicious warmth. He turned to kiss her forehead and found her lips moving to his. They kissed passionately, tongues exploring, hands pulling off sweatshirts. They kissed again, harder, and she unclasped her bra and let it drop, revealing perfect, firm breasts. Sweatpants flew away.

Gazing at each other in the amber glow of the fireplace, Luke knew he'd never seen anyone so beautiful, or wanted anyone so much. He kissed her face and neck, moved down to her breasts, her hardened nipples, exploring, touching, arousing. His hand moved over her stomach slowly, caressed her satin skin. His fingers brushed gently over her body to her vagina as it rose to meet them.

She guided him on top of her. He entered her slowly and she moaned softly. He thrust deeper with each stroke, their bodies in sync, their breathing quickening. She kissed his neck and ears. He kissed her breasts, then eased her onto him. She moved faster now, pushing him deeper. He held back. She arched her back, lifted her head, eyes closed.

Her breathing increased. They came together in surges of pleasure, losing themselves, melting into each other, collapsing, listening to the silence of their love.

After several moments, he said, "May I whisper something?"

"You just did."

"That was even better than the canoe ride."

She elbowed him in the ribs.

"One other thing," he said.

"What?"

"I love you."

She mumbled the same words into his chest. They remained in each others arms throughout the night, listening to storms come and go, making love, and drifting to sleep as a new sun peeked over the evergreens and painted Whistle Lake gold.

Now, a few days later, he feared he'd never know such happiness again.

He stared at the phone, begging it to ring. Begging her voice to be on the other end, to say she was safe, to make him laugh. He wanted it more than anything he'd ever wanted.

Instead he heard seagulls shrieking like infants being slaughtered, mocking his chances of ever seeing her again.

Six

L UKE RAN at the wild-eyed man swinging a machete toward Jenna's white neck. She twisted and ducked—as the blade slashed down, barely missing her. Luke sprinted faster, but the large man had already raised the blade again.

Luke leapt, grabbed his arm and tried to rip the gleaming machete away—but the man's arm was slippery with blood, like Jenna's face. The blade moved closer...

Luke bolted awake. He was seated in his cottage chair,

---

drenched with perspiration, trembling, jolted by the realization that one nightmare was over and the other, far more terrifying, was still going on. It was five-ten in the morning, and he felt like he'd run a marathon.

He stood, stretched his muscles a few minutes, showered and shaved. After dressing, he walked into the living room, where last night's wind had swept down the chimney and blown ashes onto the fireplace bricks... ashes from the fire that bathed Jenna's face in amber a few nights ago.

He walked to a closet and took the .38 Smith & Wesson from a locked case. Running his fingers over the handle, he felt the familiar, jagged scratch he'd put there years ago at the FBI Training Academy in Quantico, Virginia.

He placed the .38 and shoulder holster in his briefcase and walked to the kitchen, still not hungry. He drank some instant coffee, then left for the office.

At six-fifty-five Luke pulled into his underground parking slot at the Renaissance Center and went up to his office. He brewed strong coffee, poured a large mug, and sat at his desk. The Leaning Tower of Work filled his in-box: six inches of stuff to read, creative requests to assign, TV storyboards to approve, commercial reels to review. He placed the reels on a nearby credenza next to his weathered Gibson L5 guitar, which reminded him he had to work on a jingle concept for a cruise-line client.

A normal, impossible workload. A workload that wouldn't get his attention.

Jenna would.

He forced himself to sort through a pile of urgent, mindless administrative work for about thirty minutes. When he finished, he walked to the window, and watched a long, dark, ore freighter glide silently along the misty river. It reminded him that Jenna and he had planned to go rafting tomorrow.

No matter where he looked, he thought of her, feared for her. Maybe he'd recognize one of the Latins in the mug shots Redstone sent over this morning. Maybe identifying one would lead him to her. Maybe Elizabeth Blakeley had found something about the Siamese Twins in the Reference Center files.

Maybes. Lousy odds. He had to do more.

On a nearby chair, he saw a framed photo he'd planned to hang the day before yesterday. A vacation photo of his parents, his brother, Kyle, and him. He remembered the vacation, walked over and began to tack it to the wall alongside other photos.

Behind him, he heard noise. He spun around and saw Marie in his doorway.

"Redecorating?" she asked, smiling.

"Hanging my parents. Kind of early, aren't you?"

"Catching up on paperwork," she said, cleaning her horn-rimmed glasses with a Kleenex. Her blue blouse and full-flowing navy skirt coordinated nicely with her short blonde hair. He realized yet again how fortunate he was to work with her. She was smart, dedicated and organized, the real manager of the creative department. She balanced the client and agency egos with humor, diplomacy and toughness as required and kept work flowing smoothly.

He poured a cup of coffee and handed it to her.

"What's this, Secretary's Week?"

"Folgers."

"Cute."

She stared at the photo he'd just hung. "Nice picture. How old were you?"

"Six."

"Cute dimples, Luke," she said, smiling. "Where was this taken?"

"On a beach north of Port Huron."

She squinted at the photo and pointed at the red stains on his hands and shirt. "You were a stigmatic?"

He smiled. "Ketchup stains. Kyle loosened the top. Splurted half the bottle on me."

"Which is why your parents are smiling."

"We smiled a lot."

"Wow—a functional family?"

"Amazing, isn't it?"

Luke stared out the window, remembering the wonderful vacations, his normal happy childhood, his decent, hardworking parents, and realized how incredibly lucky he had been. He looked back at Marie. "And now a question for you. Answer with a 'yes,' and you'll win lunch for two at the Roma Cafe."

"Yes, yes!"

"Yesterday, after I left to see Hank Redstone, did someone phone and ask where I was?"

"Yes. A man. Maybe thirty minutes after you left. Mr. Williams. A friend of your Uncle Raymond in Grand Rapids. I'm sorry your uncle passed away, Luke. Did Mr. Williams reach you at Hank's office?"

Luke adjusted the photo. "Yes. But I don't have an uncle in Grand Rapids."

Marie stared at him over her glasses.

As he explained everything, her mouth fell open and she looked back in amazement. Before she could respond, someone knocked at the door. Luke saw a large, red-haired man in a grey uniform.

"Marie Chamberlain?" he said, looking at Marie. He had a Planterra Floral Designs logo on his coat and held a large arrangement of crimson peonies wrapped in cellophane and a red bow.

"Yes," she said, staring at the flowers.

"These are for you, ma'am."

Clearly puzzled, she said "Thank you."

The man nodded and left.

"They're from Hank Redstone," Luke said.

"Hank?"

Luke explained that the flower base had mug-shot binders that he needed to look at.

"I love peonies," she said, as she smelled the magnificent red blooms. She carried them to her office and began to arrange them.

Luke lifted out two, thick binders and placed them on his desk. He pulled off the brown paper, opened the top one and looked at the first page of faces. None resembled the men he'd seen.

Page by page, he studied the brooding Latin faces, patiently examining the eyes, scrutinizing facial features. The faces fell into three main types: Spanish, Indian, and everyone else. After reviewing the photos in both binders for an hour and a half, he repeated the process.

Finally, he sat back, rubbed his eyes and called Hank Redstone.

"They're not in the books, Hank."

"You sure?"

"Positive."

"I've got more mug shots coming from L.A. and Texas. Lots more. They'll be here tomorrow."

Luke nodded, but despair ran through him like ice water. He'd hit the wall. He wasn't going to identify the men or find any leads. The informants weren't going to uncover anything. Elizabeth wasn't going to find the right Siamese Twins reference. It felt like a two-hundred-pound barbell was crushing his chest. "Let's face it, Hank."

"Face what?"

"Jenna's seen them. They'll eliminate her."

"Not necessarily."

"They tried to kill me."

"I know, but just stay cool."

"Cool? When only two informants are searching an area with five million?"

Redstone paused. "They're reliable."

Luke wasn't persuaded. He paused, forced himself to take a deep breath and let it out slowly. "I hear you, Hank. Call me the second you know anything."

"Hang tough, pal."

"Let's hope Jenna does."

They hung up.

Luke told himself to bury his negative feelings. The only way he'd make it through this ordeal was to see Jenna being rescued, see her laughing out loud at the movies, see them in each other's arms.

He wondered if Elizabeth Blakeley had found something.

He stood, told Marie he was going to see Elizabeth. Walking down the hall, he noticed that carpenters had just finished some newly decorated offices and cubicles, a pleasing blend of light-brown woods, mirrors, and distinctive artwork. The agency had fifteen more years on it's lease and it was good to know that many work stations would always offer spectacular vistas of the winding Detroit River and Windsor. The view, Luke believed, calmed and inspired people, perhaps helped them come up with better ideas. Today, however, the view wasn't helping him come up with anything.

Elizabeth, wearing a charcoal suit, sat at her desk and waved him into her office. Her blue eyes seemed to study him as he plopped into a chair.

"You look tired," she said.

He decided not to burden her with news of Jenna's kidnapping. "A little. Any luck with the Twins?"

"Not yet. But we've only completed part of the search."

He nodded, massaged his temples, then stared out the window. "Maybe there's another way to come at this."

She tilted her head, waited.

"You and Howie Kaufman still keep the new-business prospect list, don't you?"

"Yes," she said.

"You hear which accounts are in trouble, which ones might be ripe for review..."

She nodded, brushing back strands of silver hair.

"You also probably hear which advertising accounts are locked to a couple of key individuals. Totally controlled by them. Hip pocket accounts..."

"We hear about some..."

"Suppose we focused on those accounts, say five million dollars and above. Accounts that would be likely to switch agencies—if the key client and key agency guy were suddenly gone?"

"Gone as in dead?"

"Yes."

Elizabeth's eyes hardened. "*Any* account could switch if its two key people were suddenly gone as in dead. You know the ad game. Many clients change agencies for lousy reasons. The client likes Manhattan restaurants so he picks a New York agency. The client's daughter marries the new business executive at another agency. The client likes the agency's Cayman Island Seminar villa with the cute hostesses."

"Yeah, nice profession. But the guy I overheard *knows* the account will switch to his agency when the Twins are killed."

"A *fait accompli.*"

"A done deal."

Blakeley tapped her gleaming black fountain pen against her lip. "This kind of tango takes two—a very ambitious agency type and a very powerful client."

"A top management client. Someone who can force the agency switch."

"Or a client who's being blackmailed."

Luke considered this scenario. "Very possible. So how do we find accounts dominated by two people?"

"We start here." Blakeley pointed to the latest *Advertising Age* and *AdWeek* magazines on her desk. "And here." She tapped her phone. "We make some calls."

He thanked her and left the Reference Center. As he walked back to his office, he felt like an oil wildcatter drilling holes, praying one would strike oil. Perhaps Elizabeth would turn up something. Perhaps it would lead him to Jenna. Perhaps Redstone's informant would pick up Jenna's trail and they'd reach her in time.

Perhaps. Not good enough.

He had to find some way to locate Jenna quickly.

As he entered his office, his phone rang. He rushed over and grabbed it.

"Luke, it's Hank. Any luck with the Siamese Twins?"

"Not yet. We're still trying."

"Good. We checked out Detroit Memorial. A nurse saw Jenna leave with a tall Caucasian male, a little after five last night. The nurse, Anna Benoit, got a good look at the guy."

"Did she check mug shots?"

"Yeah, but no luck."

Luke swallowed a dry lump in his throat.

"We'll do a composite drawing with her," Redstone said.

"Okay."

"Maybe it'll lead to something."

"Thanks, Hank."

They hung up. Luke stared out the window. Composite draw-ings take time, even more time to refine and distribute quietly to the right people. Jenna's life depended on how *quickly* they found her. Things were not moving quickly. *He'd* have to find her, despite the kidnapper's warning not to search.

He opened his briefcase and looked at the .38 Smith & Wesson issued to him at the FBI Academy. His mind rushed back to the those days, to *the* day that changed his life. He and his fellow trainees were doing their mandatory pull-ups during the physical training circuit.

"Thirty-six!" someone shouted at him as he chinned the bar. His arms trembled with exertion.

"Your personal best!" the instructor yelled.

Luke had a little left.

"Go for forty!" someone shouted.

Forty—the class record—was held by an ex-Notre Dame tight end with gorilla arms. Forty was impossible. Maybe thirty-eight.

Luke's pulled himself up for thirty-seven, then thirty-eight. His biceps were burning, going numb, but maybe...

"Thirty-nine!" they chanted.

He got half-way up, shaking, then a little higher. He pulled himself up, wobbling, and managed to touch his chin.

"Forty... forty... forty!"

Closing his eyes, he pulled up, his arms on fire, head swim-ming. His chin touched the bar.

"Ties class record," the instructor shouted.

"Forty-one!" they shouted.

"Luke... Luke... Luke!"

He felt dizzy, but maybe... He started up, couldn't. He stared at his muscles, willing them to tighten up. Slowly, they responded, spiking pain through his shoulders to his neck. His arms trembled wildly.

He pulled to within an inch of the bar, his vision blurring. He felt his chin nudge the bar.

"Class record!"

He heard shouting, "Luke... Luke..."

The next thing he heard was the soft hum of fluorescent lights. Slowly, he opened his eyes, saw the overhead lights, a light-green hospital room, a pink-faced doctor hovering above him, bad news seeping like black oil from the doctor's eyes.

"Luke, you need rest and treatment. You've had a serious relapse. I'm sorry son, but you won't be able to continue with the New Agent Training Program."

A day later, the FBI program director visited him in the hospital and said, "You've been an outstanding trainee, Luke. Achieved excellent grades. Demonstrated leadership. But I'll be frank ..."

Luke didn't want him to be frank.

"Our field agents, as you know, experience situations that often require extraordinary physical endurance. Situations our doctor feels might cause a relapse. You could inadvertently endanger yourself and perhaps your fellow agents. Luke, we'd like you to consider one of our inside assignments, perhaps in a technical lab."

"But I've always wanted a field assignment."

He shrugged. "Your body may not be up to it. And remember—we solve just as many cases in the lab. Please give it some thought."

Luke gave it a lot of agonizing thought, day after day, week after week, as he recovered. He'd always wanted to be an agent, but knew he could never be happy bolted to a lab chair. After weeks of soul searching, he reluctantly left the academy.

Looking back, he knew his relapse had changed him. It caused him to live more cautiously, shape his life and probably to restrict it in more ways than he realized.

For one thing, he'd decided long ago that it was unfair to subject a wife and children to someone who could keel over at any time, or worse, linger with a long debilitating illness. They deserved someone with a decent chance of hanging around.

Outside, a gull soared by. Luke walked over to the window. He watched the bird speed toward the river as though time was running out in some race.

Time was running out for *Jenna*.

He could not depend on others. *He* had to find her. He'd start where she was last seen. Detroit Memorial Hospital.

* * *

Twenty stories below in the underground garage, Izzy Janek sat in a green Mazda with his partner, Cecil Milosh, a few slots from Luke Tanner's red Mustang. Janek's heavy-lidded eyes watched the elevator doors.

"Why we gotta *wait* to grease Tanner?" Janek asked, scratching his oily blond hair. He hated waiting.

"Because we gotta," Milosh said, turning the rearview mirror toward his face and moving in on a juicy red zit.

"The longer we hang around, the more likely someone'll remember us, finger us later. Any asshole knows that." Janek wanted to do the job fast and collect the fee. "I need this money. Nino's idea of a loan reminder is a bullet in my kneecap!"

Milosh laughed. "He shot a guy in the nuts once."

Janek swallowed hard, remembering the incident. He tossed a handful of pistachios into his mouth, licked his red-stained fingers, then wiped them on his sprawling stomach.

"Hell," Janek said, "I could go up to Tanner's office, flash my police badge, close his door and just jab him with the injection needle. Bingo, bango. Heart attack. Doctor don't suspect shit." He looked over at Milosh.

"You brain-dead?" Cecil Milosh began to work on a larger pimple on his chin. "We got orders! We wait till he comes down, for Chrissakes. Just make sure you're ready!"

"Been fuckin' ready for a hour!" Janek said. "And so's my little Weed Whacker." He pulled out a nine-millimeter Mini-Uzi, checked the 32-round magazine, folded the stock back in, stroked the silencer. He loved caressing the smooth weapon almost as much as using it. "I'm ready-ready-ready—"

"—to rock-n-roll!" Milosh added, popping his zit, and smearing it on his cheek. "Remember, he gets off them elevators, we don't do jack shit."

"Yeah, yeah, yeah!"

"He walks up to his car. He gets inside. We block his car. We grease him. We leave. Got it?"

"I fuckin'-A got it."

Seven

Thursday, 10:05 a.m.

JENNA FELT something squirming beneath her leg. Leaning forward, she saw a shiny, black cockroach squiggle up her calf and under her knee. She shivered, flicked it off and watched it crawl beneath a pile of yellowed newspapers. During the night, two small green eyes had gleamed at her from behind the newspapers, then disappeared.

Her legs ached from sitting all night on the cold, concrete floor. She began to massage them with her hands which were bound at the wrists by a thick rope. Humid wind gusted through a broken window onto her soot-smeared face.

She was locked in a small, garbage-strewn room on the top floor of an abandoned warehouse. The odors of urine and vomit wrapped her like a wet blanket.

What was this all about? Was Luke really shot—or was that a pretext to kidnap her? How could he be associated with people like these? Nothing made sense—except escaping. But first she needed a weapon.

She stood, stretched her cramped muscles, then trudged slowly over the filth to a rusty, fifty-gallon drum oozing a green oily substance. If it were caustic, she might rub it in their eyes. She bent down and read the drum label. Floor cleaner. At best an irritant.

She stepped onto a damp newspaper, lifted the corner and saw two half-eaten cheeseburgers green with mold and crawling with ants. Her stomach churned. She moved over to an empty cardboard box leaning against the wall. She lifted the box and jumped back.

Four green eyes stared at her from a dark hole in the wall. *Rats.* The huge rodents, their bellies swollen, held her gaze for several seconds, paralyzing her. Goosebumps fingered down her spine. She was afraid to move or scream for fear of bringing her kidnappers into the room.

The larger rat inched toward her and looked into her eyes. Then it stared at her ankle. She held her breath. Suddenly, it turned and the two rodents waddled into the wall. She exhaled and felt her body melt.

Looking around, she saw nothing she could use as a weapon. She returned to her spot, sat and stared at the metal door. Behind it, the two men guarding her, Sonny and Leonard, spoke in hushed tones. One man stood and his footsteps faded down a hallway. The other man appeared to remain seated.

When are they coming in here again? What will they do to me?

Last night, they'd brought her upstairs after the man who picked her up at the hospital had driven her at gunpoint to this abandoned warehouse near the Detroit River. They'd bound her hands and thrown her in this room without telling her why she was here or whether Luke was alive. All they said was, behave—and they'd release her. She didn't believe them.

A key rattled into the door. She straightened up and held her breath.

The knob jiggled, the door opened and the yellow glow from the outer room silhouetted Sonny, the short, muscular man who'd bound her hands.

He strolled over, leaned close, and stared at her with tiny dark pupils, pinpoints, probably caused by drugs. His flat nose had been broken and bent left, as though it wanted you to notice the purple zig-zag scar on his cheek.

As he untied her wrist rope, she saw his left hand had the nub of a sixth, withered finger. When he realized she saw it, he curled it into his palm.

"Your boyfriend. We wanna talk to him," Sonny wheezed, bathing her with the stench of stale beer. "But we got a problem, see. He ain't sleepin' at home. We think you might know where he's at."

Luke is alive. Relief flooded her. She closed her eyes, pretending to think, assuming Luke was probably at the cottage. "I don't know."

He scrunched his thick brow. "We think you might."
"But—"

His sausage fingers pinched her cheeks like a vise. "I can *help* you remember."

Her mind searched for something to say. She remembered their rafting trip. "Maybe he's checking out rafting equipment. We were going rafting tomorrow."

"Raftin'?"
"Yes."
"Where?"
"Near Flint somewhere. I'm not sure."

Sonny's eyes narrowed and she noticed a trace of white powder on one nostril. "What about his buddies at the agency? They gotta know where he's at."

She had to think fast. If she told him about Luke's friend, Eddie, they would kidnap him.

"I met a couple of his agency friends once, but I can't remember their last names."

"Bad answer, Doctor Johannson," he said, shaking her head from side to side. "You know his agency pals good. You'll give me a name one way or another." His gaze crawled down her body, then he coughed, turned and spat into the corner.

"Talk," Sonny whispered, "or Leonard'll show you his special talent. You know what his special talent is?"

She didn't want to know.

"Tongues." He grinned. "See, crazy bastard collects 'em. One to a jar. Talks to them fuckin' tongues, would you believe? Four years in a nut house didn't fix him. 'Course he's got other talents, if you get my drift. He told me he wants to play with you real bad. And if you still can't remember any names after Leonard plays with you, he'll play with Tanner's secretary."

A hard knot formed in her throat. "There's a man in the Creative Department. Tom Lander. Tom and Luke go to Red Wings games together."

She lowered her head as though betraying Lander, who Luke told her was shooting television commercials in the Mojave Desert for two weeks.

Sonny scrawled the name on a yellow note pad, then leaned close, his body odor gagging her.

"Now you're being smart. This Tom guy better tell us where Tanner's at. If he don't, me and Leonard'll be back." As he stood, his hand grazed her breast and she jerked away.

He grinned, left and locked the door.

She leaned back against the wall and let tension seep from her body. She was being held by psychopaths, men who would think nothing of torturing and raping her to get information. Soon they would want another name when Sonny discovered Lander was in the Mojave. She'd have to give them another name. But whose? And if she didn't, they'd take Marie.

She stared up at the dim light bulb dangling from the ceiling. What was this all about? Did Luke know these people? Had Luke done something to them?

Is there a dark side of Luke? Did my attraction to him blind me to it?

He must be staying at the cottage. Its location, she knew, might be tortured out of her by Sonny and Leonard. If Luke was hurt as a result, she'd never be able to live with herself.

Her only solution was to find a way out of here.

She stepped to the window and looked out. An adjacent wing of the warehouse indicated she was six floors up. On the roof, a large billboard flashed "Mohawk Vodka" in red neon letters.

Below her was a loading zone littered with beer cans, wine bottles and fast-food bags. In the corner, a rust-eaten truck sat on tire-stripped wheels. The blue Lumina van that bought her here was hidden behind a garbage bin. Surrounding the loading zone was a crumbling, red-brick wall, beyond which stood abandoned buildings like dark skeletons sucked clean of life.

Looking down, she saw a narrow ledge about twelve feet below. Another ledge flashed in her mind. She'd been seven, walking on a skinny ledge of a half-constructed house. She'd fallen, ripped her leg on a nail and struck her head on the ground. She'd awakened in a hospital. Since then, heights, even step ladders, terrified her.

She looked down at the ledge again. To reach it, she'd have to hang from the window, drop and land perfectly on the six-inch ledge. At best, a one-in-fifty chance. Then she'd have to jump to the loading zone forty feet below.

The window was no escape route.

A mile to the west, she saw the Detroit skyline, dominated by the sun-drenched towers of the Ren Cen. To its right was the majestic Penobscot Building, and nearby, older skyscrapers. To her left, Windsor flickered in the sunlight, a smaller city squinting up at its tall U.S. cousin across the river.

Her focus swung back to the Ren Cen's 400 Tower. She counted up to the twenty-third floor where Luke's office was. Perhaps he was there now. Perhaps he was looking out his window in her direction...looking with his gentle, sea-green eyes. She'd been attracted to them, to their warmth from the moment she first saw him. She liked his natural, easy smile, how it lingered, how his thick, chestnut hair misbehaved, how *he* misbehaved now and then, how his lips curved at the corner, how his tall, athletic body moved, how his arms felt around her.

More than anything, she liked his kindness and sense of humor. At first, they'd disarmed her, and in the last two months drawn her even closer to him. Last Saturday they'd made love, and she knew her life had changed. They'd both known things had changed. They'd become serious. But cautious. They knew their careers, essential to them both, demanded their on-call, full attention.

So did a marriage. So did a family. She wanted it all, knew she could balance it all. True, friends she respected had tried and failed. But there had been reasons. Through discipline, sacrifice, and above all love, she knew *she* could balance it all.

Still she sensed Luke holding back a bit. Was it her? Or did he fear his leukemia would return and kill him like cancer had killed his mother at an early age?

A key clicked in the door, startling her.

Leonard walked in, carrying a McDonald's bag. He was well over six-feet-tall. Tiny blue veins road-mapped his broad nose. His two hundred forty pounds were stacked mostly in his shoulders and chest. The bottom of his shirt was unbuttoned and his stomach ballooned through as white as a sperm whale.

He leaned close and she flinched when she noticed a hideous purple lump where his left ear had once been. His grey lips were fat and moist. He stared at her mouth with vacant, dead eyes.

"We got you somethin' to eat," he said, ripping open the bag and placing a Big Mac and french fries on the floor beside her.

Despite the fact she wasn't hungry, she clutched the hamburger and took a huge bite, thinking he wouldn't attack while she ate. A chunk of dry bun stuck to her chalk-dry throat and she started to gag. She tried to swallow, but couldn't. Finally, she forced it

BUSINESS TO KILL FOR

down.

"Tastes good, don't it?" he said, his mouth hanging open, revealing nicotine teeth and a gray, deeply-creviced tongue. He watched her chew.

She nodded, took another bite, gulped it down.

His left eye began to twitch.

"Sonny says you gave us the name of a guy at the agency who knows where your boyfriend's at. That's real smart."

She nodded, chewing.

"Our guys are checking this Tom dude out now. Real persuasive guys." He moved closer, obviously trying to see into her mouth.

She chewed with her mouth closed and searched for a way to deflect his attention. "Do you have a cigarette?"

His eyes widened. "A doctor that smokes?"

"A bad habit, I know."

"Got a couple them my own self," he said, pulling out a pack of Camels.

She took one, her first since high school, then leaned forward as he lit it. She inhaled, let the smoke roll out slowly. She tried to hide her trembling hand, but he noticed and smiled.

"Here's somethin' to drink." He pulled a large Coke from the bag and handed it to her.

She gulped it down, burning her throat until her eyes teared. The sugar jolted her aching muscles awake.

"Thirsty? Let me help," He tipped the container, purposely drenching her white blouse and breasts.

"Real clumsy of you, Doctor Johannson," he said, staring at her breasts.

The door banged open.

Sonny stormed in carrying a cell phone, his face red and angry. He bent down and whispered to Leonard, whose eyes hardened and turned toward Jenna.

"Well, well, Sonny tells me this Tom Lander is out of town."

In fuckin' California for a week!" Sonny grunted, moving toward her. "Gonna be out there another week."

"You didn't know that, did you?" Leonard asked.

"How could I?" Her body trembled.

They stared at her.

"You know, Sonny, I ain't real sure she gets how serious we are."

"Me neither."

"We may have to like, you know, impress her."

"Yeah."

Leonard leaned close, bathing her with the scent of rotten teeth. "I may have to impress her first."

Eight

LUKE TOLD Marie he was going to drive over and talk to Nurse Benoit, Jenna's friend at Detroit Memorial, who'd seen her leave with the man. He'd also check around, ask if anyone saw anything.

Hurrying toward the elevators, he pulled out his keys and stopped. The kidnappers knew the Mustang. Bullet holes through its window were compelling proof. They could be waiting for the Mustang to pull out of the parking garage. He needed new wheels.

He walked back and phoned Connor Dow's car-pool manager, a woman who skillfully coordinated twenty World Motors vehicles and ten competitive cars.

"Barb, this is Luke."

"Hi, Luke. Need wheels?"

"Windows."

"What?"

"Expressway sniper problem."

"Luke!" her voice leapt an octave. "My God! Were you hurt?"

"Small nick," he said, touching the scab below his eye. "Got anything I could drive?"

"What would you like?"

"Fast."

"Erskine just dropped off the black Corvette."

"That will do nicely."

Minutes later, with Corvette keys in hand, Luke rode an elevator toward the Renaissance Center's subterranean parking garage. He wondered if they were waiting for him out on the street. To help conceal his face, he put on sunglasses and turned his collar up.

He reached into his pocket for a notepad on which he'd jotted a list of questions. It wasn't there. *Damn, I left it in the Mustang.* He decided to go get the notepad, punched the button and headed down. As the elevator door opened at his floor, he remembered he'd left the notepad at the cottage.

Car doors slammed. He saw two large men running from a green Mazda toward the elevator. Their eyes gave them away.

They wanted *him*—not the elevator.

One man yanked out a handgun.

Luke ducked back, reached for his gun and realized he'd left it in his briefcase. He hit the Close Doors button and flattened himself against the side wall. The doors didn't move.

Again, he jabbed the Close Doors and A-level buttons.

Slowly, the doors began to inch toward each other. Footsteps pounded toward the elevator.

The doors closed to twelve inches...

The footsteps grew louder. Any second, a large hand would reach in, trigger the doors back open.

Three inches...

The doors touched—as fists slammed against them. The elevator began its ascent and he heard the men shouting to each other and running away.

The doors opened and Luke sprinted toward the gleaming, black Corvette one hundred feet away. He beeped the doors open, leapt in and found himself surrounded by enough dazzling green and red instrument displays to fill an F-16 cockpit.

He raced out of the parking spot. They'd probably assumed he'd returned to his office. At the Exit Gate, he slid his card into the slot and drove quickly onto Beaubien. His rearview mirror was still empty as he turned right onto Jefferson. He exhaled, felt his pulse wind down a bit.

So, they were still after *him*. Why, if they had Jenna? They either thought he knew more than he did or that he might figure things out.

Minutes later, he turned into the parking lot of the massive Detroit Memorial Hospital complex on East Warren. He waited a minute to make sure the green Mazda didn't pull in after him, then entered the hospital.

Stepping off on the ninth floor, Luke caught the familiar *aire de pediatrics*—disinfectant, diapers, Desinex and baby powder. No wonder kids developed asthma. He saw Nurse Anna Benoit, ensconced as usual behind the desk in the nurses' station, filling out forms. Luke liked the energetic, pink-faced woman, who was still attractive despite her extra fifty pounds. In her mid-fifties, her silver hair and thick black eyebrows framed warm, aquamarine eyes and a wrinkle-free face. She ran her unit with a blend of intelligence, love and butt kicking as needed.

Jenna claimed Anna had taught her more practical, hands-on medicine than most medical school professors.

Nurse Benoit's eyes widened when she saw him. "Any word, Luke?"

"Not yet, Anna."

She slumped forward, lowered her eyes and shook her head from side to side. "The man said you'd been shot, Luke. He said you were critical and asking for her. Jenna was terrified."

He nodded. "Is there somewhere we can talk?"

"Sure." She handed two patient charts to a young nurse, and led Luke to a cramped lounge where they sat in frayed La-Z-Boy chairs. Next to the chairs were two rocking horses held together with silver masking tape. A wooden chest was crammed with stuffed animals and faded Fisher Price toys. Beanie Babies and other Toys of The Year formed a mountain in the corner.

She looked over at Luke and pushed her wire-rimmed glasses back up her nose. "You want to know about the man she left with?"

He nodded.

"Like I told the lieutenant, he was six-one, maybe taller. Weighed about one-eighty. Brown hair, shiny, combed back straight. He wore a grey suit. Seemed nice, concerned. But obviously wasn't."

"How old?"

"Forty-five, tops."

"Did Jenna recognize him?"

"No. He said his name was John Rasmussen and that he worked with you. Claimed he was in Research."

Luke knew a John Rasmussen in Research. Short. Bald.

"Anyway," she continued, "This Rasmussen said he happened to be driving by, saw your Mustang and the police car and stopped. He said you asked him to come get Jenna."

"You didn't recognize him in the mug shots?"

"No." She bit her lower lip and closed her eyes. "I should have suspected something."

"How could you know?"

She shrugged. "What's this all about, Luke?"

"Bad people. I overheard their plans. They don't want the police investigating. Jenna's their insurance policy."

A slow blush rose over her smooth cheeks. "Our little ones

keep asking for her. One toddler won't eat unless Doctor Jenna feeds her. And Michele, who looks worse, asked for Jenna. I told her she was out on an emergency."

She hiked her glasses up over moist eyes, picked up a rubber frog, dropped it in the wooden chest, shook her head. "She's such a gifted doctor."

Luke nodded.

"We'll get her back, won't we?" Her eyes begged for assurance he couldn't give.

"Yes, Anna, we will." He had no idea how.

He stood, thanked her and left. Downstairs, he talked to several security guards and the receptionist. They all reminded him that hospital lobbies are very busy places with hundreds of people coming and going hourly. No one recalled seeing Jenna leave with a man.

His hospital visit had turned up nothing.

In the parking lot, Luke pulled up to the pay booth where a woman attendant rested her pendulous bosom and arms on the windowsill.

"Dollar cash, or I slit your tires!" she said, smiling.

"You're a hard woman, LaTonya," he said, smiling back. "What's new?"

"Son outa rehab. Stayin' clean, too."

"Good for him," Luke said, handing her a dollar with his ticket. "LaTonya, did you see Jenna leave here yesterday evening between five and six?"

She turned and squinted toward the corner of the parking lot as though replaying a video.

"She come out early, little after five. How I know is Carmen Harlan was doing the news. Doctor Jenna, she come out with a tall man. Left with him too."

Luke felt his heart start pounding. "Did you see his car?"

"Wasn't no car."

"What was it?"

"One of them slanty vans. You know, all sloopy up front. *Chevy* van. A Luna..."

"Lumina?"

"Yeah, that's it. *Lumina* van. Dark blue. Slick lookin.' Mind having me one."

Luke's hope was rekindled. He had something. "Did a policeman ask you about Jenna and the van?"

"Nobody axked me nothin'. I only just got here."

"You sure it was a dark-blue Lumina?"

"Uh-huh. Hell, Luke, all I do is look at cars."

"Did it have a Michigan license plate?"

"Didn't look at no plate."

"Anything else?"

She rested her chins on her palm and closed her large, brown eyes. "Yeah. They was a sticker, bright yellow—shape like a spark plug—on the window where the driver sits at. Sticker had a red name smack in the middle. Name begin with a 'P'. No, wait—it was a 'B'—yeah a '*B*'!"

He tried to think of spark plug brands. ACDelco, Champion, came to mind.

"You sure it was a spark plug?"

"Uh-huh."

Then it hit him. "Was it 'Bosch'?"

"That's it."

A Bosch spark plug sticker. Something tangible. "Thanks, LaTonya. You've helped a lot."

"Doctor Jenna, she gonna be all right? I owe that girl. She got Jamal into rehab when the man said they wasn't no room."

"We hope everything's all right. But if you remember anything else about the van, or the man she left with, please call me fast." He handed her his card.

A horn honked behind him.

LaTonya glowered at the driver. "Hush up, fool! You at a hospital!" She smiled at Luke. "I remember anything, Luke, I call you."

He thanked her and drove onto East Warren, elated about the Lumina lead. He had *something*.

He gazed up at Detroit Memorial's third floor, as he always

did, and counted over to the sixth window—*the* window. Behind its grey curtains, many years ago, he'd held his mother's hand as she died on a rainy January night. He could still see her cracked lips, eyes like oily blue marbles, an IV piercing the large purple vein in her arm, the pain killer dripping slowly into the remaining eighty-five pounds of her cancer-ravaged body. Two days earlier, she had awakened for twenty minutes, long enough to celebrate her forty-second birthday.

The memory still pierced him like a red-hot poker. He'd been thirteen and the loss destroyed him. She'd been the heart of the family, a warm, comfortable, normal, middle-class family of four who loved each other without qualification. Her rules ruled: Studies first, help around the house second, then play. Sequence was everything. Exceptions were rare.

Even today, Luke missed his mother's wisdom, her clear sense of right and wrong. He still used the Mom Test—if it felt wrong, it probably was. If it felt right, do it. She would have advised him on how to balance his illness with his career, with a marriage and family. She would have helped him clarify, simplify, prioritize, and *destress* things. She would have enriched his life in more ways than he could imagine.

Beside him, a noisy furniture truck belched exhaust fumes into the Corvette. Luke sped away. He needed a place to think. Moments later, he remembered the new Normandy Bar, a few blocks away.

As he drove, he saw the former General Motors Building which General Motors had turned over to the State of Michigan and Wayne County when GM bought the Ren Cen. He recalled walking into the old building's magnificent lobby several years ago to interview for his first job in advertising at Campbell-Ewald on the fourth floor.

A friend had set up the interview three weeks after Luke had left the FBI Academy infirmary. While recuperating, he had roughed out some creative concepts for television commercials and advertisements. He showed the creative director his anti-cruelty-to-animals television commercial concept in which the camera panned a line of starving, tortured pets while the voice over said, "Their owners are animals." The creative director offered him a job on the spot. He accepted, and one week later, he was writing ads for pickles and Firestone tractor tires. He discovered he had a knack for the business and had loved it ever since.

Behind him, a Marathon Oil truck honked, jolting him back to the moment. He turned down Milwaukee, parked and walked to the Normandy Bar.

Inside, he grabbed a stool at the smokey bar and inhaled the familiar mix of garlic and cigar smoke. Just like the old Normandy. He scanned the executives and their suppliers nursing drinks or chomping on the Normandy's massive, juicy hamburgers that made the Whopper look like a cocktail cracker. Luke knew he should eat something, but he still had no appetite.

"What'd you like?" asked the rotund, white-shirted bartender.

"Molson Canadian."

"Comin' up."

As he sipped the beer, he gazed over at the massive grey-beige stones of the former GM Building, and remembered Campbell-Ewald's Chevrolet theme "Heartbeat of America..."

The song triggered something in his memory. He stood, hurried to the hall phone and called a friend, Eddie Berger, at Connor Dow. Berger was a brilliant art director and one of Luke's associate creative directors. The large, gentle man had spent some of his family's substantial inheritance amassing collections of antique cars, antique guitars and modern weapons.

"Berger," said the familiar, raspy voice.

"Eddie, it's Luke."

"You're in a saloon. I can hear."

"Good ears. The Normandy."

"Order me a libation."

"I'm coming back now. Listen Eddie, you remember your pal at Chevrolet Headquarters? The guy with computer lists of new Chevrolet buyers?"

"Lew."

"Think he could identify buyers of Lumina vans in the Detroit area?"

"Probably. What's going on?"

"It's serious, Eddie."

Luke explained everything.

When he finished, Berger remained silent for several seconds. "Jesus Christ, Luke. This is unreal."

"Will your friend help us?"

"Hell, yes."

"But he'll probably have regulations about who can access the list. Chevrolet won't want our agency guys looking at its customer lists."

"Screw regulations. Lew will help."

"I hope so. I'm coming back to the agency now."

"I'll phone Lew."

"Thanks, Eddie."

Luke paid, left, and drove off toward the agency. He felt encouraged. Soon he might have a list of Luminas in the Detroit area. With five million people living in the greater Detroit area, how many drove blue Lumina vans? Probably thousands. How many of those had a yellow Bosch spark plug sticker on the driver's window? Maybe fifty. Unless thousands of stickers were given out. A distinct possibility.

Still weighing these questions, he drove into the shadows of the Ren Cen towers. He turned onto Beaubien, checking for the green Mazda, didn't see it. He slowed near the entrance to the underground garage and drove inside.

Glancing in the rearview mirror, he saw no one follow him in. As he started up the ramp—a parked car pulled out—and moved behind him. His pulse shifted into high gear.

He checked the mirror.

A black *Toyota*. He relaxed and continued up the ramp. Glancing in the mirror, he saw the Toyota move closer. Two men inside. As garage lights lit their faces, he recognized the elevator men. The passenger pulled something metal from his coat.

Luke didn't wait to count the gun's chambers.

He floored the Corvette, squealed up the ramp, hugged the

corner, narrowly missing a concrete abutment, and raced up the second level ramp.

The Toyota raced after him.

Luke pulled away, thanks to the Corvette's speed. But speed wasn't the problem. The problem was he only had two more floors. They'd trap him unless he did something fast.

He turned, bolted across the floor parking area and raced down the exit ramp. The men in the Toyota did not see him turn down. They were heading up.

In seconds he'd be outside.

He drove around the ramp corner at frantic speed, barely missing a wall streaked with paint scuffs. He turned down another ramp and screeched to a stop.

At the bottom of the ramp—facing him—sat the Toyota.

The fat, blond passenger, jumped out and aimed his gun.

Luke shoved the car into reverse and hit the gas. Two muffled shots dinged off the ramp in front of Luke, chipping chunks of concrete onto his windshield.

He squealed the Corvette backwards up the ramp, whirled around ninety degrees. He heard the Toyota's car door slam, tires squealing, engine revving.

He sped to the other side, made a split-second decision to hide beside a shadowy elevator shaft. Five seconds later the Toyota raced by and headed up to the next floor.

He crept out, eased down the ramp, then accelerated, walls blurring past. He prayed no one was around the blind corner. Seconds later, Luke blasted through the wooden arm, knocking chunks onto the street.

He heard the Toyota behind him in the parking structure, squeal around ramp corners, coming after him.

He sped off toward Jefferson Avenue, then slammed on the brakes. Two parked delivery trucks obstructed his way. He checked the rearview mirror as the black Toyota bolted from the garage and came after him.

He was blocked—the Toyota closing fast.

Luke steered onto the sidewalk, zig-zagged around a streetlight pole, causing a wino to drop his bottle and run. Bouncing the Corvette onto Jefferson Avenue, Luke floored it and headed for the entrance to I-75.

The Toyota was just two hundred yards behind.

He pushed the Corvette to one hundred six miles an hour and the Toyota fell back a bit.

Traffic was light in the passing lane and Luke dodged cars and trucks easily. He checked the mirror. Other vehicles were blocking the Toyota in.

He relaxed a bit. He would get off at the next exit and lose them.

Then he felt like he'd caught a hockey puck in the throat.

The gas needle was below E.

It was not bouncing.

Nine

Thursday, 11:55 a.m.

FORREST KLUG fingered the white cap of his Mont Blanc pen as he sat at his massive mahogany desk, waiting for Mason Bennett. He wondered if Bennett had handled Luke Tanner and the woman yet. Tanner had to be terminated before he accidentally stumbled onto the Twins' identities, remote as that possibility was.

Klug was not worried. Bennett handled things. Klug had learned that many years ago in the steamy jungles of Vietnam.

Since then, Bennett had handled many difficult assignments for him—flawlessly. Bennett delivered. Klug could count on him.

"Mr. Carter Hunt is here," Klug's secretary said on the intercom.

"Send him in, Lucinda."

Carter Hunt, born Mason Bennett, strolled in, sat down opposite Klug's desk. Bennett's dark, reptilian eyes, capable of watching a train wreck without blinking, peered out from alabaster skin that had picked up few wrinkles since Nam. A tiny scar curled his thin lips into a slight, left-sided sneer. Brown-blond hair, thick and combed-back, crowned his chiseled, angular face. His broad shoulders and muscular biceps filled his custom-made, blue Armani suit.

A gold Rolex, silk Hermes tie, custom white shirt, alligator shoes, and silk handkerchief in his coat pocket rounded out the polished-executive look. All veneer.

Beneath was street thug. A very intelligent, competent thug. A man who understood life's basic truth, that morality is for losers.

Klug turned off his office intercom, pushed a desk button and watched the door click shut. He locked on Bennett's narrow eyes. "Tanner and the woman?"

"They'll be taken care of," Bennett said.

"I've decided their deaths must look like accidents."

Bennett nodded. "Actually, they're helping us with that."

Klug waited for an explanation.

"Tanner's secretary mentioned they were going rafting Friday," Bennett said. He detailed his plan.

When he finished, Klug nodded agreement. As usual, Bennett had done his homework. A simple rafting accident. Happens all the time.

"Do it," Klug said, opening an antique humidor and choosing a Cuban Montecristo cigar. "You asked yesterday about my overall plan." He lit the cigar and strolled over to a large wall panel covered with a purple velvet curtain.

He pushed a wall button, and the curtain folded to the side, revealing a fifteen-foot-square world map dotted with hundreds of colored push-pins. The pins were clustered in the major cities of Europe, Asia, the Americas, the Far East and the Pacific.

"You're looking at GlobeLink, my agency's beloved holding company and its many worldwide offices," Klug said, turning his good eye toward the map. "Each pin color represents one of GlobeLink's independent advertising and media networks. My network, Kennard Rickert, is represented by the red pins. R & M MultiCom by blue. WestSat Media, white. Connor Dow, green. IntraMark, yellow. Five, large, respected networks."

"Only one has more pins than yours," Bennett added.

"But that starts to change Sunday."

"With the Twins' accident?"

Klug nodded. "When my agency takes over their account—all one billion dollars worth—*I* will control more billings and more media properties than any other officer in GlobeLink. Eight hundred million dollars more than GlobeLink's Chairman, Harold Pilking. That's leverage. I'll use it and the backing of GlobeLink board members to replace him as chairman."

"You're *that* sure of their backing?"

Klug felt his lips bend in a smile. "I'm sure I have very sensitive information about each. Information they can ill afford to have made public." Klug pushed in a loose red pin near Paris and made a mental note to buy a hot new agency there.

"So the Twins' death achieves your objective," Bennett said, sliding his palms back over his slick hair like a swimmer.

"Only Phase One," Klug said. "As Chairman of GlobeLink I'll control nearly twenty-seven billion dollars worth of advertising networks and media groups globally." Saying the words rushed a delicious burst of power through him. He strolled alongside the massive wall map. "That's when I'll trigger Phase Two: Meridian Media."

As expected, Bennett's eyes widened in disbelief. "Your father's company?"

Klug nodded.

"You've got to be joking."

Klug's chest muscles tightened. "I never joke about my father."

"He won't sell," Bennett said. "Meridian's very profitable. And he spent his life building it."

"And destroyed everyone around him in the process."

Bennett stared at him. "Still, there's no way he'll sell."

"*Au contraire*. He'll *have* to sell." The thought warmed him, like twisting a knife in his father's heart.

Bennett still seemed skeptical. "Why's he have to sell?"

"Simple. Our GlobeLink agencies, which currently spend hundreds of millions in advertising in Meridian's media, will get *much* better advertising rates from my affiliate media. At the same time, Meridian will experience operational problems."

Bennett perked up like the problems might earn him fat fees.

"His television stations," Klug continued, "will experience technical problems. His newspapers will have union problems. Computer systems viruses will cause his magazines to miss issue dates. Advertisers will demand refunds. Meridian revenue will dwindle. Creditors will scream for their money."

Bennett's deep, black eyes glinted.

"Then a pleasant, elderly woman from Des Moines will offer to purchase Meridian. A *very* attractive offer. He'll jump at it."

"Is she the buyer?"

"I am. But Daddy Dearest won't know."

Bennett nodded with appropriate admiration.

"After the sale," Klug said, "I'll walk in and fire the bastard. Give him thirty minutes to clear out."

"That'll kill him."

"Yes...it will," he said, savoring the thought. *Like his betrayal killed my mother.* Klug jammed a pin deep into the map and felt the hot rush of anger.

He adjusted the gold link on his monogrammed french cuff, returned to his desk and clicked the door open, signaling that their meeting was over. Obediently, Bennett stood and walked toward the door.

Klug watched Bennett leave. A skilled, persistent doer, not a thinker. Needed direction. But he marveled at how the man always delivered time and time again over the years. Even under incredible circumstances like in Vietnam. His mind drifted back to Nam, to his days as a CIA-assigned military intelligence officer, to his comfortable life running Medusa.

His Medusa network had transported opium and heroin between Thailand, Laos and Vietnam, using a secure, brilliant, free-distribution system: U.S. military aircraft. Easiest millions he'd ever made. In fact, twenty-three million of it was still earning a healthy interest in Brussels banks.

Mason Bennett had handled Medusa's day-to-day operations, bribes, occasional wet work very efficiently—until the Siamese Twins had noticed a ripped heroin bag on the AC-47 and told the Brass. The Brass traced it to Klug and discharged him immediately, citing battle fatigue. They'd insisted he never mention Medusa or run for political office. They feared some enterprising journalist would uncover Medusa and destroy their careers by discovering that U.S. military aircraft had flown drugs which turned some American soldiers into walking zombies and some into corpses.

When Klug told his father he'd been discharged and couldn't enter politics, his father had gone berserk. Hendrick Klug had long ago ordained that he enter politics. The old man had meticulously planned each step of Klug's political career—from Vietnam hero to the Senate to the Whitehouse. Hendrick Klug, seething, red-faced, neck arteries bulging, had disinherited him on the spot and refused to speak to him since.

In the following weeks, Klug's daily calls to his father's secretary were answered with "Your father is not here." Klug was not surprised. The bastard had never been there for him. Had never cared about anyone but himself. Had never cared about the pain he'd caused Klug's mother; perhaps he had even enjoyed it.

Soon Hendrick Klug would feel pain.

Ten

Thursday, 12:20 a.m.

AFTER LOSING the Toyota in traffic near the Eastern Market, Luke nursed the nearly-empty Corvette back into the shadows of the Ren Cen.

Knowing the men in the Toyota might be waiting near the garage entrance, he parked in a small lot on Beaubien. He scanned the area and saw no one watching him, no black Toyota or green Mazda.

He adjusted his sunglasses, stepped from the car and blended in with some noisy tourists. Cars and trucks jammed Jefferson Avenue. A long queue of vehicles snaked toward the tunnel to Canada. He checked for the Mazda and Toyota again but didn't see them. Ahead, the Ren Cen's four, gleaming, thirty-nine-story towers stood around the majestic seventy-three-story Marriott Hotel.

If I just make it inside the Ren Cen, I'm safe. The Ren Cen, he recalled, had helped save the city, ignited its recovery. The sparks had taken a while, but now the city's renewal was in full bloom, along the river, in Greektown, in the Fox Theater district, in the new sports stadiums, in the new casinos, new shopping areas, new homes and neighborhoods popping up everywhere. Office rents were climbing, businesses were rushing back, new restaurants were sprouting weekly. General Motor's gutsy and brilliant purchase of the Ren Cen had greatly accelerated the rebirth.

The Motor City's renaissance was in high gear, and Luke enjoyed the vibrations more each day.

He entered with the tourists through the Jefferson Avenue door and checked the immediate area. His assassins were nowhere in sight. He took a freight elevator up and got off three floors below Connor Dow. Checking the stairwell, he saw it was empty and climbed to the agency's mailroom.

Moments later, he settled in at his desk, phoned Redstone and explained what had happened.

"So," Redstone said, "they're still interested in you."

"In my obituary."

"They must think you know the Siamese Twins."

"Or that I'll be able to put everything together."

"Which is possible."

"Hell, I know maybe a thousand people in this business. Let's assume I do know the Twins. How do I identify them?"

Redstone was silent for several seconds. "I don't know. But I do know we're running out of time."

"Like Jenna."

Redstone coughed and cleared his throat. "Unfortunately, my sources haven't come up with anything yet."

Luke's stomach churned and he slumped further down in his chair. "We've got nothing."

Redstone paused. "We got one thing."

"What?"

"You."

Luke didn't like the feel of this.

"They're anxious to nail you, right?"

"There's some evidence to that effect."

"So we help them," Redstone said.

"Spoken like a friend."

"We'll protect you."

"Spoken like a cop."

"They must be watching your home," Redstone said.

"Probably."

"So tonight you stay there. We'll plant guys inside. I'll be outside with a squad. When the bad guys come, we collar them and strongly suggest they tell us where Jenna is."

"And if they won't?"

"We suggest Jackson State Prison."

Luke thought about it and realized he didn't have a better idea. "Okay."

"I'll have someone come get your key."

"Tell them to turn left, lift and jiggle."

"One other thing."

"What?"

"I'm installing Caller ID on your phone. See if the bad guys are anxious to talk to you."

"Makes sense."

They hung up. Luke agreed that using himself as bait might be his best and only chance of finding Jenna.

"Where the hell you been?"

Luke turned and saw Eddie Berger at his door.

"I was getting kind of worried," Berger said.

"You had reason. I'll explain on the way to see your pal at Chevrolet."

"Lew'll be *here* any minute."

"Terrific."

"And he's bringing the list of Lumina van buyers."

"How many?"

"Your basic shitload."

Six minutes later, Lew Meads, a tanned, lanky man in his mid-thirties sat in Luke's office. Meads opened his buffed, mahogany-hued briefcase, lifted out a thick computer printout and fanned its green accordion-like pages.

"Here's everyone who's bought a new Lumina van in the Detroit ADI metro area."

"Luke scanned the rows of blurring names. "How many?"

"Nine thousand, seven hundred and forty-six."

Luke felt like a concrete block had dropped on his neck. He stared at the pages. "We'll never get through this list, even with police help."

"Wait," Berger said, "can this list tell us which vans are blue?"

Meads ran his finger along the letter codes at the printout's top. "No."

Luke slumped in his chair.

The list was a dead end.

Eleven

Thursday, 4:35 p.m.

FORREST KLUG'S rented Dodge Ram pickup barreled through a thicket of tall pines, hugged a curve and headed down a narrow country road. He hated the pickup. It made him look even smaller. His Jaguar XJ12's power seat raised him to normal height. But he couldn't drive it where he was going. The Jaguar would stick out like a diamond in dog turds. Klug had to blend in.

Through the thick boughs he saw the orange neon sign of the

Rendez-Booze Tavern, a redneck bar stuck beside a weed-choked pond, thirty miles northwest of Detroit. He detested the bar and the subhuman scum inside. The good news was they were stupid. None of them would recognize him or Jungle Jim, the man he was meeting.

Klug wanted absolute certainty that Jungle Jim would deliver what he'd once promised. Even if the man balked, Klug had the leverage to make him deliver.

Klug crunched onto the gravel lot crammed with pickups, vans and motorcycles. He parked next to a rusty Ford van with a "Preserve Your Right To Arm Bears" bumper sticker. Checking himself in the mirror, he decided his fake beard, wraparound sunglasses and turned-up collar obscured his face well. The disguise, one of Mason Bennett's many disguises, worked.

The bar's screen door slapped shut. Klug turned and saw a woman, mid-fifties, skeletal thin, drunk, stagger into the parking lot. Her resemblance to his mother, Rena Mae, startled him. He recalled his mother's alcohol-flushed face and straggly hair, her red-rimmed eyes focused on breakfast—a tall tumbler of scotch. He could still see her passed out on the carpet, hand clutching her best friend, a bottle of Chivas Regal, empty. Rena Mae Klug, the last months of her life. A life destroyed by his father. She was the only person who'd ever been there for him, the only person who'd protected him from his father.

The Rendez-Booze Bar door slapped shut again. A fat guy strolled out, eased onto a black Harley Softail and roared off.

Klug pulled his John Deere cap down over his eyes and strolled into the bar which appeared about two-thirds full. Even though he wore cowboy boots, everyone seemed taller. He hated them. The place smelled like someone stuffed wet newspapers into the ventilation system. Country music whined from a jukebox. A five-foot television screen replayed a Detroit Tiger home run which several customers saluted by chugging their beers.

A few people noticed Klug was a stranger, turned back to the television. He walked toward the back, crunching peanut shells on a beer-damp floor. He passed a slow-dancing couple in jeans and western shirts, three braless women in T-shirts playing pool, an old hunchback with a cowboy hat sipping beer and two red-faced dwarfs arm wrestling for cheering drunks. Human scum. Dregs. He'd love to throw a grenade at them when he left.

In a corner booth, he saw Jungle Jim. Almost fitting in with the crowd.

The man, about fifty, looked distinguished even in faded jeans and a red-plaid shirt. His face was well-concealed by dark wrap-around sunglasses and a pulled-down NASCAR racing cap. A fake, grey beard blended with a hairpiece tied in a ponytail.

Klug sat down opposite him.

"You look like a regular," Klug said. *Not*, he thought, *like the vice chairman of one of world's largest corporations.*

Jungle Jim shrugged, clearly not wanting to be here, and probably wondering why Klug told him to wear a disguise. Jungle Jim scanned the people nearby, his fingers tapping the Molson beer coasters.

A short, middle-aged waitress with carrot-orange hair frozen in a beehive, massive breasts and green tennis shoes strolled up to the table. She studied them a moment, obviously sizing them up as strangers, then yanked a pencil from her hair. A wad of pink bubble-gum popped between her nicotine-yellow teeth.

"What can I get ya's?"

Klug craved a nice Bordeau, but it would draw attention. "Pitcher of beer."

She licked the pencil lead, jotted down their order, waddled off toward the bar.

Jungle Jim checked customers at nearby tables, then turned toward Klug. "Why disguises?"

"Business."

Jungle Jim stared back, puzzled, waiting.

It's time, Klug thought, leaning close. "You said once that if your company's advertising account was ever up for review, you could help direct it to my agency."

Jungle Jim paused, then shrugged begrudging agreement.

"The account will soon be up for review," Klug said.

Jungle Jim shook his head no. "There's no reason for a review."

"There will be."

The waitress thumped down a pitcher of beer and two icy mugs. "That'll run you eight dollars, cash. Nine credit."

Klug tossed a crisp ten dollar bill on the table. "Keep it."

She snatched the bill, smiled, blinked flyswatter eyelashes at him and wandered off toward another table.

Jungle Jim whispered, "I'm telling you, our present agency is excellent."

"Not for long. Soon your advertising managers will find problems with the agency. Unsatisfactory account service. Missed magazine insertions. Billing problems. Mediocre creative work. Commercials that don't reach the networks on time. Little screw-ups that add up to major problems."

"This agency doesn't screw up. They work smart, and frankly, they create terrific advertising."

Klug sipped his beer. "Trust me. They'll screw up."

Jungle Jim's blue eyes narrowed and his jaw muscles began to twitch.

"We have access to their computers," Klug explained. "We can change their media buys, create scheduling mistakes, increase the media rates. We can even screw up your agency's financial records. Your auditors will not be amused."

Jungle Jim tapped the beer coasters faster, gulped some beer.

"Because of these serious mistakes," Klug continued, "you will direct your marketing people to put the advertising account up for review. They'll form an agency selection committee. The committee selects the agencies. Very simple."

Jungle Jim fidgeted in his chair, clearly very uncomfortable with the discussion.

Klug enjoyed his discomfort. "Then GlobeLink, our parent company, which owns both your present agency and our agency, will ask you to give us a chance to pitch for your business. This would raise no suspicion."

"And of course you happily agree to pitch."

"I *refuse* to pitch."

Jungle Jim's face froze in surprise.

Klug said, "I'll say something like 'we prefer not to compete against our sister agency.'"

Jungle Jim stared at him for several seconds, then blinked, apparently realizing Klug's ploy. "So no one suspects your agency is behind this?"

Klug nodded.

"Then what?"

"Your committee refuses our refusal," Klug said. "They quietly suggest to GlobeLink that your present agency's chances of retaining the business are slim, and strongly suggest our agency compete for your account."

"And this time you agree."

Klug nodded and smiled. "Then your committee picks five or six other global agencies capable of handling your account. The agencies, including mine, would make presentations. The committee would shortlist the agencies to three. The three agencies make final presentations. The committee says ours is best and switches the account to us. Very simple."

"Not if the committee thinks another agency is best."

"That won't happen."

Jungle Jim's thick black eyebrows lifted. "Why?"

"Because you'll give us inside information. Our recommendations will be more insightful, more intelligent, more synchronous with your company's brand strategies."

"Still won't work," Jungle Jim said, shaking his head.

Klug decided to let him run on for a while. "And why is that?"

"Your worldwide system isn't staffed to service our business. We're talking about more than one billion dollars worth of advertising and promotions annually. It's a massive assignment. Thousands of advertisements to produce each year. Fifty-eight countries. It requires specialists, people who know our business, from manufacturing to distribution. Your system doesn't have those specialists."

"Actually, it does."

Jungle Jim's eyes widened. "In each country?"

"Yes." Klug sipped the local brew and grimaced. Tasteless and cheap. Like the morons that drank it.

"But you don't handle our kind of business now. How can you get people with our product expertise on staff in all countries without raising suspicion?"

"I started months ago. I told our worldwide managers we're going after your major competitor's account. We've been hiring experienced account directors. Most are already on staff in each country. We're ready."

Jungle Jim leaned back and twisted his fake pony tail. "Still won't work."

Klug decided to play along, let him adjust to the new reality. Klug popped a handful of peanuts into his mouth and again made sure no one was paying special attention to them. "Why?"

"One *very* important fact," Jungle Jim said.

"What?"

"You know what! My chairman and our agency's chairman. They've been extremely close for many years. Since Nam. The agency's handled our business for decades. Even if they screwed up, my chairman will—and frankly should—give them another chance."

Klug fingered his beer glass. "They'll screw up too badly."

"I'm telling you, he'll give them another chance."

Klug yawned. "I think not."

Jungle Jim blinked, finally realizing he was in a very serious game of hardball. "Klug, if you're planning to blackmail my chairman, I'm–"

"Don't worry about details."

Jungle Jim's face reddened and he wiped perspiration from his lips. Angry, he stood to leave. "No deal."

"We have a deal!" Klug whispered calmly. "And sit down. Or would you rather read about your little problem in Nam on the front page of tomorrow's *Detroit Free Press?* Film at eleven. CNN, every hour on the hour?"

Hot fear flashed in Jungle Jim's eyes. He braced himself against the table, then eased down into his chair.

Klug whispered, "How would your wife and daughter and your board of directors react to what you did near Da Nang?"

Jungle Jim slumped. Color drained from his face. Beads of perspiration dotted his forehead. "You promised you'd never reveal that."

"I lied." Klug enjoyed the raw fear in Jungle Jim's eyes. The same fear he'd seen on a sweltering afternoon in the small village near Da Nang.

"Remember that day?" Klug asked, knowing it was tattooed to the man's memory.

* * *

How can I forget the worst day in my life? Jungle Jim thought as his blood turned to ice. He remembered the day every day, like a parent remembers the death of a child.

His mind drifted back to the steamy afternoon. He and his three platoon members found themselves standing over the bullet-riddled bodies of seventeen Vietnamese villagers. He remembered the bloody faces, the twisted bodies of men, women and children, the arms and legs bent oddly, the dead, questioning eyes staring up at him. He remembered being nauseated by the blood, the charred huts, the smell of burning flesh. He remembered being so crazed on LSD-laced wine that he couldn't even recall killing the villagers.

But Klug, who was there, saw me do it.

"I remember," Jungle Jim said, crushing a coaster in his hand.

Klug smiled. "So do I."

"Goddamit Klug, you promised." A bead of sweat skidded down his chest.

Klug shrugged. "No promise is forever."

Jungle Jim recalled Klug's photos of him and his platoon, rifles in hands, staring down at the bloody, insect-infested bodies. Klug would release the photos and their story if he didn't play along. It would ruin his family, his life, his career.

The nightmare of Da Nang would never end.

* * *

Klug enjoyed the flicker of resignation in Jungle Jim's eyes.

The delicious irony, Klug knew, was that Jungle Jim was innocent. The massacre had been carried out minutes earlier by the Viet Cong because a villager betrayed them. Jungle Jim and his men had been so disoriented on LSD and forty-eight hours without sleep, that Klug persuaded him he'd taken part in the slaughter and had incriminating photos. Jungle Jim saw the photos, believed him, had no reason not to.

"And finally," Klug said, "remember how I managed at great personal risk to cover up the entire incident so you and your platoon would avoid court martial and prison?"

Jungle Jim looked ill.

"Of course," Klug continued, "I don't want any of this to come out. I have no desire to ruin your life. This is simply business."

Jungle Jim stared at the floor, as though looking at the blood-soaked bodies of the villagers.

"Deal?" Klug asked.

Jungle Jim paused, nodded slowly and stood. "I never want to see or hear from you again." He hurried toward the door.

Klug followed, his lips bent in a smile. Leverage. The first rule of business. The only rule.

* * *

Three tables away, the elderly hunchback scratched his beard, removed his sunglasses, watched them leave. He reached under his black cowboy hat on the table, and flicked off the hand-sized JVC Camcorder. He'd videotaped and recorded the entire conversation through a small hole in his hat.

Mason Bennett smiled, put the hat on, slipped the camcorder into his pocket, and left minutes later.

Twelve

Thursday, 5:45 p.m.

ELIZABETH BLAKELEY couldn't believe Luke's appearance when he shuffled into her office. He was hunched over as though his spirit had been crushed. Strands of chestnut-red hair had fallen over his eyes which seemed as listless and sunken as a death-camp inmate's. Shaving nicks dotted his chin. His tie clashed with his suit which hung oddly on his tall frame. She'd never seen him so distraught. Clearly, Jenna's kidnapping, which he'd told her about, was taking a heavy toll.

What toll would her death take?

"Anything yet?" Luke asked, his eyes pleading.

Blakeley wanted desperately to give him some sign of encouragement, some hope, but her investigation had turned up nothing important. "We found seven mentions of Siamese Twins in the advertising trade media, but they were medical Siamese twins in hospital advertising. The Internet references were also related to medicine."

Luke nodded as though he hadn't expected much. "How's your list of large advertising budgets?"

She fanned a computer printout. "A lot of companies. This is a partial list of corporations with annual advertising budgets between thirty and seventy million dollars."

"How many?"

"Over one hundred and ninety-seven."

"That's more than I thought."

"Me, too," she said. "Of course, the account we're looking for could be over seventy million dollars."

"How many *over* seventy?"

"Two hundred twelve."

Luke's shoulders slumped forward.

"And if we include advertising budgets *under* thirty million dollars," she continued, "say from thirty million down to five million, our grand total goes way up."

"How many?"

She scanned another printout on her desk and saw the total. She hated to tell him. "Eight hundred three companies."

Luke seemed to sink deeper into his chair. "So roughly eight hundred three companies could be the target."

She nodded, knowing the number was overwhelming. "And checking each one thoroughly in three days is ..."

"Impossible," he added, exhaling slowly through clenched teeth.

She had to give him some hope. "Still we'll try."

"Thanks, Elizabeth." He sat up straighter. "How are you and Howie Kaufman coming along identifying the two key people running major accounts?"

"Slow. We found several people claiming they're one of the two key people, but aren't. We also found people who claim they aren't key, but are."

"Takes time to sort out."

She nodded. Her phone rang. She picked up, listened and looked at Luke. "It's Marie. She's very excited."

* * *

Luke felt his throat close shut. Maybe they'd found Jenna alive and well. Or where she was being held. Or maybe they'd ask him to come identify her body. He grabbed the phone.

"Luke," Marie said anxiously, "I have a man on the line. He *insists* on speaking with you. He says he has someone you're dying to talk to."

Luke heard a series of clicks.

"Tanner?" A man's voice. Deep, raspy.

"Yes."

Luke heard the phone changing hands.

"Luke?"

"Jenna—is that you?"

"Yes." She sounded weak, afraid, but *alive!*

"Are you all right?" Luke asked, twisting the phone cord around his finger.

"I'm—"

"Tanner," the man's voice interrupted, "You'd like to continue this conversation with Miss Johannson, I'm sure. We've decided to let you do that. In person. Interested?"

"Yes."

"Then listen good. Go back to the Ren Cen table where you unfortunately overheard our people. Reach under the table and take the envelope you find there. Inside are instructions. Understand?"

"Yes."

"Good. You see, Mr. Tanner, this whole thing is a big mistake.

You misunderstood what you overheard. See, we're in drugs. We figured you're with a rival drug group. Now that we know you aren't, we can work things out."

Luke didn't believe a word.

"A note of caution, Mr. Tanner. We know you've been talking to Lieutenant Redstone. Do *not* discuss this call with him. If you do, or if you bring the police, we'll know. Guess what happens then, Mr. Tanner."

Luke knew.

"You'll find Dr. Johannson's body in the river."

Luke stared out at the slate-grey, slippery river, the shade of a tombstone.

The phone clicked dead.

Luke hung up, but couldn't shake the image of Jenna's body in the river. Clearly, they would kill her if he didn't follow instructions. He felt Elizabeth Blakeley's eyes staring at him.

"You spoke to Jenna?"

He nodded.

"How is she?"

"Terrified."

Luke's heart pounded against his shirt. He had a chance to see Jenna—maybe *free* her—a chance he would not pass up. "Elizabeth, I've got some things to do." He stood and moved toward the door.

"We'll keep searching," she said.

"Thank you."

"Where can I reach you?"

"Try my home. If I'm not there, call Hank Redstone or Marie."

She nodded, but her eyes were tight with concern. "Luke..."

"Yes?"

"You're going to do something you can't tell me about?"

He stared at her, then nodded.

"Be careful."

"I will."

Back at his office, Luke closed the door and sat down. He'd go get the letter under the table, but he'd go armed. He took the .38 from his briefcase, slipped the harness over his shoulder and put on his sport coat.

He told Marie he was going out for a while, left the agency, took an elevator down to the floor above the alcove table. He walked along the balcony, looked over the side. The phone call, he knew, could be a ploy to pull him out in the open—out where they could get a clean shot at him. But it was also his only chance to save Jenna.

Luke studied the people around the table. A large, dark-haired man in a blue suit sat nearby, reading a newspaper, glancing occasionally toward the table. Beside him was his open briefcase. To the right of the table, stood a young couple with a black, baby carriage.

Thirty feet to the left, a powerfully built man wearing reflective sunglasses stood by the elevators, scanning the walkway every few seconds. Why was he wearing a leather jacket in eighty-two-degree weather? And why was he so tense?

Luke studied the scene for a few minutes, then, gripping his .38, stepped onto the escalator, heading down. He slid his finger near the trigger, wondering if he was over-reacting. Then he remembered that *under*-reacting had almost killed him a few hours ago.

He stepped off the escalator and walked down a long, dimly-lit hall that led to the alcove. Turning, he saw two Hasidic Jews follow him into the hallway. When Luke headed toward the alcove, the Hasidim walked the other direction.

The man reading the newspaper stared at him, then back at the newspaper. Luke checked the man in the leather jacket.

Gone.

Where the hell is he? Hiding, getting an angle on me?

Crowding the concrete wall, Luke reached the table. The young couple with the baby watched him sit down, then turned and stared over the balcony.

He reached under the table and moved his fingers over hard gobs of gum. No letter. He reached to the left. Nothing. He stretched further, still feeling nothing.

Setup! Bullet any second. Perspiration beaded his forehead.

He scooted the chair to the right, reached further, and instantly felt the tip of an envelope. He tugged the envelope away from a Velcro strip. Staring at the envelope, he realized its contents could lead to Jenna or her death. Or his.

Carefully, he opened the envelope and slid the paper out.

> *Tanner—*
> *At ten tonight come to the corner of Lafayette and Bellvine. Get out of your car and stand next to the red sign for the Church of The Redeeming Messiah. A black Lincoln Town Car will pull up beside you. It will take you to your lady. If you tell Redstone, or if we see police, she floats. Have a real nice day.*

Luke's heart pounded at the chance of seeing Jenna. He reread the note, then carrying it and the envelope by the corners, he left. Back in his office, he shut the door, placed the letter and envelope in a desk drawer, then stared at the darkening afternoon sky.

He knew what he *should* do. He should tell Redstone about the phone call and letter. His FBI training and logic told him he should leave this to the professionals, that he might further endanger Jenna's life by *not* telling them.

His logic also told him the kidnappers would kill her if he told. Perhaps they had an informant.

He walked over to the window and stared down at the river. A long ore freighter glided alongside a gleaming yacht and two sprinting speedboats. He watched the freighter head downriver and fade into the hazy afternoon.

Then he hurried toward the door.

* * *

Hank Redstone slid into the familiar back pew of Saint Mary's Church in Detroit's Greektown, and opened a prayer book. Redstone, a backsliding Baptist, reminded himself that Saint Mary's was as close as he got to church these days. He'd always promised himself that if he and his wife, Renee, were lucky enough to have a child, he'd attend regularly. God knows cops needed to strengthen their spiritual side.

He also reminded himself to call Renee and explain he'd be late for her veal scalopini tonight. Renee'd understand, bless her heart, but she'd be a little disappointed. She was so much more sympathetic than most cop wives. Somehow she handled the fear, the stress, the interruptions, the late night calls, the not knowing. He thanked his lucky stars every day. He just hoped her patience never ran out like it did with many other cop wives. He didn't know what he'd do without her. He also didn't know what he'd do if he wasn't a cop.

The church was empty except for two eighty-year-old women in the front praying to a statue of Mary. A silver-haired lady arranged yellow flowers near a side altar while another straightened an altar cloth. The sweet scent of incense hung in the air.

Moments later, he saw DuWayne Washington, a reformed addict he'd help place in a rehab center three years ago, walk in the side door. Redstone could tell by Washington's eyes that he was clean.

Redstone was proud of Washington. The young man had somehow escaped his habit, his street gang, two bullet wounds, an abusive childhood, and begun working with Project Hope in the inner city, helping kids stay off drugs.

Washington slid into the pew in front of him.

Redstone knelt, leaned forward and whispered, "I'm looking for someone."

Washington said nothing.

"Woman doctor," Redstone continued." Thirty-one. White. Dr. Jenna Johannson. Kidnaped from Detroit Memorial. Parking lot attendant saw her leave with a man in a dark-blue Lumina van."

DuWayne Washington nodded slightly. "What else?"

"That's all." Redstone made the sign of the cross.

"Ain't much."

Redstone shrugged. "I know."

"She in trouble?" DuWayne opened a prayer book and appeared to read.

"Real bad. If she isn't already dead, they'll probably kill her in hours."

DuWayne ran his fingers over the wood grain of the pew.

Redstone heard noise behind him. He turned and watched a homeless man in a heavy brown coat stumble up the center aisle, ease into a pew, lean back and konk out in seconds. The scent of wine wafted over the pews.

"They in the city?" DuWayne asked.

"Probably."

"This dude, he black?"

"White. Forty-plus. Tall, strong."

"I'll ask around," he whispered as though he didn't expect much.

"Thanks, DuWayne. You find *anything*, call me fast. This woman's in bad trouble."

DuWayne nodded, stood and left.

Redstone watched him go. DuWayne would ask around, like the other contact Redstone had briefed. But their chances of turning up something fast were getting slimmer by the hour.

Like the chances of finding Jenna alive.

Luke and Jenna. So perfect for each other. They should be walking down this aisle and tying the knot, he thought, instead of being rolled down it in caskets.

He looked up at the statue of Jesus. *We sure could use your help on this one.*

Thirteen

Thursday, 6:25 p.m.

THE DOOR swung open and Leonard's hulk blocked the
light. Jenna felt her body grow rigid. His mouth hung open,
eyes staring, glazed as though he was on something. He lumbered into the room, gut hanging over his belt, sweat glistening
on his upper lip.

He walked toward her and leaned close, his body odor suffocating her like a mildewed blanket. Her stomach began to churn.
He grabbed her jaw, turned her head and gazed at her mouth as

though it contained diamonds.

"Open your mouth," he whispered.

Leonard collects tongues...

She hesitated, tried to avoid his eyes.

His powerful fingers, reeking of cigar smoke, pinched her jaws open.

"Wider!"

She opened wider and he stared into her mouth like a demented dentist. A fat bead of sweat slid down his temple. Sensual pleasure moistened his eyes.

"Beautiful. Pink. No cracks. Sweet Jesus."

Licking his upper lip, he continued staring, then released his grip and gazed down at her breasts and body. "Everything you got's beautiful and pink."

She felt herself begin to tremble. She had to control her fear, block the nauseating thought of his fingers moving over her skin. Her rape-prevention measures would not work in an abandoned warehouse with the rapist's partner aiming a gun at her.

"But this ain't your lucky day," Leonard said, smiling.

He's going to rape me, she thought. She prepared to bolt past him to the door.

"See, the boss, he don't want me to play with you before your boyfriend comes."

Luke is coming. She muzzled her relief and happiness by focusing on an cockroach crawling under a newspaper.

"But lookin' ain't playin,' is it? Besides, your time's comin," Leonard continued. "Boss says I can play after."

* * *

Luke descended in a Ren Cen glass elevator, watching the Detroit River rise rapidly toward him. He would meet Eddie Berger at Nemo's Bar and ask him for additional firepower.

Stepping off the elevator, Luke merged into the crowd of office workers and tourists. From the corner of his eye, he saw three dark-suited men appear suddenly from behind a wall and fall in behind him. They walked close together and one gestured to the others.

He stepped onto the down escalator. The men followed. They did not speak. He got off and turned left down a shadowy hallway.

The men were still behind him. They remained silent, but Luke glimpsed one signal the others. Luke reached into his coat and gripped the .38.

Nemo's Bar was just ahead.

Luke walked faster and the three men behind him seemed to speed up and signal to each other again.

Seconds later, he ducked inside Nemo's Bar and spun around to confront them. They walked past, fingers flicking in sign language. He leaned against the door and exhaled. *A little paranoid maybe?* Not an altogether unhealthy frame of mind for a few days.

He turned and saw Eddie Berger waving to him from a corner booth. Luke walked over and sat down.

Berger sipped from a Heineken mug and wiped off a foam mustache. "You looked spooked. What's up?"

"A lot. You still collecting weapons to fight the pinko commies?"

"It's wacko terrorists these days. You need artillery?"

Luke nodded.

"What's wrong with your .38?"

"I may need more."

"Scud missiles?"

"Tough to strap around my ankle."

"What the frick's going on, boss man?"

"Jenna's kidnappers just called. They'll let me see her."

Berger bolted forward. "Jesus, you know where she is?"

"No. But they're taking me to her."

Berger leaned back and raked his fingers through his springy red hair. "They'll frisk you and find the weapons."

"They're picking me up on a busy street corner. They'll frisk me *fast* so no one sees them. They'll find my handgun. But I'm going to risk that they'll miss your .38 around my ankle."

"That's a big risk."

Luke shrugged.

Berger shook his head from side to side. "Hey boss..."

"Yeah?"

"You're nuts."

"I never promised you Einstein."

Berger's pale-blue eyes blinked, then followed a busty blonde waitress sashaying by with a tray of drinks, then blinked back to Luke. "I'm coming with you."

"No way, Eddie. They said if anyone comes with me, Jenna dies."

"But you've got to let the police tail you."

"Can't. The kidnappers will know. They already know I've been talking to Redstone. My only chance is to let them take me to her, then find a way to escape—with the help of your .38."

"Assuming you still have it."

Luke knew it was a huge assumption.

"I don't like your odds."

"Jenna's are worse."

"You're forgetting one small thing, pal."

"What?"

"These bastards tried to kill you a couple of hours ago."

"The memory lingers."

"What makes you think they won't again?"

"They want to *talk*."

Berger threw his hands in the air. "Come on Luke. Talk? About metaphysics? Anthropology?"

"They said they thought I was involved with a rival drug ring. They were talking about "twin" drug shipments. They want to clear things up."

Berger stared at him. "You believe that shit?"

Luke didn't, but shrugged. "Look, they want to talk."

"Saddam Hussein wanted to *talk*. Then he raped Kuwait and caused a crazy war that killed over a hundred thousand of his own people."

"These guys are my quickest route to Jenna," Luke persisted.

"And your coffin."

"I'm open to alternatives."

Berger stared at his beer for several seconds and shook his head. "Luke, I just don't like the idea of you against a bunch of armed hit men."

"It's the fastest way to Jenna. And I don't want to risk your buns of steel."

"They're my buns."

"I know. But think of it this way. If I get nailed, there's one major benefit."

"What?"

"You'll be promoted."

Berger smiled despite his concern. "Okay asshole, if you're hell-bent on playing Rambo, let's increase your chances of standing upright."

Twenty minutes later they pulled into the driveway of Berger's Tudor house in Indian Village, a distinguished, older Detroit neighborhood of magnificent turn-of-the-century homes, vestiges of Detroit's early automotive wealth. Berger had bought the large, handsome residence during the white exodus to the suburbs. Since then, Detroit's rebirth had tripled the value of his house.

Inside, Berger led Luke to a second-floor library with magnificent, antique guitars positioned on an oak-paneled wall. Luke noticed a beautiful, curved-top 1951 L5 Gibson gleaming beside a jet-black Les Paul Gretch.

Berger pushed a tiny garage opener. Instantly a huge wall panel hissed open, revealing a twenty-five-foot-wide, glassed-in case.

Luke saw at least fifty weapons neatly arranged and labeled. Many looked illegal. Three fully automatic assault rifles, two AR-15 automatics, a Ruger Mini-14, two compact Uzis, a range of Walther, Smith & Wesson, and Beretta handguns, plus FN gas grenades. At the top of the display were two Soviet RPG-7 rocket launchers. The wall looked like a military museum.

"You planning maneuvers?"

"We're capturing Cleveland Thursday."

"With orange shoelaces?" Luke pointed to tennis shoelaces in the case.

"They aren't shoelaces. They're C-4 explosives—enough to blow up a car."

Luke stared closer at the bow-tied shoelaces, which looked like he could lace them into his Nikes.

"C-4 explosive can be shaped into anything you want. The heel of a shoe. Pencils. Bar of soap. Transistor radio. There's even something called Foam-X which you can put inside an aerosol can and pass for shaving cream."

"Stop scaring me."

Berger pointed to a small assault weapon. "This 12-inch TEC-9 has a 36-round magazine. The threaded barrel is for a silencer. Crack gangs don't leave home without them."

Berger walked to the end of the case and pulled out a small black handgun. "Here's my custom-made Walther .38." He placed it in Luke's hand.

"It reminds me of the red-handled .38 Smith and Wesson we used at the FBI Academy."

"Why red-handled?"

"To distinguish them as practice weapons. The firing pins were removed."

"Well, the firing pin's working fine in this puppy," Berger said. He bent down and wrapped the harness around Luke's left calf. Then he reached over and lifted a small black instrument off its wall mounting.

"What's that?"

"One final insurance policy. Easy to conceal. Never needs ammo. A push-dagger."

Luke stared at its thin, gleaming blade.

"Where do I put it?"

"In the carotid artery or heart."

"I mean *wear* it?"

"Your calf."

Luke strapped the push-dagger on his right calf and Berger

demonstrated how to pull and shove the weapon. Luke was glad Berger wasn't his enemy. Minutes later, they walked downstairs to the large marble foyer.

"Eddie, they may be looking for the Corvette. Can I borrow your 4x4 Scamp?"

"Sure. I'll drive my old Jeep. And be careful."

"Have you ever known me to take unreasonable risks?"

"No. Just wild-ass ones."

Fourteen

Thursday, 8:36 p.m.

LUKE DROVE Berger's 4X4 sport utility vehicle along Jefferson Avenue, hugging the bend in the Detroit River, heading toward Lafayette and Bellvine where the Lincoln Town Car would pick him up.

He'd arrive forty-five minutes early and make sure he wasn't the star attraction at a turkey shoot.

Assuming he wasn't, he'd go with them. Then he'd wait for the right moment, use his .38 or pull dagger, and escape with Jenna.

He passed an old apartment building, its beige bricks blackened by years of exhaust fumes and grime. He knew the neighborhood. He'd filmed some United Fund anti-drug commercials here. Older homes, abandoned stores, crumbling apartments, many deserted. Older people, mostly blacks, imprisoned by fear. Parents trying to raise moral children on immoral streets.

Across Jefferson near the river, derelicts lived in deserted buildings and warehouses. Broken windows, broken lives. Prosperous in the 1920s, the area was now Blightsville. Most inhabitants sold drugs or their bodies. Strangers walking its streets at night stayed upright about as long as an NFL running back. The good news was that the city was reclaiming the area, block by block, and building new homes, new apartments, new hope.

Steering to the inside lane, Luke let a flashing ambulance shriek past. He imagined Jenna inside, IV's in arms, oxygen mask, lacerated face. He forced the image away in time to brake for a red light.

As he waited, the stench of garbage wafted into the car. Beside him, an immaculate white BMW pulled up. From the shadows, a small boy, maybe ten, emerged and handed a roll of money to a man in the car. The man flicked through the bills like a bank teller and handed the kid a brown bag. The BMW turned the corner and drove off. Luke looked back and the boy had vanished into the shadows.

Behind Luke, a car honked. The light was green. He drove ahead and moments later pulled to the curb near the corner of Lafayette and Bellvine. He stared down both streets, but saw no black Lincoln, no snipers in windows, no thugs lurking in parked cars.

Across the street, a chubby-faced man with a '70s Afro sat behind the wheel of a parked Chrysler minivan, his head bobbing to his walkman's rhythm. Down Bellvine, a skinny old man leaned against a bar doorwell and sipped from a bottle in a paper bag. Neon lights yellowed his cadaverous face. A young woman in a gold lame mini-dress sashayed up to him, placed money in his bony fingers, entered the bar.

Luke studied the area directly in front of the Church of the Redeeming Messiah. The Church sign was shadowed by overhanging oak trees and tall hedges that made the area a sprawling ebony hole. The street sign was so bent it pointed up. Scraps of yellowed newspaper swirled past the windshield.

Why *this* corner?

His dash clock indicated forty-one minutes until pickup. He had time. Why not check out the surrounding neighborhood? Maybe he'd get lucky and see the black Lincoln or the Lumina.

He pulled away from the curb and turned onto a street that looked like a Belgrade bomb zone. He saw an upstairs bedroom wall ripped away, baby bed teetering over the floor's edge, teddy bear in the railings. He wondered about the baby.

Across the river, heat lightning flashed over the Canadian sky. He crossed Jefferson and turned down Chene, heading toward the river. A large, cinder-block warehouse loomed ahead, its windows knocked out. On the ground level, someone had spray-painted "scum suckin' pigs" in orange.

As he approached another warehouse, he saw a florescent-faced guard sitting in a small gatehouse. Luke pulled up to the gatehouse. The guard, bald and obese, slid back the small window and peered out with bloodshot eyes. The scent of bourbon and popcorn wafted out along with sounds of the Red Wings game.

"Deliveries at six a.m."

"I'm not delivering," Luke said,

"No pick-ups."

"I'm searching for a blue Lumina van. Or a black Lincoln."

The guard stared back as though he'd been asked to explain relativity.

"In this general area," Luke added.

The man's fleshy brow knotted. He crammed a fistful of popcorn into his mouth, then scratched his head, leaving yellow chunks on his scalp.

"Seen a blue Lumina over to McDonalds on Jefferson yesterday."

"With a Bosch sticker on the driver's window?"

"Didn't look at no window." A black fingernail plucked a chunk of popcorn from yellow teeth. He licked his finger clean, then dug it in his ear for something.

Luke knew hundreds of blue Luminas probably drove down Jefferson each day.

"Did you see anyone inside?"

"Nope."

"He scores!" the TV announcer shouted. The guard spun around for the replay.

"Thanks for the help."

The large man belched and slammed the window shut.

Luke drove past several abandoned buildings and stores, up and down side streets, methodically checking for the Lincoln or van. Beside him, the moonlight danced along the river. Warm, humid air wafted into the car.

He turned down Lund Street and watched a dark Mercedes pull over to a tall, thin young woman wearing silver hot pants and a low-cut blouse trying to restrain considerable breasts. She bent close to the driver and discussed something. Seconds later, she stepped back and flipped him the bird. The Mercedes sped off, laying rubber.

Luke looked at the young woman, checking her lipstick. Working girls noticed vehicles. Their livelihood depended on it. He wondered if she might have seen the Lumina or Lincoln. He pulled over to her and was saddened to see she was only around eighteen. Despite wearing enough makeup for a chorus line, her natural beauty was not obscured.

"How you doing tonight?" she asked, eyes fluttering, smiling, breasts dangling near the windowsill.

"I'll do better if I find what I'm looking for."

"You found it." She smiled wider and inched closer.

"Actually, I'm looking for something else tonight."

"I can do something else."

Luke smiled. "A van."

"We can do it in a van. A trailer. Phone booth..."

"I'm *looking* for a van. A blue Lumina that might be in this area. It had a yellow Bosch sticker on the driver's window."

She backed away from the window. "You a cop?" She glanced down the street as though a squad car would appear any second.

"Not a cop. Promise."

She looked into his eyes apparently deciding if he was leveling.

"A woman in the Lumina was kidnapped. They may kill her. I'm trying to find her."

The young girl brushed back Tina Turner hair, her beautiful brown eyes never leaving his. Then she seemed to relax as though she believed him. "Lumina got one of them long hoods? Look like a Dustbuster?"

"Yes."

"Don't know nothing about no yellow sticker on no window—but they was a blue Lumina drove up that way couple hours ago."

"Dark blue?"

"Uh-huh."

"Who was driving?"

"White dude. Big. Ugly."

Luke felt his pulse increase. "Was there an attractive woman in the van?"

"Jes him."

"Did you see where it pulled in?"

"No. But ain't many cars heads up that way." She flipped open her compact and licked her cherry-red lips.

"Why?"

"Dead end."

Luke squeezed the steering wheel. "You've been a big help." He peeled off two twenties and handed them to her.

"Don't you want nothing?"

"You gave me plenty. Thanks."

Her smile was puzzled, as though it was the first time she had earned money without using her body.

He drove off and studied the first building, an old one-story office building with a AIDS billboard on the side. Its parking area was empty. He drove further, past two, four-story apartment buildings, both gutted by fire. Again, no vehicles.

He approached a large, beige brick warehouse which appeared to still be operational. The delivery entrance was huge and gave him a good view of the shipping and receiving docks. The yard contained two large GMC trucks and a red Chevy pickup with "Metro-Big-D Deliveries" liveried on their doors. No Luminas.

He wondered if the van had driven back out while the girl was with a customer.

He checked his watch. He was running out of time. Soon, he'd have to drive back to East Lafayette and Bellvine.

Ahead, he saw a crumbling red brick wall which surrounded what looked like an abandoned warehouse. Black garbage bags had been nailed over windows by the homeless to keep out winter winds. Some bags fluttered loose.

On the roof, a Mohawk Vodka sign blinked red in the ebony night sky.

He slowed near the loading-zone gate. Old newspapers clogged the wire fence. No vehicles in the loading zone. On the sixth floor, faint yellow light filtered through a ripped screen in a corner room. Probably derelicts or drug dealers.

His watch said he had four minutes. Barely enough time to drive back to the pick-up corner. If he wasn't there, they might leave and he'd blow his chance to see Jenna. He steered away from the curb, drove down the street, quickly inspected two more store-front businesses. The street narrowed and grew darker due to broken street lights. No Lincolns. No Luminas. No more time. One hundred yards later, it dead-ended at a brick wall.

He'd hit the wall too.

He turned around and drove back down the street. As he approached the Mohawk Vodka warehouse, his headlights flashed off something shiny behind the trash bin in the loading zone, something he'd missed before.

He stopped, backed up, steered the headlights toward the trash bin—and froze. He blinked to make sure he wasn't hallucinating.

His heart jackhammered against his chest.

He was staring at the rear end of a *dark blue Chevy Lumina van*. But the trash bin blocked him from seeing if it had a Bosch sticker. He had to get inside the loading zone.

He drove down the street, parked, jogged back to the wire gate. He climbed over, jumped and landed on shards of broken bottles. Beside him, a rusty "Loading Zone" sign screeched in the night wind.

He walked up to the trash bin, moved along the van's side, and stopped. His eyes focused on a mustard-yellow spark plug sticker—Bosch.

She's here. His pulse pounded in his ears.

He yanked out his .38 and moved quickly into the warehouse shadows. He inched along the wall to the open door and squinted into blackness.

Something cracked behind him.

He spun around to shoot and saw a plastic bag snapping in the wind. Exhaling slowly, he turned back, stepped inside the warehouse, and gagged. The room smelled like a latrine. He blinked, adjusting to the darkness, and saw a chipped desk cluttered with wine bottles and hypodermic needles. Beside it was a table with a leg missing and a chair, its torn cushion lying on the floor.

Luke's muscles were bricks. Raw fear was bringing back his FBI instincts fast. He crunched over broken glass and newspapers, walked to the stairwell door. Its window was soot-covered.

He started to pull the door open, then stopped. Would it creak and warn them? Maybe. But he had to get up to the sixth-floor room. Jenna was here—he sensed it.

He turned the handle slowly and pulled. The door opened with a soft sucking sound, like opening a new can of coffee.

Thunder rolled overhead.

He stepped through the door into a pitch-black stairwell. He could see nothing and steadied himself against the wall. It reminded him of when he was six in Mammoth Cave and lost his balance in the total darkness.

Lightning flashed, illuminating the stairwell through a small skylight. A putrid odor stung his nostrils. He started up the stairs slowly. After a few steps, his foot rattled an empty can and he reached down to silence it.

He listened. Only wind.

Cautiously, he continued up the stairs and reached the second level. He heard a strange, crunching sound beside him. He turned and stared into the green glowing eyes of two enormous rats, a few feet away, gnawing on the carcass of another rat.

He climbed to the fourth floor.

Starting up the fifth, he tripped over something.

Something *moving*.

A derelict, wild-eyed, bolted up, mumbling, swinging blindly. Luke avoided the man's fist, but not the vile stench of body odor and whiskey. Luke started to hush him, then saw the man had slumped back to sleep, clutching his wine bottle.

Did they hear?

Luke stared at the door above and waited. Nothing.

He stepped over the wheezing drunk and climbed to the sixth floor. He turned the handle, pushed gently and the door opened without noise. He stepped quietly into a narrow hallway, saw no one.

Moving down the hall, he saw light seeping under a door at the end.

He stopped at the door, listened.

Silence.

Then a man mumbled something and walked quickly toward the door.

Fifteen

Thursday, 10:15 p.m.

IZZY JANEK checked his nine-millimeter Mini Uzi beneath the seat, as he and Cecil Milosh waited in the black Lincoln in front of the Church of The Redeeming Messiah. Janek loved the weapon. It was like a hunk of him. He never went anywhere without it. Slept with it under the bed. It never failed him, and wasn't going to tonight when he waxed Tanner, which he'd enjoy because the bastard had slipped away from them earlier.

Glancing at his watch, he saw Tanner was already twelve minutes late. Always late, this guy. Izzy Janek hated waiting. Waiting meant bad news. He'd learned that when he was six. His momma told him to wait by the microwaves in a Toledo Kmart. Slut never came back, abandoned him. He didn't care. Taught him about life early. Made him tougher, smarter.

He sipped Tequila from a pocket flask, and turned to Cecil, the driver, who was scrunched over the rearview mirror working on another major whitehead. The guy had more zits than a high school prom. Looked like he'd scraped raspberries over his face.

"Tanner musta chickened out," Janek said, cramming pistachios into his mouth and licking the salt off his pink fingers. "Or maybe he's bringing the cops."

"No cops. And he's coming," Milosh said.

"Why you so fucking sure?"

"We got his bitch. He don't want jack shit happenin' to her."

"Don't blame him," Janek said. "Wouldn't mind some of that my own self."

"Only fuckin' way you get some of that is if she's dead."

"No problem. I boffed a stiff once."

Cecil looked at Janek's crotch and grinned. "And now it ain't stiff enough to boff!"

"Fuck you!"

Cecil laughed so hard he hacked phlegm on the mirror.

Janek remembered the dead woman, some slut he picked up in a bar. "I just hit her too hard. She was still warm and all. Warm ain't bad. Shit, man, what'd she know?"

Cecil Milosh wiped the phlegm off the mirror, leaving a streak.

"You know what worries me?" Janek said.

"What?"

"Tanner's smart. Slippery son of a bitch already lost us couple times."

"Yeah, well not this time."

"*If* he comes," Janek said.

"He'll come, asshole."

"And if he don't?"

"We do like Bennett says, for Chrissakes. Go back to the warehouse."

"Yeah, yeah, and wait. Wait for Bennett. Always fuckin' waiting. No action."

"Got the bastard!" Milosh said, wiping pus between his fingers, then reaching over to grab some pistachios.

"Get the fuck away," Janek said, slapping his hand. He looked at Milosh's butt-ugly face. "Jesus, you oughta think about a face transplant."

"Up yours, ass-wipe."

Janek laughed and pulled out his Uzi. "I ain't hangin' around here much longer."

Cecil looked at his watch. "He ain't here in couple minutes, we'll head back."

"Damn right."

"And lighten up!" Milosh said.

"Only one thing'll lighten me up."

"What?"

"Greasing Tanner."

* * *

Luke stood in a hall closet beside a mildewed mop that made him gag. Through the crack in the door, he'd watched a short, muscular man step into the hall, walk the other way and enter a room.

Now, Luke heard footsteps again. He looked and saw the man walking in his direction. As the man walked past, Luke jammed the gun in his ear.

"It's loaded," Luke whispered, yanking a gun from the stunned man's shoulder holster. "Is Jenna Johannson in that room?"

The man nodded yes, eyes straining toward the gun barrel, cheek twitching.

"How many men in there?"

He held up one finger.

"We're going in. Warn your friend, and your brains are wallpaper. Understand?"

The man nodded like a woodpecker.

Luke pushed him back to the door and listened. Inside, someone was fine-tuning a sports talk show on the radio.

Quickly, Luke pushed his captive into the room.

"Hands up. Or your partner's history!"

The man at the radio spun around and stared.

"Do like he says, Leonard! He'll fuckin' kill me!"

Leonard's hands moved up slowly.

"Take off your coat," Luke said. "Very slowly."

"Yeah, yeah," Leonard said. "But easy with the gun."

Leonard took off his suitcoat. A Magnum bulged from a shoulder harness.

"Take off your holster slow. Put it on the floor."

Leonard began taking the harness off, then his hand stopped. He smiled oddly. "Come on, Tanner. You don't shoot people. You're an ad guy for Chrissakes. Put the gun down and we'll tell you about the sweet deal we was gonna offer you and the girl. It'll make you both rich."

"Take the harness off now."

Leonard's hand was moving slowly toward the gun again. "Be smart, Tanner. You don't want no Murder-One wrap. Handsome guy like you in the slammer. Them big black bucks'll tear you a new asshole. Ain't that right, Sonny?"

"Uh-huh," Sonny whispered.

"Play it smart, Tanner. Put your gun down," Leonard persisted, more boldly now, smiling. He laughed, inched closer to his gun. "We gotta hell of a deal for you. Both of you walk out of here. Big money. Right, Sonny?"

"Uh-huh."

Leonard lunged for his gun.

Luke fired—grazing Leonard's shoulder.

Leonard yelped and spilled hot coffee on his crotch. His hand darted from his shoulder to his crotch and back. "Jesus—you shot me! My balls is on fire!"

"*Nicked* you, Leonard. We're talking band-aid. Now think hard—either the harness hits the floor or you do!"

Leonard slid the harness onto the floor, then tried to wipe hot coffee from his groin. A dot of blood appeared on his shoulder.

"Push the gun and harness over here with your foot."

Leonard pushed them over.

Luke pulled the gun from the harness. "Is Jenna Johannson behind that door?"

Both men nodded.

"Unlock it and toss me the key."

Sonny unlocked the door and tossed Luke the key.

"Now, face that wall, hands flat against it."

Both men faced the wall, hands up. Nothing like a gunshot to instill a little discipline.

Luke opened the door and saw Jenna crouched behind a chemical drum. Her face and blouse were dirt-smudged, but she appeared basically unhurt. She melted as she recognized him, and ran into his outstretched arm.

He held her, his gaze locked on the men. "You okay?"

She nodded she was.

"Really?"

"Yes, but you're sort of late for the movies."

She was okay, he realized. "Sorry. I'll buy you extra Raisinettes."

"Deal."

Luke turned to the men. "Get in the room!"

Both men stepped toward the room, glancing uneasily back at Luke's gun. "You won't get away with this," Leonard said.

"You've got three seconds to get in the room. One..."

The men hurried inside. Luke shut the door, locked it, then wedged a chair under the knob for extra insurance. He led Jenna down the hallway and stairwell, past the snoring drunk.

They stepped outside into the fresh, night air and hurried toward the gate. Jenna was alive, smiling, and they were escaping. He had never felt such incredible relief.

One second later he felt cold steel in his back.

"Bang, bang, Mr. Tanner!" a man said. "Me and Cecil was real unhappy you didn't show up on Lafayette. Back inside!"

Luke watched Cecil push Jenna back into the warehouse. He couldn't believe what was happening. In the lobby, Cecil began frisking him.

"Guy's a fuckin' arsenal," Cecil said, pulling out Leonard and Sonny's guns, plus the .38 from Luke's left calf. "Bastard's packin' a shiv too." He pulled the push-dagger from its holster. "What kinda advertisin' dude is this, anyways?"

"A dead one," Izzy Janek said.

* * *

Leonard relaxed as he watched Izzy and Cecil push Tanner and the woman against the wall.

We were lucky, Leonard thought. The last thing he needed was for Mason Bennett to find out Tanner and the woman had almost escaped. Bennett didn't like fuck-ups.

Leonard looked at the spec of blood on his shoulder. "Bastard shot me!" He felt his anger mushrooming and decided to teach Tanner a lesson, rearrange his face. He walked toward him.

"Wait!" Jenna said, looking at his shoulder. "Your wound. It could get seriously infected.

Leonard stopped and looked at his shoulder again.

"That new flesh-eating virus is in this area," Jenna said. "I must treat you immediately."

Leonard's gut twisted. The bloody spot looked big as a quarter. She was a doctor and looked worried. He didn't want no disease that ate his skin up, or that fucking AIDS.

"Quick," she said, "before infection sets in." She ripped open the bullet tear in his shirt, took some cream from her medical bag, spread the white stuff on the one-inch surface wound, then covered it with a bandage. The stuff burned like hell but he wasn't gonna let her know. Women dig strong men like him. He'd show her how strong he was real soon. He looked at Tanner and decided to handle his ass later.

Leonard called Mason Bennett as Sonny pushed Luke and Jenna in the small room and locked the door.

"We got Tanner," Leonard said, sounding cool, like nothing had happened. "Where you want us to dump 'em."

"Forget that. The man wants them to die in a rafting accident."

"Rafting?" Leonard wasn't sure he heard right.

"Yes. They were going rafting tomorrow. Still are. But you and Sonny are taking them. You *must* make it look like a rafting accident."

"Why not just pop 'em?"

"Their deaths must look accidental. Can't appear like they're linked to Sunday."

Leonard wondered about Sunday. "What's happening Sunday?"

Bennett paused. "The sun's coming up."

Leonard didn't understand, then he got it. "Can't tell me, huh?"

"Right."

As Bennett explained about the nearby river, and how they would handle the accident, Leonard felt tightness building in his neck and shoulders. He couldn't swim good and hated boats. He liked things simple. Couple bullets in the head. Knife. Poison. Hide the body. People disappear all the time. But he knew better than to push Bennett on this.

"Sonny's done some raftin'," Bennett said.

"Uh-huh. When you want us to leave?"

"Very soon. I'll phone with details." He paused. "And Leonard..."

"Yeah?"

"No screw ups."

Leonard felt his skin crawl. He knew Bennett. The guy was ice. Real crazy about doing things exactly right, which meant his way.

"Hey man, they're dead meat."

Sixteen

Thursday, 10:20 p.m.

HANK REDSTONE'S fingers drummed the armrest of the unmarked police Blazer. The vehicle was hidden behind a clump of evergreens fifty yards from Luke's Birmingham home. Two officers were positioned inside the house, three behind it. Huge oak trees arched over the street, creating a dark, shadowy tunnel. Redstone tossed two No-Doz into his mouth and washed them down with cool 7-ELEVEN coffee. He hated waiting.

"Anything?" Redstone said into a walkie talkie.

"Nothing in back."

"Nothing inside."

Redstone wanted to seal Luke inside and wait for the hit men. The house was secure. The trap was set. Everything was ready but the bait—his pal, Luke. It was unlike Luke to not show or phone.

"Where the hell is he?" Redstone muttered to his young colleague, Investigator Marcus Kincaid, sitting behind the steering wheel.

Kincaid shrugged and continued tapping on his laptop.

Redstone looked at Kincaid, a twenty-four-year-old with awesome, high-tech investigative skills. Kincaid's watery blue eyes squinted down at the screen, where he compared data on a series of rapes of inner-city high school girls. He swallowed, bobbing his adams apple like a fishing cork. His pale, youthful face and scrawny, five-eight frame made him look like the kid who couldn't buy a prom date. When Redstone promoted Kincaid instead of a fellow black, black officers had bitched and asked if he'd ever heard of affirmative action? Redstone had said, "Yeah. I'm affirming Kincaid's the best person for the job. "Any questions" There were none.

"You should have glued a LoJak to Tanner," Kincaid said.

Redstone smiled. "Human LoJaks. Wives track husbands. Implant one in every felon."

"We'd make billions."

Redstone knew the human implant idea would soon happen and that someone like Kincaid would develop it and retire a gazillionaire.

"You checked Luke's office again?" Kincaid asked, his fingers clicking magically over the keyboard.

"Not there. And he's not at his cottage."

Redstone's concern was growing. These hit men were pros. They knew how to tail and nail. Redstone flipped open his phone and called Luke's secretary, Marie, at home. She answered after two rings.

"Marie, Hank Redstone. Sorry to bother you, but do you

know where Luke is?"

"No. I saw him around five-thirty. Right after he got the phone call."

"What call?"

"Didn't Luke tell you? A man called him. Elizabeth Blakeley says it was the kidnapper. He let Luke talk to Jenna very briefly."

Redstone's grip tightened on the phone. Jenna was alive, and he sensed they might use her to get to Luke. "Did Luke say where he was going?"

"To meet Eddie Berger. You want Eddie's number?"

"Please." Redstone pulled a dog-eared notepad from his pocket and wrote down the number. "Thanks, Marie."

They hung up. Redstone punched in Berger's phone number and Berger picked up.

"Eddie, Hank Redstone. We ran a 10K fun run with Luke a couple years back."

"Oh, yeah, Hank."

"Is Luke there?"

Berger paused several seconds, too many for a simple question. "He left a couple of hours ago, Hank..."

Redstone read Berger's hesitation. "What's going on, Eddie?"

Berger sighed, cleared his throat, then told him everything.

"Jesus!" Redstone said, leaning forward, his heart pounding. "He's walking into a trap."

"I tried to stop him. But he thought it was the only way to reach Jenna."

Redstone's neck felt like a vice was squeezing it. "Where are they picking him up?"

"Some busy inner-city corner."

"Narrows it down to a couple thousand. Is he armed?"

"His .38. Plus he's got my .38 and a push-dagger."

Redstone heard the phone line click off and on.

"Hank, someone's calling. Maybe it's Luke. Hang on."

Redstone tried to think what he should do next. He rubbed his eyes. He needed more sleep but had no idea when he'd get it. Berger clicked back on the line. "That was a guy at Chevrolet

Headquarters. He's just printed out a list of blue Lumina vans in the Detroit Metro area, like the one that picked up Jenna."

"Where's this guy's list?"

"He's bringing it over now. You want to see it?"

"Yes. Did he say how many are on the list?"

"A few thousand."

* * *

Twenty minutes later, Redstone walked through Berger's front door. Berger introduced him to Lew Meads, a tall, pleasant man who led them toward a long computer printout that was spread out across the kitchen table.

Redstone hoped to reduce the number of list names to a manageable size.

"This is the R.L. Polk Detroit ADI list," Meads said. "We cross-tabbed it with some Chevrolet assembly-plant manufacturing lists. Together they tell us how many blue Lumina vans there are in the Detroit metro sixty-mile area."

"How many?" asked Redstone.

"Three thousand, eight hundred, seventy-three."

Redstone exhaled slowly. "Damn popular color." He scanned the list for a few seconds and shook his head. "If we concentrate just on Detroit and the closest suburbs, how many?"

Meads studied the back page of the printout. "About two thousand six hundred."

Redstone's throat tightened in a hard knot. "Not enough time to check out this many. Or enough people."

"Still, this people'd like to help," Berger said, pointing to himself.

"Me, too," Meads added.

Redstone looked at both men. Eagerness burned in their eyes and there were no extra bodies at the precinct that could help. "You're hired. Who knows—we may get lucky."

"Thanks," Berger said. "What about the Bosch stickers?"

"They were handed out at two hundred twenty-six Shell stations in southeastern Michigan. Also at the Detroit Auto Show and the Grand Prix."

"How many stickers?" Berger asked.

"Over two hundred ten thousand stickers," Redstone said as the phone in his pocket buzzed. He pulled it out and hit the receive button.

"Redstone."

"DuWayne..."

"What's up?" Redstone asked, knowing Duwayne Washington didn't make useless phone calls.

"You remember Jesse, my pal from rehab?"

"Yeah."

"Jesse saw a blue Lumina van like you said."

"Where?" Redstone's pulse kicked up a notch.

"Front of a liquor store down on Jefferson near the Belle Isle bridge. Big white dude driving. The van had some kinda yellow sticker up front."

"Was it a Bosch sticker?"

"He don't know. Anyways, I'm dropping some kids off at STJ rehab on East Jefferson. I'll check around."

"DuWayne..."

"Yeah?"

"*We'll* check it out."

"Man, I'm already down in the area. Just gonna look."

Redstone knew he couldn't stop DuWayne Washington. "If you see the van, DuWayne, drive on by. Call me fast."

"You got it."

They hung up. Redstone was worried. DuWayne wanted to be a cop, but his drug record still blocked him. And when he tried to protect kids from drugs, he sometimes acted like he wore a badge.

This time it could be very dangerous.

Seventeen

Friday, 8:40 a.m.

LUKE HEARD another beer can phizzst open in the outer
room. The boys liked their breakfast oats and grains in the
form of Budweiser. Liked it enough to consume nine cans in the
last forty minutes.

Morning sunlight filtered through the grime-smudged window
and turned Jenna's thick, brown hair gold. She was cradled in his
arm, sleeping. Squalor accentuated her beauty sculpted fluidly
over elegant, high cheekbones and slender nose. Her piercing

blue eyes rested beneath gossamer-thin eyelids. He saw a tiny scar on her lip and wanted to know where the scar came from. He wanted to know everything about her, everything she'd done, everywhere she'd been, everyone she'd loved. Would he get the chance?

He reached down and took a fleck of lint from her hair. Her eyes fluttered open, she smiled and nuzzled into his shoulder. The warmth of the moment was broken by an empty beer can clanging onto the floor in the outer room.

"The boys are awake," she whispered.

He nodded.

She closed her eyes and burrowed deeper into his side.

He stared at the door. How much more time do we have, he wondered? Hours? Minutes? They had one choice—escape. And they couldn't wait for an opportunity. They had to *create* it.

The problem was he'd searched every inch of the room twice and found nothing he could use as a weapon. He glanced around the room again. Filthy, stained newspapers and moldy food lay everywhere, a chemical drum oozed dark-green sediment, black insects darted beneath papers. His clothes looked like he crawled through a garbage dump.

The window overlooked a concrete loading zone, six floors below. No escape route. His only chance was to attack—catch one man off guard and grab his weapon before the other man shot him. Lousy odds. Zero odds if he didn't try.

A key jiggled in the door.

Jenna bolted up as Sonny and Leonard walked in. Leonard, who still looked angry for being nicked by Luke's bullet, glared at him, holding a Colt 357.

Leonard strolled to the window, looked out, then faced Luke. "Tanner, you're gonna phone your cop pal, Lieutenant Redstone. You're gonna tell him you and your girlfriend are fine, that her kidnapping was a big misunderstanding. Every word you're gonna say is right there on that page."

Sonny handed him a cell phone and a sheet of paper filled with double-spaced typing.

"Say only what's on this page. If he asks you something that ain't here, make your answer fit." His breath was thick with beer.

Luke read the script quickly. He hoped Redstone didn't believe it.

"Any questions?" Leonard asked.

"No."

"One last point, Tanner," Leonard said. "If you try to warn him in any way, I'll grease your bitch." He spun a silencer onto the barrel of his .357, strolled over to Jenna, and held the gun a few inches from her temple.

"*On* her head," Sonny advised. "Don't splatter your shirt."

Leonard glanced at his grey polyester shirt, then jammed the silencer against her temple. Luke watched her eyes close, and her body begin to tremble. His muscles turned to hot steel. He wanted to leap across the floor and smash Leonard's head through the wall.

Sonny dialed and handed the phone to Luke.

"Redstone."

"Hank, it's Luke."

"Jeezus, Luke. Where the hell you been?"

Luke checked the script. "Last night I got a call from the people who took Jenna. They picked me up and took me to her. Everything's sorted out now."

Luke spoke slower than usual, praying Hank detected it. "As it turns out, this whole thing is a big misunderstanding. The guys I overheard are into drugs. They thought I was with a rival drug gang. They figured I was giving you information that could lock them up. So they took Jenna to make sure I didn't. When they found out I was not in drugs, they phoned me. We worked things out. I'm with Jenna now. We're fine."

Redstone did not respond for several moments. "What about the plan to murder the Twins in a jungle? What about the big advertising account switch?"

Sonny pointed further down the script to the word "Twins.'

"*Twins* was just a code word for two drug shipments," Luke

said. "They wanted to terminate the two shipments over a jungle path and *switch* to delivery by air. Advertising was just a cover."

Again, Redstone was silent.

Luke prayed he wasn't buying any of this crap.

Sonny nudged Luke to continue. Leonard pushed the gun harder into Jenna's temple.

"Hank, Jenna and I are going away for a few days. Do a little white-water rafting. I'll see you when we get back."

"Let's get together *now*."

Sonny pointed down the script.

"There's no time now, Hank. I've got an appointment."

Sonny checked his watch and signaled Luke to end the conversation.

"Gotta run, Hank. I'll phone later."

Redstone paused. "Yeah, okay."

Luke hung up, hoping Redstone had enough time to trace the call.

Leonard pulled the gun away from Jenna's temple, leaving a red welt. "You did good, Tanner."

"You too," Sonny added, patting Jenna's buttock as he passed her.

"Oh, by the way," Leonard said, "Redstone can't trace the call. It's an out-of-state cell phone."

Triumphant, Leonard and Sonny strolled from the room and locked the door.

"You okay?" Luke asked.

She nodded, rubbing her temple.

Luke placed his arm around her as they sat down and stared out the window. Clearly the boys were planning a rafting accident. A deadly accident. If Redstone believed the rafting trip, he'd stake out all the main rafting rivers, like the Menominee River's rapids in the Upper Peninsula. But what if the boys chose a little known river like the one near his cottage? Even Redstone probably didn't know about it. Not many people did.

He suddenly remembered another rafting accident with someone he'd cared a great deal for a few years ago. Mamie. They'd somehow managed to capsize a tiny raft in three feet of calm water and when they stood—discovered the raft on their heads.

Mamie had worked for a film production company he'd hired to shoot some tourism commercials. She'd directed the commercials, which turned out as breathtaking beautiful as she was. Tall and slender, like the model she'd once been. Dark hair and green eyes. Outgoing and friendly. They'd dated about six months, becoming serious. She was looking for commitment. He wasn't ready, or maybe his physical condition was holding him back. He was never sure. After suggesting to her that a recurrence of his condition did not lend itself to marriage and family, that he wasn't exactly the Everready bunny—she said she could handle that. He wasn't sure that she fully understood the potentially debilitating effects of his disease. He asked her to give him some time. She did.

Five months later she asked again. He still wasn't ready. The next week, she took a job in New York and soon after married an NBC news journalist. It had hurt. And he'd known he'd made a major mistake.

And then he discovered he hadn't.

Jenna.

In the outer room, Luke heard Leonard punch in a number on the cell phone and say, "Tanner just read your script real good. Redstone bought every fuckin' word."

Leonard listened for several moments.

"Yeah," he said, "Rains swelled up the river bad. Real dangerous."

Eighteen

MASON BENNETT walked into the den and rechecked the carefully-arranged items he would take to Mexico. He grabbed the shaving kit, lifted the false bottom and examined his custom-made Glock. The gun, ninety-seven percent plastic, had breezed through hundreds of airport metal detectors undetected. He closed the bottom and placed some toiletries on top.

Opening the theatrical kit, he checked his AFTRA ID card, the beards, hairpieces, tinted contact lenses, latex noses, and collagen implants to puff out his lips and cheeks. He'd probably never need any of it, but he liked the insurance.

He placed everything in his large green Cabela backpack and zipped it shut. He was ready.

Turning, Bennett gazed out his apartment window at the towering Ambassador Bridge linking Detroit with Windsor, Canada. Cars flicked past thick iron girders, flowing smoothly, like his plans. Tanner and the woman would soon be victims of a rafting accident. The Twins would soon be victims of deadly *cuatro narices* venom.

And Forrest Klug will soon fall victim to my new demand.
Klug would go ballistic, but he could not refuse.

Bennett had kept in contact with Klug since Vietnam, handling special assignments for him from time to time, making problems and certain people go away, helping grease the skids of Klug's career path, which resembled a Cambodian killing field; bodies stacked on bodies, careers decimated at whim.

Klug treated clients like deities; charming them, cajoling, fawning, taking care of their every desire. He treated employees like Kleenex. Used them, threw them away. Klug acted as though his wealthy birthright anointed him with some divine authority to rule lesser beings.

On the other hand, Klug paid excellent fees. Like this sweet, one-million-dollar fee for dispatching the Twins. By far, Bennett's most lucrative fee ever. After all, the Twins were national figures, whose death would result in one billion dollars in business annually for Klug's company. *One billion. Year after year.*

The more Bennett had thought about the one billion, the more he knew his fee was inadequate. He had to pay the assassin and others from *his* million. And if the cops ever suspected murder, he'd have to disappear and that would be costly. Clearly, the assignment deserved a larger fee. An additional million felt about right. He'd demand it when he visited Klug in a few minutes.

Klug would explode of course. But he'd agree. He'd have to. It was too late to replace Bennett. If Klug threatened him, and Klug threatened anyone who disagreed with him, Bennett was ready. He'd learned to think survival with Klug in Nam. He'd learned survival by age six.

Bennett walked into the small kitchen and saw Shoshanna pouring him a cup of coffee. A most inspiring sight. Long legs, wasp-thin waist, full breasts, silky, milk-chocolate skin. Her tan eyes turned toward him and he was pleased to see they were still clear. When he'd first seen them, they were red and swollen shut—the result of a vicious beating by her pimp, who'd dumped her unconscious in an alley for saying she wanted to quit. Bennett had brought her to his apartment, told her she could stay as long as she wanted, then went out and rearranged the pimp's arms and legs. Two weeks later the pimp moved to Houston in a body cast.

"You travelin'?" she said, handing him the coffee.

"Mexico," he said, sipping some. "You staying here or with your mother?"

"Here. Her boyfiend's back, drinking bad." She pointed to an ugly, one-inch scar behind her ear. "He's a mean drunk."

Bennett nodded.

"Man's *crazy* mean," she said, "like my daddy."

"I understand."

She seemed to doubt he really could understand. "Figured your daddy one of them "Father Knows Best" dudes."

"What he knew best was *hurting* people. My first memory is him breaking my jaw with his Jim Beam bottle. I was four."

Her eyes widened. "Where your momma at?"

"On the sofa, drugged, watching."

Shoshanna shook her head and put her coffee cup down. "She try to stop him?"

"Yes, but he beat her unconscious."

"Bastard!"

Bennett felt the old anger, the frustration that he'd never personally repaid his father. Thankfully, cancer had done a beautifully slow and painful job for him.

"He beat you?"

Bennett nodded. "A lot. Made me do every job perfect or he'd beat me. No job I did was perfect."

Even now, Bennett knew that fear of his father drove him to

complete *every* assignment to perfection, sometimes at great risk. But the obsession had stuffed his bank accounts. He completed jobs, some impossible tasks. His clients knew it and paid him exorbitant fees.

Shoshanna reached over and placed her long fingers on his hand. "Where your folks at now?"

"Dead. When I was nine, they went to the liquor store and never returned. I waited at home. Four days. Alone."

"Bastards!"

"My Aunt Charleen came by, took me into her home. When I was fourteen, she took me into her bed. Three years later, I joined the army and found myself in the Mekong Delta, shooting at twelve-year-old Cong in black pajamas. Everybody shot everybody. Didn't know the good guys from the bad. If it moved, we shot it."

She stared into his eyes.

"After a while, I didn't feel *anything*."

"Gotta feel *something*."

"I didn't," Bennett said, knowing he still didn't *feel* things like other people. Maybe he never had. He knew that wasn't normal. He didn't care.

"See you in a few days," he said, grabbing his Cabela bag.

"You be careful," she said, hugging him.

He couldn't remember the last time someone said that to him.

Fifteen minutes later Bennett walked into Klug's office and sat down. Klug remained buried in the salmon-pink pages of the *Financial Times of London*, even though Bennett knew he'd seen him walk in. It was as though Bennett didn't exist. People existed when Klug wanted something from them.

Soon, Bennett thought, I'll have your undivided fucking attention.

Bennett looked around the plush, fifty-by-forty-foot office. A long, teak conference table gleamed from the corner. Surrounding it were several leather chairs. Klug's chair, of course, was built four inches higher than the others. Expensive paintings decorated the walls, along with photos of Klug smiling with the titans of industry and the last three presidents. Klug was easy to spot. The shortest, stretching his neck up to appear taller.

Bennett smelled cigar smoke and saw butts in the copper ashtray. The agency's no-smoking rules didn't apply to Klug. No rules applied to Klug.

The phone rang and Klug picked up and listened. His glass eye turned down and in as though checking something on his nose. The natural eye had been slashed beyond repair when his father threw a glass paperweight at him for stuttering. Klug had been nine.

Klug shouted directives into the phone, hung up and turned toward Bennett. "Are Tanner and the woman handled?"

Bennett nodded. "Their rafting accident is arranged."

"And Mexico?"

"Everything's ready."

"The satellite phone?"

"Functioning perfectly. Carlos checked it out twice."

"Caller ID and PIN numbers can't be traced?"

"No way."

Klug nodded.

"In two hours," Bennett said, "I'm flying to Mexico to make certain everything goes as planned."

Klug stood, raised his chin and strutted on custom-made, twelve-hundred-dollar shoes. The shoes, which lifted him two-inches, unfortunately tilted him forward like a man hurrying to take a shit. He put his hands on his hips, stuck out his jaw, and looked at his massive wall map like a dictator studying troop movement.

"Soon it will all be mine," Klug said.

"Yes, but we need to discuss something."

Klug gazed at the map as though Bennett hadn't spoken.

"We need to talk," Bennett said.

Klug pushed in a red pin and seemed annoyed. "What?"

"This Twins assignment is by far my most important."

"Tell me something I don't know."

"Eliminating two of the country's most respected corporate leaders is much riskier and more complex than I first thought. It warrants a larger fee."

Klug's hand froze on another red pin. "I already increased your fee eighty thousand for Tanner and the woman."

"I need more."

Klug stood stone still for several seconds, his neck growing rigid. He turned and riveted on Bennett. Klug the Intimidator using his do-you-realize-who-you're-talking-to stare. "You're getting one million, plus eighty. That's more than adequate."

Calmly, Bennett straightened his silk tie, enjoying Klug's irritation. "I need another million."

The eyelid covering Klug's glass eye suddenly fluttered like a window shade. Crimson mushroomed up his neck. He stormed over to Bennett and stopped inches from his face. "Forget it."

Bennett shrugged and shifted forward as though preparing to leave. "Then forget Sunday."

The good eye blinked and Klug's jaw dropped open so wide Bennett saw his silver fillings. The little man was obviously adjusting to a big reality—that there wasn't time to hire someone and get him to an obscure jungle thousands of miles away.

Blackmailing the blackmailer. Bennett could *feel* Klug's rage and it felt sublime. Bennett had put up with the man's arrogance, insensitivity and abuse for too long.

"One more thing," Bennett continued. "In case anything should happen to *me*, the police will know everything."

Klug stepped back as though shot. He sat down, flipped open a humidor, and fumbled for a cigar. Shaking, he lit one and puffed shafts of smoke toward the ceiling ventilator.

"I've kept a dossier on this entire Twins situation," Bennett continued. "Sort of my life insurance. The dossier contains taped recordings of our conversations, plus deposit slips from your accounts to mine, and from my accounts to Mexican banks."

Klug shrunk further into his chair.

"It also contains a videotape of you and Jungle Jim at the Rendez-Booze Bar."

Klug closed his eyes.

"Oh yeah," Bennett continued, "I know Jungle Jim is John Shelby. Lip-readers can tell the police every word you both said. I've even thrown in some material from Nam that details your Medusa network."

Klug coughed out smoke as though slapped on the back. He stood slowly and began to pace, bent over.

"My dossier," Bennett said, "has everything a prosecuting attorney needs to convict you. If I don't phone a certain individual each week—and repeat a specific phrase—he'll deliver the dossier to the police."

Klug's cheek began to twitch. His upper class attitude had tumbled several social strata. A fat vein pulsed on his temple. He didn't appear to feel well.

Bennett felt terrific.

"You forget one thing," Klug said.

"What's that?"

"If I go to jail, you go."

"Wrong again. By the time the police have the dossier, I'll be in another country under a new identity. I've transferred my money there and bought properties. I could live there tomorrow, quite comfortably, for as long as I want."

Klug exhaled again, then stared out his window. "Is this how you repay me? Christ, Mason—we were in Nam. I thought you trusted me."

"As you once said—trust is for retards."

Klug slumped deeper into his chair and faced Bennett for several moments. "I'll transfer the additional million today."

"I'll check for it," Bennett said, walking to the door. "And don't worry about Mexico. Everything will go as planned. After all, I have a lot more incentive."

Klug, ashen-faced, stared at the floor. "J-J-Just d-d-do the goddamned assignment!"

Nineteen

Friday, 10:07 a.m., Yucatan

CARLOS RAMOS jerked the red Jeep Cherokee down a rocky, chuck-holed trail through thick Mexican jungle. He cursed as the truck bottomed out, snapping his head back again. The tires had hit every fucking hole since Cancun and given him an ice-pick-in-the-eye headache.

He looked over at Paco and hated him. As usual, the man was dozing and his round, hairless face showed no discomfort. Paco was too stupid to feel pain. If you yanked his silver eyebrow ring, he probably wouldn't wake up.

Carlos checked his watch. He had to pick up the *cuatro narices*, deliver them to the snake pit and drive back to Cancun Airport to meet the *gringo*, Mason Bennett.

Carlos steered through steamy shafts of sunlight, followed the path around some banyon trees and one-hundred yards ahead saw the familiar long, thatched-roof buildings clustered beneath palm trees. A skinny man stood beside the first building, watching the Jeep. Carlos parked and he and Paco got out. The skinny man wore faded jeans and a stained T-shirt. He strolled over and shook hands.

"Everything ready?" Carlos asked, looking around the camp.

"*Sí,*" The man had deep acne pits and a cobra tattoo on his right hand. Snakeskin suspenders held up his jeans.

He led them behind the building, past a bloody, half-butchered wild boar, and pointed to a walled corral about fifty feet wide. The corral, shaded by large trees, contained hundreds of glistening, brownish-black snakes entwined like rubber bands between large chunks of limestone. One slithered up the steep bank and Carlos noticed the serpent had openings beside its nostrils, creating the appearance of four. Beside the snake, fat white maggots squirmed in the half-eaten stomach of a large rodent.

"Never seen so fuckin' many *cuatro narices*," Carlos said.

"And they attack," the man said. "Want proof?"

Carlos nodded, remembering Bennett's insistence that he *see* the snakes' aggressiveness.

The man turned and shouted, "Chico!"

Seconds later a short, fat man limped from behind the building holding a gun to the head of a frail old man with tied hands. The fat man grinned oddly at no one, then bashed the old man's head with his gun and flipped him into the snake pit. Dazed, the old man rolled down the incline, landed on several serpents, then tried to scramble to his feet.

It was too late.

The snakes had circled him, moved in, hissing, their eyes enraged, fixed, fangs exposed. The old man looked behind him where more snakes moved in for the kill.

A snake lunged.

The old man leapt back, but Carlos saw the fangs sink deep into his leg, injecting their lethal venom. More fangs tore into his arms and neck. He clawed a few inches up the hill, fell, collapsed. Snakes ripped into his neck and face.

Carlos swallowed hard as the old man's eyes froze. The old guy knew he was toast and slumped forward on his face, his right leg trembling as more fangs ripped into it

Carlos was impressed. These snakes were very *agresivo, colérico*. Big angry bastards. He nodded his acceptance and paid the man.

Minutes later, he and Paco drove off with seven plastic containers. Each held a dozen snakes. Carlos heard the containers bouncing around on the floor, the snakes hissing angrily. One might get loose, bite his leg.

He eased off the gas a bit and wiped sweat from his face.

Twenty

LUKE LISTENED at the door but heard only the groan of a fog horn from the Detroit River. Sonny had left twenty minutes ago, leaving Leonard snoring in the outer room.

Luke reviewed the escape plan he and Jenna had developed. Everything depended on surprising their captors. And a ton of luck.

"Let's run through it again," he said.

Jenna nodded, they walked through the sequence twice, then

rehearsed at actual speed several times, refining their moves. When the moves felt fluid, they sat down.

"Maybe we should wait," she said. "Look for a better opportunity."

"We may not get one."

"But Leonard's furious at you. You grazed his shoulder. He'll use any excuse to shoot you."

"He'll have to shoot through Sonny, who's not exactly anorexic."

She nodded, but fear lingered in her eyes.

"Just keep that fifty-gallon drum between you and Leonard's gun," Luke said.

Footsteps clicked down the hallway and entered the outer room. Sonny and Leonard mumbled something, then stepped toward the door.

"Get ready," Luke said, nodding toward the door, realizing their fate might be decided in the next few seconds.

"One last thing," she said, touching his hand.

"What?"

"I love you."

He embraced her. "My sentiments exactly."

The key jiggled in the door and Jenna moved as planned to the window. She sat down and positioned her dress so the sun spotlighted her long, tan legs.

The door banged open and Luke looked at the hulking silhouettes of Leonard and Sonny. Leonard, his Colt 357 drawn, walked in beside Sonny who carried two Burger King bags. Sonny's gun remained in his shoulder holster.

"Room service," Sonny said, walking over to the open space near Luke. He ripped open the food bag, grabbed two burgers and fries, and stuffed them in his pockets. He placed the food and drinks on the floor.

"Eat!" Leonard said.

Jenna leaned forward, purposely brushing her dress halfway up her thighs, and took a burger. Leonard stared at her long, shapely legs. Then Sonny noticed them and began to gaze.

Slowly, Luke reached as though taking a burger—then bolted for Sonny.

Sonny sensed him coming and tried to lunge away. But Luke grabbed him from behind, reached for his gun, grabbed the handle.

Leonard turned, gun raised, as Luke spun Sonny between himself and Leonard.

Luke tried to yank Sonny's gun out, but the man's massive bicep clamped the barrel to his ribs. Luke couldn't budge the gun.

"Duck, Sonny!" Leonard yelled, leaping to the side.

Luke twisted Sonny between him and Leonard.

"I can't!"

Luke wrestled the gun's handle partly out of the holster.

Leonard, aiming at Luke and Sonny, leapt toward the metal drum—and grabbed for Jenna—but missed. She ran to the window.

Yanking with all his strength, Luke jerked the gun from Sonny's holster. Sonny stumbled backward and fell.

Luke aimed toward Leonard—who'd cowered behind the drum.

Luke rolled right to get a better angle.

"Drop the gun or she's dead!" Sonny shouted.

Luke spun around and saw Sonny pressing an eight-inch switchblade against Jenna's neck. Her eyes were riveted on the knife.

"Drop the fuckin' gun!" Sonny screamed.

Luke's options were zero. Even if he shot Sonny, Sonny could still slit her neck and she'd bleed to death while Leonard pumped a few bullets in his back.

Luke put the gun on the floor.

Leonard stepped from behind the drum, scooped it up, then turned toward the door. Luke looked back at Sonny, who removed the gleaming blade from Jenna's neck.

Suddenly, Luke's back exploded in pain as Leonard kicked him.

"Bastard!" Leonard shouted, kicking him in the stomach.

Luke buckled over, fell to the floor, unable to breathe. Jenna screamed. Pain curled him into a prenatal crouch. He gasped for air.

Leonard's shoe whacked the side of his face. Luke tasted blood. Leonard kicked again. Pain shot down Luke's spine. His head was numb, everything going grey, fading.

"Stop!" Jenna shouted.

"Fuckin' asshole," Sonny yelled, ramming his boot into Luke's neck. "I'm a black belt."

Leonard laughed. "Easy, Sonny. There's a better way to teach this dude."

"Yeah?"

Luke felt himself slipping, his vision tunneling, the room going black.

Leonard jammed the barrel of his Magnum into his bloody ear. "Next time you try this shit, you'll watch me cut your bitch's tongue out—before I blow her brains out!"

Twenty One

Friday, 3:40 p.m. Yucatan

MASON BENNETT grabbed his large Cabela backpack from the first-class storage area and stepped outside the American Airlines 737 into the sunshine. The Cancun air hit him like a hot damp towel and reminded him of sweaty afternoons in the Mekong Delta. He merged with the tourists squinting their way across the tarmac toward the *Aeropuerto Internacional de Cancún,* where Carlos and Paco awaited him.

They'd take him to check out the snake pit and make certain

the Twins began their hunting trip on schedule.

Inside the terminal, the cool air jolted him and he found himself engulfed by passengers rushing toward the customs lines. He moved to the shortest line and passed through customs without incident. In the mobbed reception area, he searched the crowd of swarthy faces for Carlos and Paco. He saw Carlos first. The man's coal-black eyes were pressed into his pudgy face like raisins in a bran muffin. Beside him stood Paco, shorter, darker, quieter, eyebrow ring glinting above almond-shaped Indian eyes.

Bennett nodded without speaking and followed them outside. They walked toward a red Jeep Cherokee outfitted for off-road jungle driving; a row of high-beam headlights across the roof, a grille screen, wide, deep-tread tires. Bennett got in, felt an icy blast of air-conditioning—and icy steel against his ankles. Looking down, he saw two floor-mounted assault rifles.

Carlos sped along the highway that cut through the jungle and headed south on Highway 307 along the Caribbean coast.

"Is the pit ready?" Bennett asked.

"*Sí*," Carlos said, grinning. "As ready as the *serpientes*."

* * *

Forrest Klug paced behind his desk, still fuming that Mason Bennett had blackmailed him into a higher fee. He'd underestimated Bennett, a minion who'd executed orders without questions for twenty years.

Klug had to hand it to him. Bennett had street smarts. He'd correctly sensed that something might happen to *him* after the Twins' accident. In fact, Klug had planned to neutralize Bennett. But now things were different. Bennett had a dossier. Its contents could destroy everything Klug had worked for.

Klug had to find the dossier, destroy it and eliminate Bennett before he could assemble more incriminating evidence. The dossier was apparently with a man Bennett phoned every week. Phone records would reveal such a number. Klug flipped his Rolodex to the "R's" and dialed.

"Hello," said a raspy voice.

"Russer, this is Mr. K. Are your friends still with the phone company?"

"My friends are wherever you want."

Klug explained what he needed, and Russer assured him he'd have his information within hours. Klug relaxed a little, knowing Russer would deliver. As Klug hung up, his executive assistant, Lucinda Breck, walked in. Her blue suit seemed slightly disheveled.

"You wanted to do your correspondence now, Mr. Klug."

"Yes." He noticed her face seemed splotchy and drained of its usual energy. Strands of grey hair had fallen from her always perfect chignon. One earring was missing and her puffy red eyes suggested she'd been crying. He sensed her mother's illness had worsened. "Your mother?"

She nodded and closed her eyes.

"What's happened?"

Her face flushed. "Her insurance plan just called her. They stopped payment for her weekly antitrypsin treatment—even though the doctor said it's the only thing that keeps her breathing."

Klug knew the insurance game: refuse payment enough times and people stop requesting. "How much is the treatment?"

She dabbed her eyes with a damp Kleenex. "Nine hundred seventy dollars a week."

"And she's on social security?"

Breck nodded, her eyes filling. Lucinda was a trusted and indispensable assistant, whose mother had once worked closely with Klug's mother for many Manhattan charities, and who, like Klug's own mother, had been divorced and left penniless late in life by her philandering husband.

"Lucinda, tell your mother not to worry. The insurance company will pay the bills. I'll talk to the CEO."

"But they already refused—"

"They'll change their mind."

She nodded. "Thank you, Mr. Klug." She dabbed her eyes with

a Kleenex. "You know, my mother still speaks so highly of your mother. Such a wonderful woman."

"Yes...until my father destroyed her."

Breck's eyes widened. Klug realized he'd never told her why he and his father never spoke. She seemed eager to know more.

"Their divorce?" Lucinda Breck whispered.

Klug nodded, his mind drifted back to the night. "My mother's life shattered the night she came home from a charity function and found my father in their bed with a young woman."

Breck looked down at the carpet.

"Mother had sort of tolerated my father's affairs for years and always held her head high. But when he flaunted a woman in their bed, *knowing* she would find them, *wanting* her to see, *wanting* her to feel the pain—well, it destroyed her."

Breck closed her eyes. "How humiliating."

"He was gifted at that. He actually announced to her from the bed that he was going to marry the giggling slut. He told mother he'd filed for divorce that day, and that according to their pre-nuptial agreement, this was now *his* domicile, and that she had to leave in the morning."

Lucinda Breck gasped.

"Cruelty was his other talent."

"How long were they married?"

"Thirty-one years."

"What happened then?"

"Two days later, I moved my mother into a new apartment that looked out over Central Park. Unfortunately, the only thing she looked out over was a whiskey bottle. One year later, she died from a massive dose of Valium and alcohol."

"I'm so sorry, Mr. Klug." Breck's eyes moistened again.

"But I didn't see it as suicide. I saw it as murder."

A murder, Klug reminded himself with pleasure, his father would soon pay for.

Twenty Two

Friday, 9:45 p.m.

"**H**OW'S YOUR list coming, Eddie?" Redstone asked, stuffing half a Big Mac into his mouth and hanging up his office phone.

Eddie Berger and Lew Meads had come up with a time-saving idea of calling Lumina van owners and asking if they wanted to be in a Chevrolet television commercial. Most owners did and quickly disclosed whether their Lumina had window stickers which might be competitive to General Motors ACDelco spark plug brand.

The list was shrinking amazingly fast, but Redstone knew it wasn't fast enough.

"We're whittling it down," Berger said. "Our agency guys have eliminated ninety-seven more."

Redstone nodded and wiped mayonnaise from his lips. "Lew?"

Lew Meads flipped shut his cell phone and checked his list. "Our team's phoned eighty-nine."

Redstone ran his finger down the master list. "Which leaves roughly three hundred eighty to go."

"Actually more," Berger said. "I'm getting quite a few answering machines."

Redstone nodded that he was too. He bit off another chunk of Big Mac and wiped perspiration from his forehead. He wasn't hungry and was still eating. He always did when stressed. And Luke and Jenna's chances were stressing him out. The room was stuffy, the smell of burgers and fries hanging over them like a cloud of grease. He walked over, opened the window, then faced the two men. "Guys, we're running out of time."

The two men stared back.

The phone rang and Redstone punched the speaker button.

"Hank, it's Kincaid." He was excited. "Got something."

"Talk."

"I cross-checked the Lumina phone numbers against the phone numbers on Luke's home Caller-ID."

"A match?"

"Yeah. Company called Telecenter. They have a blue Lumina van and they called Luke's home."

Redstone's heart kicked into high gear. "Did you call Telecenter?"

"Three times. No answer. Phone company says the number's good. It's a telemarketing company. You know, people making lots of phone calls. But get this. Telecenter has *one* phone. A one-phone telemarketing company makes no sense."

Redstone stood and paced. "*When* did Telecenter call Luke?"

"A few hours before he disappeared last night."

"What's Telecenter's address?"

"Thirty-nine DeWite Street. Deserted warehouse off Jefferson near the river."

"No-man's-land." "Meet us at DeWite and Heldrum in ten minutes."

Redstone hung up and faced Berger and Mead. "Keep phoning just in case this Telecenter Lumina doesn't pan out." They nodded and turned back to their phones.

He hurried outside into the warm, humid night and smelled rain coming. Overhead, a fat yellow moon slid from behind thick clouds and illuminated the anti-riot squad awaiting him in the parking lot.

They split into three unmarked vehicles and sped toward the warehouse. Traffic was light. Minutes later they turned up DeWite Street and picked up Kincaid and two other officers.

Looking ahead, Redstone saw the darkened warehouse looming like a massive, black mountain. As they drove closer, he noticed faint light behind a corner room on the sixth floor. They had to get up there without alerting the occupants.

"We can enter a coal chute in back," Kincaid said.

Redstone nodded and spoke into the police radio. "Darnell, you and Parker cover the front. We're going in the back."

Redstone's car and the third vehicle drove to the rear and parked. They got out, cut the chain lock on the back gate, stepped inside, and squeezed through the coal chute. One minute later they entered the sixth floor and moved silently down the hallway to the room.

They positioned themselves on both sides of the door. Redstone listened, but heard nothing. Weapons drawn, the men burst into the room.

Empty. A second room, even filthier, was also empty.

Redstone saw crumpled fast-food bags, beer cans and half-filled coffee cups on the table. He walked over and felt the coffee cup. Warm. A fleck of ash burned on a cigarette butt.

Someone had been in the room minutes before.

Twenty Three

Saturday, 10:10 a.m.

L UKE'S MIND moved like sap down a tree. He was in a bed,
drifting in and out of sleep, trying to lift his eyelids and
determine where he was, where Jenna was. His eyes felt
crazyglued shut and he wondered if they actually were.

The last thing he remembered was Leonard handing them
Cokes around eleven p.m., then feeling drowsy moments later.
Jenna had slumped against his shoulder, mumbled, "drugged,"
and passed out, seconds before he did. After that he could only

recall a brief, blurry image of being jostled around the interior of a car.

Straining, he forced his right eye open. He blinked, saw the fuzzy outline of his watch. Was it ten-after-ten or ten-to-two? Beyond the watch, he saw a knotty-pine wall with photos of fat, grinning men holding strings of large walleye. To the left, sunlight filtered through the sheer, fluttering curtains of a small window. He heard birds, smelled pine. A cabin?

Was Jenna here?

He rolled over—and snapped to a stop. His right wrist was handcuffed to the brass bed rail. Turning, he saw Jenna on a nearby bed. *Thank God*. She was asleep, her wrist also cuffed to the headboard.

"Jenna."

She didn't respond.

"Jenna," he said louder.

Nothing.

He studied the white sheet covering her for several seconds. No rise and fall. No hint of breathing. Dead still. Cold sweat blanketed his skin and his heart pummeled against his chest. They'd given her too much sedative.

They killed her!

Crazed, he jerked his handcuffed arm away from the brass railing. The cuff rattled loudly, but held. He jerked it again.

"Bastards!" he shouted.

Jenna gasped, her eyelid fluttered.

Every inch of his body melted. Her eyelid flickered again and slowly, her eye opened and turned toward him.

"Enjoy your coma?" he asked.

"Uh-huh." She rubbed her eyes. "Where are we?"

"Not in Kansas, Dorothy."

She squinted toward the window.

"Based on the knotty pine walls and other stuff," he said, "I'd say we're in a cabin."

She yawned, stretched and rubbed her handcuffed wrist. "Our Cokes must have been pure diphenhydramine."

"Will I need Viagra?"

She smiled. "The stuff in sleeping pills, butthead."

Sitting up, he saw two sun-bleached wicker chairs, a small bamboo lamp table with a faded *Fishing World* magazine, a rattan lamp, a painting of small blue ship sailing into a red sunset, a wood-plank floor covered partly by a worn area rug, and a pine chest beyond Jenna's bed. Nothing that could pry off the handcuffs.

"Can you reach that pine chest?" he asked.

She stretched toward it, but her fingers stopped several inches short.

"There's another way," Luke said. He stood, lifted his bed, and scooted it toward the chest. Suddenly, a bed slat fell and slapped against the wood floor.

Did Leonard and Sonny hear?

Luke listened. Nothing. He fixed the slat and continued inching the bed toward the chest. Opening the top drawer, he found a tattered *Guns & Ammo* magazine, an empty Coppertone tanning tube, a Nissan key chain with two rusty keys. The bottom drawer revealed three bars of Dial soap, a tattered Ronald McDonald coloring book, broken crayons, and more kids' stuff.

"Find anything?"

He tossed a Kermit the Frog doll at her. She caught it and said, "Kermit, when we need Arnold Schwarzenegger?"

"We need divine intervention," he said, looking out the window at a pristine, turquoise-blue lake about one hundred feet away. The lake was surrounded by tall evergreens, a sandy beach and a grey, weathered cabin on the opposite shore. Even if he had a cell phone what would he tell the police—we're on a beautiful blue lake? Michigan had eleven thousand beautiful blue lakes.

He tried the front door and discovered it was locked from the outside. Dragging the bed back, he sat down and looked around the room again. No weapons, no way out. They were trapped.

He faced Jenna who brushed back her hair, looked out the window a moment, then faced him and calmly said, "They're planning our rafting accident, aren't they?"

He nodded, but was amazed at how calmly she said it. Perhaps being a doctor somehow conditioned her to accept death.

He wondered what level of white water they'd be rafting in. Would they have life jackets?

If they were thrown into class five or six without life jackets, their chances of surviving were slim.

Twenty Four

ELIZABETH BLAKELEY, working at her computer, heard someone behind her. She turned and saw Howie Kaufman, the agency's point man on new business, lumber in, carrying a large mug of coffee. He'd been helping her search for the Siamese Twins by compiling two lists; one of large advertising accounts controlled by two key men, the other of major ad agencies that didn't have a client in a major product category.

Kaufman, a former All-Pro NFL defensive tackle dropped his

two hundred eighty pound, six-foot-seven frame in a nearby chair, hissing the cushions flat. His ruddy, moon face was dominated by a nose which had slammed into too many helmets. His muscular arms hung like tree trunks from his massive shoulders. Kaufman, one of the few Orthodox Jews to play pro football, had an uncanny skill at tackling evasive runners, which earned him the moniker—Yom Klipper.

No one was sure whether Howie's new business success was due to his gentle, relaxed sales manner, or the prospective client's fear that Howie might fall on them.

She noticed his large blue-grey eyes seemed tight with worry. He avoided looking at her and she knew something was wrong.

"They have Luke," he whispered.

Elizabeth felt like the wind had been crushed from her.

"He met Jenna's kidnappers," Kaufman said. "The police traced them to a deserted warehouse near the river, but got there too late." Kaufman rubbed the white scars on his knuckles, vestiges of football cleats. "Lieutenant Redstone says Luke called him and said everything was okay."

"Did Redstone believe him?"

"Not a word. Luke also said Jenna and he were going white-water rafting. Redstone thinks the kidnappers are setting up a rafting accident."

Elizabeth's heart skipped. She leaned forward and rubbed her temples. The last two days were insane. How could a plot to kill two unknown businessmen escalate into the strong possibility that two people she really cared for would be murdered? Luke had nothing to do with the plot. He simply overheard something he shouldn't have. She felt nauseated and frustrated.

"What can *we* do?" she asked.

"For starters we can find every damn white-water river in Michigan."

"Aren't the best ones in the Upper Peninsula?"

"Most are. But the kidnappers probably want to handle this fast, close to home."

Blakeley nodded, pressed her intercom and spoke to her young assistant, Maggie. Seconds later the competent, perky brunette walked in.

"Maggie, we need some information fast," Blakeley said, and quickly explained why. "Please search the Internet and our files for *White-Water Rafting—Michigan*. Also ask Scotty Morton at the Detroit Free Press. We need the name of every white-water river in the state. Also check northern Indiana, Ohio and Ontario."

"And the *Michigan Tourism* Web site," she suggested.

"Good idea."

"Maggie," Kaufman said, "Ask Scotty if he has a list of rafting outfitters. Chances are they'll rent or buy a raft."

"Will do," Maggie said, walking from the office.

Elizabeth continued pacing behind her desk, trying to think what else she could do. She stopped and stared at an executive group photo on the wall. Luke smiled from the middle row.

"When was that picture taken?" Kaufman asked.

"Couple of years ago at Harsen's Island."

"Luke looks happy."

"He was just promoted." She brushed back strands of hair, recalling how surprised and pleased he'd been.

"And deserved it," Kaufman said, stretching his massive arms. "Baines Thomas says Luke creates and sells creative work as well as anyone he's known. And he's known everyone."

She nodded. "I agree, but...."

Kaufman scrunched up his eyebrows. "But what?"

"Sometimes I think Luke is too...consumed by his work. It's all he does. Weekends. Late nights. He leaves little time for anything else. It seems to overwhelm him sometimes. He needs more balance in his life." Elizabeth knew about balance. She'd learned about it the hard way. She'd worked too many nights and weekends in her early career and her family had suffered. Reprioritizing her life twelve years ago, and disciplining herself to stick to the new priorities and new balance, had transformed her life, made each part better.

"Balance like Jenna, maybe?" Kaufman said, winking.

"No maybe. She's the one. She's shifting his priorities fast. They're perfect for each other."

"I couldn't agree more."

"But..." Blakeley said.

"Another but?"

"Luke seems to hold back from commitment, seems to fear it."

Kaufman stared back. "No way. Luke's smitten by Jenna. I saw it in his eyes. And Jenna digs him. Take it from a major sex symbol."

Blakeley smiled. "Luke was smitten by another lovely girl a few years ago. I think she moved to New York because he wouldn't commit. Luke was hurt by it."

Kaufman shrugged. "Today, a lifetime commitment lasts about eight years. Kids are afraid to commit. They act like it's Ebola."

"Which is odd for Luke," Blakeley said. "He's never feared anything." She walked back to her desk, sat down and scanned the list of Siamese Twins references she'd found. "If only we could identify the Siamese Twins."

Kaufman reached in his briefcase, pulled a green folder and opened it. "This might help."

"What?"

"The list of major advertising agencies that don't have a client in a major product category."

"Like an airline or a fast-food chain?"

"Exactly."

"How many agencies?" Blakeley asked.

"One hundred twenty-eight large agencies so far. Each is missing a major product category they'd kill to get." He slid the list in front of her.

She recognized all of the prestigious agencies, then locked her eyes on one. "Why is *our* agency here?"

"We don't have an airline account," Kaufman said.

"But who'd *kill* to get one?"

"Have you met some of our new young MBAs?"

Blakeley smiled. "They'd strangle the Pope with his rosary for the United Airlines business."

He smiled, rubbed his scarred knuckles again and shifted his weight, causing the cushion to wheeze. "But who wants to hang the Siamese Twins?"

She shrugged and fingered her silver bracelet. "This Twins name is driving me crazy."

"Why?"

"Because a few years ago, I read about two businessmen called Siamese Twins. I saw a photo of them. They were wearing dark jackets, standing next to a boat, or truck, or something big. I woke up at three-thirty this morning with the damn picture in my head. But I can't remember who, or where I saw it."

"It'll come to you."

"Hopefully in time to save Luke and Jenna."

* * *

Sonny stepped from his Ford Bronco and strolled past a row of new sailboats, fishing boats and a gleaming, medium-sized Chris-Craft in front of Maynard's Marine & Outdoor, a sprawling boating and hunting store a few miles from the Holloway Dam, northeast of the Flint River.

He breathed in the cool air. It smelled clean and nice. He liked being outside. He also liked this job. Buy a raft and diving gear, then after the accident, keep everything. He liked jobs when he got to keep stuff.

He stepped inside Maynard's, smelled leather and new rubber. *Man* smells. He filled his lungs and gazed at the wet suits, fishing poles and jet skis. Along one wall he saw a bunch of gleaming Mercury outboard motors. Along another were display cases filled with new rifles and handguns. The guns looked beautiful. He wanted to feel them, all smooth and cool. Turning, he saw what he was looking for, walked over and ran his fingers over the slick fabric surface of a fully inflated raft.

"Thinking 'bout a little raftin'?" said a deep, gravelly voice behind him.

Sonny turned and stared at a silver Roy Rogers belt buckle.

Slowly, he raised his eyes until he stared into the bullet-grey eyes of a giant. The man stood at least six-ten and weighed over three hundred fifty pounds, most of which was stuffed into his faded bib overalls. The guy's springy hair hung like fat copper wires over his forehead. His neck looked like white birch. Sonny stepped back. He didn't like people bigger than him.

"Oh yeah," Sonny said. "Couple friends. They like rafting."

"What class?"

"Nice people."

"No. What class of *rafting* they like? Class One's smooth, then she gets rougher with Class Two, Three, Four, Five. Class Six is real Depends time."

"Depends?"

"Depends—adult diapers—scares shit out of you!" The giant chuckled into a laughing fit, accidentally knocking a bowling ball off its display. He reached down and lifted the ball one-handed, without using the holes, and placed it back on the display.

Sonny swallowed and took another step backward. "Yeah, they like scary."

The large man thumped the raft with his meaty fist. "This here Zodiac'll handle it. Tough as a humpback mule. Comes fitted with everything. Seats six to eight. Special stitching—stuff's like iron. And she's on sale."

"Can it handle rough white water?"

"She can probably handle Niagara Falls. A pal down in West Virginia took his Zodiac down the New River. Them's mean rapids. Run 'em like she was on rails."

"I'll take it."

The giant smiled. "Guarantee you'll like it. Now, if you're wantin' scary water around here, try Indian Claw. That's some serious white water, thanks to the new river diversion. Plus she's swelled up real fat from the rains and all." He turned to a wall map and ran bratwurst-sized finger down a squiggly blue line. "Start about here and run her down to here."

"Sounds good," Sonny said, even though he'd already decided

on Indian Claw, since it was fed by the lake beside their cabins.

Sonny looked around the store at the other equipment. "I'll need a few more things."

Minutes later, the behemoth totaled Sonny's purchases on the cash register. "This stuff bottoms out at three thousand nine hundred eight. How you fixin' to pay?"

"Cash," Sonny said proudly, pulling a thick wad of hundred dollar bills from his pocket. The giant's eyes widened. Sonny liked impressing people with his hundreds, making sure they knew he was no low-life, even though they could see he wasn't.

"God is good," the giant said, his eyes locked on the money. Sonny peeled off the bills and handed them to the man who flicked through the money like a bank teller, then stuffed them under the cash register tray.

"Thanks, fella. We don't get many cash sales this big. Anything don't work, I'll replace it right quick."

Outside, the man loaded the purchases into Sonny's Bronco, then secured the raft to the roof. He leaned against the Bronco, tilting it, and stared at Sonny. "One word about the river, son."

"Yeah?"

"Indian Claw's been running extra angry here late. Be careful. And don't go as far as Devil's Backbone 'less'n you got a river pilot. That's real serious white water. Class six. Could ram you into them big rocks."

"Right," Sonny said. He wasn't worried. He'd rafted before, and could swim like a shark. He could handle any stuff the fucking river threw at him.

Sonny drove away and stared at the beautiful countryside. The sun had burned off the morning mist, revealing dark green pine trees. Fresh, clean evergreen smell. He could even taste it. He liked this area of Michigan. Not many cops. Lots of gun and hunting stores. Good drinking holes with real men. Life is good. Soon he'd be rafting along the Indian Claw.

And Tanner and the woman would be scrapin' along the rocky bottom.

Twenty Five

Saturday, 11:30 a.m.

HANK REDSTONE watched the three evidence technicians conduct their forensic investigation of the garbage-strewn warehouse rooms. The mid-morning sun burned through the grimy window, illuminating millions of dust particles. The stench of stale beer, rotten food and urine forced him to stand near the window.

Redstone had to find some clues fast or he'd find Luke and Jenna dead. They were running out of time—if they hadn't

---

already.

He watched a slim, bald print man brush grey powder on a wooden table and look up smiling. "Big fat sucker here."

"AFIS it," Redstone said, hoping the computer system could quickly identify the print.

The hall door swung open, and an excited young police officer darted over to Redstone, gasping. "I found a guy who saw Tanner and Jenna leave here with two men last night."

"Where is he?"

"Across the street in that abandoned grocery. But he was here last night, sleeping in the stairwell. Someone stepped on him. Another guy kicked him in the gut and told him to get the hell out. So he did."

"What'd they drive?"

"A dark slanty van."

Redstone turned to Marcus Kincaid. "Put out another APB on the Lumina. State wide. And have someone watch this place in case they come back."

Kincaid nodded and made the call.

Redstone looked out the window toward the abandoned grocery where two officers were talking to the old homeless man in a long, tattered brown coat. As Redstone turned, he noticed a crumpled yellow note snagged on a rip in the window screen. He opened the note by the corners. Blank. As he looked closer, sunlight picked up faint indentations. Gently, he rubbed his pencil over them, and watched white numbers emerge in the grey shading. He tilted the note toward the sunlight and saw the hint of more numbers.

"Marcus, see if our document guys can pull up these last four numbers—fast!"

Kincaid clutched the corner of the note, put it in a plastic bag and gave it to a young officer who hurried from the room.

For the next thirty-five minutes, Redstone and the tech people filled bags with trace evidence. They found good prints on the playing cards and beer cans. Some prints were already being run through Detroit's AFIS computerized fingerprint-checking system which could check millions of fingerprints in seconds.

Redstone knew that even if the police computer identified a kidnapper's fingerprints and had his address, the guy wasn't sitting at home watching *Masterpiece Theater*. But still they'd have a name and face.

"Hank, we got the rest of the Post Em numbers," Kincaid shouted from the corner of the room. "It's a phone number—Maynard's Marine and Outdoor. They sell rafts."

Redstone's heartbeat jumpstarted. "Where?"

"Near the Flint River. Few miles from the Holloway Dam. One hour drive."

"Too long. Get a chopper," Redstone said.

Four minutes later, he heard the thumping clip of the Detroit Police Bell helicopter.

As they boarded, Redstone couldn't shake his fear that the kidnappers were already on the river, that they'd already staged the rafting accident, early, before the river got busy with possible witnesses.

Then they'd clear out.

Twenty Six

Saturday, 3:40 p.m.

LUKE'S FINGERS burned from bending the bed spring brace back and forth. He licked them cool, then reached back through the slit in the box frame and resumed twisting the hot metal brace. He wanted to snap off the brace and use it as a weapon.

But the brace refused to break off.

It was about six inches long and slightly curved. He tried bending it the other direction and fiery shivers shot up his fingers.

Again, he cooled them in his mouth.

"Try gripping it with the blanket," Jenna suggested.

He squeezed the thick blanket partly through the slit but it wouldn't go further. "Too bulky."

He pulled it out and continued twisting the brace, wondering what he'd do if the metal refused to break off. Without it, he had one weapon. His hands.

"Listen..." Marita said, looking toward the window.

He heard a strange, scraping sound outside, something dragging over the grass beside the cabin. He looked outside but saw nothing.

"What is it?" Jenna asked.

Luke shrugged, stood, pulled his bed to the window, but still couldn't see anything. The odd scraping noise grew louder. He leaned left and froze.

Sonny and Leonard were dragging a large, black raft toward the river.

* * *

Hank Redstone watched the ground rise as the Detroit Police Bell helicopter approached the narrow landing strip near the Flint River. Gusting side-winds buffeted the aircraft, rocking it. The pilot tilted the control stick, dropped airspeed, descended to a few feet over the runway, then eased the skids onto the ground.

Redstone looked over at Marcus Kincaid whose scrunched up body seemed to inflate now that it was back on Mother Earth. Kincaid hated flying. He hated most things cops have to do, like shoot at people, high-speed car chases, paperwork. But he loved catching criminals, was better at it than most, and his high-tech smarts put every crook in Detroit a little closer to the slammer.

"Look," Redstone said, pointing outside at a field. "God's own *terra firma*."

"The firma the better. Let's just hope Luke and Jenna are around here. All we got is RGF."

"RGF?"

"Redstone Gut Feeling."

Redstone smiled. "Hey—did I have time for a probability study? The bad guys made Luke tell us he was going rafting. Somebody in that room called Maynard's Marine. Maynard's sell rafts. This is not nuclear physics." He squinted out the window at three small, private aircraft beside a long Holiday Rambler motor home that appeared to serve as the airstrip terminal.

"Maybe," Kincaid said, "someone up here saw them."

"Maybe they roll up the sidewalks after dinner."

Beside the motor home, Redstone saw a white Chevrolet Impala police car with black and gold stripes and mud-splattered door panels. He pointed to the car. "The county mounties,"

"Right on time."

Redstone and Kincaid deplaned and walked toward the terminal. The door opened and a blond, three-year-old boy wearing a dinosaur sweatshirt and holding a soccer ball ran out and stared up at Redstone's six-feet-three-inches of black skin.

Redstone smiled down and said, "Hi, there."

The toddler continued gazing at his face and hands. Redstone suddenly felt very black. "Mus' not be many us darkies up here, I be guessin'."

"You be smart as a whip, Boss," Kincaid said.

"Les' see mah best watermelon-eatin' grin works." Redstone grinned like a maniac.

The toddler's face exploded in a giggle and he tossed him the soccer ball, ready to play.

"Not now, son. Maybe later." Redstone handed it back.

"Oki-doki," the toddler said, kicking the ball and chasing it down the airstrip.

A tall police officer, sandy-haired, fortyish, in a chocolate-brown shirt and tan pants stepped from the terminal and walked toward them. He peeled open a pack of gum with one hand.

The officer removed his wrap-around sunglasses, revealing the palest-blue eyes Redstone had ever seen. An easy smile creased the man's bronzed face as he slid a stick of gum between white teeth. He dropped the wrapper in a nearby container.

"Juicy Fruit?"

Redstone and Kincaid each took a piece and thanked him.

"Deke Martin, Deputy Sheriff. You fellas must be Lieutenant Redstone and Sergeant Kincaid."

"I'm Hank Redstone. This is Marcus Kincaid."

"Pleasure to meet you." Redstone could tell the man meant it. They shook hands.

As Deputy Martin led them over toward the police car, Redstone asked, "Do you know where Maynard's Marine & Outdoor is?"

"Spittin' distance."

They got in the car and sped off down a two-lane dirt road, lights flashing, dust rooster-tailing behind them. Two minutes later, Deputy Deke Martin skidded the Impala to a stop in the gravel parking lot of Maynard's Marine & Outdoor. Redstone noticed a "Live Bait" poster and a blue neon "Mercury Outboard Motors" sign flashing in the window. An Irish setter dozed on the deck of a Chris Craft cruiser. They walked inside where a thin, young man with horn-rimmed glasses was folding orange hunting vests. Deputy Martin approached him.

"Hey, Billy," Martin said.

"Hey, Deke."

"Wasn't Jimmy workin' this morning?"

"Yep, but he's driving up to the U.P. to see his sister in Iron Mountain. You remember Inez. Married that upholstery guy."

"Oh yeah."

"Can I help you fellas?"

"Maybe," Deputy Martin said, gesturing to Redstone.

Redstone handed Billy a police ID-photo of Sonny, whose fingerprints had been pulled from a warehouse beer can and identified by AFIS. "This man may have come in here early this morning. Name's Sonny Slater. Sometimes uses Daryl Lee Miller."

Billy studied the photo a few seconds. "Never saw him. But Jimmy mighta."

"You have Jimmy's sister's number?" Redstone asked.

"Right there," he said pointing to a yellow note stuck to the cash register. "But he won't be there for a few hours."

"He have a car phone or cell phone?" Redstone asked.

"Nope," Billy said. "What'd this Sonny fella do, anyways?"

"He's kidnapped some people. Plans to kill them rafting."

Billy's eyes shot open. "Sweet Jesus. Wonder if he's the fella Jimmy told me about?"

"What fella?"

"Stranger. Bought a shitload of stuff early this morning."

"What kind of stuff?" Redstone asked.

"Zodiac, wet suits, scuba gear. Run over three thousand bucks! Fella paid cash!"

"Zodiac?" Redstone asked.

"A raft."

Redstone's muscles turned to bricks.

"Did Jimmy mention where the man is rafting?" Kincaid asked.

"Nope. But you got the Flint and Indian Claw Rivers. Indian Claw's closer and meaner."

"If Jimmy calls in, please have him call this number immediately," Redstone said, handing the young man a card.

"You got it."

Redstone turned to Deke Martin. "Deke, we need a lot of police checking the rivers."

"We ain't got a lot, but you got what we got. Plus I'll ask the lads down near Mott Lake to start looking."

As they walked toward the door, Redstone stopped. "Damn!"

"What?" Martin said.

"Our chopper."

Deputy Martin's eyes lit up. "That sucker'll skim the river like an hawk huntin' dinner."

* * *

"They're coming," Luke said, pulling the bed back in place and sitting down.

This was it. He'd get one chance. He'd watch for the best moment, overpower one of the men, grab his weapon. Failing that, he'd use the bed brace which he had finally broken off. And maybe Jenna could attack with the brace he'd given her.

The key jiggled in the slot. The door swung inward and slammed against the cabin wall.

Leonard and Sonny stood there, wearing black, gleaming wet suits. Leonard's Colt was pointed at Luke.

"You guys need fresh air," Leonard said.

"Yeah, perfect day for a raft ride," Sonny added.

"Course we might get a little wet." Leonard winked at Sonny.

Sonny grinned, and unlocked Jenna's handcuff. She rubbed the red welts on her wrist. He walked over to Luke, slipped the key into his handcuff, popped it open.

"Outside!" Leonard commanded, pointing with his gun.

Luke and Jenna walked out of the cabin into cool wind.

"Head toward the water!" Sonny said.

Looking around, Luke saw no other people. He and Jenna walked slowly down the gentle slope toward the lake. As they approached the raft, Luke saw a paddle leaning against the side. He considered grabbing it, but knew bullets would rip into him before he reached it.

"Turn around," Leonard said.

They turned around.

"Spread out, five feet apart."

They moved a few feet apart. From the corner of his eye, Luke watched Sonny step into the raft, lift a green tarpaulin, pick up something heavy with both hands, carry it over beside Jenna and drop it on the ground.

A concrete block with a long rope attached.

Luke felt like the block landed on his head. His body went numb. The concrete would pull them straight to the bottom. He had to do something fast. If he bolted for Sonny with the brace, Leonard'd shoot him in the back.

Luke noticed an oxygen tank in the front of the raft. Now he understood. After the concrete took them to the bottom, Sonny or Leonard would dive, untie the ropes and release their bodies to make their deaths look accidental.

Sonny wrapped the rope tightly around Jenna's waist, then tied a series of knots behind her back. She looked terrified.

"These blocks was on sale," Sonny said, chuckling. "Got me two for the price of one." He stepped back into the raft, grabbed the other block. As he turned, the block slipped from his hands, rocking the raft.

Leonard faced Sonny.

Luke gripped the brace in his pocket and started toward Leonard.

Quickly, Leonard swung the gun in Luke's face. Luke froze. The two men stared at each other, knowing what almost happened.

"Bad fuckin' idea," Leonard said, placing the gun barrel on Luke's forehead, fingers tightening on the trigger, eyelid twitching. "Very bad!"

"Don't!" Jenna shouted.

Luke held his breath as Leonard's jaw muscles hardened into angry knots. Seconds later, he lowered the gun. Luke exhaled through his teeth.

Sonny picked up the concrete block, dropped it beside Luke, wrapped the rope tightly around his waist and tied several knots in back.

"Raftin' time," Sonny said. "Carry your blocks with you. Sit up front, opposite each other."

Luke gestured for Jenna to board the raft. Clutching her block, she stepped slowly into the raft and sat at the front right-hand side. Luke sat across from her.

Leonard and Sonny got in the back. Sonny shoved off, then paddled a few feet into the lake. A gentle current eased the raft into a narrow stream, that carried them, three minutes later, into a swift-moving river.

"Indian Claw," Sonny said. "Exciting ain't it, Leonard?"

"Fuckin'-A!"

Luke saw no life preservers in the raft. He looked at Jenna. She was chalk white, staring at her concrete block. Her body was rigid, her eyes tight with fear.

Twenty Seven

JENNA WATCHED Sonny steer the raft through the swift, dark current. He seemed experienced, even skilled, piloting through the rapidly moving water. Beside him, Leonard looked nervous, gun in hand, staring at the water, then at the magnificent pine forest along the banks, then in front of the raft.

She noticed large, jagged rocks below the water's surface. She swam well, but negotiating churning water spiked with sharp rocks, while tied to a twenty pound concrete block, was a death sentence. Goosebumps shimmied down her back.

Her only hope was to find a way out of the tightly-bound rope without being discovered by Leonard and Sonny. She'd tried wriggling out, but the rope hadn't budged.

Fingering the rope at her side, she estimated it was about an inch thick. Slowly, she rubbed the rope against the coarse edge of the concrete block. After a few seconds, she felt only a thin, frayed fiber. It would take an hour to cut the rope this way. She didn't have an hour.

Checking Leonard and Sonny again, she saw they were increasingly mesmerized by the scenery. City boys at day camp. Any distraction helped. She leaned back and felt the brace in her pocket nudge her thigh. *Could it cut this rope?* She reached into her pocket and felt the sharp, jagged edge.

Keeping her eyes on the forest, she eased the brace from her pocket and began scraping it against the rope she'd wedged against the concrete with her leg. She moved only her fingers, to avoid detection. After several seconds, she felt a tiny ball of fuzz. The brace was *cutting. But what if the rope, like some ropes, has a thin wire running through it?*

She tried to signal Luke to use his brace, but he was looking down river. She coughed to get his attention. No reaction. She coughed again and he faced her. She glanced at her fingers cutting the rope. He saw what she was doing, but refused to reach for his brace. *Why?*

Seconds later, he moved his leg, and she saw he was already scraping his brace over the rope.

Her relief was short-lived as a soft, low hissing filled her ears. It quickly grew into the angry roar of water crashing against water. White water. She fingered her rope, only half-cut. *What if they forced them to jump in these rapids?* Her heart pounded as the churning water grew louder. She sliced faster.

"What's that noise?" Leonard asked, his thick brow furrowing.

"Fun," Sonny said, grinning. He pulled out a small map, checked it, then whispered something to Leonard.

This is it, she thought, slicing faster. In these rapids the blocks would yank them straight to the bottom.

"It's getting mighty fuckin' choppy," Leonard shouted, clutching his seat.

"This is silk, man. Just wait," Sonny hollered, clearly enjoying Leonard's fear.

She saw white water exploding off rocks one hundred feet ahead. Cold spray hit her face. The raft gained speed as it was sucked toward the roar.

Seconds later, they dropped into the rapids and her stomach whooshed up to her throat. The raft heaved, dipped, slid around rocks into slashing waves, dropped a few more feet, darted into even swifter current.

Jenna squeezed the seat. A massive wave slammed them from the side, drenching them.

"Son of a bitch!" Sonny yelled, eyes maniacal. He pushed off a boulder with his paddle, then back-paddled furiously as the raft reeled into a twisting current between two boulders. Leonard was frozen to the seat, eyes wide, mouth open.

Jenna sat rigid, paralyzed, watching Luke, looking for some assurance they'd get through this.

He nodded. "It's okay."

But it wasn't okay. One big dip would flip the raft and send her and the concrete block straight to the bottom.

Ahead, she saw an enormous black boulder piercing the surface. The raft sped straight toward it. They were going to hit. Suddenly, another wave broadsided them, then catapulted them around the boulder into more turbulent water. Cold water hit her eyes.

Laughing, Sonny back-paddled wildly to the left. The raft squirted around a souse hole into surging waters.

Then calm.

Soothing, serene, smooth-as-glass calm.

The raft glided peacefully ahead, as Jenna listened to her heartbeat and the hiss fade. Sonny howled at the sky like a coyote and slapped Leonard's thigh. Leonard looked catatonic.

Jenna exhaled slowly. She felt her rope. It was drenched, except where she'd gripped the cut surface. Luke's cut portion looked totally soaked. He resumed cutting, but his expression suggested the wet rope was harder to cut.

The raft swept on down the river, which twisted and sometimes bent one hundred eighty degrees in the opposite direction.

Minutes later, Sonny pulled out a small map and squinted at it. The raft's constant bobbing apparently made reading it difficult. He angrily stuffed the map back into his pocket. "I'm pulling into that lagoon ahead," he said.

"What's wrong?" Leonard asked, water dripping from his purple ear lump.

"Nothin'. I need to check this fuckin' map out good."

Leonard seemed pleased to reach land. "Gotta take me a shit anyways. Rapids shook a load loose."

Jenna was worried. If they forced her out of the raft, they might see the frayed rope.

Sonny steered the raft into the small lagoon and eased onto a flat, mushy bank. The lagoon was hushed and shaded by cathedral-arched weeping willows and thick evergreens. Leonard stepped from the raft and wandered into the forest. Sonny remained, studied the map, his gun aimed at Luke.

Moments later, Jenna heard laughter behind her. She spun around, and through the branches saw several large grey rafts with yellow *Argosy* logos, carrying smiling passengers heading down river. The rafters were too preoccupied to notice them.

"Don't even think about callin' out," Sonny said.

His gun had already convinced her not to.

She looked at Luke. His uncut rope looked as thick as it had ten minutes ago.

Twenty Eight

THE DETROIT Police chopper's downwash flattened the long, silky grass beside the Holiday Rambler terminal. Redstone, along with Kincaid, Deputy Deke Martin and a local pilot, Shep, who knew the rivers, boarded and strapped themselves in.

Redstone's ears filled with rhythmic thumping as the chopper glided up over the Flint River meandering as far as he could see.

He turned to Shep, a thin, young man with pale-blue eyes, sparkling ear studs and carrot-colored hair yanked back tight in a pony tail. "We're looking for four people in a raft. One's a

---

183

young woman. Two of the men are probably going to push her and the other man overboard. Fake an accident."

Shep's eyes widened as he looked from Redstone to Kincaid, then said, "They may not need to fake. Indian Claw is wicked water." He banked the chopper right, leveled off at about one hundred fifty feet and darted along the river at ninety miles an hour. Two miles later, he banked right again and headed down another, narrow, but faster-moving river.

"Indian Claw," Shep shouted.

Redstone looked down on the river swollen with rainwater. Pine trees blurred past as the chopper skimmed over the sun-sprinkled water below. The river was dark, clear and clean, its shoreline dotted with white asters and violets. An old man fished from an algae-covered boulder. Redstone felt like he was in a commercial for bottled water.

Moments later Redstone saw a young girl snorkeling near shore and felt bile rise in his throat. Four months ago, he'd pulled a teenage girl's nude corpse from the Rouge River near Detroit. Acid had eaten away her face and breasts. Later, when her killer laughingly called it cosmetic surgery, Redstone lost it and broke the asshole's jaw, causing the guy to eat through a straw for three months. The girl's half-eaten face was forever burned into Redstone's memory. And people wonder why cops drank.

"River traffic's light. Few fishermen," Shep said.

Redstone realized the kidnappers had probably chosen this river because there'd be less chance of an eyewitness. He pointed ahead at some white water.

"Red Dog Run," Shep said.

As they flew over the rapids, Redstone studied the turbulent, pounding water. It was as though someone had deliberately placed obstructions beneath the surface to make it more treach-erous. He searched the banks for any hint of a raft. He saw noth-ing.

"There's more white stuff down river," Shep shouted.

The chopper swooped along the river like a pelican searching for dinner. They turned abruptly south for a few miles. The forest grew thicker along the banks.

Suddenly, Shep bolted upright and pointed ahead. "Raft with four people at one o'clock!"

Redstone couldn't see them. "Where?"

"Right bank," Kincaid said, pointing. "Beneath those trees."

Redstone squinted, shielded his eyes and saw the raft. "Let's get closer."

The pilot peeled right, swept down. As the chopper moved in, Redstone saw two middle-aged couples picnicking in the shade. He signaled the pilot to pull away, but not before a frightened man dropped his sandwich in the river.

"Detroit Cops Harass Innocent Rafters," Deke Martin shouted.

"Film at eleven," Redstone added.

The pilot hurled the chopper over the sun-dappled water. Several minutes later they passed two shorter white-water runs, but saw only a small, orange canoe.

"Any other white water?"

Deke Martin paused a moment. "Well, there's Devil's Backbone. Quarter-mile of real *mean* water. Drops off ten foot. Rocks. Boulders. You name it. Souse holes you could sink a bus in. Nobody rafts over Devil's Backbone less they're an expert or nuts."

"Or maybe planning to kill someone," Redstone suggested.

Deputy Martin nodded.

Minutes later the pilot flew over Devil's Backbone. Redstone was amazed to see the river suddenly collapse several feet to a lower level, convulse in several directions and spit up angry, twisting shafts of water. It looked like Niagara Falls—flat.

Water bashed against boulders and rocks jutted up through the surface like shark's teeth. A large tree branch flipped over the waterfall and disappeared in the foaming, cascading gorge. The branch did not reappear. He realized that any human passing through the raging water would emerge as hamburger.

Decayed chunks of logs and debris littered the muddy bank,

like tombstones of unsuccessful attempts to negotiate the violent water.

"Look at that!" Kincaid said, pointing to an enormous whirlpool.

"We call it Kenmore," Martin said.

"Kenmore?"

"As in Kenmore Washer," Martin explained. "If someone's falls in, it's like they're sucked into a washer. You see their head, then their foot, then their arm, then their head again, and pretty soon you don't see squat. People die in there."

The chopper passed over the gorge three times, then hovered for several seconds. Redstone stared into the vicious, swirling water, scrutinizing every angry inch for any trace of a raft, paddle, lifevest, clothing. He saw nothing. Perspiration skidded down his chest and a dull pain began to squeeze his neck muscles. "Where the hell are they?"

Deke Martin shrugged and looked back the way they'd come. "There's more river way up north. Even some heading south."

"Maybe they're rafting tonight," Kincaid said. "Dirty work's easier in the dark."

Redstone nodded. "There's another possibility."

"What?"

"They're done and gone."

The cockpit was silent, except for the clip of the rotors.

"Let's keep looking," Redstone said, his stomach churning like the whirlpool below.

Martin lifted his sunglasses and squinted up river. "Well they mighta started farther up river and are coming down."

The pilot nodded, swung the chopper around and headed up river.

Minutes later it swooped over the shaded lagoon where Luke, Jenna and Sonny sat in the raft, waiting for Leonard.

Twenty Nine

LUKE HEARD the clip of a chopper pass overhead and fade upriver. Leonard got back in the raft, rocking it. He plopped down, lit a cigar, then tossed the match onto some wet leaves. Sonny paddled out of the shady lagoon and the raft was sucked into the current surging downriver.

Luke fingered his soggy rope. The wet strands were harder to sever; like cutting rope with a butter knife. He sensed he had only minutes.

He watched Sonny scratch his jaw, study the map again, then look downriver. Leonard still seemed intimidated, and stared at

187

the shore. Both men were distracted just enough to let Luke and Jenna whittle their ropes.

"Watch that fuckin' tree!" Leonard shouted, chomping on his wet cigar.

Sonny hooted with laughter and steered around a partially submerged tree trunk lodged between boulders. As he shifted to the side, his pantleg lifted, and Luke saw two nickel size scars, probably bullet holes, just above a Cobra tattoo.

"Devil's Backbone ahead! I knew it!" Sonny shouted, pointing to a sign on the bank.

"You weren't sure?" Leonard asked.

"Fuckin'-A, I was sure! Just checkin' we didn't drift up Morgan Creek."

Sonny leaned over and whispered to Leonard who whispered back, then the two men stared at Luke and Jenna.

Luke realized Devil's Backbone was Jump Time. How far away? How much time? He still had a quarter-inch of damp rope to slice and his fingers were already numb from gripping the brace.

He signaled Jenna to cut her rope faster. She blinked back that she was. Her forehead was dotted with perspiration.

The raft glided along in silence for several minutes, until Luke heard the hiss. The heavy, angry roar of white water. Much louder than before.

Devil's Backbone.

Moments later, fingers burning, Luke felt his rope split in two. But Jenna was still cutting. She looked exhausted and he feared her red face might alert the boys.

Sonny's eyes grew hard as he squinted ahead. He whispered to Leonard and steered toward the bank where the current slowed. Leonard scanned the river, then the banks, apparently looking for eyewitnesses. There were none.

Jenna coughed. Luke looked over as she uncurled bleeding fingertips to reveal her severed rope. Every muscle in his body melted. Then re-hardened as the raft bounced through three jagged rocks, sticking like spikes through the water.

"Showtime!" Sonny yelled, training his gun on Luke. "Stand up with your blocks."

Luke realized they'd have to lift their blocks without revealing the severed ropes. He signaled Jenna to watch him, bent down, clutched both ends of the rope in his fist, and lifted the block. Jenna did the same.

Turning, he heard Devil's Backbone. A soft hiss growing into a mean growl, water exploding against rocks. The roar was louder than anything he'd ever heard, louder that a 747 taking off. They were only one hundred yards away.

"You have a simple choice," Leonard shouted. "Jump in or fall in with a lot of bullet holes."

"And you got ten fuckin' seconds to jump," Sonny screamed.

Leonard began yelling. "One...two...three...four..."

Luke and Jenna stood up. He watched Jenna grow terrified as she looked down at jagged chunks of granite sweeping beneath the raft. Her body shaking, she stared at Luke. He tried to calm her with his eyes, but it wasn't working. She was sweating, gulping for air, hyperventilating, panicking.

If she didn't jump, they'd shoot her.

He locked on her eyes and shouted, "Jump. I'll find you."

Leonard and Sonny laughed.

"...five...six...seven..."

Her eyes were fixed.

"...eight..."

She's not going to jump ...

"...nine..."

As Luke started to push her, she leapt in.

Luke jumped. As he hit the icy water and went under, he dropped his cement block and looked for Jenna.

She was a few feet away, eyes wide, holding her concrete block, sinking. Finally, she dropped her block.

The raft still above him—Luke jabbed the sharp brace into the raft's underbelly twice. Bubbles exploded from the rips.

He turned for Jenna. She wasn't there. He looked down, left and right, didn't see her. He swam deeper, saw nothing. He spun around. Still nothing. Lungs bursting, he raced up for air. He surfaced beside a rock and scanned the river, but couldn't see her.

Sonny screamed back at him. Leonard fired his gun.

Luke ducked under as bullets ripped into the water. More bullets tore past his shoulder. Where was Jenna? Did Leonard shoot her? Did she strike her head on a boulder?

Was she being swept toward Devil's Backbone?

He should have grabbed her *instantly*.

He surfaced, looked.

More bullets sliced the water twelve inches away. He dove under, searching and swimming toward a boulder sticking above the surface. The powerful current pulled him down toward the gorge.

His lungs burning, he surfaced and grabbed onto the slippery boulder. Gasping, he still couldn't see her.

He shimmied up the boulder for a better view. Nothing. She'd disappeared. A bullet ricochetted off the boulder.

Then he saw her.

Face down. Near the middle of the river, drifting into the swift current toward Devil's Backbone. He pushed off the boulder and pulled water with all his strength.

If he didn't reach her in seconds, she'd be swept over the falls onto the crushing boulders of Devil's Backbone.

Luke churned the water harder, but Jenna was being pulled into faster current. Sharp, hot pain shot through his lungs. He was only six feet from her motionless hand. Kicking faster, he lunged for it and missed. She was drifting away, sliding toward the gorge, just ten feet away.

Swallowing water, he touched her finger. He stretched, grabbed her wrist, flipped her on her back and tried to swim toward the shore.

Suddenly, a powerful current spun them around and slammed Jenna's back against another boulder, exploding water from her mouth.

He held her against the boulder.

She jettisoned out more water. She coughed, gasped for air,

clutching him, semiconscious. More water poured from her lips.

Clinging to the boulder, he gasped, "You're...okay."

"Lu..." She sputtered, coughed.

He glanced over her shoulder and saw Leonard and Sonny clutching the deflated sides of the sinking raft as it plunged down toward the sharp, granite bluffs.

The raft disappeared momentarily as it dropped over the waterfall, hit bottom, reappeared, spun wildly and crashed into an enormous five-foot wave. The violent wave crushed the flimsy raft and flicked it like a leaf against nearby rocks. Fat waves swept over the collapsed sides. The raft dipped, and slammed into a large round boulder that looked like a submerged Volkswagen beetle.

Sonny and Leonard were hurled head first into the water. Sonny's skull struck a boulder and turned the water to pink foam. Leonard's head whacked the same boulder and split open like a melon. They were swept ahead toward a massive whirlpool that sucked them in and appeared to devour them.

Luke watched for several seconds, saw Leonard's arm emerge, then Sonny's legs, then nothing. He never saw either man again.

Against his chest, he felt Jenna breathing more regularly. He looked at the shore. Even though it was only fifty feet away, the current was too swift to risk swimming it.

"How long can you hang on?" he asked.

"Till Thanksgiving."

He laughed. Minutes later, he watched the Police chopper pilot wave to them, then land in a nearby clearing. Three men deplaned and ran toward them. Luke was overwhelmed to see Hank Redstone.

A local police officer hurled a life preserver attached to a long rope over toward him, who snared it as it floated by. They pulled Jenna to shore first, then Luke.

"We happened to be in the neighborhood," Redstone said, embracing them both. "Where are your two pals?"

"They stayed with the raft."

As Luke walked toward the chopper, he felt the icy downwash

from the blades and shivered. He took Jenna's hand and they looked at each other, realizing how incredibly lucky they were to be breathing air instead of water.

Luck. Leonard and Sonny's had run out.

Had it also run out for two businessmen hunting in a jungle?

Thirty

MASON BENNETT'S binoculars locked on the Beechcraft King Air C90A as it touched down on the sun-baked dirt airstrip carved through the dense Yucatan jungle. Swirling white dust rooster-tailed after the sleek aircraft as it roared down the strip.

Bennett wanted to make sure the Twins deplaned and headed into the jungle on schedule.

The afternoon sun baked his pale skin. Beads of sweat skidded down his neck. His shirt clung to his skin like Saranwrap. Beside him, Carlos and Paco peered through bushes, watching the aircraft.

Suddenly, at the far end of the runway, a young man and woman with a small girl strolled into view and watched the Beechcraft taxi toward them.

"Who the hell are they?" Bennett asked, concerned. He didn't want any witnesses to see the Twins landing.

"Nobody," Carlos said, shrugging. "They clean the airstrip."

The plane taxied to a stop, the cabin door popped open, and two white-coated stewards stepped out. They opened the rear compartment and began unloading hunting gear.

Bennett flicked sweat from his chin and watched the empty doorway. He waited another full minute, growing anxious. Where the hell are they?

A smile creased his face as the Siamese Twins entered the doorway, stepped down from the aircraft. Baines Thomas had rugged good looks, a tall athletic body, grey-black hair, and was outgoing. Donald Mackay was two inches shorter, stocky, silver hair, more reserved. They walked around, stretching their well-conditioned, sixty-year old bodies. Bodies that would soon pulse with deadly *cuatro narices* venom.

Bennett watched the Twins scan the surrounding jungle and wave to the family. The little girl waved back, smiled, then scooted behind her mother's dress.

A third man stepped into the doorway. Bennett recognized him from the photo. Cesar Torres, *el guía*, the guide.

Torres was a tall, wiry man whose dark eyes seemed to devour everything on the airstrip in a glance. His narrow, mahogany face suggested a Spanish-Indian heritage and many years in the sun. His biceps were large and looked chiseled. The corner of his left eye was scarred and pulled down.

Torres turned, stared directly at Bennett and nodded.

Jesus—he sees me through one hundred yards of thick jungle. Perhaps the reflection of the binoculars. Bennett moved further behind a thick branch. He watched Torres glide effortlessly onto the dirt runway and stretch his long arms and legs. He scratched the stubble on his jaw and looked toward three red World Motors SUV Off-Roaders speeding across the runway toward the aircraft.

The Off-Roaders stopped beside the aircraft. The stewards began loading hunting gear into the vehicles. Torres and the Twins climbed into an Off-Roader that drove over to the family. The Twins got out, chatted with the little girl and handed her a chocolate bar. She smiled and held her mother's hand.

The Twins got back in and the three vehicles drove down the airstrip. Halfway down, they turned onto a one-lane jungle trail.

Bennett turned to Carlos and Paco. "Let's go."

They hurried back to their dark-blue Ford Econoline van, got in and drove off. As they turned onto the runway, Bennett saw the young girl and her parents were picking yellow flowers just a few feet away. The family stared at him and the van.

Big problem, Bennett thought. They'd seen the Twins and his face. They'd seen where the Twins went. They'll watch us follow the Twins. They'll tell the cops if asked. Wrong place, wrong time.

The family would have to be handled.

Carlos drove across the runway and followed the three Off-Roaders through the jungle. Thirty-five minutes later, he pulled to a stop behind a small hill. Ahead, Bennett saw a solid wall of jungle. Stepping out, Carlos led them though palm trees and underbrush, then stopped and lifted a thick branch.

One hundred feet further, Bennett saw the Off-Roaders beside a grey, brick hunting post with a thatched roof. The Twins chatted with an old woman in a white, Mayan dress with red hem and collar border. Her thick silver hair, pulled back in a tight bun, framed a tawny, beaming face. She directed a group of workers unloading the camping equipment and stuffing it into backpacks.

Minutes later, Cesar Torres led the Twins, along with four small *cargadores* carrying backpacks, on foot, down a jungle trail heading south.

Bennett walked over to the van and took out a briefcase. He opened it and took out a square satellite phone dish and aimed it skyward. He turned on the phone, punched in the ID and PIN numbers, then turned the dish until it beeped with the signal from the Astar-East satellite. He called Forrest Klug's private line.

"Klug."

"The hunt has begun," Bennett said and hung up.

* * *

Klug placed the receiver down and whispered to himself. "So has my hunt. We will find your dossier and destroy it. And then we'll destroy you."

Thirty One

Saturday, 7:55 p.m.

ELIZABETH BLAKELEY flinched when her phone rang. She grabbed it, listened a moment, felt all tension drain from her and exploded in a smile.

"Luke and Jenna are okay!" she shouted to Howie Kaufman.

Kaufman's large hands clapped together like a thunderbolt.

She pushed the speaker phone and asked, "Did they discover who the Siamese Twins are?"

"No. The kidnappers drowned in the Indian Claw. We found

their bodies and drivers' licenses. We're trying to link them to someone who knows the Twins."

"Where are Luke and Jenna?"

"Flying back with Redstone and Kincaid. The chopper will land near the Ren Cen in minutes. We wondered if you've turned up anything on the Siamese Twins."

"Not yet," Blakeley said, wishing she had something.

Hanging up, she felt as though an anvil had been lifted from her back. Luke and Jenna were alive, safe. Perhaps this ordeal would bring them even closer, and perhaps close enough to realize how important they were to each other, important enough to want marriage. She hoped so. It was so obvious they were a perfect match.

She looked at Howie Kaufman who was staring out the window, rocking on his heels, smiling like they'd won the lottery. "We should be able to see their chopper soon."

"That's it!" Elizabeth Blakeley said, standing, excited.

"Where?"

"No—*flying's* it.

"Flying's what?"

"The photo of the Siamese Twins. They were standing next to an *airplane*. A fighter. And I remember *where* I saw the photo."

Kaufman's eyes widened. "Where?"

"In our archives. I'll go check. You wait for the police helicopter."

Encouraged and hopeful, Blakeley hurried from the Reference Center, sped down the stairwell two floors and opened the archive door. She stepped inside the musty room and walked along the creaky, shadowed aisles filled with magazines, advertising photography and artwork from seven decades. She loved the archives, and often lost herself paging through the faded, ancient advertisements for Buick cars, Mum deodorant, Congoleum floors, GE washing machines and many more—glimpses of a simpler, kinder, gentler America.

She stepped between two crammed book shelves and flicked on the lamp. Yellow light spilled over the dusty magazines.

She'd seen the photo in this aisle. Which meant it must have been in the old *Advertising Age* magazines. But there were over nine hundred old issues. It would take her hours to go through them all. She grabbed some tattered *Advertising Age* magazines and began to page through them.

The wood floor creaked oddly a few aisles over. She turned and the sound stopped. Could someone be here with her? Other people were in the agency. She'd seen some signatures in the guard's sign-in book.

Another loud creak. She wished the room weren't making strange noises and that it wasn't so dark.

* * *

Luke gazed out the police chopper window at the lake-sprinkled countryside creeping past. The last rays of sun painted the forests and lakes in a soft rust-orange. Far to the left, he saw Port Huron's two majestic bridges to Canada and the cobalt-blue water of Lake Huron sprawling north for hundreds of miles.

Beside him, Jenna dozed, her head resting on his shoulder. He noticed the red handcuff welts on her wrist and the dried blood on her raw fingertips and knew they would heal faster than her memory of Leonard and Sonny.

He marveled at how the last two days had brought them even closer, forged their relationship in ways he'd never envisioned. Their ordeal had also reminded him that life evolves in ways you may not imagine, that it doesn't follow your nice, logical game plan. At any time, life can rip away the person you love. Before you tell them the things you want to tell them, before you do the things you want to do, before you undo things you've done. Like the old song says—*Now* is the hour.

Meanwhile the problem that nearly got them killed still gnawed at him. Two innocent men would be slaughtered in hours. Common sense suggested that he leave the investigation to the police and FBI teams. They were well-equipped and experienced to handle these things.

On the other hand, new Leonards and Sonnys might be out there looking for Jenna and him. He'd have to be alert, remain on guard, at least until Sunday.

Hank Redstone hung up the phone. "We're running Sonny and Leonard through our records now."

"Anything yet?"

"No."

"The Lumina?" Luke asked.

"Sonny was listed as primary driver."

"What about Telecenter Corporation?"

"Dummy corporation," Redstone said. "No paperwork. No names. No tracks. These guys know how to hide."

"Let's hope the two businessmen do."

Redstone stared at him for several seconds. "Luke, you realize our chances of saving these two men are lousy?"

Luke nodded. He turned and stared out the window, knowing he would feel guilty if the two men died.

Thirty Two

Saturday, 9:05 p.m.

THEY HURRIED into the Reference Center. Luke watched Elizabeth Blakeley, eyes brimming, rush up and embrace them. Over Elizabeth's shoulder, he shook hands with a grinning Howie Kaufman whose massive fingers engulfed his like a first-baseman's mit. Everyone plopped into leather chairs around the conference table.

"Safe at last," Blakeley said.

Luke smiled. "But two men somewhere are not."

Elizabeth nodded. "I've been in the archives searching for two men standing beside an older aircraft. I'm sure the men were referred to as 'Siamese twins.' But I found nothing. I've got Sue and Nan going through old issues. We've also been phoning the P.R. directors of major companies and asking if their CEOs are hunting. So far, only one's fishing with his sons."

Luke tapped his fingers on the walnut table, then stared outside at the dark night sky. "You know the best guy to ask about CEOs who hunt?"

"Baines," Blakeley said.

"Who?" Redstone asked.

"Our chairman," Luke said. "He knows most of them."

"But Baines is still in Sweden," Blakeley said, glancing at her watch. "Where it's now three in the morning."

Luke shrugged. "It's worth a wake-up call. You know his hotel?"

"No."

"His wife, Moira, should," Luke said.

Elizabeth flipped open a Roll-a-Dex, punched in Thomas's home number and hit the speaker button.

The phone rang several times before Moira picked up.

"Hello?" she said, out-of-breath.

"Moira, Luke Tanner."

"Oh...hi, Luke. Sorry I took so long. I was in the garden."

"No problem. Listen, Moira, something important has come up. Do you know Baines' hotel in Sweden?"

"He left Stockholm today."

Luke's hope rose. "Is he home?"

"Not for another week."

"More business?"

"No. He's hunting."

Luke fell back in his chair as though shot. Hot pain gripped his chest. Elizabeth Blakeley gasped and lowered her head.

"In Mexico," Moira continued. "The Yucatan jungle."

Luke's throat was chalk, he tried to swallow, couldn't. Beside him, Howie Kaufman dropped his head into his hands.

"Baines is hunting in the Yucatan?" Luke asked. He wanted to hang up before she confirmed it.

"Yes. He and Don Mackay are there for a few days. Wild turkeys or some damn thing like that."

Luke slumped further. His chairman *and* the chairman of World Motors were hunting in the Yucatan jungle. "Can we phone them?"

"Impossible. They go there partly to get away from the phones for a few days."

"He's totally unreachable?" Luke asked.

"Until Monday. What's wrong? Client giving you problems?"

Luke didn't want to suggest her husband might be in grave danger without absolute proof. "Yes. Someone's giving us problems."

He also didn't want to ask the next question, even though his chairman's life might depend on it. "By the way, Moira, were Baines and Don Mackay ever referred to as the Siamese Twins?"

Moira did not answer for several seconds. "No. Not that I recall."

Luke felt like someone lifted barbells from his chest. Blakeley and Kaufman exhaled audibly.

"But they were thick as thieves before I met Baines," Moira added. "Chuck Cutter would know. Chuck flew with them in Vietnam. You want his number?"

"Yes," he said.

Moira gave him the number, then asked, "Luke, why on earth do you want to know if he and Don were called Siamese Twins?"

Luke searched for a way to answer without alarming her. "Oh, we're doing an agency brochure. Someone thought that they were referred to as Siamese Twins a long time ago, because they're close friends and all."

Moira paused. "I see."

Luke sensed Moira did not quite buy his explanation. "Well, thanks, Moira, and if by some chance he calls home, please have him phone me or Elizabeth Blakeley immediately here at the office. Or at home. It's quite urgent."

"All right," she said, her voice taut with concern.

Luke hung up and looked across the table at the others. Their faces mirrored his fear. Howie Kaufman's ruddy complexion had turned ash-grey, his clenched hands bone white.

Blakeley dialed Chuck Cutter's phone number and Cutter answered immediately.

"Mr. Cutter?"

"Yes..."

"I'm Luke Tanner. I work with Baines Thomas at Connor Dow Advertising. Moira Thomas suggested I phone you."

"Sure, Luke. How's Moira?"

"Just fine."

"Good for her. How can I help?"

"You flew with Baines Thomas and Don Mackay in Vietnam, didn't you?"

"You bet."

"I wonder if you ever heard them referred to as the Siamese Twins?"

Cutter paused, then chuckled into a rattling cough. "I'll be damned..."

"What?"

"Haven't heard that in a while. Thomas and Mackay flew wing to wing, even touched a couple of times. Flew so damn close we called them the Siamese Twins."

Luke's pencil dropped from his hand, rolled across the table and fell to the floor. Kaufman slammed his fist down on a folder, nearly cracking the table and causing a coffee cup to move several inches. Then the room fell silent.

Luke tried to speak over the hot lump in his throat.

"Damn good pilots, Baines and Don," Cutter said. "F-4 Phantoms. Backed each other up. Helped a lot of MIGs buy the farm. Almost forgot we called them the Siamese Twins."

Luke felt like a belt was tightening his chest.

"Good guys, too," Cutter continued. "Not many people know but they uncovered a major drug network called Medusa that was smuggling dope into Nam using U.S. military aircraft. The dope was turning our boys into zombies, getting 'em killed. Military brass hushed that mess up damn fast. The Twins were fearless."

"Uh-huh," Luke muttered. Blakeley's eyes were wet.

"The day before they were scheduled to return to the states, they flew a big Huey with food and medicine to an orphanage surrounded by the Cong. Saved those kids' lives."

Luke whispered, "Well, thank you, Mr. Cutter. I've got to run."

"You're welcome."

"Tell Baines I'll see him at the July reunion."

"Okay," he said mechanically.

Luke hung up, sat back and felt the remaining strength drain from his body. Silence hung over the group like a burial shroud. "It all fits. They were called Siamese Twins. They're hunting together right now in the Yucatan jungle. The consolidated World Motors Corporation advertising account at Connor Dow is worth over one billion dollars."

"And," Howie Kaufman added, "if both men were suddenly gone, the advertising account might be up for grabs."

Luke felt nauseated. His boss, whom he'd liked and respected enormously, and Donald Mackay, whom he heard was a decent man, were walking into an assassin's trap.

"There *must* be a way to reach Baines," Elizabeth Blakeley said.

Luke tried to think of ways. "Maybe his secretary, Louise, helped organize the hunting trip."

Luke phoned Louise and explained what had happened. Louise did not respond for several seconds. When she finally spoke, her voice was cracking with emotion. She explained that Don Mackay's executive secretary coordinated the hunting trip through World Motors' Travel Department.

"Do you or her remember any trip details?"

Another deep breath. "Not much. Baines told me they were flying from Sweden to Cancun. In Cancun they meet the guide.

The guide will take them hunting in the Yucatan jungle. After hunting, they're going to Mexico City where they'll award some college scholarships."

"Did he say *where* they're hunting in the Yucatan?" Luke asked. Howie Kaufman slid a map of Mexico in front of him.

"No."

"Do you recall the name of the hunting guide?"

"No."

"What about the hunting outfit?"

Louise was silent for several seconds. "Something like Rodriguez, or Romero. Wait, I wrote it down in my planner."

Kaufman leaned closer to the phone speaker as they heard footsteps fade and return, then pages flip. "It's *Expediciones de Caza Ramírez!*"

"Do you have a phone number?"

"Yes."

Luke took down the number, thanked her and hung up.

He quickly dialed *Expediciones Ramírez.* After several seconds of international clicking, he heard the phone ring. He hoped his high-school Spanish would be understood. The phone continued ringing. He glanced at his watch, wondered if Cancun time was one or two hours behind, checked the map legend and saw it was one hour.

"Don't tell them too much yet," Redstone said.

"Why?"

"*Expediciones Ramírez* might be involved in the assassination."

Luke realized they could be. "If they are, perhaps phoning them will make them call it off."

"Or do it sooner," Redstone said, rubbing his knuckles. "But we're down to hours. We have to risk telling them."

Luke nodded. "There's no one to tell. It's still ringing. Probably closed."

"And tomorrow is Sunday. Closed again," Redstone said.

Forty seconds later Luke hung up. He dialed again and still got no answer. He drummed his fingers on the table as his stomach did cartwheels. They'd hit the wall again. He saw no way tonight to determine exactly where in the jungle they were.

Baines Thomas, the man who'd meant so much to his career, guided him, taught him so much, was walking into a death trap. He owed Thomas, and would do everything possible to save him and Mackay. But Sunday was only two hours away.

Suddenly, Hank Redstone pulled a tattered phone directory from his coat, flipped to a page, grabbed the phone and dialed a number. "I just remembered a police pal in Mexico City. Juan de los Santos. Juan's an official with Mexico's PGR, the *Procuraduría General de la República*, sort of like our FBI. They can operate anywhere in Mexico. Juan and I were classmates one summer at the National FBI Class many years ago. Since then, we've worked together on a couple of drug cases. He'll get someone over to *Expediciones Ramírez*."

The phone rang four times, then he heard Juan's recorded voice. At the beep, Redstone started to leave a message when the phone was picked up by a man breathing heavily, huffing for breath.

"*Halo!*" he said, sucking in air.

"Juan, you old *bandido*—it's Hank Redstone."

"Hank. How are you? I was running on my treadmill. Our outside air is not so good." His voice was deep and slightly accented.

"I'm fine. We should be sucking the fresh air at the Amigo Bar."

"And a few cold beers maybe, *gringo*."

Redstone smiled. "Sanchez still sweating in the Acapulco jail?"

"*Sí.* You got some *hombres* who belong with him?"

"How'd you guess?"

"*Qué pasa*, Hank?" He gasped for more air.

"Two very important U.S. businessmen are hunting somewhere in the Yucatan jungle. They will be assassinated tomorrow. We can't reach them by phone, and we're not sure *where* they are. The trip was arranged by *Expediciones Ramírez* in Cancun, but no one answers the Ramirez phone."

"What kind of huntin'?"

"We don't know."

"These businessmen—who are they?"

"The Chairman of World Motors Corporation and the Chairman of a large advertising agency, Connor Dow."

"Ayeeeee..." De los Santos paused. "You got *no* idea where they are?"

"None."

Juan de los Santos breathed out hard. "Hank, the Yucatan has several thousand square miles of jungle."

"Sorry, Juan, it's all we know."

"One thing I know."

"What's that?"

"I can get the full support from the *Policía Nacional* and the *Policía de Yucatan*."

"Why?"

"Killing *these* two men could kill our twelve billion dollar tourism business."

"I hear you. I'll fax photos of both men."

De los Santos paused. "I need more than faxes, *amigo*. I need you down here and someone who can positively identify these men."

Redstone looked at Luke. Luke nodded that he'd go. Jenna's hand touched his arm and he saw her concern.

"We'll be there," Redstone said. "I'm sure my boss'll green-light me to fly down. Don Mackay and Baines Thomas are respected national figures."

"I'll get emergency authorization for you to bring your weapons in. We'll work together. In the meantime, we'll check out this *Expediciones Ramírez*."

"Thanks, pal."

"*De nada.* Let me know when you land at Cancun airport. We'll meet you. *Vaya con Dios*."

"You too," Redstone said, hanging up.

"Where do we fly out?" Luke asked.

"City Airport," Redstone said. "The DPD can charter an aircraft."

"No need to," Elizabeth Blakeley said. "I just talked to Don Mackay's secretary. World Motors has placed one of its corporate jets at your disposal. It'll be ready at City Airport in an hour."

"I'm going, too," Jenna said.

Everyone turned and stared at her.

The last thing Luke wanted was to risk Jenna's life more than he already had. Because of him, she'd nearly died on the river and suffered at the hands of Leonard and Sonny. "But Jen—"

"But nothing," she interrupted, ice in her eyes. "There are a lot of ways you could get injured in the jungle—snakes, scorpions, gunshot wounds, knives, coconuts falling on your head—and no medical help. You need a doctor."

She smiled her non-negotiable smile.

Luke looked at Hank for help.

Hank smiled. "Don't argue with your doctor."

Luke wouldn't argue. He'd worry a lot.

Thirty Three

Saturday, 10:25 p.m.

JENNA GRABBED the Reference Center phone, called the hospital and was put through to the head night nurse in Pediatrics.

"Nelly, it's Jenna."

"Oh, Doctor Stevens, we've been so worried. Are you all right?"

"I'm fine. How's Michele?"

Long pause, papers ruffling. "Not good. Woke up a few minutes ago, asked for you, then sort of drifted off. Want me to see if she's awake?"

"No. I'm coming over to see her now. Please tell her if she awakens."

"Okay."

"And, Nelly, please prepare a field emergency kit. Include everything I might need in a jungle."

Nelly coughed. "As in bananas and snakes?"

"As in. I'll need vials of antivenin polyvalent. Also a Sawyer's Extractor, insect repellants and the like."

"I'll put them in our basic Detroit emergency kit."

"That should do fine."

"What's going on?"

"I'll explain later."

They hung up.

Outside, Jenna got into a police car and was driven toward Detroit Memorial. On the way, she phoned Dr. Alex Dubin, a close friend, and asked him to fill in for her tomorrow. He gladly agreed when she promised to have dinner with his wife and him.

At Detroit Memorial, she stepped off the elevator and hurried down the empty, dimly-lit hallway. Faint light filtered out beneath Michele's door. Jenna wanted to comfort her and explain she'd be away for a day. She opened the door to Michele's room and saw a colleague, Doctor Carvell, and a nurse hovering over the young girl. Michele's cheekbones, like grey tissue, were bathed in soft chalky light, her eyes were closed. An IV dripped into her emaciated arm.

"Sinking?" Jenna whispered.

Doctor Carvell shrugged his shoulders and checked her IV catheter. "We're doing everything we can."

A hot lump burned in Jenna's chest. She took the girl's frail, cool fingers in hers and stared at her for several moments. *I'm here Michele. Stay with us until I get back...please.*

Jenna wondered if she would get back in time. Her mind drifted back to other instances in her life when her belief she could work everything out in time had caught up with her.

In college she'd *known* she could persuade a close friend to stop using cocaine, but hadn't. The friend, twenty-three, died from a cocaine-induced heart attack. She'd *known* she could work forty hours and study ninety-five hours a week for her medical school exams. She'd picked up A's, and a viral infection that put her in bed for a week.

Perhaps she was doing the same with Luke. Deluding herself with the belief she could pursue her demanding medical career, with its long, unpredictable hours, interruptions and emergency calls—*and* be a loving mother, *and* be a loving wife.

She'd always believed she could balance things. *Known* it.

Could she, realistically? The answer she knew required that she think a lot more about what was really important in her life.

She kissed Michele, walked from the room, headed down the hall, turned the corner and saw Dr. Norman Stickles walking directly toward her. Trapped again.

"Ah, Doctor Stevens," Stickles said, rubbing his stubby fingers together. "We heard about your ah...absence...er abduction." He raised his eyebrows as though he didn't believe it.

"I *was* abducted."

"Of course." He rolled his eyes.

"I'm fine now."

Polite nod. "Good. Take an extra day with your paperwork. But have it on my desk Monday morning."

"I'm afraid I won't be able to."

"Why's that?"

"I have an emergency in Mexico. Dr. Dubin is filling in for me."

Stickles' face grew pink. "Mexican emergencies. Missed work. Alleged abductions? It's just too much. Doctor, may I remind you that you work in *this* hospital. If you don't have the paperwork Monday morning, we'll have to reevaluate your status at the hospital."

She stared into Stickles' tiny pupils and realized it was time to level with him.

"Actually, Norman, I've been reevaluating the hospital's status with me. I'll let the Chief of Pediatrics and the Chief of Medical Administration know what I decide to do within two weeks. And why."

Stickles fleshy jaw began to twitch, then dropped open.

"*Hasta la vista*, Doctor." She left him standing in the hall.

In the parking lot, she unlocked her car, drove home accompanied by the police car and changed into lightweight, loose-fitting summer clothes.

The police drove her to City Airport. Minutes later, she, Luke and Redstone strapped themselves into the comfortable seats of a World Motors Corporate Learjet. It raced down the City Airport runway and soared into the clear night sky.

She watched the twinkling Detroit skyline fade away.

Everything's fading away, she thought. *Michele's life. My career at Detroit Memorial Hospital...*

Thirty Four

Sunday, 7:25 a.m.

THE WORLD Motors Learjet banked right and began its approach into Cancun International Airport. Luke looked down on the puffy morning clouds hanging over the jungle like a flokati carpet. Soon, the clouds slid apart and he glimpsed the dense emerald treetops stretching as far as he could see.

Beneath those trees, somewhere, a friend and his colleague, were walking into a death trap.

Jenna touched his hand. "What's Baines Thomas like?"

"Terrific guy. Nice, easy-going. Comfortable with ditchdiggers and presidents. Started in our mail room, worked his way to the top. Very smart."

"Smart—but he hired you?"

"Ha ha."

"Can he handle the heat down there?"

"I think so. He keeps in excellent shape. Played college football. He's tough a lot of ways."

"How?"

Luke thought a moment. "He takes risks. Backs breakthrough, provocative creative work, sometimes at the risk of losing clients who think safe, boring ads are good. I owe him a lot for supporting my work."

The aircraft bounced through some turbulence, rattling Redstone's glass of orange juice, then leveled off. Redstone's eyes, staring blankly at the jungle, suggested the hopelessness of their mission.

"What about Don Mackay?" Jenna asked.

"I've met him a few times. Smart, decent man. Word is, Mackay's a brilliant automotive engineer with tons of patents."

"He'd need more than patents to become chairman of World Motors."

"Mackay has more. Baines says he senses the cars and trucks Americans want, then shepherds those vehicle concepts through nit-picking committees and management levels. He was rocketed to the chairmanship five years ago as a result of a number of successful new-vehicle launches. Under his leadership, the company's gained market share, done quite well."

Jenna pointed to a copy of *World Motors Times* in the seat pocket. "Says here that Mackay set up a college scholarship foundation to help kids in a group of inner-city schools. If a student maintains a B-plus or higher grade average, the company picks up two-thirds of college tuition."

"Our company also contributes to that fund."

The aircraft banked suddenly and descended through the hazy clouds. Luke pointed down at Cancun's long line of towering hotels jutting into the Caribbean.

Jenna nodded. "They look like a string of pearls."

"A necklace dedicated to the new Mayan Goddess of Tourism."

"Look, joggers in front of the hotels."

He saw the tiny figures running along the road and remembered jogging the same road once in the blistering Mexican sun. "Better now than after nine a.m."

"You know about jogging in Cancun?"

"I ran forty minutes down there around noon once. Crawled back six pounds lighter." Which reminded him that the jungle would be blazing and that they should drink enough water.

The plane touched down and taxied to a spot near the terminal at the *Aeropuerto Internacional de Cancún*. As they deplaned, Luke saw a slim, dark-haired, handsome man in a blue shirt and khaki pants approaching them from the terminal. His tanned, chiseled Latin face broke into a smile as he waved to Redstone. Beside him, a short, pudgy man in royal-blue uniform skip-stepped to keep pace and dabbed perspiration from his face with a white handkerchief.

De los Santos threw his arms around Redstone and smiled. "Hank, you look good, but maybe you add a couple pounds."

"Steel, *amigo*." Redstone introduced him to Luke and Jenna. De los Santos introduced everyone to Jaime Hernandez, a police official with the *Policía de Cancún*.

Juan de los Santos turned to the group. "We go now to *Expediciones Ramírez*. If we determine what they hunt, we might discover where."

Hernandez escorted them past long queues of jealous passengers waiting to clear customs, then outside to three police cars and two motorcycles. The police caravan sped out of the airport and darted through the dense forest toward Cancun. Luke was amazed at the number of new buildings and construction sites, many geared toward the massive growth of tourism, an industry which would be devastated by the death of two prominent Americans.

A few miles south of the city they turned into the jungle, drove a quarter mile and stopped beside a long, white stucco building with a roof of thatched palm leaves.

Getting out, Luke saw a stable in back, and a small corral where men were feeding pigs, donkeys and chickens. A gust of humid morning wind warmed his face and squeaked a sun-faded red sign, *Expediciones De Caza Ramírez.*

Inside, Luke caught a whiff of leather and saw two teenage boys rubbing Neats Foot Oil into saddles. A red macaw screeched from atop a large black radio pumping out an uptempo Rickie Martin song. The smell of fresh manure wafted through an open window. Behind the cash register, a small spider monkey watched them, then hid his half-eaten banana.

A back door swung open, and a lean, hard-muscled man about five-ten strolled in. Juan de los Santos introduced him as Miguel Ramirez. Ramirez, about forty, smiled easily, revealing perfect white teeth. His thick, black hair fell forward above dark, relaxed eyes that seemed to miss nothing. Years of jungle sun had bronzed his narrow face and powerful arms reddish-brown. He wore a bone-handle knife on his belt and two large animal incisors on a leather strap around his neck. He reminded Luke of a Mexican Crocodile Dundee.

"Miguel, please tell these people what you told us," said de los Santos. "Who first phoned you about the hunting trip?"

"The man from World Motors Travel. Mr. Kearns. Nice man. He phoned about two months ago. He ask me to make a hunting trip for these two very important men, Mr. Mackay and Mr. Thomas. So I did. He approve trip. Everythin' okay."

"Then what?"

"Then a week ago, I get call from different man. Mr. Kyzer. He said he is with World Motors and they want to use their guide instead of me. He said I still get paid full guide fee and the guide will buy supplies from us."

"Why were they using their guide?" Redstone asked.

"He said guide was friend of Mr. Mackay."

"Did the guide buy the supplies here?" de los Santos asked.

"*Sí.*"

"Do you know him?"

"No. He has Belize accent. But he pay me the full guide fee in cash and buy the supplies. Plenty food, water, ammunitions."

"What kind of hunting?" de los Santos asked. "Wild turkey, quail?"

"We plan *temazate*, white-tail jungle deer. But the guide's assistant, he say wild boars."

"Where would they hunt wild boar?" Redstone asked.

Ramirez shrugged and fingered the handle of his hunting knife. "Many places, *señor.*"

"Around here?"

"Yes."

"They no hunt here," said a voice in halting English. Luke turned and saw it was a thin young boy oiling a saddle.

"The guide," the boy said, "he tell assistant to put supplies in airplane."

Luke slumped against the counter. A airplane meant they could be hunting virtually anywhere in the Yucatan. Reaching them in time just became even more impossible.

Juan de los Santos walked over and stared out the window. "Okay, let's assume they took a private plane."

"Then probably," Officer Hernandes said, "they took off from Cancun International or Isla Mujeres. May I use your phone, please?"

"*Sí,*" Ramirez said, pointing to the phone near the cash register.

Hernandez phoned the Cancun Airport manager, spoke to him and hung up. Hernandez explained that more than two hundred flights had departed in the last twenty-four hours, and that the manager would print out a flight list.

"These men, they in danger?" Miguel Ramirez asked.

Luke nodded. He explained about the assassination attempt and asked Ramirez if he'd be their guide.

Ramirez studied them a few moments. "You already pay me the guide fee. Also, assassinated hunters not so good for my business. We go."

As they stepped outside, Luke nearly bumped into a heavyset worker stacking saddles near the door. The group piled into the police cars and drove off.

* * *

The heavyset worker watched them drive away, then walked to a nearby tool shed and went inside. He pulled a cell phone from his pocket and made a call.

Thirty Five

"THIS WAY," said the airport traffic control manager, a thin, balding fifty-year-old with the calm assurance of a man who juggled several crises hourly.

Luke and the group followed him to a long oak table on which he fanned out spreadsheets for both area airports.

"These," the manager said, "are the private and charter flights that departed, and their final destinations over the last twenty-four hours."

Luke was astounded by how many commercial and private flights had taken off in one day. He wanted to identify the right flight, fly the World Motors jet there, then take a chopper directly to the hunters.

"Here," the manager said, circling a flight number. "Three passengers to Chichen Itza. Mr. Thomas and Mr. Mackay are passengers."

"This man, Chico Canara, he must be the guide," Officer Hernandez said, pointing to the third name.

"I never hear of him," Miguel Ramirez said.

Hernandez said, "Maybe he is not a licensed guide. I will check his name with the official Yucatan and Belize hunting guide lists."

Three minutes later, Luke, Jenna, Redstone, Juan de los Santos and Miguel belted themselves into the comfortable seats of the Learjet. It whooshed down the runway and glided southwest over the jungle, leveling off at thirteen thousand feet and quickly reaching a cruising speed of five hundred and ten miles per hour.

Luke checked his watch. It was already nine. Time was running out. Miguel had said there were many hunting trails, each with offshoots, and many hunting groups. Picking the right trail might prove difficult. Eye witnesses might be their only hope.

Minutes later, Juan de los Santos tapped Luke on the shoulder and pointed out the window at massive, grey stone ruins that emerged in a sprawling jungle clearing.

"Chichen Itza. Ancient Mayan city. Very mysterious. Started about 450 A.D."

Luke looked down at the amazingly well preserved buildings and temples. "What are those long stone things in front of that building?"

De los Santos looked where Luke pointed. "Altars."

"For what?"

"Human sacrifice. Men, women, even children were sacrificed to the Rain God. The altars had bowls on them."

"For rainwater?" Luke said.

"No," de Los Santos said, looking away.

"What were they for?"

"You don't want to know."

"I do."

De los Santos shrugged. "Beating hearts taken from living human beings."

Luke swallowed. "I don't want to know."

Moments later, the Learjet landed, using every inch of the small, Chichen Itza *Aeropista* runway. The aircraft turned and taxied over to two tiny white buildings outlined with blue stripes. One building had a thatched roof and was attached to a shaded open-air waiting lounge, where a taxi driver sipped a Coke and read a newspaper. He looked up and his eyes widened as though the arriving aircraft meant a juicy fare. A skinny cat, ribs pushing through tan fur, darted past him and hid under a Chevy Suburban with a *Policía* insignia.

They deplaned and were instantly baked by the hot air. Luke saw heat waves squiggling up from the runway.

A twenty-foot radio tower with a long, orange flag sat atop a second building. Its door swung open and a short, heavyset man wearing a loose white shirt and pants and a grey eye patch greeted them in English. "I'm Hector Blanca, airport manager. Please to come in."

In his hot, narrow office he introduced them to Diego Garcia, a smiling, stocky forty-year-old officer with the local *Policía Estatal de Yucatan*. Garcia shook hands and chewed on an unlit cigar.

Luke looked around the office crammed with aviation books, photos of airplanes and pilots. A signed photo of Chuck Yeager sat on Blanca's desk beside a large fan that whooshed humid air and the sweet, heavy fragrance of potpourri onto Luke's face. He noticed a vivid painting of a bullfight beside a wall thermometer registering ninety-six degrees. All skin glowed with perspiration.

"*Señor* Blanca, can you tell us whether a specific flight landed here yesterday?" Juan de los Santos asked.

"Yes, of course," he said proudly, smiling.

"We're looking for a Beechcraft King Air C90A. Three men

should have deplaned between five and six o'clock in the afternoon. These are two of the men." He handed him the photo of Thomas and Mackay.

Blanca studied the photo for a few seconds and bit his lower lip. He grabbed a flight log and flipped it open. His pudgy finger slid down the page, then his large, mahogany eyes rolled up and looked at Juan de los Santos.

"No such plane landed here in the last three days, *Señor*."

"You sure?"

"Positive."

Luke's hands clenched. The aircraft did not land here. *We're back at ground zero.*

"Perhaps," Redstone said, "they landed somewhere else first, then flew here late last night."

Blanca tapped his desk as he checked another page. "We had one flight last night, *Señor*. A small Piper Dakota with engine trouble. Pilot only."

"But the Beechcraft's flight plan was to land here," Redstone persisted.

"*Sí*," Blanca said. He shrugged and adjusted his eye patch. "But sometimes an aircraft must change destination en route. You know, weather. Emergencies. Engine trouble. Or..."

"Or what?" Luke asked.

"Something illegal, like the drugs."

"Or maybe," Redstone said, "to *kill* someone."

Blanca sat up straighter. The fan hummed more warm, damp air onto everyone's skin.

"Any other airports near here?" Luke asked.

"Only one. An old landing strip in the jungle maybe fifteen kilometers away," Blanca said.

"Could a Beechcraft C90A land there?" Redstone asked.

Hector Blanco grabbed a volume of *Janes Aviation*, flipped to a page and studied it for a few seconds. "Yes, the C90A needs about one thousand feet to land. The airstrip, she is just over nineteen hundred feet. And Pepe, the man who clears the strip, he would certainly know if a C90A landed there. He doesn't get so many big aircraft as we do."

"Let's phone him," Juan de los Santos suggested.

Blanca frowned. "Sorry, no telephone."

Luke's stomach clenched tighter. More lost time. "How far by car?"

"Twenty minutes," Officer Garcia said, fingering his black mustache. "That road outside goes by the airstrip. Pepe and his family live there. I take you now."

Garcia stood, rubbed his ample belly, thanked Hector Blanca and ushered the group outside to his polished red Suburban. They all piled inside, where Luke inhaled the overwhelming scent of three pine air fresheners propelled by blissful air-conditioning.

As they drove beneath the shade of the overhanging trees, Luke turned to de los Santos. "What if Pepe says no C90 landed?"

"Then we phone all airports within two hundred miles and check their records. And we keep trying to reach their pilot. He is not answering his phone. It will take time."

Time we don't have, Luke thought, as branches scraped the window.

Minutes later, Garcia turned off the main road and careened onto a rough, dusty trail that snaked into the jungle. He maintained the same speed, as though still on pavement.

"How much further?" Redstone asked, bouncing off his seat.

"Five minutes," Garcia said, chomping on his cigar. "Looks like someone visit the airstrip this morning."

"How do you know?"

"Fresh tire tracks, they come and go."

Thirty Six

AS CESAR Torres squeezed through a thicket, he brushed against some zapote trees, picking up a gob of white, sticky *chicle* on his muscular forearm. He scraped off the gooey substance and flicked it away. He hated *chicle*. It reminded him of someone he despised. His mother. She'd made him chew it when other children in their *barrio bajo* slum got Doublemint. His mother made him do many things he hated.

He glanced back at his hunting party and smiled.

225

The two old *gringos*, Don Mackay and Baines Thomas, were experienced hunters and kept up with his pace, no trouble. They were in amazing condition for sixty-year-olds. But conditioning didn't mean shit when *cuatro narices* venom pumped through your veins.

All Torres had to do was lead the old men to the snake pit. The *cuatro narices* would do the rest. Which, Torres knew, would be excruciatingly painful. First the *gringos* would feel the burning near the fang marks, then icy, numbing paralysis would creep up their bodies, slowly squeezing life from them. The beautiful thing was they would be alert, knowing they were dying, knowing they could do nothing, knowing their lives would end in this fucking jungle. It would be most pleasing to watch, Torres knew.

He checked the rest of the hunting party, four experienced local *cargadores* carrying provisions and gear.

The group had gained extra miles yesterday by walking late into the surprisingly cool evening. This morning they'd broken camp two hours early and covered many more miles in the cool morning air. As a result, they were three hours ahead of schedule. The sooner he collected, the better. And he would collect a lot. This was his most lucrative hunting trip ever. The two *gringos* must be very important.

He still couldn't believe his good fortune. Mason Bennett agreed to pay his two hundred thousand dollar fee without haggling. Two hundred thousand just to make sure two old men fell into a fucking snakepit. Life had some luck.

Ahead, something moved in the bushes. Something big.

Torres raised his hand, halting the hunting party.

Slowly the reddish-brown head of a puma rose above the bushes forty feet ahead. Its ears flicked as it scanned the area. The cat was large, maybe nine feet long, two hundred pounds. Any second it would catch their scent.

Torres gestured toward the puma. The group nodded.

The big cat remained motionless for several seconds, then crouched and ripped flesh from the carcass of a white-tailed deer. Torres saw a problem. The puma was blocked from behind by a cliff. Blocked-in, many cats attack. He signaled the hunters to move slowly behind a clump of trees.

The puma's head came up, dropped and disappeared. It was probably still eating, but one never knew with a cat, especially one who felt trapped or thought you wanted its food. The cat could be moving toward them now. Torres grew concerned. He couldn't let the puma touch the Twins. It would screw up the *cuatro narices* accident, and his fee.

Something snapped behind Torres. He turned and saw a *cargador* standing on a broken branch.

The puma's head shot up. It saw them, roared, then charged the closest person—Mackay.

Torres raised his rifle and fired. His shot barely grazed the animal's ear.

The cat leapt for Mackay.

Baines Thomas fired.

The bullet entered above the puma's left eye, dropping the big cat instantly inches from Mackay's feet.

Torres walked over to the animal and stared at the bullet hole issuing fresh blood. He felt the warm, pleasing rush he always felt when life seeped away. He watched the animal's chest slowly rise, fall, stop. He looked into the eyes, watched them dim and fade, then transform as he knew they would, into the cruel, black eyes of his mother.

Baines Thomas walked up and knelt beside the cat.

"Excellent shot," Torres said.

"Lucky," Thomas said, running his hand gently along the cat's reddish brown coat. "Sorry we interrupted dinner, pal. But you'll get a position of honor in Wayne State University's science department."

Don Mackay knelt down.

"This makes us even," Thomas said.

"For what?"

"The North Vietnamese MIG you knocked off my ass near DaNang."

Mackay smiled. "Took you long enough."

"Hey, don't forget who dragged you out of that Saigon bar one second before those MPs would've tossed your butt in the slammer."

"I could've handled them."

"Unconscious?"

McKay laughed.

Laugh while you can, amigos, Torres thought. He watched the *cargadores* strap the puma on the game wagon, then signaled the group to resume the hunt. They walked for another twenty minutes through mango and papaya trees plump with fruit and soon they found themselves in thicker jungle.

Torres heard screeching from high in the trees. Looking up, he saw the familiar blue and gold feathers of a macaw. Little bastards always warned his prey. As a kid, he enjoyed slitting their throats and listening to them wheeze to death. These days they were too valuable. On the illegal bird market, he got twenty thousand dollars a piece for them.

Minutes later, Torres led the hunting party onto spongier ground where he'd seen wild boar. He hoped they'd find boar today. He'd give his victims one last hunt, a little thrill—before they gave him a big one. After several minutes he knew the boar had moved north, and they were not going to see any.

Checking his watch, he realized they were hours ahead. "We stop for lunch."

The *cargadores* immediately made camp, took out the cooking gear, and began preparing the meal. Soon Torres smelled steaming *huevos motulenos*, Yucatan tortillas topped with beans, fried egg, ham, sausage, cheese and *poc-chuc*, thinly sliced flanks of wild boar served with onion chunks and a spicy sauce.

They ate in the shade of three *flanboyan* trees.

"This boar is delicious," Mackay said.

"Fresh. Caught yesterday," the cook said, smiling.

Torres took a beer from the dry-ice container and chugged down several gulps. Suddenly, he felt the silent pulser in his backpack vibrating against his shoulder. Someone was calling on his satellite phone. Only two people knew the number.

He stood, walked a couple hundred feet away from the group and stepped behind some thick bushes. He took the briefcase from his backpack, opened it, took out the small satellite dish and phone and turned it on.

"Torres," he whispered.

"Bennett. We got trouble."

"What trouble?"

"The police are looking for your hunting party."

Torres felt his muscles tighten as he scanned the immediate area. "How'd they—"

"Never mind how. They don't know who you are, or where you are. But you must speed things up. How far are you from the snakepit?"

Torres looked at his watch. "Four hours, maybe."

"Too long. Find a new location. Then separate the Twins from the rest of the hunting party. Figure out a legitimate reason to lead them away. You know, a special view, an old temple, whatever."

Torres recalled the area around him. "There's a Mayan ruin a few miles ahead."

"Perfect," Bennett said. "They like Mayan history. Tell them how fantastic the ruin is. When you get near it, stop. Have the *cargadores* wait while you take the Twins to the ruin. Kill them there. Then rough yourself up, and run back to the *cargadores*, shouting you were attacked by robbers."

Torres considered the plan. It could work. There had been a few robberies in the area. "What about the police group tracking us?"

"We'll handle them."

Torres paused, then saw a golden opportunity to squeeze this rich yankee for more money. "There's one small problem."

"What?"

"Things have changed."

"How?"

"Now *I* must kill the Twins. And the police are involved. I take much greater personal risk."

"So?"

"So my price just doubled. Four hundred thousand dollars." It felt good pushing this gringo.

Bennett did not reply.

"Take it or leave it," Torres said, as he mashed a bug against a tree. He could feel Bennett's anguish, knew the man had no alternative.

"You'll get the money," Bennett said softly. "And Torres?"

"Yes?"

"If you don't handle the assignment, I will kill you."

The line went dead.

Torres felt his skin crawl. This Bennett was a bad man. He might mean what he said. It didn't matter. The Twins were dead men. This assignment was turning out to be even more profitable than he'd anticipated. Double the money. And *he*, not the snakes, got the pleasure of killing the men. He put the satellite phone back in the backpack and strolled back toward the campfire.

He sat down, resumed eating, and studied his prey. They were laughing with the *cargadores*, enjoying themselves, obviously content with life. Why shouldn't they be? Everything had been given to them in life. Perfect lives, wonderful parents, happy childhoods, excellent educations and successful careers. All the advantages of wealth, all the things he'd been denied.

He thought of his childhood, of his *puta* mother who'd slept with any man who tossed her a few pesos. The mother, who, when he was six and asked her who his father was, pointed at the all the men in the bar and said, "Take your pick." Everyone had laughed at him. The mother who pushed burning cigarettes into his arms when he refused to sleep with older men who smelled of expensive cologne.

The same mother who drove him to a remote jungle village, said it was his new home, gave him twenty pesos and drove off. She never came back. He had been ten. For the next few years, he lived in the streets of the village, doing odd jobs, hunting for something to eat, learning to survive.

Learning to hate. He found pleasure in killing small animals. He learned to *love* killing because each victim was his mother.

Then one day the victim *was* his mother. The happiest day of his life. Torres could still see the clean, red bullet hole he'd placed between her disbelieving eyes. He'd read that experts claim that killing a parent causes more guilt than any other crime. The experts hadn't met his mother. Torres had never felt such pleasure. Never would again. But each kill rekindled a little of that sweet ecstasy.

He looked back at Thomas and Mackay. He hated them for their comfortable, easy lives. Soon, he thought, I will balance their soft lives with some serious pain and suffering. A plan began to form in his mind.

After lunch, they broke camp and continued into the thick brush. Torres walked alongside Thomas and Mackay.

"There's an old Mayan ruin ahead," Torres said. "Just uncovered a couple of years ago. It's very interesting."

"I'd like to see it," Thomas said.

"Count me in," Mackay added.

Thirty Seven

Sunday, 10:42 a.m.

THE THICK, dark jungle seemed to close in around Jenna as Diego Garcia bounced the Suburban past a row of towering *palma* trees. With each mile, she was more certain her decision to come was correct. Someone would need medical attention. The question was who, and whether she was equipped to handle it.

Ahead, she saw a narrow, sun-bleached airstrip flickering white through the jungle green. Beside it in the shadows, sat a small, white stucco house with a roof of thatched palm leaves. Three hand-made wooden chairs were clustered beneath a tarpoleum roof porch. On one chair she saw a small, hand-made dollhouse. Beyond the chairs, rows of green, leafy vegetables sprouted from a garden.

Garcia skidded to a stop next to the home, swirling dust into the breeze.

She hoped Thomas and Mackay had landed here and were nearby. The sooner she got to them, the better. If they were bitten by a pit viper, time was critical. She had enough antivenin to counter a normal level of poisoning. But numerous viper bites would be fatal.

She followed Garcia and the others to the front door. Garcia knocked and called out, "Pepe, it's Diego Garcia."

There was no response.

"Pepe? Maria?"

Behind Jenna, wind hissed through the trees and she watched a large black bird swoop onto a nearby branch and stare at her as though trying to tell her something.

Garcia called again, waited, then he and Luke stepped inside and froze. Garcia whispered something and crossed himself. She moved beside him and gasped.

Sprawled on the floor in a massive pool of blood lay a young man, face down. She dashed over to him, traced the blood to two bullet wounds, one directly in the heart, the other above the ear. She bent down to detect a pulse she knew wasn't there and watched an insect crawl from his mouth. His pupils were fixed and dilated, his skin purplish and waxy, almost translucent. Looking closer, she saw early signs of rigor mortis in his neck and face.

"He's probably been dead a couple of hours," she said.

Garcia moaned from the bedroom door.

Jenna hurried over, looked in, and felt bile rise in her throat. A young woman and a small girl, presumably Pepe's wife and daughter, lay on a blood-drenched bed. Their throats were slashed, like someone had run a thick red marker from ear to ear.

Blood had gushed from their severed carotid arteries and collected in dark pools. The woman's wrists were bound, her face bruised, her blue dress ripped open, her vagina smeared with semen.

The three-year-old girl's tiny eyes stared vacantly at the bloodied, one-eared Snoopy dog clutched in her arm.

Nauseated, Jenna had to steady herself on the bed post. The one medical problem she could never handle was physical violence to children. She closed the child's eyelids and brushed back her silken hair. *What kind of monster can do this? Did the daughter watch?* Jenna's eyes brimmed as she turned away. "They were killed when he was."

Again, she felt woozy and felt Luke's arm ease her away from the carnage.

Garcia pointed to several open dresser drawers, clothes strewn about the floor, a small crucifix on the floor. "This is no robbery. These people have nothing to steal."

"They were killed," de los Santos whispered. "So they couldn't tell us the C90 landed here!"

"Their death tells us it landed," Luke said.

Garcia nodded, his face red with anger. "I phone this in." He ran outside to the car.

* * *

Luke led Jenna over to a small window where they looked out at the dense, green jungle. If the family was murdered because they saw the C90 land, then Thomas and Mackay were hunting in this area. But which direction? He'd seen at least six trails and footpaths leading from the airstrip. And each had offshoots, Miguel said.

"In here!" Miguel Ramirez shouted from the other room.

The group hurried into the room and saw Ramirez lifting Pepe's fingers. Scratched in blood, were the letters *P A N C H.*

"What's *PANCH?*" de los Santos asked.

Garcia stared at the letters. "Pancho, maybe. The old man who takes care of the other end of the airstrip. He lives down there."

"Could Pancho have done this?" Redstone asked.

"No. He loved these people. They were his only family."

"Maybe Pancho saw the murderer," Luke said, "and Thomas and Mackay."

The group hurried outside, jumped into the Suburban, sped down the dirt runway. Fifty yards ahead, Luke saw a small hut made of hundreds of tightly bound, vertically stacked, tree trunks with thin gaps to let cooling breezes flow through. The roof, corrugated plastic, was supported by long poles. Beneath the roof was a faded-green nylon lawn chair and an oil drum with a tiny radio on top.

As they walked toward the home, the door opened and a small, white-haired man in his late seventies shuffled outside. His dark-brown, clear eyes peered at them from a prune face. He spat tobacco into the tall weeds as he shuffled toward them. A threadbare grey shirt and tattered pants flapped against his skinny frame.

"Pancho, it's me, Diego. These people are police." Garcia said in Spanish which Luke was able to follow. Garcia walked close to the old man, placed his arm on his shoulder and whispered, "I'm afraid there's been a terrible accident at Pepe's."

Pancho wobbled backward as though stabbed.

As Garcia explained, the old man's eyes dimmed. He appeared dizzy, ready to collapse. Jenna hurried to his side, helped him into the lawn chair. Tears flooded his eyes as he stared at Pepe's cottage.

"Did you see anyone at Pepe's in the last couple of hours?"

Pancho seemed not to hear. A tear vanished into a crevice in his parchment cheek. He nodded and whispered, "*Sí*. A couple of hours ago. A long blue van. Two men got out and talked to Pepe. I walked back to my garden. When I returned the van was gone."

"Did you hear gun shots?"

"No."

"Could you recognize the two men?" Garcia asked.

"No. They were very far away."

"What about the van? Chevy? Volkswagen? World Motors? Ford?"

He shrugged.

Garcia nodded. "Pancho, we think Pepe and his family may have been killed because they saw a Beechcraft King Air land here yesterday. Did you see an aircraft that looks like this?" He handed the old man the photo.

The old man blinked red eyes. "*Sí*. It landed yesterday. Late afternoon."

Luke's hope surged.

"Did these two men get off?" Garcia showed him the photos of Thomas and Mackay.

"*Sí*."

"Where did they go?" Garcia asked.

"They got in three small trucks. The trucks drove into the jungle."

"Which direction?" de los Santos asked.

The old man scratched his grey cheeks, stood slowly, hobbled about fifty feet in front of his cottage, and pointed to a trail about halfway down the airstrip. "Down that middle trail by the palm trees."

"Where does it go?" Luke asked in awkward Spanish.

"Domingo's," Miguel Ramirez said, "An old hunting post. The owner died two years ago. His wife runs it now."

"Can we phone Domingo's?" Luke asked.

Garcia nodded. He moved to the Suburban, grabbed his mobile phone and called the station for the number. He called the number, spoke a minute and hung up.

Garcia nodded. "Rosa Domingo says they stopped there late yesterday afternoon. Left a half hour later on foot."

"Does she know *where* they're hunting? Luke asked.

"No. But she will ask some workers."

Luke helped Jenna ease Pancho into the nylon chair. She handed him a small bottle of pills and explained directions in fractured Spanish. The old man nodded without taking his moist eyes off Pepe's cottage.

As they drove away and turned down the trail toward Domingo's, Luke glanced back at Pepe's cottage. The dead bodies flashed in his mind. He felt nauseated by the death of the young family and small girl. And he felt anger. Whatever happened with Thomas and Mackay, Luke would not rest until the killers of Pepe and his family were brought to justice.

Thick, dark vegetation, clusters of palm trees, then white flowers blurred past. They drove around large chunks of limestone, vestiges of ancient Mayan buildings.

The car phone rang. Garcia picked it up, listened for a couple of minutes and hung up. "We just heard from the *Dirección General de la Fauna Silvestre.*"

"From what?" Redstone asked.

"The Mexican Hunting Bureau. The Bureau says the hunting party had all the necessary licenses and permits. But the guide, he used someone else's name. Cesar Canara is the name of a guide whose been in the hospital for three months."

"Do we know the guide's real name?" Redstone asked.

"*Sí,*" Garcia said, turning and looking at Miguel Ramirez. "Cesar Torres."

Ramirez sucked air through his teeth and shook his head from side to side.

"Who's Torres?" Luke asked.

Ramirez's eyes turned hard. "An evil man."

"And a *wanted* man," Garcia said. "The Veracruz police think he murdered some prostitutes. Older women."

"Also two in Acapulco," Ramirez said. "And I think he murdered some clients on hunting trips. Three of his customers died in very suspicious accidents. The police could never prove Torres caused them."

"What kind of accidents?" Luke asked.

"The first one was a rich businessman from Mexico City. A mountain climber. He died when his rope broke on a Guatemalan cliff. A new rope. His partner, in jail two times, he inherit the business. The second businessman was a very good scuba diver. He dived in one of the *cenotes*, the underground pools of water near here. His oxygen tank did not work. His wife collected two million dollars in insurance. Then, one month later, she married a man who was, how you say, making the romances with her for two years. The third man, a New York *arquitecto*. Torres says the man walked away from the campsite one night. Two weeks later they found his body so ah ... *putrefacto* the doctors could not determine how he die. Not accidents–murders."

"No evidence against Torres?" Redstone asked.

"None," Garcia said.

"There is some," Ramirez added. "Two expensive villas he bought on the Belize coast over the last three years. And a Hatteras yacht. Not bad for a hunting guide."

"A guide who *kills* people!" Garcia said, chomping angrily on his unlit cigar. "I will find this man."

A half hour later, the truck pulled up to the small lodge at *Caza Domingo*. Next to the lodge, in the shade of a tin roof, Luke saw two women hacking open coconuts and carving out the meat. Young boys chased sqwaking hens. Near the lodge steps, a scrawny cat lifted its eyelids and shut them again. In back, Luke saw a corral with mules crowded into the shade of two thick banyon trees.

As the group exited the van, a portly, grey-haired woman in her late fifties, wearing a full white dress with red, Mayan borders, stepped onto the porch. She looked like she'd stepped out of a painting Luke had once seen.

"Hello, Rosa" Garcia said in English.

"You drive fast, Garcia," she said, smiling.

He nodded, introduced the group to her and handed her the photos. "Are these the two Americans you saw?"

She studied them a second. "*Sí*. Nice men."

"Which direction did their hunting party take?"

"There," she said, pointing to a ten-foot wide dirt trail in the jungle.

"Are there wild boar in that direction?" asked de los Santos.

"In all directions, *Señor.*"

"And *cuatro narices?*"

"*Sí.*"

"May I use your phone, *Señora?*" de los Santos asked.

"Inside."

"I'll phone for a military chopper. We'll catch the hunting party in minutes."

"Chopper won't help," Ramirez said.

"Why?"

"The tree tops are too thick. Like a roof. Can't see hunters. Only one way to find hunters. On ground."

Thirty Eight

MASON BENNETT studied a map in the back seat of the Ford van as it bounced along the road to the jungle airstrip. Beside him sat Carlos. In the front passenger seat, Paco snored.

The driver, Manny, was a dark, powerfully built local hit man. His forehead and jaw jutted out, the result, Bennett suspected, of excessive steroid use. His massive biceps had split open the sleeves of his gray T-shirt. He stared ahead, his eyes black slits, void of emotion.

A few hours earlier, Bennett had ordered Manny, Carlos and

Paco to execute the family at the airstrip. Bennett hadn't felt good about it, but he had no choice. The family could have identified him, told the police which trail the Twins had taken. Of course, the police might have guessed the trail. To be sure they didn't, Bennett was driving to Domingo's hunting post.

He looked over at Carlos. The man was polishing his TEC-9 machine gun as though it were Waterford crystal. Around his shoulder hung a black leather case stuffed with 36-round magazines.

"Carlos," Bennett said, "You're positive the airstrip family was dead by the time the police group could have reached them?"

"They were dead when we left."

"So no one could have told the police which path the Twins' took."

"No one."

"Maybe the old man," Manny said, steering around a rotting stump.

Bennett tensed up. "What old man?"

Carlos looked at Manny as though he should have kept his fucking mouth shut. "Guy named Pancho. Lives down the airstrip. Helps clear it."

Bennett was concerned. This Pancho would have been intrigued by the KingAir C90A. He would have come out and watched it, seen the Twins, seen which trail they took. If the police asked him, he'd tell.

"Let's see what he knows," Bennett said, rubbing the stock of his M16-CAR assault rifle.

Minutes later, they pulled up to Pancho's hut. Bennett saw an old man sitting in a lawn chair beside his shack, watching their van. They got out, walked toward him. The old man's empty eyes continued to stare at their van as though he recognized it. Perhaps he did, Bennett realized, from when it was parked at Pepe's.

Flexing his muscles, Manny strutted close to the old man and spoke in Spanish. "*Señor*, did you have visitors a little while ago? Some North Americans."

The old man stared ahead as though Manny had not spoken.

"*Señor?* Did some policemen visit you?"

Bennett saw the old man's eyes flicker with understanding.

"Make him talk," Bennett said, checking his watch.

"Tell us about the visitors," Manny shouted, grabbing the old man's shoulders. "Did they ask you about an airplane that landed here?"

The old man remained silent.

Carlos lit his cigarette lighter and held the flame near the old man's eyes, then up to the cottage's dry thatch roof.

Pancho looked at the flame, then at Carlos, then turned back toward Pepe's home.

"No fire," Bennett said, not wanting to draw police to the area. He noticed something on the oil drum next to the old man. Walking closer, Bennett saw it was a small brown prescription bottle. He picked it up and read the label, "Detroit Memorial Hospital. Dr. Johannson." The woman doctor had been here.

"The police were here. He probably directed them to the hunting post. Let's go."

"What about him?" Manny asked in English, nodding toward Pancho.

"Handle it," Bennett said, walking toward the van. Getting in, he heard two muffled shots. He looked back and saw the old man slump against the oil drum, crimson drops streaking down its black side.

As they drove away, Bennett realized things had changed. The police group was in hot pursuit of Torres. But how close they were depended on *when* they'd reached Domingo's and *how* they were tracking him—by vehicle or on foot.

Clearly, the police group had to be eliminated. Before they reached Torres and the hunting party. Then Bennett would make their bodies disappear with the help of the scorching jungle heat. In Nam he'd watched the blistering Mekong Delta sun reduce a corpse to bones in three weeks.

Twenty-six minutes later they pulled into the clearing at Domingo's. Bennett remained in the van. Using his fake police

ID, Carlos easily learned from the old woman which direction the police truck had taken.

"How far can they be?" Bennett asked him as Manny steered onto the pathway.

Carlos looked at his watch, then at a map. "If they left here around eleven, they could be near where Cesar Torres stopped for lunch."

"Will the police figure out Torres changed direction toward the Mayan ruin?"

"*Sí*, if they have a good guide."

Bennett pulled a paper from his pocket and read the name. "Their guide is from Ramirez Expeditions. A man named Miguel."

Carlos bit his lower lip. "Miguel Ramirez will track Cesar like a jaguar."

Bennett felt his muscles tighten. He didn't like the idea of an exceptional tracker following Torres. "Can he catch Torres before Torres kills the Twins?"

"No chance," Carlos said, studying the map. "Torres is too far ahead. The police can only drive a few more miles. Then they must walk."

"But what if the hunting party stops and rests for several hours?" Manny asked, sweat sliding down his Cro-Mangon brow.

"Torres won't let them stop," Bennett said. "I told him the police are following him." He pointed to the satellite phone on his belt.

The van bottomed out in a large sinkhole, snapping everyone forward and whacking Paco's MAC-10 machine gun against the dash. He cursed and gripped the weapon with both hands.

"Also," Carlos continued, "the police must drive very slow to search for the hunters' broken twigs and branches. We drive faster, just follow tire tracks. Catch them easy."

Within minutes, Bennett and the men had found the hunters' campfire. He saw that the Suburban's tire tracks turned south-east, toward the Mayan ruins. The police group was following

Torres.

As they followed the tracks, Bennett looked down at his M16-CAR assault rifle and checked that it was on full-auto mode. He ran his fingers along the stock. So similar to the M16 stock blown from his hands years ago in another jungle, near DaNang. He'd been cleaning mud from the stock of his M16 when he and his platoon were caught in a triggering explosion of seven land mines and blown into the air. He'd awakened seconds later with a severed arm, lying across his mouth. He thought it was his, then noticed the quivering fingers were black. He turned and saw the rest of the soldier, skull split open, grey-pink brain sliding out, bleeding, buzzing with flies. To the left he saw another young soldier, chunks of metal stuck in his hamburger face.

He heard the Cong running toward them, knew what was coming. He crawled beneath bleeding soldiers, causing some to shriek in pain. He squeezed under a man staring into a blinding sun, and froze as Cong machine guns opened up on the bodies above him.

Two bullets ripped open Bennett's left thigh. He bit his arm to keep from screaming.

When the Cong left, he felt where the bullets had lodged in his leg. He reached over, tore a strip of shirt from the corpse next to him and tied the strip around his upper thigh to control the bleeding. He lay there, trapped beneath the corpses, the warm blood of the soldier above dripping onto his lips.

As Bennett listened to the screams turn to moans, then whispers, then silence, he confirmed what he'd long known. Life was *surviving*. At all costs. How is a detail. Right or wrong is a fool's question. You grab what you want—any way you can—before one of life's howitzers nails you. He promised himself, if he survived, he'd take what he wanted and never look back.

He *had* survived, thanks to Medevac choppers. And he'd survived comfortably ever since, as his numerous Curacao savings accounts could attest.

The Ford van bumped into another log, snapping Bennett back to the present. He noticed the vegetation had grown much thicker and through the dense, green canopy above, black clouds were rolling in.

"In two miles we find the Suburban," Manny said. "Then we catch the bastards fast."

Bennett nodded. They would catch them. But if, for some unforeseen reason they couldn't, he'd play his ace.

His satellite phone.

He'd simply call Torres and have him eliminate the Twins immediately.

Thirty Nine

A DEEP sinkhole swallowed the Suburban's right front tire, snapping Luke's head back against the headrest and spritzing Coke onto Jenna's face. He watched tiny fizz drops skid down her nose, hang there a moment, then plop onto her blouse.

"Jou put your leeps on de hole and leeft de can up," he said in his best Mexican accent, smiling, handing her a Kleenex.

"Thanks, smart ass," she said, wiping her face.

They were sitting in the back seat of Garcia's Suburban, bouncing down the narrow jungle path. Redstone and Juan de los Santos sat in the middle row chatting about their FBI training days. Beside Diego Garcia, Miguel Ramirez rode shotgun, watching the path ahead like a hawk.

A call came in for Redstone, and he took the phone.

The four-wheel-drive Suburban clawed easily through the rugged, thick underbrush. They were gaining on the hunting party, but Luke knew the assassin could kill Thomas and Mackay at any time.

As they passed a thicket of palmetto trees, branches screeched along the windows, sending goosebumps down his spine. A tire struck a large rock, freezing stomachs and conversations. Redstone looked like he'd reswallowed lunch.

Luke noticed Garcia had to steer around trees and underbrush every few feet. The speedometer dropped to four miles per hour. Ahead Luke saw a line of trees as thick as the Wall of China.

Garcia crawled to a stop beside the dense trees. "The end of the expressway, *amigos*."

Getting out, Luke felt like he'd stepped into a blast furnace. The heat wrapped him like a hot wet towel. The group grabbed backpacks containing supplies and huddled around Miguel Ramirez, who bent down and examined some broken branches and flattened foliage.

He signaled them to follow him down a four-foot-wide path. They trudged ahead through steamy shafts of sunlight.

Luke swatted gnats swarming around his face, some clinging to his damp skin. The heat was overwhelming. He knew this was going to be an endurance test some might not endure. Redstone walked alongside Luke.

"My phone call," Redstone said, "gave us a bit more on Leonard and Sonny."

"Like what?"

"Your basic model citizens. Assaults and rapes for both. Leonard was special. He collected tongues. Paid some guy at the county morgue to let him in. Leonard'd slice off the tongues, shove the body back in the drawer and leave. Nobody'd know."

Luke stepped over a large boulder green with algae. "Have you connected Leonard or Sonny to anyone at World Motors or an advertising agency?"

"No," Redstone said, ducking under a tree limb. "Any thoughts about which agency?"

Luke shrugged. "Not really. I guess you start with those agencies which have the most to gain."

"Which are?"

"Major agencies that don't have an automobile client."

"A lot of agencies?"

"Yes."

"How long has your agency had the World Motors account?"

Luke calculated the years. "Sixty-one years."

"Isn't that a long time?"

"Very long," Luke said, pushing thick, grey-green vines to the side. "Today, the average client-agency relationship is about seven years."

"Why so short?"

"A lot of reasons. Sometimes the agency does lousy work. Or takes the client for granted. Sometimes a company hires a new advertising manager and he hires his pals at another agency. Sometimes the agency is a convenient scapegoat for the *company's* problems. Sometimes the company is dumb."

"Sounds like the police department," Redstone said, brushing spider webs off his glistening face. "So how come Connor Dow and World Motors have lasted sixty-one years?"

"We grew up together. Helped make each other successful. A real partnership, not one of today's pseudo partnerships. If one of our agency people is counter-productive to the partnership, they tell us, and we move the person off the business. If one of their people is counter-productive, they reassign their person out of the way. We replace the person, not the agency."

"Makes sense. Speaking of replacing the person, who would succeed Don Mackay if he doesn't make it out of this jungle?"

"Hard to say." Luke stepped toward a thin chunk of limestone that amazingly transformed into a large lizard which scurried into the weeds. "Mackay would be tough to replace. He's a real car guy, a superb engineer with terrific marketing savvy. A rare combination. He's demanding, but fair. His staff reveres him."

"One of them doesn't."

Luke looked at Redstone and nodded. "Mackay's still got five years before he retires. His successor hasn't been named. Quite a few names have been tossed around." Luke peeled a gnat from his eyelash.

He heard a loud, cracking sound—one hundred feet ahead.

The tall bushes began separating, and something large and unseen bolted directly toward them. Suddenly, a white-tailed doe and her fawn sprang from the thicket, sped off and disappeared behind some trees.

"*Temazate*, jungle deer," Miguel said.

Luke was mesmerized by the graceful, leaping animals. He stared at the surrounding jungle, which pulsated with life and mystery, and wished he had time to savor it.

"So how would World Motors go about switching to a new agency?" Redstone asked.

Luke shrugged. "Probably start with an agency review."

"How's that work?"

"The World Motors agency-review committee would pick five or so large agencies and evaluate their capabilities." He stepped over some sticky mango fruit.

Redstone asked, "Would this World Motors committee automatically place any one agency on the list?"

"Ours, probably."

"Yours? Why, if they're considering replacing your agency?"

"Out of respect for our long years of service, they'd probably give us one more chance to keep the business."

Redstone nodded. "Any other agency?"

Luke pushed through some bushes thick with brilliant yellow flowers. "I suppose GlobeLink, our parent company, would request that our sister agency, Kennard Rickert, be placed on the list."

"Time out. Your sister agency would compete against you for *your* business?"

"Sure."

"That seems counter-productive."

"Not from GlobeLink's perspective. They would have *two* chances to win the World Motors business—Connor Dow or Kennard Rickert."

Redstone paused. "So World Motors might put Kennard Rickert on the list?"

"Probably. Kennard Rickert is an excellent, worldwide system, almost as large as ours."

"What about other agencies? Any been real aggressive in going after the World Motors business?"

Luke considered the question as he stepped over a decaying log crawling with shiny, black insects. "A number have. One in particular. And I'm told they've been schmoozing some of World Motors younger marketing people for years."

"Which agency?"

"Standfield Draper & Partners out of New York. Their chairman would sell his firstborn for a major car account."

"Think Standfield Draper might be behind this?"

Luke thought a moment. "They're very competitive. But murderers? I don't think so."

"We're talking a billion bucks here. People kill for tennis shoes today." Redstone pushed moss-covered vines to the side.

Luke nodded agreement. He heard thunder, then screeching. Looking up, he saw magnificent red and blue birds, spreading their wings, squawking at the approaching storm. Lightning illuminated the dark sky.

Suddenly, the bushes next to him rustled loudly and quail exploded through the branches and soared skyward. He followed their flight and saw black, menacing clouds racing in fast.

His stomach tightened. Rain, he knew, would obliterate the footsteps they were following.

Forty

JENNA FOLLOWED Luke through a grove of towering rubber trees. The heat was suffocating, humidity pushing ninety. She felt like she was walking in a steam room. Luke, Redstone and Ramirez seemed impervious to the heat. Garcia's pink face suggested his weight was taking a toll. Despite the heat, she had to keep pace in case anyone needed medical help.

Luke reached over and presented her with a crimson, orchidlike flower. "Tarzan like Jane."

She placed it behind her ear, batted her eyelids, "Jane like cold shower."

Miguel Ramirez halted the group. They stood at the brink of a trench, maybe nine to eleven feet wide, and at least thirteen feet deep. The bottom was thick, swampy marsh extending in both directions as far as she could see.

"We run, we jump over, *sí?*" Ramirez said.

Luke, Redstone and de los Santos nodded they could.

Diego Garcia stared at the swamp below. "Not me."

"Nor me," Jenna said, relieved the chunky Garcia was along.

"No problem," Ramirez said. "Luke and I jump to other side. We make vine bridge. You crawl over."

"Crawl?" Garcia asked.

"*Sí.* You grab the vine, put your legs over, and pull to other side. Very simple. Just a few feet."

Garcia stared at the trench, then nodded he could do it.

"Jenna, can you crawl over?" Ramirez asked.

"Yes," she said, telling herself she *could* control her fear of heights.

Ramirez and Luke walked back about fifty feet, sprinted, and leapt over the trench, landing with two feet to spare. They headed into a thicket and came back minutes later with a long, one-inch-thick grey vine.

Ramirez swung one end of the vine over to the other side where Garcia and Redstone tied it around a small tree. The vine was more than long enough to span the trench, and strong enough to support a human.

Hank Redstone and de los Santos sprinted and leapt over the trench.

"Go ahead, Jenna. We steady vine for you," de los Santos said.

She knelt at the edge of the trench, wiped her sweaty palms on her pants, grabbed the vine with both hands, then locked her legs around it at the knees.

"Ready?" Redstone asked.

"Yes," she said, a knot forming in her throat. She tightened her grip and began to inch herself out over the trench, hanging by her knees and hands, looking up, reminding herself not to look down.

"Doing great," Luke shouted.

She focused on her hands, pulling herself forward in three-inch increments, doing well. Perspiration dripped from her chin and elbows and the humidity seemed worse. She grabbed a sharp knob, slid her fingers over it, continued.

She was one-quarter of the way.

It was harder now. Her fingers and neck muscles burned, her palms slipped a little. She dragged herself forward another three inches, then another. Overhead, birds shrieked down at her.

"That's it!" Luke shouted.

Nearly half way.

Her biceps were on fire. A sharp knot dug into the back of her knee. She lifted her leg over it, took a deep breath and advanced.

Suddenly, sharp tiny claws crawled onto her wrist. She saw a six-inch chameleon, green as the vine, creep onto her knuckles. She began to tremble as the chameleon turned the color of her skin and then scampered up her arm and leaped into her hair. She shook her head hard several times and felt the chameleon fall away. Gulping air, she tried to calm herself.

"Keep coming," someone said.

Snapping her attention back to the vine, she continued, but her hands slid more with each grasp.

"You're doing fine," Luke said.

I'm doing lousy.

"It's not far," Ramirez said.

She tilted her head sideways—ten feet more to go. As she turned her head back, she saw her reflection in the swampy water below and the jungle started to swirl. She blinked, closed her eyes, breathed deeply, froze.

They shouted for her to continue, but their words sounded like echos. Pain bolted up her forearms and legs. She was paralyzed.

Move, she commanded herself.

She sucked in air. Reaching ahead, she grabbed the vine, pulled forward. She reached again, gripped, but her sweaty palms slipped off.

Suddenly, she was dangling upside down like a trapeze artist, hanging by her crossed knees, which were slowly slipping apart.

Luke leaned over and reached for her hand, but missed by three feet.

Her head pounded with blood.

She swung her arm up, missed the vine, felt her left leg slip off, then her right.

She was falling.

Tucking her legs in like a diver, she landed on her knees and hands a few feet down on the soft, sloping bank. She skidded down a few feet, and grabbed an exposed tree root.

But her fingers were too wet. Slowly, she slid down the root, bounced off the bank and landed on her hands and feet in four inches of muck. She checked her arms and legs.

She was fine.

Then she wasn't.

Something moved between her fingers.

She yanked her hand from the mud, pulling out a long brown snake curled around her wrist—its mouth twisting toward her face. She flung the snake off. It landed a few feet away, hissed, coiled, moved toward her. She stepped back—and heard hissing behind her.

"Don't move!" Ramirez shouted. "*Cuatro narices.*"

The angry serpent hissed louder, its eyes riveted on her.

More snakes slid through the weeds around her. She was in a nest. Her heart pounded in her ears and she was having trouble breathing.

A large snake lifted its head, exposed its fangs, slid closer, angry eyes locked on her.

"Stay still," Ramirez whispered.

She had no choice. Her feet were locked in mud. She suddenly felt cold despite the heat. She waited a minute, two, losing all sense of time. The snakes, coiled to attack, waited for her to move.

She stood like a trembling statue dripping perspiration. She knew the snakes sensed her fear. Slowly, a cough tickle began to creep into the back of her throat. She swallowed it, but it came back stronger.

She tried to hold it, couldn't.

The cough exploded from her throat.

Angered, the snakes hissed and slid closer—and coiled for the kill. She heard something above her.

"Raise your arm," Luke whispered a few feet above her. His arm was held by Redstone whose arm was held by Ramirez.

She lifted her hand.

A closest snake's mouth opened wide, exposing its glistening fangs.

It sprang.

Jenna felt herself being yanked upward. The snake's fangs pierced the tip of her tennis shoe and stuck in the rubber.

The five-foot snake dangled from her shoe.

She looked up and saw Luke gripping her arm. Ramirez and Redstone were pulling them upward.

She shook her leg, but the serpent's fangs were still locked in the rubber. Had the fangs pierced her toe?

Luke whacked the snake, dislodging it. The serpent splashed into the muck below and slithered into the weeds.

Luke pulled her up over the bank, fell back on the ground, and she collapsed on top of him. They remained there, gulping air, listening to each other's heart pound.

Seconds later, she looked up. "See. I made it."

Ramirez fell against a tree, laughing.

Garcia was not laughing. "I think I wait here," he shouted from the other side of the trench, watching the snakes.

"No," de los Santos said, "We need you to make the arrest. You're local."

"We build you a bridge, *amigo*," Ramirez said.

Minutes later, he and de los Santos had fashioned a primitive bridge of four narrow tree trunks, bound by vines. Garcia sat down and scooted on his considerable butt across to the other side of the trench.

Jenna walked alongside Luke. "Sorry I panicked," she whispered. "We lost time."

"Not much. Besides, Miguel says that's serious rain ahead. The hunters must have stopped."

As she pushed on through the jungle, she saw black clouds swirling overhead. Thunder rolled like a gutter-ball. Her clothes clung to her. The darkening trail made it more difficult to follow footprints. The wind twisted nearby trees where parrots shrieked at the approaching storm. Lightning popped overhead and Jenna moved closer to Luke.

The rain hit like a waterfall.

She opened her mouth and gulped down several refreshing mouthfuls. It tasted cool and wonderful.

They were drenched instantly, but continued trudging forward, their visibility limited to five feet. Miguel slowed his pace. Lightning exploded, slicing off the top of a nearby tree and hurling the fiery wood to the jungle floor. She smelled the lightning's pungent ozone.

Three minutes later, everything grew strangely silent, and the rain diminished to mist. The winds fell silent. The sky turned an eerie, greenish yellow and looked like it was falling. She knew this sky. Tornado sky. What she didn't know was whether tornadoes struck the Yucatan. Trudging ahead, she prepared herself for anything.

Thunder and lightning exploded again, bringing back heavy rain. Her shoes slid on the rain-slick ground. Luke held her closer.

Ramirez stopped and examined broken branches every few feet. Rain had flattened the foliage and blurred the hunters' footsteps.

Lightning ignited, blinding everyone momentarily. They watched a tree incinerate and blacken. She knew people were electrocuted by standing too close to trees. They tramped up a steep, rain-drenched hill, stepping over logs and slick chunks of limestone.

Jenna tightened her grip on Luke's arm as he followed Ramirez's soggy footprints. The hill grew steeper and rocky. Her foot slipped again and Luke grabbed tree branches to anchor them.

She leaned into the slanting rain which stung her face. Water streamed over her tennis shoes. Ramirez, four feet ahead, looked as blurry as an impressionist painting.

As they neared the summit, she heard sudden movement behind her. Glancing back, she saw Juan de los Santos slip and fall backwards down the hill, grasping wildly for something to hold on to, tumbling down the ravine, landing hard on some boulders half-way down.

She stepped to the edge and looked down. Juan did not move.

Luke and she slid down the slippery, forty-foot slope. Ramirez and Redstone followed.

De los Santos was semi-conscious, his eyes fluttering. "Leg," he gasped.

His left leg had lodged between two large rocks. Halfway down the thigh, his leg, clearly broken, bent outward.

Jenna knelt beside him, fearing a spinal injury. "Juan, can you move your right leg and arms?"

He moved both his arms and good leg and she exhaled slowly with relief.

"Good." She ran her hand gently along his left thigh where it twisted between the rocks. "Luke, can you try to move this rock away?"

Luke, Redstone, Ramirez, and Garcia grabbed the slippery, suitcase-sized rock and tried to pull it back. It wouldn't budge. Luke grabbed a nearby tree limb, pried the rock up slightly, and the three men flipped it down the hill.

Jenna wiped rain from her eyes, took out a pocket knife, cut open Juan's pantleg and studied his thigh. She didn't need an X-ray. The break was bad. She touched the protruding skin gently. De los Santos winced.

"Juan, your femur is broken," she said. "It looks like a clean transverse break. You must remain stationary until we can get some medical help."

Juan de los Santos nodded, his handsome, angular face gripped with pain.

"I'm going to apply a traction splint now, Juan," Jenna said, blinking rain away. The splint, she knew would help keep the leg muscles from contracting and moving the broken bones, which would cause him unbearable pain.

He nodded.

But how can I create a traction splint here, she wondered? She squinted through the torrential downpour at the dripping trees. Moving into the brush, she saw something that might work. "Miguel, could you please cut these two branches off.

Miguel pulled his machete out, slashed off two three-foot branches and trimmed off the leaves in thirty seconds. She placed the branches along each side of Juan's injured leg, knelt at his foot and studied the broken bone for a full minute. She told him to grit his teeth, then gently she grasped his ankle and calf and slowly pulled until she felt the broken femur ease back into position.

"Ahhheeeeee," Juan hissed as mud squeezed between his fingers. Tears and rain slid from his eyes. "Hurry, I play soccer tonight."

"Okay," she said, smiling. She opened her medical bag, took out long wide strips of adhesive and taped the branches to his ankle, knee, and thigh. Then using her bandanna, she constructed a makeshift device beneath his ankle. She placed a small twig in the bandanna and began to twist the twig, tightening the tension and pulling his foot down, very slowly, until he signaled it felt better.

When she finished, she turned to Luke. "I should stay with Juan."

"No," de los Santos said emphatically. "You must go with the group, Jenna. I'll be fine. I have my gun if starving beasts come by."

She reached into her medical bag, took out a small bottle of white pills. "Take one now and as you need them for pain."

"*Gracias.*"

The group tramped back up the hill and continued into the jungle. The rain had let up slightly. Luke walked alongside her.

"Don't worry about Juan," he said. "Redstone says he's tough as a railroad tie."

"He better be. His leg needs professional attention."

"We'll get him some later," Garcia said. "Meanwhile, we've lost a lot of time."

Jenna glanced at her watch and saw that applying the splint to Juan's broken leg had taken eighteen minutes. Added to the time lost when she fell into the pit, this put them well behind the hunters.

She was exhausted. Her lungs felt heavy, and her legs and arm muscles burned with fatigue.

She wasn't sure she could maintain this pace much longer.

Forty One

CESAR TORRES'S machete slashed through thick vines like they were spiderwebs. He glanced back at the violent thunderstorm hammering the jungle a few miles behind. The storm had slid northeast, missing them, but refreshing them with a cool mist.

Everything was proceeding well. Soon he'd be at the ruins, handle the two Americans, then return to Belize.

He was amazed the older Americans hadn't asked to stop in the heat. They didn't seem to need to. Odd, he thought, that their excellent health would help them die sooner. And he knew exactly *where* they would die. Isolated. Enclosed. An excellent location.

Despite the fact that the police were tracking him, Torres was not worried. They had no idea where he was, couldn't see him from a chopper and couldn't catch up. Besides, cops were morons. He'd outwitted them since he was nine. By the time they found the Twins' bodies, he'd be sipping rum on the veranda of his Punta Gorda villa, looking out at the ocean, thinking about how to spend his four hundred thousand dollar fee.

He pulled out a small map, studied it and realized that soon he'd take the path to the ruins. Soon...

"Cesar," Baines Thomas said, as he and Mackay walked up beside him, "can you tell us a little about these Mayan ruins?"

Torres flashed his helpful-guide smile. Why not give them a little history before *they're* history, he thought.

"I'm not Mayan," Torres said, scratching the thick stubble on his chin, "but Luis Martinez back there, he is. He knows Mayan history good. Sometimes he is a guide at Chichen Itza. And he speaks English." Torres faced a small *cargador*. "Luis, come tell our friends about the Maya ruins."

Luis, a thin, oval-faced man, five-five, jet-black hair and almond-shaped eyes walked up beside Thomas and Mackay. He shook hands, smiled with perfect white teeth.

"I know a little," Luis said.

"We'd be interested," Thomas said.

"Well, about four thousand years ago my ancestors in this area were farmers. At first, they build small villages. Later, big cities."

"Like Chichen Itza?" Thomas asked.

"*Sí*. With its big temple, *El Castillo*, for Kukulkan, the Snake God. He bring the Toltecs to Chichen Itza."

"I thought Chichen Itza was *Mayan*?"

"Mayan and Toltec. The Toltecs came from central Mexico. Very aggressive." Luis winked and gestured toward Torres. "Hey, Cesar, you look a little Toltec, huh?"

Torres grinned appropriately. "You are half-correct, Luis. I am part Toltec." *But I inherited all their aggressiveness, as our two gringos will soon learn.*

"What about this Mayan ruin we're walking to?" Thomas asked.

"Toxuum," Luis said. "It's excellent."

For killing, Torres thought, as he brushed spiderwebs from his mouth. He'd been to Toxuum three times, and it was ideal for what he planned. The ruin was secluded, difficult to reach and rarely visited. Buildings were only partly excavated. Each had dark, cool, silent rooms. They reminded him of tombs.

"Toxuum was discovered only four years ago," Luis continued. "It's much smaller than Chichen Itza, but has great how you say *potencial*. Many buildings are still under the ground. One is sealed, so we hope the paintings are in good condition."

"Many buildings?" Mackay asked.

"*Sí.* The radars show many. Only sixteen locations have been digged out. Like the temple and the Well of Sacrifices."

"They sacrificed people at Toxuum?" Mackay asked.

"*Sí.* It's difficult to understand, but sacrifice was an honor. They believed the gods need fresh human hearts. They throw people in well."

Cesar Torres listened to each delicious word. Sacrificial death always excited him.

"Who'd they throw in?" Thomas asked.

"Everyone."

"Women and children?"

"*Sí.*"

Torres watched a flock of huge vultures soar overhead, sqwaking angrily at the storm raging behind them. The rains, he knew, would slow the police and make tracking him very difficult, perhaps impossible. He smiled. Luck was with him today. Even without luck he could outwit them. The jungle was his world, his sanctuary. He could live in it without supplies for months.

Baines Thomas turned to Luis. "Cesar says you're a guide at Chichen Itza?

"Yes. These hunting trips give us a little extra money. Cesar, he pays good."

"You have a family?" Thomas asked.

"*Sí, Señor*," Luis answered, his eyes brightening. "My wife, Teresa, and I have six childrens. Teresa, she sells the Coca-Colas at Chichen Itza. We save for my oldest son, Jose, to go to university maybe. Jose is *número uno* in his school."

"What does he want to study?" Thomas asked.

"Ah...how you say—*ingeniería?*"

"Engineering?" Mackay said, sounding interested.

"*Sí.* He wants to be an engineer."

Who cares? Torres thought as he led the group around the decaying carcass of a wild boar crawling with hundreds of glistening maggots. In two weeks animals and heat would reduce it to bones.

"Luis," Don Mackay said, "does your son speak any English?"

"*Sí, Señor.* Very good. Eight years he studies the English."

Cesar Torres sensed Mackay was about to help Jose's kid. Big deal. Torres had never needed help. Never would.

"We're opening a new engine assembly plant near Merida in three months," Mackay said. "I can arrange for Jose to work there while he goes to college. If he's interested, have him talk to a Mr. Estrada. We also pay eighty percent of his college tuition while he works at the plant. Would Jose be interested?"

Luis started to speak, but emotion seemed to choke his response. Finally, he whispered, "Yes. We will never forget this, Mr. Mackay. I promise you."

Torres smiled to himself. Poor Luis. His son's gift would never be received. The job offer would die with the Twins, rot like a banana. Jose would sweat his balls off in the jungle like his old man. Such is life. Still, Torres wondered what his life would be if he'd gone to college years ago. He'd been good at school, *inteligente* the teachers said, but he had to leave at eleven. Knowing where your next meal came from was more important than knowing where Simon Bolivar came from.

Torres stopped the hunting party. Something was stirring in the bushes ahead of him. Slowly, he raised his Rugger 77.

Within seconds, a family of agoutis, rabbit-sized, reddish-brown animals, scurried from bushes forty feet ahead and began munching on fallen mangoes.

Watching them, he recalled Pepito, his pet agouti, the only pet he ever had. His mother, in a drunken rage, had clubbed Pepito to death, skinned him, put him in a stew and forced Torres to eat him. Torres had become sick and vomited. His mother laughed. But the *puta* had paid later.

Torres took out his map, studied it, then called the hunting party around. It was time to separate his prey.

"The ruin is down this path," Torres said, pointing. "I will take Mr. Mackay and Mr. Thomas to the ruin. *Cargadores* stay here. No sense carrying all the equipment there and back here. We will come back and continue the hunt."

"Shouldn't Luis come?" Thomas suggested. "He knows the ruins."

Torres hesitated, trying to think of an excuse not to bring Luis, but couldn't. "Yes, of course, Luis must come. He can give us the history." *Unfortunately, he must also give me his life.*

The *cargadores* slid their gear off and began setting up a temporary camp. Torres led Thomas, Mackay and Luis down a path toward Toxuum.

An hour and twenty minutes later, they approached the outskirts of the ancient ruins. Thomas pointed to a grey ruin partially covered with mossy algae and surrounded by shallow groundwater.

"What's that building?" Thomas asked.

Luis looked at the ruin. "A bathhouse. There's water inside, from a *cenote*. Very deep. People went swimming in it."

As they strolled toward Toxuum, Torres reviewed his plan. Beautifully simple. They would walk to his special place. Luis would begin explaining the surroundings. *I move behind them, take out my gun, squeeze the trigger. Pop, pop, pop!*

So simple. *Beautiful.*

Forty Two

RAIN HAMMERED the van roof as Mason Bennett watched Manny steer the vehicle around a fallen tree. Branches raked against the fenders. The windshield wipers slapped away fat sheets of rain as thunder exploded overhead.

Beside Manny sat Paco, wide awake now. Bennett was in back with Carlos whose eyes were riveted on the map. Bennett wanted to eliminate the police as soon as possible, then make certain Cesar Torres had handled the Twins.

Bennett turned to Carlos. "How far could the police drive?"

Carlos slid his finger to a dark-green shaded area of the map.

"Here. End of path."

"Absolutely no farther?" Bennett challenged.

"No. Too many trees."

"But they could drive around this way."

"No. Ruins *other* way."

Bennett saw he was right, but wanted to make certain the police could not take a shortcut to Cesar Torres's hunting party. "So, if the police parked here, how far could they have walked by now?"

Carlos glanced at his watch, checked the map, then pointed to a spot. "Here."

"So they're in this storm."

"*Sí*." Lightning exploded ahead.

"Is Torres's group also in the storm?"

Carlos fingered the barrel of his handgun as he gazed down at the map, then out at the sky. "Probably."

Paco turned from the front seat. "What if Torres's group stops and the police keep going?"

"Torres won't stop," Bennett reminded them.

The van suddenly bottomed out in a hole, jerking everyone to the left. Paco's head bumped against the window. "This road *es un hijo de puta!*"

"A whore like your cousin, Rosita?" Carlos said, laughing.

"Fuck you!" Paco's black eyes ignited with anger, the first emotion Bennett had ever seen in them.

"You wan' me to slow down?" Manny asked.

"No," Bennett said.

Lightning cracked a few yards away. Manny yanked the steering wheel left, then right, barely missing a chunk of limestone. The storm was getting wilder. Thunder boomed, wind howled through trees. Rain slammed against the windows as though they were stuck in a car wash.

One hundred feet later, a tree limb thudded onto the hood and everyone flinched. Manny hit the brakes, sliding the limb off.

"How long do these fucking storms last?" Bennett demanded.

"They come, they go fast," Carlos said unconvincingly, squinting up at the black sky.

"Look!" Manny shouted.

"Where?" Carlos asked.

"Through the trees, you see?"

Bennett saw only rain gushing down the windshield.

"Their truck. They stop, like I say," Manny shouted. "Too much trees."

Lightning flashed and Bennett caught the glint of a cherry-red fender.

Manny parked behind some trees, a short distance from the Suburban. They stepped out into the rain and walked to their van's rear. Manny opened the back door, crawled inside, rolled out a blue Yamaha Razz mini-motor scooter. Carlos and Paco lifted it down onto the ground. Manny wheeled out three more of the small, two-foot wide scooters.

The scooters, Bennett knew, could squeeze through any jungle a man could—but up to thirty miles per hour faster. The deep-tread tires could claw over any terrain, even the muddy soil sucking at his shoes.

Suddenly, the rain slowed to a drizzle. A little luck, Bennett thought.

The four men grabbed their weapons and shoulder bags stuffed with ammunition clips, mounted the scooters, turned the keys and smiled when the engines purred to life.

Manny examined some broken twigs and branches and pointed down a trail. Following him, the four scooters roared down the narrow path into the jungle. Bennett relaxed as his speedometer climbed to sixteen miles per hour. At this rate, they'd catch the police group much sooner.

Minutes later, the rain stopped. Their speed increased and they splashed through puddles of groundwater, spraying roostertails to the sides.

Ahead, Bennett saw a small hill. They drove up its rocky ridge. Manny approached the top, turned hard right and headed down the other side. As Paco turned, his front tire skidded on a rain-slick stone, flipping him off the scooter.

Bennett tried to swerve away, but caught Paco's back wheel. Bennett spun out, fell off his bike onto some small rocks and skidded down a sloping hill into waist-deep water.

The other three men ran down and pulled him out.

"You okay?" Carlos asked.

"Yeah. Just wet. Fucking scooter skidded out!" He rubbed his hip where he'd hit the rocks.

Carlos picked up Bennett's rifle and handed it to him. They trudged back up the hill, checked out the two bikes and their weapons. Everything was undamaged. They mounted the bikes and continued into the jungle.

Soon the sun burned through the hazy clouds. Bennett's confidence rose with the speed, twenty-one miles per hour.

Three minutes later, Bennett couldn't believe his eyes. He was looking at a massive, fast-flowing river—like a goddamn Mississippi flood. It was about one hundred yards wide and extended as far as he could see. "What the fuck's this? There's no river on the map!"

"Rainwater," Manny said. "Come from high ground."

"How deep?"

Manny got off his bike, snapped off a tree branch and plunged it down into the water. He pulled the branch out and Bennett saw the water line was over three feet, too deep to drive through.

"Goddammit!" Bennett shouted "We've got to get around this water!"

"This way," Manny said, leading them along the bank.

Twenty-three minutes later, after going around the rain-lake, they returned to their original trail. Bennett seethed over the lost time. The Twins and the police group had probably passed here before the rains. And now the jungle was thicker, slowing his speed, forcing changes in direction every few yards. He slowed to six miles an hour, then four.

"Stop!" Bennett yelled.

The group pulled their scooters to a stop beside Manny.

"Check your map." Bennett said.

Carlos spread the map across his handlebars.

"Where are we?" Bennett asked.

Carlos and Manny studied the map closely. Carlos placed his thick finger on a location.

"And where's Torres's group?"

Carlos checked his watch, studied the map for several seconds, then pointed to a spot. "About here, if they did not stop for the rain. If they did stop, they could be about here."

"And what's the closest the police could be to Torres?"

"Back here."

Bennett saw the police could be within three miles of Torres. Even though this meant Torres would kill the Twins at least forty-five minutes before the police got near the ruin, Bennett knew numbers could deceive. Numbers didn't consider thunderstorms or rainwater rivers. Numbers didn't factor in the unforeseen—a twisted ankle, heat exhaustion, another flood. Torres could have been *forced* to stop—while the police kept going.

Bennett didn't like his margin of safety. The Twins *had* to be killed. He would phone Torres, tell him to find a reason to separate the Twins from the group immediately and eliminate them.

Bennett reached down, took his small briefcase from his backpack, opened it, pulled out the satellite dish and set it up. He then grabbed the phone unit attached to his belt and dialed Torres's number. There was no sound.

He dialed again. Nothing. His ear felt wet. He pulled the phone away and watched water pour from a small crack in the casing. He'd cracked it when he fell!

"This fucking thing is ruined!"

"Don' worry," Carlos said. "There's no way the police can catch Torres in time. No fuckin' way, man."

"How can you be sure?"

"Because Manny, he knows a shortcut."

Forty Three

LUKE STEPPED briskly up a steep incline, turned and looked at the others. Sweat-slick faces gleamed back at him. Hair was glued down like helmets. Mouths sucked in humid air. Bodies dragged along through the suffocating heat. Luke hoped they could hang on at this pace until they reached the hunting party.

Redstone walked alongside. "Problem."

Luke prayed it was minor.

"What if," Redstone said, "this is not the hunting party's trail?"

"Miguel thinks it is."

"Miguel also thinks there are many campers around. Which means many footprints—that the rain is distorting. Maybe we're following some campers."

Luke knew it was possible and signaled Ramirez. "Miguel, you still think this is the hunters' trail?"

Ramirez shrugged, his eyes riveted on the muddy path. "I think so, but this much rain...footprints hard to read."

Luke realized there was simply no way to be positive. "Can we still catch them before the ruins?"

Ramirez wiped a gnat off his tan, leathery cheek. "If we maintain this pace, we should catch them about three miles before the ruins. We drove in, and we're walkin' twice the normal speed. But everything depends on the 'ifs.' *If* they started this morning at a normal time. *If* they stopped during the storm. And *if* they walked past here when these broken branches indicate."

"They *must* have stopped in the storm," Garcia huffed, perspiration dripping from the folds of his double-chin.

Despite the logic, Luke still had an uneasy feeling. Too many 'ifs' *had* to occur to reach Thomas and Mackay in time.

Luke walked through a clump of yachee trees and dazzling, yellow flowers. Large white butterflies fluttered above fallen logs. The sun sucked vapors from the jungle flora, unleashing the thick, sweet forest scent that helped make the heat a little more bearable. The jungle was incredibly beautiful. Every inch screamed life.

And every black shadow seemed to hide death.

Ramirez stopped and knelt down.

He examined a plant. Then two others. He fingered the tips of some broken branches and his brow tightened. He pawed the ground, rubbed the dirt between his fingers, then stared up at Luke and Redstone and shook his head from side to side.

"What's wrong?" Redstone asked.

"Too dry," Ramirez said, fingering a footprint.

"So?"

"So the rain back there fool us. Make us think branches cut

more recent."

Redstone's eyes narrowed. "You're saying the hunters passed through here *earlier?*"

"Yes."

"How much earlier?"

Ramirez touched the soil, felt more cut branches. "Hard to say. Maybe an hour. Maybe more. They must leave camp *very* early this morning or go far last night."

Luke slumped against a tree. Their time cushion had just disappeared. He started to ask Ramirez if there was any way to make up the time, when the man raised his hand to hush everyone. He pointed ahead, cupped his right ear, listened, seemed to sniff the air, then stepped soundlessly up the path a few feet and stopped.

The group followed. Ramirez squinted ahead for several seconds, frozen like a bird dog, then pointed and whispered, "White smoke."

Luke stared for several seconds before he finally saw a pencil-thin wisp of smoke weaving up through the trees eighty feet up the trail.

Ramirez signaled the group to follow silently.

They crept through the foliage and stopped within fifty feet of men's voices. Luke heard Spanish. The hunting party. They *had* stopped. They were laughing. Relief washed through his tired body.

Redstone and Garcia drew their guns. Inching closer, the group squinted through the foliage. Luke saw three small men sitting around a campfire with hunting equipment and rifles stacked nearby. He scanned the area, but did not see Thomas and Mackay, nor anyone fitting Cesar Torres's description.

"Hunting party," Ramirez whispered.

Luke squeezed a nearby branch. They'd been following the *wrong* hunters.

Ramirez walked up to the men sitting around the campfire. "*Amigos*, any luck hunting?" he asked in Spanish.

The startled men turned and looked at them.

"A little luck," said a short man with glossy black hair, pointing to the game wagon. "That puma. He attacked us several kilometers back."

Luke was able to follow the Spanish.

Ramirez nodded. "We're looking for a hunting party with two sixty-year-old Americans. We think they're heading toward the ruins. Did you see them?"

"*We* are the hunting party," the man said.

Luke snapped his head around, half expecting Cesar Torres to leap from the bushes with a blood-drenched machete.

"But where are the Americans?" Ramirez asked.

"Walking to the Toxuum ruin with the guide, Cesar, and Luis, a *cargador*. After they see ruins, they'll come back here, and we continue the hunt."

"*When* did they leave here?" Miguel asked anxiously.

The little man pulled out an ancient pocket watch tied to a frayed black shoelace. "They left one hour and twenty-two minutes ago."

"By now, they are at the ruins," another man said.

Forty Four

CESAR TORRES'S eyes focused on the grey stone marker that pointed toward Toxuum's ruins eighty meters ahead. Through the trees he saw an ancient ruin jutting into the late afternoon sky. Soon his fingers would feel its cool limestone. Soon the cool limestone would feel warm blood.

Behind him, Luis stuffed the old *gringos* with more Mayan history. The history would die with them.

Torres felt his senses snapping alive. They always sharpened before the *moment*. He heard animals moving around him, recognized them without seeing them, smelled flowers he didn't notice, felt a breeze before it cooled him, saw insects crawling on leaves fifteen feet away. Power crackled through him like electricity.

"What's this open field?" Baines Thomas asked, as the strolled onto an enormous, grassy area, one hundred yards by thirty yards, surrounded by a high stone wall.

"The ball court," Luis said. "See the stone rings near the top of the wall?"

Thomas and Mackay nodded.

"The players tried to knock the ball through."

"Like basketball," Mackay added.

"*Sí*. But the players could not touch the ball with their hands."

"How big was the ball? Mackay asked.

"Maybe baseball size. Rubber."

"A *rubber* ball a thousand years ago?" Mackay asked.

"*Sí*. Before that, Mayans have no balls."

Thomas smiled. "Like certain clients."

Mackay laughed. "You're fired."

"Again?"

Thomas ran his hand along the wall. "So if they couldn't use their hands, it was like soccer?"

"*Sí*. But very different."

"How?"

"The losers have their heads chopped off. But some experts think *winners* have heads chopped off—as a *reward!*"

Thomas shook his head. "I wouldn't know whether to shit or go blind."

"Go where?" Luis asked.

"Old *gringo* expression, Luis. It means you lose both ways."

And both of you will soon lose, Torres thought. He was excited by the talk of beheading. He'd often thought how pleasing it would be to behead someone. He'd heard that a freshly decapitated body jerked about and briefly tried to run. With luck, he might see that some day.

"Come," Luis said, leading them to an ancient building overlooking a courtyard. Part of the building was covered with earth and large stones shaped like boots. He guided them down through the elaborate entrance into a large room where they saw a sprawling, carved frieze of a grey-green jaguar on a wall. The colors, one-thousand-years-old, looked like they'd been painted last week.

"The jaguar is incredibly well-preserved," Thomas said.

"So is *this* mural," Torres said, pointing to a wall painting of headless soldiers. "It shows what happened to Mayan enemies."

Torres stared at the two men facing the painting. *In many ways, you are my enemies. You were given all the things I was denied. Things I deserved as much as you. And now you stand between me and my fee.*

Torres's pulse quickened as he stepped behind them and studied their heads. Three little heads in a row. So perfect. So easy. So clean. Thump—thump—thump. He could do it now.

But this wasn't *the* location.

Luis ushered everyone back outside to a building with a circular tower that had part of its wall missing. "This is the observatory. The Mayans precisely calculated the movements of the stars. Scientists are astounded that one-thousand years ago, the Mayans, without calculators, predicted recent eclipses in North America to the exact hour."

"What's that thing?" Thomas asked, pointing to two large stone sculptures depicting long poles with skulls on top.

"Human skull racks. Similar to the Aztec skull racks. They stick thousands of enemy heads on them!"

Torres was exploding with excitement. He had to wipe his damp palms on his trousers. He couldn't wait any longer. "Luis, show them the friezes in the Temple of the Soldiers."

"*Sí.* The best is last," Luis said, smiling.

Torres followed them into the Temple, reached into his knapsack, gripped the .45, and slid it into his pocket. They moved into a large room with a partially collapsed roof through which a shaft of sunlight lit swirling dust particles.

Using his flashlight, Luis led them down a hallway which descended into another dark hall. At the hall's end they walked through an ornately carved entrance into a shadowy chamber.

Torres fingered his .45's cool, steel barrel. His eyes were riveted on the backs of their heads. He saw the precise location each bullet would enter, saw the bullets entering their skulls in slow motion, saw the hot metal ripping through brain tissue, destroying memories, saw the blood soaking the stones.

Luis played his flashlight beam over the wall, revealing an enormous frieze of spectacularly bright colors. Thomas and Mackay stepped up to the frieze.

"It's like they were just painted," Mackay said, leaning close.

"*Sí*. This room was sealed tight until a year ago. No outside air to eat the paint. Last year the professor, he put a special coating over the paintings. We see them as my ancestors saw them."

"What are the eagle and jaguar doing?" Thomas asked.

"They offer fresh human hearts to the Gods."

Like me, Cesar Torres thought, moving behind the men.

Forty Five

LUKE'S LUNGS were on fire as he and Redstone ran down the twisting jungle path, sucking in hot, suffocating, ninety-eight-degree heat. He felt like he was breathing furnace flames.

He and Redstone had left the others behind and were making one last effort to stop Cesar Torres.

Luke realized that running to the ruin was probably pointless. Torres had been there for nearly an hour and wouldn't waste time. He'd kill Thomas and Mackay and leave quickly.

Luke glanced at his watch. Twenty-five minutes more to run. Maybe more, if the terrain ahead was as hilly as the *cargadores* said. Could he last in this heat? Reason and logic told him he'd arrive too late. Hope told him to keep running.

Behind him, Redstone gulped air like a wounded buffalo. They were running through near-impenetrable, treacherous vegetation. They could only see about four yards ahead and had no idea of what their feet would land on.

Luke estimated they were running a nine-minute mile, nearly two minutes slower than his normal pace, but with more pain and perspiration. No wonder Mexican marathoners did so well.

He dodged a cluster of thorn bushes and saw hanging vines closing off the narrow path ahead. Slowing, he gauged how to knife through.

He jumped past, vines clinging to his arms, and landed safely. Redstone bolted through seconds later.

"How you doing back there?" Luke shouted.

"Lungs died ten minutes ago."

"They'll adjust to this air."

"Air?"

Luke knew their energy was draining fast. It was insane to run in this kind of blistering heat and heavy humidity. Heat stroke was a lousy way to cross the finish line of life.

"How much further?" Redstone huffed.

"Maybe three miles."

"Tell Renee I loved her."

They sprinted over rolling terrain for several minutes, adjusting their speed and direction to what the jungle permitted.

Luke felt like he was running through a field of land mines, leaping, slowing, speeding, changing pace every few strides. His lungs were hot lead, his thighs cement.

Redstone now sounded like he was having an asthma attack, but Luke knew his friend would rather drop before stopping. Luke prayed he wasn't killing one friend to save another.

"You in pain?" Luke shouted.

"I'm in a jungle. My people know jungles."

"Your people aren't eating two Big Macs a day."

"I can pass your honkey ass, anytime."

They sprinted through thick, waist-high grass which clung to their sweaty arms. As Luke ran out of the grass, he pushed aside a bush and saw he was in trouble.

Two yards ahead, an obscured, fallen tree blocked his way. "Jump!" he shouted, as he hurdled it with only an inch to spare.

Redstone saw the tree trunk too late. He leapt, caught his foot on it, flipped and landed oddly on one foot. He immediately rocked to his side, eyes closed, clutching his left ankle, and let out a slow, deep groan.

Luke knelt beside him.

"Foot..." Redstone gasped, pulling down his sock and rubbing his ankle.

"Did it crack?"

"It *scrunched*."

"Maybe you only sprained it."

Redstone huffed out hard through his teeth. "Let's see if I can walk."

Luke helped his large friend to his feet. Gingerly, Redstone eased his injured foot onto the ground, shifted a little weight on it, jerked back in obvious pain.

"Shit! Shit! Shit!" Redstone screamed at the sky.

"You're benched, ace."

"Yeah, yeah...Go ahead—I'll catch up later."

Luke helped him over to a tree where Redstone sat, leaned against the trunk, and rubbed his ankle as sweat poured from his face.

"I'll be back," Luke called, sprinting ahead. He hated leaving Hank behind, but there was no other choice.

Luke ran into heavier, thicker brush that pulled at his legs, slowing him. Long, thin weeds raked his hands and forearms. He prayed his feet didn't land in a hole.

He was running in a sauna. His lungs were searing, his body's resources depleting fast. He was punishing his body in exactly the way his doctor and Jenna had told him to avoid, the way that might help trigger a relapse of his leukemia.

Common sense shouted stop. Common sense said it was too

late to save Thomas and Mackay. But there were times, like now, when you told common sense to take a hike.

He kept running—right into a long, spiky green leaf that sliced across his right forearm, leaving a track of razor-sharp thorns imbedded in the skin. He tried to pluck them out as he ran. The plant toxin stung his arm.

Looking up—he knew Murphy's Law applied to jungles.

He was staring at a long, steep hill. He started up the incline, his body fighting the added exertion, his chest burning. He commanded his rubbery, sweat-slick legs to keep pumping.

Sixty excruciating seconds later, he looked up and saw he was only one-third of the way up the hill.

His legs were concrete.

He was hitting the wall, the twentieth mile of a marathon. His mind and body were shouting stop. He punched his mind's pause button, locked on automatic, blocked out the pain, forced one leg ahead of the other and continued up the hill.

Someone was driving nails into his lungs. His heart pounded in his ears. He glanced up and saw the summit still one hundred feet straight up. Would he pass out before he made it?

He saw three, then four paths...many legs...ears ringing. He shortened his stride, kept going, vision blurring, losing it.

Then, strangely, his legs seemed lighter. *Were* lighter. He was floating... The summit. He'd made it.

He coasted, going down now, gulping fresh air, letting gravity ease him down the hill. He filled his lungs and his head began to clear. His heartbeat left his ears, a little strength returned.

He would make it.

He looked up and saw a circular ruin building jutting above the trees a quarter mile ahead. Toxuum. Just minutes away. He reached the bottom of the hill, followed the path around a wall of tall, dense trees, then nearly collapsed in shock.

Dead ahead was another steep hill.

Forty Six

CESAR TORRES drank in the dank, cool air of the Temple. His finger slid over the cold steel of his .45 and around the trigger. He watched Luis explain the wall painting to Mackay and Thomas, who were clearly mesmerized by the artwork.

Torres moved behind them.

It was time. Time to quench his thirst, to quench the thirsty stones with blood, mix it with the blood spilled centuries ago. Time to balance out the fat, privileged lives of these two gringos with some very bad luck, and end Luiz's worthless life.

Torres's heart hammered against his chest. He enjoyed the

pounding, prolonged the moment, like good sex, savoring the escalating moments until ... Staring at the back of their heads, he took a deep breath, then eased the gun from his pocket, raised it slowly, tightened his finger on the trigger, started to squeeze.

Then he heard it. Very faint.

Was he imagining?

No, he heard it again. A noise. Louder now. Someone outside. Shouting.

Shouting my name!

Luis and Thomas turned their heads toward the noise as Torres slid the gun back into his pocket.

"Listen," Luis said, looking at Cesar. "Someone calls you, Cesar. Do you hear him?"

Torres nodded, trying to conceal the anger contorting his face. Who the fuck was calling him? Only the *cargadores* and Mason Bennett knew he was here. The accent was American. Why was Mason Bennett here? It could only be bad news.

Torres led Thomas, Mackay, and Luis back through the hallway and rooms leading to the temple entrance. Stepping outside, Torres saw it was not Mason Bennett.

Instead, a tall, chestnut-haired man, drenched in sweat, anxious, stood on the bottom step, his green eyes locked on Torres.

"Luke?" Baines Thomas shouted, "What the hell are *you* doing here?"

Torres knew and jerked out his gun.

"Look out!" Luke shouted. "Torres wants to kill you."

Thomas leapt behind a massive sculpture.

Torres grabbed Mackay from behind, pulled him back and fired two shots at Luke which ricocheted off an enormous Chac Mool statue. Torres remembered an escape route. He jammed his gun against Mackay's head and jerked the man back inside the temple.

* * *

Luke watched them vanish in the temple blackness. He pulled

out his gun, ran up the stairs, paused at the opening. He peered around the door.

Torres fired, chipping off a stone fragment that stung Luke's jaw. Luke leapt back behind the Chac Mool statue with Thomas and Luis.

"What the hell's going on?" Thomas asked.

"Torres was hired to kill you and Mackay," Luke whispered. "I'll explain later. Right now, let's get Mackay back."

Thomas nodded.

"Do you have weapons?" Luke asked.

"No. Torres said we wouldn't need them here."

They climbed back up to the entrance. Luke sensed Torres was probably just inside, waiting to blow his head off. Luke borrowed Thomas' straw hat and jerked it into the doorwell.

Nothing. Perhaps Torres had moved further inside.

Crouching, Luke bolted into the temple, swept the room with his gun. Nothing. The blackness blinded him momentarily, but then he saw the room was empty.

Thomas and Luis entered. Luis pointed at the door leading to other rooms. They moved to the door, listened, heard nothing. Again, Luke shoved the hat in the doorwell but nothing happened. He stepped into the room, saw more blackness. Thomas and Luis followed.

Luis pointed to footprints which skidded as though someone was being dragged. He followed them to a long narrow hallway, stopped, and whispered, "He go to tunnel. Tunnel go to jungle exit. We go behind him, wait."

Luke and Thomas nodded. They hurried back through the rooms, ran outside, sprinted along the temple into the jungle and stopped at a steep, narrow stairwell which led underground. Luis led them down the stairwell and into a dark, murky tunnel. Dusty light sliced through a ceiling slit.

Luke noticed the tunnel was at least thirty degrees cooler. It felt good, then his soaked shirt felt like ice and he began to shiver. They moved silently over the stone floor, turned a corner, took a few steps.

Luis stopped and raised a hand.

Luke was about to ask him why, when he heard why. The soft shuffle of shoes moving toward them in the darkness. He squinted, but saw nothing.

The shuffling grew louder, and soon he glimpsed the silhouettes of Torres and Mackay, backing around the corner. Torres's gun glinted beside Mackay's head.

As Luis moved to the side, his shoe kicked a small rock across the stone floor.

Torres spun around and fired twice.

The shots were deafening, and dust rained down from the ceiling, blocking Luke's vision, but not before he saw Torres yank Mackay back around the corner.

Luke felt someone slump against his leg. Looking down, he saw blood seeping from Luis's upper-right chest, below the shoulder. Luke eased the small man down flat onto the stones. Thomas yanked a bandanna from his pocket and held it against the bullet wound.

"I'll go after them," Luke whispered.

"Be careful."

Luke hurried down the long hallway and peered around the corner. The hall was empty. He crouched, turned the corner, and continued, hugging the wall, moving into a large room. He saw no one. He moved through the room to a short passageway open on one side. Was Torres waiting for him?

He found a pebble, tossed it down the hall.

Nothing.

He ran down the hall and into the room. Torres and Mackay were not there.

Where the hell are they?

Luke stepped to the door of the main entrance room and froze. He heard a man moaning, gasping for breath. Luke spun into the room, nearly tripping over the prostrate body of Don Mackay as he tried to get up.

"You shot?" Luke asked.

"No. Just whacked," Mackay said, rubbing the back of his

head. "And pissed off. Bastard ran outside. Get him."

Luke hurried outside and scanned the ruins. Torres was nowhere in sight. Luke continued to search, but found no hint of the man. As he ran down the temple steps, something tan flashed against the jungle green. Torres's shirt. He was at least a quarter mile ahead, sprinting on the path that led from the ball court.

Luke started to run, but his tight, dehydrated leg muscles began to cramp. He slowed his pace and one hundred yards later, his muscles loosened and he ran faster. But Torres had put more distance between them.

Seconds later, Luke saw a wet, fresh footprint beside a pool of rainwater, another print a few feet away, then several more. The distance between footprints indicated Torres was sprinting. He was thin, ideal for running distances. But how far could he sprint in this heat?

Torres's footprints soon disappeared in ankle-deep grass.

Luke continued running in the same direction, searching for footprints in the grassy area which was about half the size of a football field. He found no footprints. Torres must have changed directions in the grass. Luke ran along the fringe of the grassy area, searching for an exit footprint. He found none.

This was crazy. Torres couldn't run on moist ground without leaving footprints. But he had, and he was getting away, gaining time.

Luke ran back to Torres's last footprint, got on his hands and knees, and studied a four-foot area surrounding it, looking for any hint, a plant pushed into the ground or twisted oddly, an indentation, anything.

He saw nothing.

It was as though Torres had been pulled into a helicopter.

Forty Seven

LUKE CRAWLED along the ground, searching for some hint of a footprint, finding nothing. Had Torres removed his shoes to avoid leaving prints? Even his foot should leave some indentation. Maybe he should let the bastard go. Thomas and Mackay were safe, and he should concentrate on getting medical attention for Luiz, de los Santos and Redstone.

But he couldn't let Torres escape. For one thing, Torres might return to finish the job. And Torres was the key—the link to those behind this, to those who'd slaughtered Pepe's family. If Torres got away, he'd flee Mexico, change his identity and disappear.

But looking down at Torres' last visible footprint, Luke could find no further prints, no trace of the man.

He walked around so daylight hit the ground differently. Still nothing. He shifted a bit to the left and saw it immediately. A small, broken twig pushed oddly *through* a leaf. The leaf seemed mashed into the soil. He lifted the leaf and saw a fresh, round heel indentation. Torres *had* removed his shoes. Three feet ahead was another crushed plant with a heel print beneath, and beyond that, a flattened red flower.

Torres had moved from plant to plant.

Painstakingly, Luke tracked Torres, step by step, stopping every few feet to confirm the man's direction. Overhead, thunder rolled and he saw threatening clouds moving in again. Rain would wash out the faint indentations.

Luke followed the heel prints about two-hundred yards to the ancient bathhouse he'd passed earlier. He stopped beside the shallow groundwater surrounding the bathhouse, and saw two clear, fresh *shoe* prints.

Another shoe print shimmered just beneath the water's surface. He stepped into the water and tracked the prints to a narrow patch of ground bordering the bathhouse. He followed the prints alongside the grey stone bathhouse, which appeared to contain several chambers. The footprints led up to the entrance and pointed inside.

Luke tightened the grip on his gun.

Torres was inside.

Or had he *planted* the footprint, then *backed out* on his footprints to make it look like he was inside? Luke walked back up a few yards, re-checking Torres's footprints. They were not smeared as they'd be if he'd backtracked.

Torres was inside.

He was waiting.

He was armed.

Light rain started falling as Luke stared through the opening. He let his eyes adjust to the inky blackness inside where dark *cenote* water lapped gently against the stone floor. Was the lapping caused by Torres? He searched the water for any reflection, any hint of human form, but saw nothing. Heavy, humid air oozed out through the door.

Going in I'm most vulnerable, he thought. Torres would shoot any form that appeared in the door. Solution: Give him very little form to shoot.

Luke squatted and grabbed a small, leafy tree branch. He jerked the branch into the doorwell. Nothing. Maybe Torres was in another chamber. Luke saw a long, low stone bench just inside the door. If he got behind it, he'd probably be safe. Taking a deep breath, Luke slid inside and lay behind the bench.

Silence.

He could not see and waited for his eyes to adjust. Crouching, he inched into the blackness, and nearly fell over another stone bench. He squatted behind it and focused on the water reflections snaking up the walls.

Where is he?

He scanned the room again, did not see Torres. Twenty feet away, a small door slowly came into focus.

Silently, Luke stepped on the algae-slick stones to the side of the door. He peered in and saw a much larger room with a similar pool of water. A tiny shaft of sunlight slid through a roof crack and lit a six-inch patch of water.

He listened for Torres's breath, but heard only water washing softly against stones. Luke squinted into the shadows, unable to discern shapes. Bending down, he felt along the slimy stones for something to toss into the room. He found nothing.

Torres was *close.* Luke felt the man's presence. Just feet away. Waiting. But where? Beside the door? Farther back in the room? In the water? Wherever, Torres had a clear shot at him.

Walking through this door was walking into a bullet. And the door was the only way in.

Or was it? Luke studied the water. The level was identical in both rooms, suggesting it might flow through or under the wall between the rooms. If he could swim underwater into the room, he might surface *behind* Torres. Even if he couldn't swim under the wall, he could surface silently at the wall, and possibly see if Torres was behind the door.

The water was Luke's only possible advantage.

But dangerous. Miguel had mentioned how *cenotes* were often connected to underground rivers and caves—large enough to swallow five or six houses.

But I'm only going under a few feet. He walked back near the entrance, gripped his gun, and eased silently into the water. The cool water jolted his heated body. Something squiggled between his legs and swam away.

He took a deep breath and slid underwater.

He swam toward the wall, groping for the stones. His fingers touched the slimy wall. He moved down its surface about seven feet until he felt water flowing through a massive, square opening into the next room.

He crawled through the opening, gripped his gun and pushed off the wall, heading up. He exploded through the surface of the water.

Torres, ten feet away, spun around, gun in hand. Eyes crazed, he fired, ripping the water beside Luke's shoulder.

Luke fired back twice, missing.

The sound was deafening.

Suddenly, horrific, terrifying sounds—shrieking and flapping of wings—filled the chamber. Hundreds of bats had come unglued from the ceiling. Furry wings scraped Luke's lips and neck, tiny claws dug into his hair. He slapped them away.

Bats locked on Torres's face. Swatting at them, he slipped on the slick stones, fell backward, hit his head hard against a stone bench, then slid, unconscious, into the water, his gun splashing beside him.

Luke treaded water, watching where Torres went under. Was he unconscious? Luke waited twenty seconds, searching the swirling black water. Thirty seconds. Forty.

Still nothing.

Did Torres swim into the other chamber? Luke paddled to the

right, checked the entrance, did not see him. Torres was still under water. Sixty seconds.

An eery hush filled the chamber. The bats had flown away.

Luke heard only the water. Then he *felt* it—behind him.

Turning, Luke saw Torres rocket out of the water, sucking in air, eyes wide, slashing a hunting knife down toward Luke's face.

"*Bastardo!*"

Luke caught Torres's wrist, stopping the blade just inches away.

Torres jerked Luke underwater, slashed again, nicking Luke's gun hand, causing him to drop his gun into the depths.

Take control! Luke commanded himself.

The knife slashed toward him again in slow-motion. He grabbed Torres's wrist and tried to wrestle the knife away, but it seemed welded to the man's hand.

Both men surfaced, gasping for air.

Torres kneed Luke in the stomach then yanked him under again. They wrestled for the knife, twisting and spinning for several seconds.

As they re-surfaced for air, Luke had an idea. Perhaps his only chance. He filled his lungs to the bursting point. Feigning exhaustion, he let Torres pull him under again. Then, abruptly, Luke swung his body on top of Torres and swam the surprised man *down*—toward the deep, black depths of the *cenote*.

You're going home, bottom-feeder.

Torres seemed confused by Luke's tactic, and fought the descent.

Luke counted on his runner's lungs to outlast Torres. He would keep Torres underwater until the man panicked and tried to save his own life.

Luke's momentum pushed them into darker, cooler water.

Then something unseen pulled at him. Something powerful.

What the hell? A strong current was sucking them sideways and down into an opening. Down into a cavern.

Luke fought the brutal current, but Torres's thrashing made it difficult. They were sucked deeper into the cavern—to an underground river. Torres's eyes bulged with panic. Bubbles slid from his mouth. His arms grew less forceful, his kicks weaker. Soon his body grew limp, then still. He lost consciousness.

Finally.

Luke reached for Torres's knife—and realized his mistake.

Torres flipped him and slashed open his right shoulder. The icy water jolted Luke's open flesh. Raw fear rammed adrenalin into every cell of his body.

With brute strength, he spun Torres beneath him again and swam the man still deeper. They descended faster than the current. Torres struggled wildly.

In seconds, Luke knew, one of them would die.

Suddenly, Torres's body jolted to a hard stop.

What did he hit?

In disbelief Luke saw the bloody tip of a pointed stone rip up through Torres's chest.

Torres was skewered on a stalagmite. His eyes stared at the bloody stone in his chest as bubbles screamed from his gaping mouth. His arms and legs flailed to extricate himself, then stopped and began to float like corks. Luke felt warm blood spewing from the man's chest and mouth. Torres's eyes rolled back...

Luke's lungs were exploding.

Air! He swam toward the end of the cavern, turned up, struck his head on the cavern roof. Dazed, he swallowed water, but managed to crawl along the cavern roof to the main pool of water. Bubbles squirted from his mouth.

He looked up but couldn't see the circle of sunlight. He turned, lungs on fire, and still couldn't find it.

He swam blindly, his chest splitting. Was he swimming up or down? He was losing it.

He wasn't going to make it.

He swam left, thought he saw light. Was he hallucinating? He soared toward it, swallowing water, blacking out.

Forty Eight

THE GENTLE breeze came from nowhere and cooled Mason Bennett's face. He smiled as his speedometer climbed to twenty-one. The trail was smooth, wide and free of obstacles.

They'd averaged over fifteen miles per hour for the last twenty minutes and had more than made up the time lost circling the massive rainwater lake.

Soon they'd reach the police group. He visualized exactly how he'd eliminate them and dispose of the bodies so that no trace of them would ever be found.

Fifty feet ahead, Manny pulled to a stop at a large limestone boulder which split the trail in two. The main trail continued to the right. A second path, wider and smooth, bent left into more open, flat jungle.

Carlos spread the map across his handlebars and studied it with Manny. Manny pointed to a spot on the map. Carlos pointed to another spot and mumbled machine-gun Spanish Bennett couldn't follow.

Angrily, Manny shook his head no, explained something, ran his finger over the map and pointed to another location. Carlos looked at him for several seconds, then shrugged.

"What's going on?" Bennett asked.

"Manny says this new path is the shortcut. It can save us ten minutes, maybe fifteen."

"Take it," Bennett said. The sooner he handled the police, the better.

He followed Manny, Carlos and Paco down the path. Bennett's speed climbed to an exhilarating twenty-three miles per hour.

He would reach the police group in minutes.

Forty Nine

LUKE HURLED more water from his stomach as he clung to the greasy stone walk. Gulping air, he managed to hoist his chest up onto the walk and collapse, drifting in and out of consciousness. He sputtered more water out and felt something slither between his thighs. He opened an eye and watched a snake slip away.

My *life* almost slipped away, he thought, pulling himself further out of the water.

Minutes later, he crawled to his feet, lumbered outside and squinted into the brilliant daylight. Dazed and exhausted, he headed back toward the ruins. His mind was as numb as his body. He'd never killed a human and didn't like the empty, nauseating crater it left in his gut. He also didn't like the piercing headache creeping across his forehead.

But he was alive. So were Baines Thomas and Don Mackay. Their would-be assassin was dead. The injured *cargador*, Luke hoped, was hanging on.

All he wanted now was to get quick medical help for Luis, then get everyone safely out of the jungle. As he straggled onto the ball court, he saw Baines Thomas waving him over to the entrance of the large temple. Beside Thomas, Mackay was bent over Luis, who lay on his back in the temple shadows.

Luke walked over, and saw that Luis was worse.

"Jesus, Luke," Thomas said. "Your shoulder's cut bad."

"I'm fine."

"Where's Torres?"

"He sort of drowned."

"Sort of"

"Actually he's parked on a stalagmite twenty feet under water." Luke quickly explained what happened, then knelt beside Luis. The small man was conscious, his eyes terrified and glassy. Mackay held a large, blood-soaked towel against the bullet hole in his upper chest.

"Hang in there, Luis," Luke said.

The small man blinked.

Luke heard voices. Turning, he saw Jenna, Ramirez, Garcia and the *cargadores* trudging from the jungle. In their midst, Hank Redstone hobbled on a tree-limb crutch. A *cargador* pointed toward Luke and the others.

Jenna broke into a jog, climbed the temple steps two at a time and threw her arms around him.

"What happened?" she asked, staring at his wet shirt.

"I got Torres before he got Thomas and Mackay."

"I mean your shoulder," she said, ripping open his bloody shirt and examining the four-inch gash. "That's a serious laceration."

"Luis is more serious."

Turning, she saw Luis, quickly knelt beside him and studied the bullet wound in his extreme upper-right chest. After a few moments, she stood, ushered Luke and Garcia a few feet away.

"He needs medical attention fast," she whispered. "He's lost a lot of blood. The bullet may have hit his subclavean artery or lung."

Garcia said, "But we are two hours from a village phone."

Luke watched her eyes darken. She walked him and Garcia over near the *cargadores* and whispered, "Luis may not have two hours."

Garcia said something to the *cargadores*. A thin, young *cargador* said, "To village I run. One hour. I phone for the help."

"Yes, please," Jenna said.

"Wait!" another *cargador* said, pulling a square satellite dish from a case. "See what I find in Torres's backpack."

"What the hell's that?" Garcia asked.

Luke's hope soared. "A satellite phone. We use them on remote television commercial locations. They work where cell phones can't." Luke punched in the Caller ID and PIN numbers taped to the case, aimed the dish until it identified the satellite signal, then handed the phone unit to Garcia.

Garcia dialed.

The group crowded around as though he held the Hope Diamond. Everyone waited several seconds, faces frozen. Finally, Garcia's eyes smiled and he spoke in rapid Spanish.

Hanging up, he said, "They send the Merida medical helicopter. "She is near Izamal. We are lucky."

Jenna whispered the good news in Luis's ear.

The small man blinked, but Luke noticed he seemed greyer, more listless. Blood had pooled on the stones from his shoulder to his waist, like he was floating on a purple lake.

Twenty-two minutes later, Luke heard the rhythmic pulse of the MedEvac chopper skimming over the trees toward them. The chopper nestled down near the temple, swirling clouds of dust skyward. Three young medical personnel quickly moved Luis into the helicopter and left with Diego Garcia who would show them where to pick up Juan de los Santos.

"*Vaya con Dios, Luis,*" Luke whispered as the chopper lifted over the trees and disappeared into the late afternoon sun. He slumped back against the Temple wall and exhaled with relief.

Luis might make it, but he was beginning to wonder whether he would. His legs felt like an earth mover had rolled over them. His headache pounded, his shoulder cut burned, his nausea seemed to cartwheel and his body shivered despite the ninety-six-degree heat. Clearly, he'd pushed himself too far, perhaps into triggering a relapse of his disease. His joints ached like they had when he'd relapsed at the FBI Academy.

Jenna walked over to him with her black bag and stared at him.

"Now *you,*" she said.

"Now me what?"

"Now we pluck you from the jaws of death." She leaned over and applied an antiseptic creme to his shoulder laceration. It burned like hell, and he flinched.

"Wimp," she said, applying a lotion to his dry, cracked lips. "You're lucky you didn't suffer heat stroke."

"Heat stroke creates character."

"It also creates *death*. Seventy percent of heat stroke victims die. You're seriously dehydrated."

"No, just thirsty," he said, hoping for a laugh he didn't get.

"You've lost at least five, six liters."

"So bring me Lake Michigan with a slice of lemon."

She asked a *cargador* to bring her water. The young man reached into the provisions wagon and handed her two large bottles of Evian which she handed to Luke. "Drink. Then we'll talk."

"Yes, doctor."

Luke started chugging down a bottle. Jenna was right. He felt the semi-cool, clear water race miraculously through his dissipated body, refreshing parts he didn't know he still had. He gulped down the second bottle and asked for more.

"Take these," Jenna said, handing him two aspirin and a can

of orange juice. "Running several miles in this heat made your blood more viscous. These will help. They'll also help your headache."

"How'd you know I had a headache?"

"Your brow's scrunched up like an accordion."

He swallowed the aspirin and leaned against the temple wall. After a few minutes, his trembling slowed, his pain and nausea eased, and he began to feel almost human. He drank another two liters of water and felt there was a decent chance he would rejoin humanity.

From beside the temple, Miguel Ramirez shouted, "We pitch camp here tonight."

My camp be pitched, Luke thought.

"Yeah, enough fun for one day," Baines Thomas said. He turned and faced Luke. "Luke, what the hell is this all about?"

Luke explained how he'd overheard the conspirators in the Renaissance Center, how Jenna and he had been kidnaped, how they escaped, discovered Thomas and Mackay were the assassins' targets, traced them to the Yucatan and tracked them to the ruin.

Thomas and Mackay stared back as though he'd confided that aliens abducted the president.

Thomas walked over and placed his hand on Luke's good shoulder. "First of all, thanks for saving our asses. Second of all, your raise is approved."

"I just got a raise last month." Luke smiled.

"And you just earned my exceptional performance raise."

"Can't argue with the boss."

Thomas ran his fingers through his black hair, then turned toward Redstone. "Hank, do the police have any idea which advertising agency is behind this?"

"Not yet," Redstone said, rubbing his swollen, blue-black ankle. "We're trying to determine which agency has the best chance of getting the World Motors account if you and Mr. Mackay were ... no longer around."

"That's damn near impossible to determine," Thomas said.

"But," Luke said, "we identified major agencies that would love an automotive account."

"Over fifty, I bet," Thomas suggested.

"Over one hundred."

Thomas's eyebrows raised.

"We also believe," Redstone said, "someone at the agency is working with someone at World Motors. Someone very high up. Someone who could *force* the agency switch. Any thoughts on who, Mr. Mackay?"

Mackay stared back somewhere between shock and amazement. "No. I can't believe *any* of our top people are capable of this."

"Who's most likely to gain from your disappearance?"

Mackay's eyes narrowed. "Impossible to say. I've got five years left, and we haven't determined my successor."

"No clear choice?"

Mackay rubbed his beard. "Not really. And these days who can predict what a board of directors will do. You saw them take over GM a while back."

"What about your top people?"

"I've known them for over thirty years. They can't be involved in this. They're trusted, loyal colleagues."

"So was GM's Ignacio Lopez," Thomas said. "Before he snuck off to Volkswagen with what people said were secret plans."

Mackay smiled. "*Touché.*"

"Even so," Redstone said, "we're checking out your top management."

Mackay nodded, clearly stunned by the strong probability that one of his top people had conspired to kill him.

"What about Torres?" Thomas asked.

"The Belize police are checking his home and bank accounts," Redstone said. "We'll try to link him to an agency or someone at World Motors."

A *cargador* walked up and smiled. "Time for the dinners."

Luke realized he was famished. The aromas of garlic, onions and spices filled the air. The group walked over to the small campfire and sat on folding stools. The *cargadores* brought over huge serving dishes filled with Yucatan specialties.

Baines Thomas pointed to a dish covered with leaves. "What's under the leaves?"

"*Cocinita pibil,*" the cook said, "pork marinated with the juice of sour orange and special flavorings. *Delicioso!* And here is some *pavo relleno negro,* turkey with spicy chopped pork and beef."

"What's this?" Jenna asked.

"*Papadzules*—corn tortillas stuffed with chopped eggs and cucumber seeds, covered with tomato sauce. *Buen provecho!* Enjoy them all!"

Luke did, and each bite pumped new strength into his dissipated muscles. Several platefuls and bottles of potent, red, Mexican wine later, they finished dinner.

He looked at the early evening sky beyond the observatory, the shadows creeping across the ball court. Through an opening in the trees, he saw an magnificent indigo and purple sunset. The fading sun anointed the grey buildings with warm, tawny-red hues. Toxuum was seducing him and he was almost too exhausted to enjoy it.

He turned to Jenna and said, "I be sated."

"Me too."

They stood, said good night and walked over near the temple where the *cargadores* had hung hammocks in a small clump of trees.

"Hammocks?" Luke said. "A sleeping bag would be more comfortable."

"Miguel said poisonous snakes might crawl into it."

"Gee—I was hoping someone else might." He helped her into a yellow, nylon hammock, then rolled himself into another hammock two feet away.

He lay on his back, exhaled slowly. Not your basic day at the office, he thought. Amazingly, he was still a living, breathing part of the universe. From the ebony jungle, insects chanted their nightly mantra. Frogs croaked a Gregorian chant. Stars sprinkled the Mexican night sky like tossed diamonds.

"Look," Jenna said, pointing up. "The Big Dipper."

He nodded.

She reached over and held his hand. "You okay?"

"Very okay. Everything's worked out. Thomas and Mackay are safe. Garcia called and said there's a good chance Luis will live. Tomorrow we'll return to Cancun and fly back to the good old U.S. of A. and determine who's behind this."

"We're lucky."

"Uh-huh," he whispered, but something he couldn't define told him they may need more luck soon.

Fifty

MASON BENNETT'S knuckles whitened on his binoculars as he watched Luke and Jenna settle into their hammocks. Bennett stood with Carlos, Paco and Manny in the jungle blackness about sixty yards away. More than anything, he wanted to empty his gun into Manny's stupid face.

Manny's shortcut had taken them six miles out of the way, wasted twenty-three minutes and prevented them from catching the police in time. His reward would be an eye opener—a .44 caliber bullet through his cornea. But first Bennett needed Manny and the others to handle the police and find out whether

Torres had killed the Twins.

Bennett studied the group of men sitting around the campfire, particularly two men he thought were Mackay and Thomas. He needed to see their faces. He heard chatter, bits of Spanish and English. What concerned him was their tone. It was not subdued or mournful. He watched three short men stand and carry serving pans to a nearby table and begin cleaning them. *Cargadores.* Four men remained seated.

Minutes later, the two men stood and faced the fire, the flames flickering onto their faces.

Donald Mackay and Baines Thomas!

Torres fucked up.

Bennett gripped a branch so hard it punctured his palm. He closed his eyes and forced himself to calm down. Soon his breathing returned to normal, his muscles loosened, his anger dissipated.

He would still complete his assignment. They'd kill everyone at the campfire, drag their bodies into the blistering jungle, cover them with branches. The jungle would do the rest.

He watched Thomas and Mackay walk over and roll into their hammocks. The *cargadores* finished cleaning the dishes and walked to the sleeping area. Within fifteen minutes everyone had bedded down for the night.

Carlos nudged Bennett. "Now?"

"No. We wait until everyone's been sleeping a while."

Two hours later, the campfire had shrunk to red embers. Darkness blanketed the sleeping area and the temple. Everyone had been asleep for at least an hour.

"Now," Bennett whispered to the three men.

"You coming?" Carlos asked.

"I'm staying here in case anyone tries to escape along this path. Meet me here when you're done."

They nodded, stepped from the jungle and moved silently across the ball court toward the campfire. A large cloud slid over the moon, further shrouding them in darkness.

Bennett watched them move closer. Fifty yards, thirty, fifteen.

Carlos stopped and pointed toward the people each man would kill. Manny and Paco nodded and inched toward their sleeping prey. This should be quick, Bennett thought.

Then suddenly he saw a shadowy form—human—dart from behind a ruin wall and stop behind Paco. Paco, Carlos and Manny dropped their guns, put their hands up.

Bennett's gut twisted. *This is not happening,* he thought, pulling out his handgun.

* * *

Luke felt someone shaking his arm. He heard voices, rubbed his eyes, saw Jenna pointing toward Miguel Ramirez, gun in hand, escorting three men toward the fire.

Luke reached for his gun, then remembered it fell into the *cenote* water. He rolled from his hammock, grimacing as sharp pain spiked through his shoulder gash. Other sleepers began to awaken.

As Ramirez led the three intruders close to the fire, Luke studied their sweaty faces in the flickering yellow light. Two men looked vaguely familiar. Walking closer, he realized he was looking at the two Latins he'd seen in the Renaissance Center. His hope rekindled. They could provide important information, like who hired them.

"We have visitors," Ramirez said.

Thomas, Mackay, Redstone and the *cargadores* approached the campfire.

Then it happened.

The dark, muscular man yanked a gun from his boot.

"Duck, Miguel!" Luke shouted.

Miguel leapt sideways as two bullets whisked past his head. He fired back, hitting the man above the left eye. The man froze, stumbled and fired twice into the ground, then collapsed face first into the burning embers, showering fiery sparks fifteen feet into the night darkness.

Thomas and Mackay ran over to Miguel, who appeared

unhurt. Luke pulled the heavy intruder from the fire, turned him over and grimaced at an ember burning into the man's eye. He flicked the ember off as Jenna brushed more crimson coals from his face and hands.

Luke turned back to the other two intruders.

They were gone.

* * *

Bennett saw Carlos and Manny running toward him. He waved them over, and they all sprinted down a narrow pathway toward their motorscooters two hundred yards ahead.

He saw no one chasing them and let Carlos and Manny run slightly ahead. They were morons! Major liabilities who knew too much. Risks he didn't need.

Bennett ran closer to them, lifted his gun and shot each man in the back of the head. They collapsed like sacks of cement. He leapt over their bodies and sprinted toward the scooters.

He heard footsteps behind him.

Looking back, he saw the silhouette of a man—a tall, thin man—fifty yards back, running fast, gaining.

Bennett jumped over a log and saw the glint of the motor scooters just thirty feet ahead. He reached the four scooters, pumped bullets into three engines, jumped on his scooter and drove off.

Turning, he saw the tall man—Luke Tanner—was only twenty yards behind.

Bennett spun out of the small clearing, kicking up pebbles and dirt. He hit the gas and pulled away. To his astonishment, Tanner had anticipated his direction, cut the angle and was on him.

Tanner dove.

Bennett turned left, felt Tanner's fingers scrape his leg and tennis shoe, pulling on a lace, as the scooter roared away. Bennett fired two shots back at Tanner, who jerked and rolled under some bushes. *Got him!*

He fired three more shots and the bushes went stone still.

Bennett sped off and breathed out slowly through his teeth. A little closer than he liked. But he was safe. They couldn't pursue him on foot, but they'd use Torres's phone to warn local police to look for a man on a scooter. He hoped they did. Soon, he'd be driving out of the jungle in the van. Then he'd take Highway 180 northeast to Cancun.

There, he'd concentrate on his *backup* plan. He'd always preferred it anyway. Klug had insisted on the jungle accident.

The backup plan was also an accident. But cleaner, smarter, easier to execute, and best of all, no evidence would ever be found.

Fifty One

LUKE WATCHED helplessly as gas and oil poured from the motorscooters. He smelled cordite and gasoline. Ramirez tried, but couldn't start them. Luke stuck his finger in a bullet hole and realized a bullet had nearly put a hole in him.

"*Muerto*," Ramirez said, fingering an oily crankcase. He threw his hands in the air and kicked the useless scooter on its side.

Luke memorized the license number in case they'd been bought or rented with a credit card.

Back at camp, Ramirez phoned in a description of the man on the scooter to the Chichen Itza *Policía*. Luke knew his description was sketchy, but at least the police knew they were looking for a man on a red motorscooter. How many people drove out of the jungle on a red Yahama scooter in the middle of the night?

Where would he drive out? Would he drive out? Perhaps he had a hideout.

Luke and Ramirez walked past *cargadores* carrying the two dead men toward the temples. Luke approached Jenna near the campfire and explained how the man escaped.

"What if he comes back?" she asked.

"If he does, Ramirez and the *cargadores* are standing guard all night."

"While you *sleep*."

He saw concern in her eyes. "Yes, Doctor."

They strolled back and flopped into their hammocks. After chatting a few minutes, he closed his eyes and tried to sleep, but he was too wired. His body craved rest, but his mind roller-coastered from hissing vipers to slashing knives to choking on *cenote* water. Every few seconds he would jerk awake. Finally, exhaustion pulled him into a nightmarish sleep.

* * *

Dishes clattered and he awoke. Luke squinted into brilliant shafts of sunshine and heard voices. How long had he slept? His watch said over seven hours. Amazing. Birds whooped and chirped and cawed and whistled like a cacophonous jungle alarm clock. His muscles were stiff, but rested. The aroma of fresh coffee and bacon brought saliva to his mouth. Looking around, he saw the others were clustered around the campfire, eating breakfast.

Then he saw Jenna. She sat nearby on a large block of limestone, sipping coffee, staring at a temple as though she'd formed a spiritual bond with it. The morning sun washed her face and hair in soft gold. The effect was overwhelming. How could anyone who'd nearly drowned in a river, fallen in a swamp, and trudged miles through a steamy jungle look so beautiful? Despite her beauty, the woman clearly needed a full-time bodyguard. He was available for the job. He was ready.

She turned and smiled at him and in that instant, he knew. Some life decisions are made instantly, others take a lifetime. Easing out of his hammock, he stretched, walked over and planted a serious kiss on her cheek.

"You're after my coffee," she said, pulling her cup away.

"Your affections, ma'am."

She smiled.

"But coffee will help me get over my nightmare," he said.

"About what?" She handed him her cup.

"Us," he said, sipping some and watching sun dance on her cobalt eyes.

"Tell me more."

"We didn't live happily ever after."

"Why?" she asked.

"Godzilla ate Cleveland."

"Bet it gave him gas."

"Yep. But it made me think—"

"The gas?"

"No," he said, smiling and trying to dial up the appropriate seriousness to his voice. "It made me think that these last two days from hell have been a wake-up call."

"You haven't exactly been sleeping."

"But I have..."

She brushed hair back off her forehead and looked at him. "So tell me, Rip Van Luke, what have you learned?"

Although she appeared to expect a humorous response, it was time to level. "I'm not quite sure. But I know I've been living my life...sort of part-way. Holding back, I guess."

"Holding what back?"

"The rest of living. There's a better, smarter way to live. Living means living fully, all the way, taking certain risks."

"Such as?"

"Marriage and family."

"These are risks?"

"They are when my condition might cut them short."

Her right eyebrow arched as she clearly caught his seriousness. "So now you'd like to live life fully?"

"Yes, but ..." He was unsure how to proceed.

"Yes, but?"

"It's unfair to ask a woman to share her life with someone who might not be there in a few years. Someone who might leave her alone with children."

"This woman," she said, her eyes playful, "have you asked her yet?"

He swallowed the lump in his throat. This was harder than he thought. "Not quite yet."

She nodded, smiled. "So what else have you learned?"

"That I could be hit by a falling television commercial light. That you could pick up one of a hundred fatal diseases at the hospital—next week. That I love you. Stuff like that."

She smiled. "You should have more nightmares. So what are you really saying?"

"What I'm really saying is that before radiation seeps through the hole in the ozone layer and shrivels our reproductive organs to sterile raisins, I'd like to ask you to marry me and maybe even do the family thing."

"Wow, do I hear a proposal in there?"

"You do."

She stared at him without blinking. "Luke, this is so sudden!" She cupped her hands over her eyes, then shook her head from side to side for what seemed like a month.

She wasn't ready. He should have known. He began to panic, realizing he should have asked her later, at a more appropriate time and place. How could he expect her to think clearly after she'd barely escaped death twice in the last twenty-four hours.

She removed her hands from her eyes and looked up grinning. "I'm not doing anything for the next few decades."

His body melted. "Do I hear an acceptance in there?"

"You do."

They kissed and embraced, and Luke was overwhelmed with

love for the woman in his arms. Whistles, hoots and applause rocketed over toward them from the breakfasters. Luke and Jenna stood and bowed.

"The choppers will be here in minutes," she said. "Why don't you grab some breakfast?"

"I'll use a fork," he said, sauntering away.

"Fork-get I asked," she shouted.

"Knife comeback."

"Wanna spoon later?" she asked, smiling.

He was still laughing as he stacked his plate with scrambled eggs, thick strips of crispy bacon, fried Mexican peppers and onions, and hot, buttery biscuits. He scarfed it all down and went back for seconds. He calculated he'd consumed a gazillion calories and burned off just as many in the last twelve hours. He also noticed, with enormous relief, that he didn't feel the frightening nausea and joint pain he'd felt last night. Perhaps he'd escaped a relapse.

Ten minutes later he watched two large helicopters nestle onto the ancient ball court. Garcia stepped from the first, ran over and shook hands with everyone. Medics jumped from the second chopper.

"Everybody okay?" Garcia asked.

"Everybody but them," Luke said, pointing to the corpses in the Temple shade.

"How's Luis?" Jenna asked.

Garcia smiled. "The doctor, he said Luis will be okay. The bullet miss his important things. Also we pick up Juan de los Santos. His leg will be okay too, thanks to you, doctor."

Jenna blushed slightly.

Minutes later, with everyone on board, the two choppers floated up over the jungle. As they flew over the bath house, Luke looked down and felt his chest tighten. Cesar Torres's body was probably still down there, skewered on the stalagmite, arms and legs flailing.

Luke turned to Garcia. "What about Torres?"

"This afternoon the divers go down and remove his body.

Maybe they find clues in his clothings."

"If they find him."

Garcia stared back.

"The current was fast, pulling us down into that river."

Garcia nodded. "*Sí*. If the current pulled him into the underground river, we never find him."

At Chichen Itza, the helicopter carrying the corpses landed at the *Aeropista*, while the chopper carrying Luke, Jenna, Redstone, Garcia, Ramirez, Thomas and Mackay sped over the jungle canopy toward Cancun.

Baines Thomas and Don Mackay broke out a fresh deck of cards and began playing gin rummy.

Luke turned to Garcia. "Anything on the guy on the scooter?"

Garcia shook his head from side to side. "Nothing. Police are watching the main jungle paths. They've seen no red Razz motor scooter. No tracks either."

"Could he have driven out somewhere else?" Redstone asked.

"*Sí*. Sixty miles of jungle. Or maybe he still hides in the jungle."

"Or maybe he left the scooter and drove out with someone," Luke suggested.

Garcia nodded. "On Pepe's airstrip, we find fresh tire tracks coming *out* of the jungle. Firestones. They come on some new Ford vans. We look for such vans now."

Minutes later the chopper drifted over *Aeropuerto Internacional de Cancún* and touched down beside the main terminal buildings. Through the window, Luke saw tourists streaming from the parking lots and busses into the terminal.

The chopper set down on the tarmac and they stepped outside. They were suddenly surrounded by two phalanxes of armed *Seguridad de Aeropuerto* police and nervous officials, who hurried them toward the airport. Luke saw police marksmen, weapons drawn, poised on the roof and enough sun-glassed security men for a presidential visit. Cancun was making damn sure there were no last-minute assassination attempts on *Señor* Mackays and *Señor* Thomas, whose safe departure ensured the safe arrival of tourist dollars.

The airport manager led them down a long marble corridor, and into his office where a smiling white-coated waiter offered them strong Mexican coffee and freshly-baked chocolate cookies. Luke grabbed a cookie.

The manager gestured for all to sit, then smiled nervously at his two important guests. "I hope you enjoyed your hunting trip before the...ah...unfortunate incident?"

"We were promised an exciting trip," Thomas said.

"Which we got," Mackay added, smiling.

The manager's rigid face collapsed in a smile. "We apologize for any difficulty this despicable guide, this ah...Cesar Torres, caused you. He's from Belize, you know." He said "Belize" as though it were a leper colony.

"Remember Belize, Don?" Thomas asked. "Deep-sea fishing in that storm."

"Hard to forget," Don said, and began telling the story, which Luke had heard before.

Yawning, Luke checked his watch. The World Motors corporate jet wouldn't be ready for thirty minutes. His legs were stiff, and his bladder was maxed out, thanks to Jenna who'd made him drink enough water to hydrate a herd of yak. He stood, stretched, and whispered to her, "I'm going to take a walk."

"Want company?"

"Sure, if you don't mind standing at a urinal."

"My life's dream."

They left the room and strolled down the long, gleaming marble corridor toward some boarding gates. Stretching his legs muscles felt good. They walked in silence and Luke tried to put the last few days into perspective.

Jenna nudged his elbow. "What's wrong?"

"Nothing. Just thinking."

"Thinking what?"

"That the person I love is alive and walking beside me. That Thomas and Mackay are safe and will be protected by the police in Detroit. That Luis and Juan de los Santos will recover. That many of the bad guys are pushing up daises. And that the good guys have basically won."

"But ..."

He felt her eyes on him, wondering how she always knew when he held something back. "But we still don't know which agency is behind this. Or which World Motors executive is involved. Or if the assassins will strike again."

"Which gnaws at you?"

"It gnaws," he said.

They turned a corner and were engulfed in a crowd of noisy tourists. Most were American vacationers—tanned, burned, peeled; college kids and brain-fried parents dragging squealing toddlers with red, blistered noses.

"Hang on," he said, grabbing Jenna's hand and weaving her through the avalanche of flight bags, sequined sombreros, wood carvings, bulging suitcases, a blurring mosaic of multicolored bermudas, short shorts, sweatshirts, tennis shoes and sandals. A blend of cigar smoke, coconut suntan lotion and Novocaine filled his nostrils.

They escaped for a couple of feet, but quickly found themselves swallowed up in another group of boisterous tourists.

Luke stopped. Something freeze-framed in his mind. Something he'd just seen. Something on a man passing him—also worn by the man on the motorscooter. What was it?

"Luke, what's wrong?" Jenna asked.

He turned and looked back at the crowd. A tall man was staring back at him.

"It might be him."

"Who?"

"The man on the motorcycle."

"Which man?"

"The tall one with the backpack."

"I don't see him."

Luke started walking toward him. The man glanced back again, saw Luke following, picked up his pace.

It is him.

The man disappeared behind some people, then around a corner. Seconds later, Luke turned the corner and found himself engulfed by a swarm of grade-schoolers holding hands and three older nuns. He squeezed between the nuns and kids and resumed the chase.

But the man had vanished.

Luke saw the restrooms.

He's in one. Or down a side hallway. Luke entered the men's restroom and checked under the stall doors. Empty. He checked the woman's restroom, apologized to a woman breast-feeding an infant, dashed outside and tried the janitor's door. It was locked.

Luke ran down the hallway toward the main check-in area, searched every cranny without success. In the main shopping area, hundreds of tourists milled about the shops. Small children darted between groups of adults. Art poster display units partly blocked his view of the area. It was impossible to see one person in the sea of hundreds. The man could be ten feet away, watching him.

Luke checked some shops, then the ticket counters. Nothing. After a couple of minutes he knew he'd lost him. Luke ran back to the airport manager's office.

"What's wrong?" Redstone asked.

"I just saw him."

"Who?"

"The man on the scooter last night."

The airport manager pushed a phone button and spoke rapidly. The head of security ran into his office thirty seconds later.

Fifty Two

BENNETT HAD been standing on a toilet tank when Tanner burst into the men's room and looked under the stall door. Tanner had pushed the door open a few inches, then hurried to the next stall. Life was a game of inches. Two more, and Tanner would have caught a bullet between the eyes.

Bennett stepped down and walked to the mirror. How had Tanner recognized him? Tanner hadn't seen his face last night, and he'd been looking down when they passed in the airport crowd. Bennett looked at his shirt and pants. They were different from last night. He straightened the strap of his backpack.

The backpack! It was strapped to the scooter last night. I'll ditch the backpack and change my appearance.

Quickly, he returned to the stall, locked the door and unzipped the large, green Cabela. He took off his shirt and pants, stuffed them deep into the backpack, then pulled on a beige shirt and pants. He grabbed his theatrical kit, removed a grey wig and beard, put them on. He stuffed several more items into a yellow, duty-free bag, tucked his plastic handgun under his shirt, and hid the backpack beneath newspapers in the trash bin.

He opened a small mirror, adjusted the wig and beard, applied grey paste to his eyebrows. His face was older, fuller. He stooped a little. He opened the stall door and checked himself in the large mirror.

He was a different person. Twenty years older and no backpack.

He opened the door and shuffled out into the hallway. Tanner was nowhere. Merging in with some noisy tourists, Bennett headed toward the main check-in counter area.

He knew Tanner would have described him as an Anglo-American. The police would be waiting at gates for U.S.-bound flights, studying each male passenger closely, conducting passport-to-face checks. Even though he had a passport that matched his new face, he wouldn't risk it. He knew a safer way out.

He walked to the main check-in area and got in line behind a family at the AeroMexico counter. Four policemen rushed past and headed down a corridor, checking out each male.

Bennett saw another cop outside briefing taxi drivers. The cop touched his shirt and trousers, then gestured as though carrying a large backpack. One taxi driver nodded yes and pointed toward the parking area. Excellent. The police would be diverted for a while.

The ticket agent handed boarding passes to the family and pointed them toward the gates. Bennett stepped to the counter and smiled at the young, dark-haired attendant.

"Good morning, sir," she said, smiling, somehow knowing he was American.

"Hi there. I'd like to get on that Acapulco flight, if possible."

"Oh, Acapulco may be filled, sir. Let's see." She tapped away at her keyboard.

Bennett glanced over his shoulder and saw *Seguridad de Aeropuerto* police teams positioned at the major passageways leading to the departure gates. They were also guarding the airport exits, checking the passport of each male.

He looked outside and saw several *Policia de Cancún* vehicles swerve up to the curb. Police officers jumped out and took up positions along the front of the airport. He noticed a number of police dragnetting the parking lot.

"You're lucky, sir," the agent said. "We have two seats left. Name please?"

"John Davis."

"How will you be paying, Mr. Davis?"

"Cash." He pulled out a thick wad of one hundred dollar bills and paid.

"Any luggage?"

"Just carry-on."

Bennett watched two policemen stop a middle-aged American wearing a grey shirt and blue pants. The policemen asked him questions, and the American became a little defensive, which caused the police to become even more interested in him. Perfect.

"Departure is at Gate 8, Mr. Davis," she said, handing him his ticket and boarding pass. "The flight is boarding any minute."

"Thanks." He walked toward the passageway.

Ahead, he noticed the policemen were studying each man walking through the passage. Bennett blended into a cluster of people and shuffled past the police without incident. He stepped through the metal detector, which again failed to detect his plastic Glock.

He saw cops briefing duty-free store clerks. He stepped into a crowded souvenir shop, bought a white *I Luv Cancun* sweatshirt and put it on. He walked back toward the departure area, more relaxed, knowing he'd board any minute. Four cops in a golf cart beeped past going the other way. Outside, sirens blared.

He strolled into the sprawling departure lounge. Hundreds of vacationers and business people were scrunched down in chairs or milling about waiting for their flights. Children scurried around thier parents. The departure gates were fanned out in a circle. He walked over and blended into the crowd of passengers near Gate 8.

Bennett breathed out slowly. He had his boarding ticket. The attendant appeared ready to board passengers. The police were searching for a younger man with a backpack.

Looking back, he saw more people streaming toward him into the already jammed gate area. Only three policemen scanned the massive crowd.

Within minutes he'd be flying to Acapulco.

At the same time, his pursuers would be flying home on their shiny Learjet. They'd be celebrating, congratulating themselves for stopping the assassination, sipping champagne perhaps. They would not notice the black AM/FM radio cassette player hidden in the small luggage compartment. Even if they did, they would not know it contained four pounds of CX explosives and an altitude trigger mechanism.

At thirteen thousand feet, the radio would, so to speak— turn on with a bang—and sprinkle the Caribbean with tiny pieces of aircraft and passengers.

"We're boarding now," said the attendant as she opened the departure door to his flight.

Fifty Three

LUKE, REDSTONE, Jenna, and two policemen followed Pablo Munoz, *Director de Seguridad de Aeropuerto*, down the long passageway to the departure lounge. Luke noticed that Munoz, an athletic forty-year-old with gleaming black hair and brown eyes, carefully screened each male he passed. Munoz had assumed command immediately and mobilized airport security forces within sixty seconds. Although he limped slightly, everyone had difficulty keeping up with him.

Luke knew they had to arrest the man before he boarded a flight or left the airport. So far, the police had found no one fitting the man's description at U.S.-bound gates. Luke feared he'd changed clothes, dumped the backpack, avoided security, and was halfway to Cancun by now.

Entering the departure area, Luke saw throngs of passengers, at least five hundred, swarming around the nine gates. Many looked American. Many had buried their faces in newspapers and magazines.

Flights at Gates 1 through 4 wouldn't leave for more than forty-five minutes. Gates 5 through 9 were departing soon. Pablo Munoz approached the ticket attendant at Gate 5.

"Francisco, we're looking for a man, around forty, wearing a grey shirt and blue pants. He was carrying a green backpack."

The attendant, a middle-aged man with a port-wine mark on his right cheek, stared at the floor, then looked up. "Lots of grey shirts and blue pants. No green backpack."

"If you see him, hold the aircraft and call me."

The attendant nodded.

Luke and the group followed Munoz to Gate 6, where Munoz interrogated the tall young female agent with rose-colored glasses.

"I saw someone like that five minutes ago."

"Where?" Munoz asked.

"He got off the flight from Veracruz."

"Got *off*?"

"*Sí*. A teenager."

Luke heard the loudspeaker click on, then a soft-voiced female announcer said in Spanish, then perfect English:

> *Ladies and gentlemen, AeroMexico Flight 332 to Acapulco, departing from Gate 8, is boarding at this time. And AeroMexico Flight 649 to Mexico City is departing from Gate 9 at this time. Please have your boarding passes ready.*

Luke and the others followed Munoz to Gate 7, where the ticket agent recalled no one fitting the description. Luke scanned the crowd of laughing tourists and rowdy U.S. college students directly behind him. None resembled the man.

Jenna touched his shoulder. "He's probably driving to Cancun."

Luke nodded. "If he's still here, he's changed clothes and ditched the backpack." Luke thought of the backpack, but sensed he'd recognized something else about the man. Something the man had worn then and now. *What was it?*

They stepped up to the Gate 8 counter. The chubby ticket agent said the only backpacks he'd seen were worn by two ten-year-old school girls.

As Munoz led the group to Gate 9, Jenna pulled Luke aside.

"I'm going to check this flight monitor," she said, pointing behind her to a monitor suspended from the ceiling.

"For what?"

"Flights he might have *just* taken. The stewardesses could check passengers. Police in the destination cities could check departing passengers."

"Makes sense," Luke said, following Munoz over to Gate 9.

As Munoz talked to the agent, Luke studied the passengers mulling around the door to the aircraft. Most were tourists, the rest appeared to be Mexican and American business travelers. They inched toward the door. All shapes: thin, muscular, heavy, tall, short, old, young, male, female. None resembled the man.

He turned and scanned the Gate 8 passengers handing their boarding passes to the agent. Again no one looked remotely like the man. Turning back, one body shape caught Luke's eye. Roughly the same shape, weight and height as the man, but a completely different man. This guy was *old*, stooped, grey-haired, different clothes, a full beard. And he carried a yellow shopping bag—no backpack. Couldn't possibly be him.

Still something about the man seemed familiar. The shape of the head, maybe? Nose and eyes? Luke wasn't sure. The man's legs were obscured by the massive, red-plaid suitcase of the young woman ahead wearing a St. Marys College of California sweatshirt.

Passengers inched closer to the door and the young woman rolled her red suitcase forward, revealing the old man's shoes.

Luke looked down at them and felt his stomach clench.

He was looking at high-top Converse tennis shoes, robin's-egg blue—the exact same shoes worn by the man on the motorscooter. The shoe Luke's fingers had scraped. How many of those shoes could there be in this airport?

Is that him?

Luke needed a closer look.

The old man seemed to sense Luke staring at him. He glanced at Luke, turned back and calmly inched closer to the door.

A young, excited policeman brushed past Luke and grabbed Pablo Munoz's arm.

"We have him!" the policeman said.

"Where?" Munoz asked.

"Main check-in lounge. Green backpack. Blue pants. American. Trying to leave the airport. He fits the description."

"Let's go," Munoz said.

"Wait," Luke said, grabbing Munoz's arm. "A man directly behind me in the Gate 8 line is wearing the same light-blue tennis shoes the motorscooter guy wore last night and the guy I saw earlier. He's about the same shape. He's older, has grey hair and a beard. Could be a disguise. But the blue Converse shoes...they're not common."

"Which old man?"

"In the white Cancun sweatshirt. Yellow shopping bag. Behind Jenna."

Munoz looked at the line and frowned. "I don't see him."

"I don't see Jenna," Redstone said.

Luke spun around.

Jenna and the man were gone.

Luke ran to a young woman in the St. Mary's sweatshirt. "Where's the old man who was standing here?"

"Down there." She pointed to a narrow hallway ten feet away.

"Did he take the woman standing here?"

"Yes. I don't think she wanted to go."

Luke's heart slammed against his chest. He sprinted with Munoz and the group into the hallway. It was empty. They ran to the corner, peered around, saw the man pushing Jenna toward the end of the long hall.

"Stop!" Munoz shouted, showing his handgun.

The man pushed a gun against Jenna's temple. He spun her between himself and the police and continued backing down the hall.

"She's dies if you follow."

The police froze.

Luke watched helplessly as the man dragged Jenna around the corner. Leaning against the wall, Luke felt his body turn to mush. Perspiration blanketed his skin. Jenna was being held by a physcopath who'd kill her the moment he didn't need her. Munoz spoke into his walkie-talkie in rapid Spanish, directing security people to seal off the area.

"We won't follow," Munoz said, "We *wait*."

"Remember," Luke said, "he killed his own people last night."

Munoz nodded. "Our people are well-trained in hostage situations." He ordered two men to remain in the hall, then led Luke and others quickly back through the passenger lounge, down the long corridor toward the main terminal.

Two hundred feet down the corridor, Munoz unlocked a door. The group followed him inside a dimly-lit hallway that seemed to wind back toward where Jenna and the man were last seen. Gun drawn, Munoz led them down a short staircase and paused beside a corner. He peered around it, then glanced back, puzzled. "He's not there."

"Where could he be?" Redstone asked.

"In one of two offices. Or heading back toward the departure lounge." Munoz whispered into his phone, "You see him?"

"No," crackled a voice.

"Keep watching. We're checking out the hall offices now."

Munoz led them down the hall to the first office door. Munoz and Redstone positioned themselves on either side; Luke and the others stood back.

On a count of three, Munoz and Redstone bolted into the office. Two terrified secretaries spun around from their computers.

"Everything okay, Felicia?" Munoz asked.

"*Sí*," Felicia whispered, her gaze riveted on Munoz's gun.

"You see a man holding a young woman?"

"No."

"Okay. Relax. Lock this door. Don't let anyone in unless you know them."

She nodded.

Munoz led the police group down the hallway to the second office door. Munoz and Redstone again positioned themselves on each side of the door, then bolted inside. The office was empty except for some used chairs and desks stacked along a wall.

Luke saw a door to a storeroom. Munoz stepped to the door, opened it, flipped on the light, and burst in.

One wooden chair.

They dashed back outside to the hallway, where Munoz spoke into the phone. "Any sign of them?"

"No."

"Did you check the hallway?"

"*Sí*. They are not there."

Munoz looked puzzled.

"Where are they?" Luke asked.

"Only one possibility. The back stairs."

"Back stairs to where?"

"Outside."

Fifty Four

BENNETT DRAGGED Jenna down a stairwell to the airport's ground level. He'd use her as a hostage until he escaped the airport. After that she was excess baggage.

His threat to kill her was working. The police had not followed. But they would, and they'd alert all security personnel to look for a bearded man wearing a white *Cancun* sweatshirt and light-blue high-top tennis shoes.

The *shoes*—the fucking tennis shoes—is what Tanner recognized, Bennett realized. Last night he scraped one when he dove for me.

Bennett pushed her down a dark hallway, turned the corner, and saw a luggage rack stacked with baggage tagged "Caribe Sun Tours." He told her to face the wall, then pulled off his beard and sweatshirt, unzipped a suitcase and looked inside.

Kids clothes!

He unzipped another suitcase—woman's clothing. He opened a third case and rifled through men's shirts, suits, ties. He grabbed a pair of tan shoes and put them on.

As he pulled Jenna toward the door leading outside—the door swung open. Two baggage handlers stepped inside and stared at them. Wrong place, wrong time.

"I'm lost...," Bennett said, smiling. *"Dónde estan las departure gates?"*

The shorter handler pointed upstairs.

"Gracias," Bennett said, then pulled his silenced gun and shot both men in the head. They stared blankly, then slumped beside the rack, eyes locked open, blood skidding across the tile floor to a drain.

Jenna gasped and started to scream.

Bennett shoved the gun against her temple. "Another sound, and you die." *Which is probably the smart thing to do,* he thought, since the police were looking for him *and* her. Alone, he'd draw less attention, especially in the baggage handler's uniform. She was slowing him down.

He should do her now.

Fifty Five

"IT'S BEEN kicked open," Munoz said, as they reached a metal door.

Luke pushed the door all the way open, and followed Munoz down the cramped stairwell to the ground floor. As Luke passed some baggage carts something red on the floor caught his eye.

"Wait!" he said, swallowing hard, staring at a stream of blood worming its way over gray tiles to the drainage slits.

Everyone turned and looked at the blood.

His heart in his mouth, he leaned against the wall, unwilling to follow the blood to its source behind the cart. *Please, no.* Slowly,

Munoz rolled the luggage cart back and Luke saw that it was not Jenna. He melted with relief, then felt somewhat guilty for feeling it as he gazed at the bloodied bodies of two young men in their underwear.

Munoz bent down, fingered their necks for a pulse, shook his head from side to side. He barked into his phone for a doctor. Standing, he slammed his fist into a hard-sided suitcase, then hurried the group outside to a young mechanic working on a tractor.

"Hector," Munoz asked, "did you just see an Anglo, grey beard, maybe, six feet, probably wearing baggage handler overalls? He had a woman with him."

The mechanic ran his fingers through his straight, black hair. "I saw a new guy with a woman over near those three AeroMexico planes. But this man, he didn't have no beard."

"Thanks." Munoz said, and led the group over to the closest AeroMexico aircraft, a Boeing 737. They dashed up the stairs to the passenger compartment, where the crew was preparing to board passengers. Munoz flashed his badge to the chief stewardess, an attractive middle-aged woman. He explained the situation.

Luke studied her eyes as she tried to recall.

"I saw no such man or woman."

Two nearby stewardesses said they hadn't either.

"I saw them," said a deep voice.

Luke turned and saw a slender, dark-haired pilot leaning against the cockpit door.

"Where?" Munoz asked.

"They walked beneath my aircraft. Then they went over near that AeroMexico 767. Never saw them before. They looked Anglo."

"Did he wear light blue, high-top tennis shoes?" Luke asked.

"Regular shoes, tan I think."

"I saw his blue tennis shoes behind the luggage racks," Redstone said.

Munoz thanked the captain, hurried the group outside, then up the stairs of the 767. Inside, Luke saw the plane was filled with passengers. The chief stewardess approached them with a puzzled look. Munoz explained.

"Sorry. I've seen nobody like that," she said.

"He might have taken off the overalls," Luke said, "Did you see a man in a white *Cancun* sweatshirt?"

"*Sí.* Yes," she said, glancing over her shoulder. "In 6-C."

Luke turned and saw an obese, bald man paging through *TIME.* "Not him."

Luke heard a curtain zing open. He turned and saw a young dark-haired stewardess in the galley. "I saw two people like that."

"Where?" Munoz asked.

"By our baggage conveyor belt at the forward hold."

"What were they doing?"

"The man was looking at the belt. They rode up the belt, you know, like they were checking it, or the luggage."

"How long ago?"

"A few minutes."

"Did they ride it down?"

"I don't know. I've been very busy."

Munoz looked at Luke and Redstone, then turned to the pilot, who'd joined them. "Is the luggage compartment still open?"

"Yes," said the pilot, who'd joined them. "We're waiting for some Chicago baggage."

"Can you stop the Chicago baggage until we check out the luggage compartment?"

"Certainly," he said, turning and issuing instructions to his copilot.

"Can we enter the luggage compartment from here?" Munoz asked.

"No," the pilot said. "The only entrance is through the cargo door."

One minute later, Munoz, Redstone and Luke huddled with three anti-terrorist squad members beneath the tail of the aircraft. A baggage handler unfolded a diagram of the cargo hold, showed them where luggage, commercial cargo and mail pouches were stored and where the man might hide. Munoz rehearsed how they would enter and search.

"Remember, we assume he still has the woman," Munoz said. "We must *talk* him out of the plane. No shooting, unless he endangers her or others."

The group nodded, but Luke sensed the man would not surrender peacefully. As the group moved to the creaking conveyer belt, Luke's muscles hardened. He watched the anti-terrorist team climb aboard, ride the belt up to the cargo door and disappear inside. Then Luke followed Munoz and Redstone up the ramp.

Stepping inside, Luke bumped his head against the five-foot, nine-inch ceiling. When his eyes focused, he saw that luggage was stacked solidly to the front of the aircraft. The anti-terrorist men were already checking luggage, stacking it in the space by the door, tunneling a narrow pathway toward the front. Dusty, humid air blanketed him.

The group burrowed its way through suitcases and trunks. Many were large and plastered with colorful vacation stickers.

Luke's senses were on hyper-alert. Was Jenna in pain? Injured? Alive? Was she even on this plane? Sweat poured from his face as he looked behind a large suitcase and trunk. Ten feet further, he came upon a black storage chest, six-feet by three-feet. Its ornate brass clasp was open.

The anti-terrorist team surrounded the chest and aimed their weapons at the lid. Munoz tried to nudge it with his foot, but it was too heavy. He reached down, grabbed the lid, and jerked it up to reveal flowery red dresses, silk blouses, antique porcelain dolls, several books and tattered photo albums. An elderly woman's belongings.

Leaning back, Luke nudged a stack of luggage and something thudded behind him.

They spun around and aimed their weapons at a hard-sided red suitcase wobbling noisily on the floor.

"Why did that fall?" Munoz asked, his gun frozen on the case.

"I bumped it," Luke said. "Sorry."

Munoz nodded, still staring at the suitcase as though it would explode.

The heat was stifling as they neared the front of the cargo hold. Luke saw huge cartons of commercial cargo and sacks of mail large enough to conceal a man. The police group searched carefully, inch by inch, carton by carton, sack by sack. Everything appeared in order. Everything looked normal. There was no hint of Jenna and the man.

Luke remembered three other large aircraft moored nearby. Perhaps the man had taken her over to one or escaped elsewhere.

As Munoz and the others checked the last few cartons, Luke looked back toward the cargo door. Sunlight poured through the opening like a fat laser beam, bleaching nearby stacks of luggage. The rays reflected off something shiny in a wall cranny.

He walked back and saw it was a new shirt wrapped in cellophane. To the right, he saw two more shirts and a pair of folded jeans jammed into a crevice. A few feet away, more clothing was stuffed between bags. A suitcase had probably popped open, or a baggage handler had found his size but ditched it when he learned the police were boarding.

But something bothered him: *how* the clothes were lodged—and how they were placed in so many locations.

His eyes moved to a large green, military duffle bag. The bag was five-and-a-half-feet long, with "J. RAMOS" stenciled in white letters. The bag was full, but packed oddly, solid in some areas, sagging in others. Atop it, lay light luggage. He walked close to the duffle bag, saw more shirts and socks stuffed between nearby suitcases.

Placed there.

Something was wrong.

He stared at the area for several seconds before he realized the stenciled "R" on the duffle bag was *moving*, almost imperceptibly, up and down. Were his eyes playing tricks? Was a breeze ruffling the bag? No. The movement was too rhythmic.

The "R" was *breathing*.

A walkie-talkie crackled to life at the front end of the cargo hold where Munoz and the others were opening a large carton. Munoz took the walkie-talkie from his belt.

"We're holding an American with tan shoes and a white Cancun sweatshirt," said a faint, static-filled voice. "He's wearing a grey toupee, and he's very nervous."

"Where'd you find him?"

"Trying to board a Dallas flight."

"We'll be right there."

Munoz and the police started back toward the cargo door.

Luke hurried down the aisle and stopped them. "Wait!" he mouthed. Leaning close to Munoz, he whispered about the breathing duffle bag.

Munoz's eyes narrowed as he looked over Luke's shoulder. "Show me."

As Luke turned to show him, a cough erupted near the duffle bag, then a loud zip.

The man leapt from the bag, threw a large suitcase toward them and fired off two shots. Bullets thumped into baggage beside Luke's head. He hit the floor.

The man vanished behind suitcases.

Munoz and Redstone returned fire, but the shots missed. The man darted behind some hard-sided trunks near the door, then fired. Two bullets ripped past Luke's shoulder, pierced the ceiling.

Luke dropped behind some luggage, his eyes glued to a sticker of a bikini-clad sunbather inviting him to "Come Play In Acapulco!" He peered between two suitcases, saw the man's shadow moving on the wall.

Where is Jenna?

A few feet away, Munoz, Redstone, and the others were pinned down behind luggage. They couldn't move without being shot. Silence filled the cargo hold.

Then above him, Luke heard passengers start screaming.

Suddenly the man shot at something *outside* the cargo door. Police on the conveyer belt, Luke thought. But the police didn't fire back.

The man fired three more shots outside, pinging metal. No return fire. What the hell was he doing? And where were the police?

The man fired outside again. Ping! Ping! He was shooting at something metal beyond the conveyer belt. Luke tried to gauge where the bullets were striking. When he realized, he felt like he'd been speared in the heart.

The bastard was firing at the wing's *fuel cells*—filled with thousands of gallons of gasoline. *Trying* to set the wings on fire—so he could escape in the confusion while his pursuers burned in an inferno.

Luke shouted, "He's trying to ignite the fuel cells!"

"Bastardo!" Munoz cursed, as he rolled behind some bags and fired off three shots. The police unleashed a barrage of bullets toward the man, hoping to keep him from shooting at the wings. But the man pinged two more bullets into the wing.

Luke heard passengers screaming as they squeezed down the aisle to the door. Infants and children shrieked. The loudspeaker told passengers to leave their luggage and deplane calmly. But Luke sensed they knew they might get caught in the gunfire if they deplaned—or burned alive if they stayed. They were trapped and knew it.

The man fired again at the fuel cells.

"Fuego!" shouted a voice outside.

Fire, Luke realized. Bullets *had* ignited the fuel cells.

"Bomba de incendios!" Fire engines. Luke heard their distant sirens.

"Fuego!" a woman passenger screamed.

Luke knew the aircraft could explode in flames any second. He also knew he had the only possible angle on the man. Luke signaled Munoz that he was going to rush the man.

Munoz nodded, then gestured to wait a second. Munoz picked up a brown suitcase and threw it to the opposite side. The man mistook the bag for a policeman, leaned out and shot toward it.

It was all Luke and Munoz needed.

They shot him in the chest and face. The man went still, then stumbled backward, fired off three wild shots into the floor.

Redstone fired, striking the man in the temple and stomach. The man froze, tripped backward over a piece of luggage, then tumbled out the cargo door.

The police hurried to the door.

Luke ran to the duffle bag area and searched for Jenna, but couldn't find her. *She isn't here.* He's killed her and hidden the body somewhere in the airport. Looking outside, Luke saw the man's limp, unconscious body, overalls caught in the conveyor belt, inching down toward the chain mechanism on the ground.

"Where is she?" Luke shouted at the unconscious man.

He watched in horror as the man's shoulder and neck were crunched into the belt mechanism. His arm popped backward loudly, his body squeezed deep into the groaning mechanism. The belt began to vibrate and whine as the machine mangled him.

Finally, someone pushed the stop button.

Firemen hosed fire retardants onto the flames licking the wing. Within seconds, the flames were extinguished. Passengers rushed down the stairs and ran with children toward the terminal, a few glancing back at the mutilated, dead man on the conveyer belt.

Behind him, Luke heard a slow zip. He turned and saw strands of disheveled, auburn hair emerge from a second duffle bag hidden in the shadows beneath soft luggage in the far corner of the cargo hold. Jenna rubbed her head, blinked. He hurried over, helped her stand and embraced her for several seconds. He started to speak, couldn't. He'd never felt such overwhelming relief.

"My head," she said. "Where are we?"

"In the cargo bay. You're okay now."

She rubbed the back of her neck. "You keep saying that."

Luke smiled with moist eyes, then helped her over to the bay door where boarding stairs had been rolled up. They walked down to the tarmac. Sirens wailed from several directions. An ambulance stopped a few feet away.

Luke walked over and looked down at the man's blood-smeared face. It looked very familiar. Leaning closer, he recognized him. "That's the man I saw in the Ren Cen."

"And the man who picked me up at the hospital," Jenna said.

"Asshole got around," Redstone said, pulling out the man's wallet and checking its contents,

Luke saw a small, black booklet beneath the man's elbow. He took it and paged through the names and phone numbers.

Redstone pulled his driver's license from his wallet. "Meet Mason Bennett."

"Never heard of him," Luke said, as he leafed through the E's and F's, recognizing no names.

"This guy's a passport office," Redstone said, studying two passports.

As Luke flipped to the Ks, one name—Lucinda—caught his eye. It was next to a large "K." The phone number had a Detroit area code. Luke felt a sinking feeling in the pit of his stomach as pieces of the puzzle drifted together.

Was it possible?

He turned to Munoz who was checking the man's handgun. "Can I use your cell phone?"

"Sure." Munoz handed him the small black phone.

Luke pushed on the power, and watched green lights flash across the screen.

"What's up?" Redstone asked.

"I'll know in seconds."

Luke dialed the number, waited for the international clicking, then heard the phone ring. Three rings later it was answered.

"Mr. Klug's office. This is Lucinda."

Luke felt like he'd caught a line drive in the throat. "Sorry, wrong number." He hung up.

Forrest Klug. The man had once offered him a job. Charming, very persuasive, very bright, but something about Klug had turned him off.

Luke felt Redstone's large brown eyes burning into him.

"Talk to me."

"We may know who's behind this," Luke said.

"Who?"

"Forrest Klug. Chairman of Kennard Rickert. "This," Luke said, pointing to the booklet number, "is his direct line."

"Sweet Jesus. We'll get on Klug like Crazyglue." Redstone grabbed the phone and punched in a number.

Moments later, Luke and Jenna turned and strolled toward the World Motors corporate Learjet parked one hundred feet down the runway.

"Where you go?" Pablo Munoz asked.

Luke said, "To the Learjet. We just want to get everyone on out of here."

"No, Señor."

Luke stared back.

"No Learjet. Dogs found a radio cassette player loaded with explosives and an altitude trigger. Twenty minutes over the Caribbean..." Munoz threw out his arms imitating an explosion.

Luke swallowed hard, stared at the gleaming Learjet for several seconds and shook his head.

Taking Jenna's hand, they strolled toward the terminal. "Taken the train lately?" he asked.

"Sleeper car'd be kinda nice."

Epilogue

Two months later

THE BLUE-SKY sun warmed Luke's face. A fresh breeze rolled off Whistle Lake, weaved through some wild flowers and drenched him with the sweet scent of honeysuckle.

He followed the late afternoon sunlight dancing over the water to a chunk of bleached driftwood. A few feet away sat a pudgy, pink faced guitarist wearing a gold-sequined sombrero, along with six other mariachi musicians pumping out an uptempo rendition of *Spanish Eyes* for the sixty-three party guests beside

Luke's cottage.

Luke and Jenna had invited them to the first annual celebration of *Los Toxuumarados*. Beside him, Jenna looked magnificent in her blue floral blouse, denim skirt and thin red suspenders. Her eyes looked like pools of blue scooped from the lake. Her tanned skin seemed to glow.

Nearby, Elizabeth Blakeley, Howie Kaufman and Nurse Anna Benoit and spouses played a game of take-no-prisoners croquet against Miguel Ramirez, Juan de los Santos, Diego Garcia and their wives. Luis Martinez, nearly recovered from his bullet wound, and World Motors newest Mexican employee, talked with Donald Mackay, who'd graciously flown him and the Mexican contingent up to Michigan on a World Motors corporate jet.

Luke turned and saw his father down by the lake showing Marcus Kincaid the finer points of fly casting.

Luke whispered to Jenna, "Our guests are festive, *si?*"

"*Sí.* And mucho relaxed," she said, pointing to Eddie Berger dozing in a lawn chair, his index finger stuck in an empty Carta Blanca bottle

Luke noticed Baines Thomas waving them over. "I think it's time we made the rounds again," Luke said.

"Hey—this doc doesn't make rounds any more, remember?"

He smiled at her reference to resigning from Detroit Memorial three weeks earlier—thanks to Donald Mackay's incredible offer. World Motors, GM, Ford and Chrysler-Daimler would fund three new child abuse centers on the condition that she agree to run them. She'd agreed on the spot, resigned the next day, and hadn't stopped grinning since.

They walked over to Baines Thomas, Donald Mackay and Hank Redstone.

"You *gringos* appear recovered," Luke said.

Baines Thomas lifted his margarita. "The healing elixir of Mexico's ancient gods."

"I'll drink to that," Redstone said, sipping his margarita. "By the way, Mexico's banking gods called today."

"About what?" Luke asked.

"They released bank records that implicate Forrest Klug big time. It confirms a lot of what's in the dossier Bennett had compiled against Klug. It arrived by mail at police headquarters three days after Bennett died."

"What was in it?" Thomas asked.

"A solid financial trail linking Klug to Bennett and Cesar Torres. Plus a video of Klug blackmailing John Shelby into shifting the ad account to Klug's agency."

Everyone digested what Redstone said for several moments.

"The prosecutor is absolutely *convinced* they can lock Klug up for life?" Luke asked.

Redstone nodded. "Yep. And his old man."

"Hendrick Klug?" Thomas asked. "I never liked that old bastard."

"The man himself. Forrest Klug somehow got detailed records of his father's illegal activities at Meridian Media. Sonny Boy turned the records over to the police. Serious stuff. Daddy Dearest will do twenty to thirty. Probably croak in the slammer."

"What about John Shelby?" Donald Mackay asked.

Redstone sipped his beer. "The video proves Klug blackmailed him. After they met in the bar, Shelby feared Klug might try to harm you, Mr. Mackay. He didn't know when or where. Sunday morning, when we were in Mexico, he phoned the police about his fear."

"What did Klug have on Shelby?" Luke asked.

"Photos. They show Shelby obviously zonked on drugs, standing over the bodies of slain Vietnamese villagers. Klug had brainwashed Shelby into believing that he'd slaughtered them in a drug-induced state of mind. But a villager who survived said three Cong killed them ten minutes before Shelby's platoon ever showed up."

Donald Mackay nodded. "John resigned last week. I'm trying to talk him out of it, but he's hell bent on returning to Vietnam to set up some orphanages. He's been talking about it for years."

Elizabeth Blakeley lifted her glass. "I toast John Shelby."

"I'll drink to that," Redstone said, sipping more.

"You'd drink to a Vegamatic sale," his wife Renee said.

Luke laughed and realized there was something else they should all raise a drink to. He squeezed Jenna's hand and she smiled back, sensing what he was about to say. He held up his drink. "There must be something more we can drink to."

"Just name it," Redstone said.

"Our *next* party," he said, peaking interest on their faces.

"What party?" Thomas asked.

Elizabeth Blakeley smiled and seemed to guess what was coming.

"Our wedding reception," Luke said.

The group stared back in silence, then broke into smiles and applause. The news raced through the guests like electricity. Everyone surged closer, cheering and congratulating them.

After all the congratulations, Nurse Benoit and Michele Krammers, the cancer patient, walked over. Jenna embraced the young girl who looked twenty pounds heavier and amazingly healthy.

"I hear you'll be discharged soon," Jenna said.

Michele smiled and nodded.

"So will Doctor Norman Stickles," Nurse Benoit said, trying to keep the smile from her face.

Jenna stared back in disbelief.

"Turns out Dr. Hissy Fit," Benoit said, "has a naughty habit of writing lots of strong prescriptions for very dead people. Lucrative little narcotic business. His idea of niche marketing."

Jenna shook her head in amazement, then turned to Michele. "Well, Michele, now that you're a healthy, free woman, would you consider working in one of our safe homes?"

Luke watched Michele's eyes fill as she whispered, "Yes."

Jenna embraced her for several seconds.

"I smell food," Benoit said. "Hungry, Michele?"

She nodded and they walked off toward the kitchen.

Luke looped his arm through Jenna's and they strolled over near the lake. He heard loud honking. Looking up, he saw a flock of Canadian geese skid down onto the dark-blue water and drift toward the small island. He took in a deep breath and was rewarded with the rich aromas of garlic, onions and beef drifting from the open kitchen windows.

"This scene looks like a commercial," he said.

"Spoken like Connor Dow's new worldwide creative director."

"I'm still amazed Baines Thomas offered me the job," Luke said.

"No one else is."

"Dinner is served," someone shouted from near the kitchen.

They walked over and joined the group for a dinner of several varieties of enchiladas, cheese and chicken quesadillas, fried chalupas, thick gorditas stuffed with chopped beef, and tongue-searing chili. The second wave brought corn on the cob with melted cheese, tamales with sausage and potatoes, marinated pork and shrimp in garlic butter. Dessert was mango ice cream, fried bananas and flan and apple pie. Everything was washed down with several bottles of Mexican wine.

When finished, Luke, Jenna and those still awake, sat and watched the orange sun melt into the lake. Crickets began their nightly chant, fireflies flickered like tiny swinging lanterns. The mariachis floated a soft, intoxicating version of *Besame Mucho* into the clear, purple-red sky.

Luke leaned over to Jenna. "You mentioned you'd already picked our honeymoon location."

She nodded.

"Where?"

"Guess."

"Promise me it's Cleveland."

"Ever hear of the Yucatan?"